OCT - - 2011

DEEPLY DEVOTED

BOOKS BY MAGGIE BRENDAN

HEART OF THE WEST

No Place for a Lady
The Jewel of His Heart
A Love of Her Own

THE BLUE WILLOW BRIDES

Deeply Devoted

DEEPLY DEVOTED

A NOVEL

MAGGIE BRENDAN

Revell

a division of Baker Publishing Group
Grand Rapids, Michigan

Published by Revell
a division of Baker Publishing Group
P.O. Box 6287, Grand Rapids, MI 49516-6287
www.revellbooks.com

Printed in the United States of America

Library of Congress Cataloging-in-Publication Data
Brendan, Maggie, 1949–
    Deeply devoted : a novel / Maggie Brendan.
        p.   cm. — (The blue willow brides ; bk. 1)
    ISBN 978-0-8007-3462-6 (pbk.)
    1. Mail order brides—Fiction. 2. Cheyenne (Wyo.)—Fiction. I. Title.
    PS3602.R4485D44 2011
    813'.6—dc22   2011016898

Unless otherwise indicated, Scripture quotations are from the King James Version of the Bible.

Scripture quotations labeled NASB are from the New American Standard Bible®, copyright © 1960, 1962, 1963, 1968, 1971, 1972, 1973, 1975, 1977, 1995 by The Lockman Foundation. Used by permission.

This book is a work of fiction. Names, characters, places, and incidents are the product of the author's imagination or are used fictitiously. Any resemblance to actual events, locales, or persons, living or dead, is coincidental.

Published in association with Tamela Hancock Murray of the Hartline Literary Agency, LLC.

11 12 13 14 15 16 17   7 6 5 4 3 2 1

In memory of Colonel Alexander Richard Christine (July 2, 1932–July 22, 2010), for his deep devotion to his country, the United States of America, and the tremendous suffering he endured for many years so that we might have our freedoms.

What I tell you in the darkness, speak in the light; and what you hear whispered in your ear, proclaim upon the housetops.

Matthew 10:27 NASB

1

Cheyenne Territory, Wyoming
Spring 1887

Catharine Olsen sipped the last of her tea from the bottom of her cherished Blue Willow teacup, then carefully placed it on the saucer on the table next to her. She leaned back on the settee, shoving her curls away from her face, and slipped a letter out of her Bible. Though she knew the words by heart, she reread the letter, now worn and discolored from time.

> *Catharine,*
>
> *It is hard for me to contain my joy that soon we shall meet and you will be my bride. I feel like I already know you well from our correspondence. I pray you will have safe travel on the Union Pacific. You should have a day to rest after the long, arduous journey. I will promptly call for you at the hotel the next day. Until then, I remain affectionately yours,*
>
> *Peter Andersen*

Had it been just yesterday when she stared from the train's window at the prairie that seemed to stretch as far as her eye could see? The relentless wind whipped the unending gold-tipped grass, and there was not a tree in sight . . . just open fields with an occasional cabin dotting the landscape and perhaps deer or elk grazing in the distance. Peter had told her to keep a lookout for them, and maybe a herd of bison. She wondered how she would adjust to such surroundings after leaving her beloved Amsterdam with its lush meadows and myriad of tulips . . . and the memories, not all of them good. An image swam before her eyes, and her heart tightened. *I can't think about it today or I won't be able to go on . . . What purpose could it possibly serve?*

Would her heart ever heal? A single tear slid down her cheek, but she hastily swept it away before her sisters could see. She sighed and glanced over at them sitting with their heads together, reading a newspaper they'd picked up at the last stop. She prayed silently that all would work out as she hoped, but she knew from experience that only the Lord could see what was in store.

"Next stop, Cheyenne!" the conductor announced as he walked the aisle. He lifted his pocket watch from his waist-coat. "In about ten minutes." Passengers began to gather their reading materials, satchels, and personal belongings in preparation for their arrival.

True to the conductor's word, the train slowed its approach at the Union Pacific depot. Catharine decided that it was one of the most beautiful railroad depots she'd ever seen. The impressive structure looked fairly new with its multicolored sandstone, stone arches, and steeply pitched roofs that resembled a castle. Peter had written in his letters that the stone was quarried from west of Fort Collins, Colorado. Along the opposite side of the train, the rail yard was a profusion of trains narrowly wedged between one another, which could make disembarking dangerous.

Finally, with a squeal of metal on metal and a belch of steam, the engine halted, then passengers immediately scrambled to the exits, happy to have arrived in Cheyenne.

"Finally! I'm ready to get off this train," Greta exclaimed, but she lowered her voice after a stern look from Catharine.

"Stay close to me, girls. The train tracks are really close together, and walking could be treacherous." Catharine led the way, and the conductor assisted them after reminding them to take care as they stepped off. The wind howled, scattering dust and debris and threatening to rip their skirts from their slight forms in the bright April morning.

All three paused a moment amid the throng of people and soldiers and looked about wide-eyed. A foreign soil and a foreign city. The contrast here in life and in customs would be hard at first, no doubt, Catharine thought. Straightening her shoulders, she motioned to her sisters to follow her into the depot. Greta and Anna struggled with their heavy satchels, huffing and puffing.

Catharine stopped to watch them, shaking her head. "I told you not to carry too much on the train. Will you two ever listen to reason?"

Greta laughed, and the vibrant sound echoed throughout the vast waiting room. "We will, dear sister, just as soon as you have something sensible to say. You're such a worrier."

"Don't be mean, Greta," Anna scolded her sister. "I wish I hadn't stuffed all my paint into this satchel. I hope nothing leaked out. But I just couldn't leave it behind." The youngest of the three hiked her bag up to her chest and used her other arm to support it.

"Okay, let's find out where we're to go," Catharine said, looking around the large room. "Peter has a room waiting for me at the hotel. I'll just need to ask about further instructions."

The waiting area was filled with travelers, some being greeted as they arrived and others bidding their goodbyes before their respective trains departed. Catharine and her sisters stood stock-still to admire the beautiful room with its large fireplace, making it appear homey and restful for the many travelers who milled about. The depot was enormous, and no expense had been spared on the elegant fixtures. Catharine admired the pine and red-oak carved woodwork and ample windows that flooded the room with bright light.

A group of soldiers in army uniforms stood milling about near the ticket window and openly admired the three young women. One offered to help with Greta's bags, but when she started to say yes, Catharine stayed her by the arm. Greta smiled at the soldier and he shrugged with a grin, but his eyes followed them. Greta glanced back with a flirtatious tilt of her head.

Peter wouldn't arrive until the next day, which would allow Catharine a chance to rest before their meeting. He would not be prepared for her sisters in tow as well. That was one little detail that Catharine hadn't told him about, for fear of rejection. Peter had paid for her travel fare, and by closely watching her budget after her father's shipping business failed, she'd managed to save enough funds for her sisters' fares as well. Her parents' untimely death at sea six months ago, during a buying trip to the Indies, caused catastrophic loss for his shipping company, and it hadn't helped the situation when Catharine scrutinized the ledgers and found that her father's accountant had embezzled most of the profits, leaving them with very little to live on.

She tightened her lips in a fine line and looked around the busy depot for someone to ask about directions to their hotel. Over a window with metal bars across it was a sign that read INFORMATION, so Catharine spoke to the clerk there. "Excuse me, sir. Can you tell me where the Inter Ocean Hotel is?"

The clerk looked up and smiled at her and her sisters, straightening his bow tie. "The hotel's one block north on Sixteenth Street, ma'am. Will you need assistance?"

"If you would be so kind, I would be most grateful. We have two large trunks that need to be transported." As Catharine gave him her name to make arrangements for their luggage to be taken to the hotel, the clerk's pen paused as he squinted over his spectacles at her. "So . . . you're Miss Olsen." He leaned toward the front edge of the window, then scrutinized her with an approving gaze.

"Yes, sir, I am, and these are my sisters, Greta and Anna." Greta and Anna bowed their heads slightly in his direction, and his smile broadened.

"Well, it's very nice to meet you ladies. Name's Joe Willis." He bobbed his head. "I'm to tell you Peter Andersen has a carriage waiting to carry you the short distance to the hotel . . . but I don't think he mentioned any sisters." He studied the three of them, his eyes sweeping from one to the other. "Maybe I can be of assistance with your carpetbag there."

Catharine smiled back. "I believe we can manage. If you'll just see to it that our trunks are delivered, then we'll be going."

"Will do. You'll enjoy your stay at the Inter Ocean. It's one of our finest in Cheyenne, and I reckon Mr. Andersen spared no expense on your behalf. Welcome to Cheyenne, ladies."

So here they were enjoying all the comforts the fine hotel had to offer while Catharine waited anxiously to meet her future husband. She had been mildly surprised but pleased that Peter had reserved a room for her at such an opulent hotel. That made her wonder about him. *Isn't he just an ordinary farmer?*

Greta strode over to Catharine and plucked the letter out of her hands, rattling the Blue Willow china cup and bringing Catharine sharply back to the present. She gasped in horror and quickly reached to steady her prized china to keep it from tumbling to the floor. It held sentimental value for her, and she had always admired the Blue Willow pattern.

"*Alstublieft*, for goodness' sake, Catharine!" Greta said with a pointed look at her older sister. "Pull yourself together. How many times are you going to read that letter? You'll be meeting your beloved Peter in the flesh any moment now."

"*Langzaam aan!* Slow down! Honestly, Greta, you act as though you were raised in a barn with the milch cows."

Greta flounced over to the chair next to Anna. Her younger sister barely glanced up from the book she was reading, shook her head, and watched as the letter fluttered onto the rug. "Just leave her alone, Greta. If she wants to read it until it disintegrates, then let her." She picked up the letter and handed it to Catharine.

Catharine glanced at her sisters and sighed. She folded the letter and placed it back in its proper place in her Bible. *Lord, how am I going to be both mama and papa?* Greta, for all her impatience and impulsiveness, was a bright, pretty, but not always logical seventeen-year-old. Anna, fifteen, was in her usual oblivious state to what revolved around her, being content to ramble outdoors, read poetry, and let others wait on her. It wasn't that Anna thought they *should*, it was more that she felt she had much better things to do than the mundane. That included just about everything.

But Catharine held fast to her decision that no matter what, she would care for her sisters. She absentmindedly pushed back a curl from her eyes that had escaped its pins. Now that they'd left Holland, she hoped that she could keep a tight rein on Greta's adventurous spirit and offer motherly guidance to sweet Anna.

"I'm sorry!" Greta tucked her skirt under her bent legs. "It just seems that you can't know the *real* Peter just by the letters he wrote." She sniffed. "Ha! He could be an old widower with a bent back and a brood of children. I wouldn't believe anything that was written to me in a letter. Best wait until you're actually in his home and can see for yourself. On the other hand, maybe he's a wealthy farmer, or he wouldn't have put us in this grand hotel. This may not be as bad as I thought after all."

"Don't you have any faith at all?" Catharine answered gently. "I'm sure Peter is who he says. The truth comes out in what we write or say."

"Did you tell him that you'd been married before?" Greta pursed her lips until the corners of her mouth lifted.

"Greta, it's none of your business what we discussed in our correspondence these last couple of months." Catharine started to say more but clamped her mouth shut. She hadn't meant to speak so sharply to her sister, and she wasn't in the mood to argue with her today. She had more pressing matters on her mind.

Anna gave Catharine a quick squeeze about the shoulders, smoothing her red curls. "I thought we were going to read from Hebrews this morning. It does seem so appropriate, considering . . ."

Catharine opened her Bible. "I suppose there's a little time before he arrives." Catharine patted the spot next to her.

Anna snuggled up close, and Catharine's heart warmed at the trust her sister placed in her. She must not fail her sisters, and she wouldn't. They were depending on her.

She slid her finger to the passage marked by the lace cotton handkerchief that had once belonged to her beloved mother and read, "By faith Abraham, when he was called to go out into a place which he should after receive for an inheritance, obeyed; and he went out, not knowing wither he went—"

Greta cleared her throat, interrupting her sister. "I have no idea what that means, but I'm sure you'll be able to explain it to us."

"I know!" Anna jumped up and leaned forward, hands on her hips. "It means Abraham obeyed the Lord without knowing where he was to go, *ja*?"

Catharine looked fondly at Anna's maturing, round face and shining eyes and answered with a smile, "*Ja*, you are exactly right. I feel like we are doing the same thing as Abraham, stepping out in faith where God leads."

"You mean *you* are stepping out and dragging us with you!"

"*Nee!* No. And I don't appreciate the sarcasm or your tone of voice, Greta. Whatever is the matter with you? We discussed this thoroughly when I saw Peter's ad for a bride, and we were all in agreement that we might have a better future in America." Catharine stared at Greta, who squirmed under her scrutiny. "As I recall, Greta, you were hoping for a bit of adventure."

Greta's small mouth twitched at the corners. "*Ja, ja!* I know, but now that we are here, I'm having doubts. Why, there's nothing here but brown prairie, dust, and cattle. It's dreary, flat, and drab!"

"I'm sure it's not that way year-round. We'll miss our home, but I believe the Lord has led us all here for a fresh start." Catharine reached over and patted her on the hand. "We must trust Him."

Anna sat back down. "And we should pray that we can take the same faith that Abraham demonstrated to follow God's leading—"

A sharp rap on their hotel room door made all three of them jump, and Anna giggled.

"He's here!" Catharine hopped up, placing her palms to her burning cheeks. "Do I look all right?" She fussed with the hair pinned at the nape of her neck.

"You look wonderful, especially with the flush on your cheeks," Greta said.

Catharine smoothed her skirts and bolted to the door to swing it open. "*Hallo.* You must be Peter." Anna and Greta stood behind her.

Peter whipped off his brown hat, revealing a head full of thick, sandy brown hair with eyes the color of the ocean they'd just crossed. He had a mustache cropped close to his full upper lip, and he smiled back timidly at the three women assembled before him. "Good morning, ladies. Yes, I'm Peter Andersen."

Catharine's heart leaped to her throat, and her corset seemed to be cutting off all of her air supply. She pressed her hand to her abdomen as though it could pump the much-needed air into her midsection. Why did her stomach feel strange? Would he know she was hiding something by the look on her face?

Catharine swallowed hard. He was deliciously handsome and tall, with eyes that pierced right through her. She chided herself for having foolish notions about falling in love. It was really all about Peter, who needed a wife. And she needed a new beginning. Simple as that. Best not to entertain such thoughts about him.

Peter shifted his weight in the awkwardness of the moment. "May I come in?"

Greta hastily stepped aside. "Pardon, forgive my manners."

Catharine's legs felt as stiff as peppermint candy sticks, but she was finally able to move forward to greet the man who was to become her life partner. "Peter! It's so good to meet you at last," she said, suddenly feeling reticent as she extended her hand.

But Peter stepped closer to her and tightly grasped her hands in his. "My dear Catharine, I'm so glad you've arrived!"

His chest expanded as he drew in a deep breath. Was it in anxiousness or agitation? Catharine couldn't be sure and was almost afraid that he was going to bestow a bear hug on her, which would be unseemly since they'd just met face-to-face. She felt heat touch her face and flash down her neck as her eyes traveled up his towering frame. His warm smile was inviting, and the small cleft in his chin lent charm to his sharply defined jaw and tanned face. He swallowed, and she noticed his Adam's apple move.

"Oh! Where are my manners? Do have a seat," Catharine said, leading him to the nearest chair. She looked nervously at her sisters, fully aware that his eyes were following her. "Can I take your hat?" Her hand shook as she reached for the black Stetson hat, then placed it on the hall tree. Glancing back, she stifled a laugh at his hair flattened from the hat, which created a natural band all around his head. He seemed a tad uncomfortable in his dark suit with matching string tie. His wedding suit, perhaps? She doubted this was true farmer attire. The suit coat hugged his body, and it was easy to see he was well-muscled. "Peter, these are my sisters, Greta and Anna."

His eyes held an expression of surprise, but he only bowed stiffly in their direction. "I'm happy to make your acquaintance."

"Greta, was there any more tea, or do we need to ring for room service?" Catharine asked, trying to divert his questioning look for now. He would find out about her sisters soon enough. She hoped he would be in agreement to take them into his household as well, since he'd told her in their letters that his farmhouse was large.

Peter sat down and folded his long legs under the edge of the chair. "Please don't go to any trouble for me. I thought perhaps we could go have some lunch. We've a lot to discuss before we marry." His eyes held hers with a level gaze for a long moment, then traveled discreetly down her form.

Catharine's heart thudded against her ribcage. Was he pleased at the way she looked or sounded with her accent? Maybe he didn't like her freckles or red hair! More importantly, could she do this again?

Why were these doubts plaguing her now? She had felt so confident through their correspondence. But what if Greta was right? It had been a long time since she'd given her heart to a man, and she *had* made a terrible mistake before . . .

2

Peter ushered his bride-to-be, with her two younger sisters trailing behind, outside onto the congested streets of Cheyenne. He hoped his face didn't reveal his complete surprise that her sisters had journeyed with her, but he thought it best not to voice what he was thinking at the moment. At least not until they were alone. He was certain Catharine would make the perfect wife. Her letters were thoughtful and sweet, and her intelligence was apparent in the way she wrote. She was so unlike most of the ladies he'd courted in Cheyenne, and he'd felt a definite connection with her. He'd been dreaming of a long life with a companion to fill the emptiness he felt.

Now he wasn't feeling so convinced. Had he let his feelings run away with him? Did he really know the true Catharine through six months of letters? He still had a few unanswered questions.

Putting these thoughts out of his mind, he turned to the ladies. "We'll just have lunch at the Depot Exchange. It's a short walk down the street, unless you all prefer that I take you in the carriage." He paused on the sidewalk, waiting for an answer.

Peter watched as Catharine lifted her head of thick auburn

hair to look up at him demurely with her green eyes. Her appearance had somewhat shocked him earlier. He'd envisioned a blonde with soft blue eyes, much like her sisters who had true Dutch looks. Instead, Catharine's hair was burnished crimson and seemed to have a mind of its own, escaping the confines of the fetching green bonnet she'd donned before leaving the hotel.

"Walking would be fine, Peter," she said, assuring him with a look through thick, sweeping lashes. "We've had too many hours on the train this last week, and walking is good for the constitution, right, girls?" She turned to her sisters and they nodded in agreement.

Peter held out his arm to Catharine, and she took it timidly as he guided her across the busy street, then started in the direction of the restaurant.

Whatever would his mother say? Hopefully that meeting could wait a day or so. Then he would know more about Catharine's plans for her sisters. Perhaps the girls would be gainfully employed or otherwise engaged. He hoped so. He wanted Catharine all to himself.

Peter had waited a long time for just the right woman to become his wife. The single men outnumbered the women five to one in Wyoming. Out of the ones he'd courted, none of them were right for him. Either they didn't want to marry a wheat farmer or they preferred living in town with the social elite that Cheyenne had to offer. Peter didn't think he was unhandsome, but he was beginning to worry. He knew his mother had chosen Dorothy Miller for him, and at every turn she contrived to get them together. He had a feeling Dorothy liked the idea, but he felt only friendship for her. One evening after reading an article in the *Cheyenne Daily Leader* about mail-order brides, he got the idea that he might find a suitable wife that way. After all, nothing else had panned out.

From what he could tell from their six months of correspondence, Catharine was excited about their future, in spite of a flicker of sadness he'd caught in her eyes. How could a man be so lucky?

Luck's got nothing to do with it, he heard in his head. *Didn't you pray for a mate?*

"We may have missed the crowd, as it's well after twelve now," Peter said. Catharine's hand on his arm felt light as bird, barely touching him, as though she thought her weight was too much for him to support. He couldn't help but notice how slender and fine-boned her hands were, with neatly filed oval nails. Gentle hands, he wagered.

Greta and Anna followed behind, chattering as they looked and gawked at what was to be their town now.

"Is it always this windy?" Catharine held a hand against the front of her skirt to keep it from billowing up.

"Yes, I'm afraid it is. It's worse on the prairie without the protection of the buildings. Once we ride out to the farm, you'll see how windy it really can be. But there's a certain calming beauty to the prairie. I hope you'll come to love it as much as I do," Peter said. "Watch your step, ladies," he added as they crossed the street. "The recent rains have made a mess of the streets."

"How far is it to your farm, Peter?" Catharine asked, stepping carefully over a mud hole as she held the hem of her skirt up. They reached the plank walk, strolling past townsfolk, who nodded briefly and stared openly but then moved on down the sidewalk, busy with their own afternoon ventures.

Peter smiled, glad that Catharine wasn't afraid to talk, and as long as it wasn't as much as his mother, this would work out nicely. Besides, he enjoyed the sound of Catharine's voice, smooth and soothing. Definitely a change from the grating sound he was used to hearing from his mother. "Not too far. About three miles outside of town. You'll still be close enough to come into town whenever you feel the need to. We have lots of new shops, and more are being built every day." He stopped in front of the restaurant and turned to face them. "We're here. I hope you're all hungry."

As they paused on the sidewalk, a passing wagon's wheel slung mud directly onto Greta's skirt, splattering the entire side, and she jumped back in horror. "Ooh . . . now look at what he's done!" She clenched her hands next to her sides. "I'll look like a waif going into the restaurant."

"Don't fret, Greta. It's down near the bottom where no one will even see," Anna said.

Peter was already taking out his handkerchief, then he knelt down to wipe the mud away, which only made it streak all the more. "I'm sorry, but it's really not that bad, Greta. Besides," he said, standing, "everyone will be looking at your pretty face and not your dress, I'm afraid."

Greta tilted her head sideways, enjoying the compliment. "*Dank U wel*. Thank you, Peter."

He bowed slightly. "Shall we go in now?"

Catharine surveyed the busy dining room with pleasure, admiring its lavish furnishings of damask on the tables and the thick drapery framing the windows. Tall ferns in huge ceramic pots graced the corners of the room. Dark mahogany chairs and deep wood accents and molding lent a cozy atmosphere to the sounds of tinkling glass, the clatter of china, and the chatter of patrons. Delicious smells tickled her nose, along with the pungent smell of coffee, and her stomach rumbled. She hoped Peter hadn't heard. She hadn't realized she was so hungry. They followed the maître d' to a nearby table, and he handed them a menu once they were seated.

"The food smells wonderful," Anna said, taking her seat. "*Dank U wel*. Thank you very much for inviting us along for lunch. I'm sure you'd much rather spend your time with Catharine."

Catharine looked gratefully at Peter. "Yes, it's very kind of you to take us all to lunch." She could feel the heat rising to her face and knew that with her fair complexion, her freckles stood out even more.

"It's my pleasure, really." Peter gently pushed Catharine's chair to the table as she adjusted her skirt, then took his seat next to her. "Were you comfortable at the hotel?" Peter asked.

"*Ja*, the accommodations were very nice indeed," Catharine said.

"It was owned by Barney Ford, a former slave who moved here from Denver. I thought you might enjoy the atmosphere after your long journey, so I took the liberty of reserving a room."

"It was much more than what we—I mean I—expected." Catharine's throat felt dry and she reached for her water glass. Peter appeared to be well spoken and educated. For some reason, even though his letters conveyed a certain sophistication, she thought farmers in America were not educated. Maybe she had a lot to learn about these Americans.

Greta joined in. "Quite true. We never expected such a lovely room. This place must cost a fortune."

Peter shifted in his chair. "It's the best hotel we have in town," he said.

Anna, who'd mostly kept quiet, spoke up. "When do we leave for your farm? I can't wait to see it and explore the countryside."

Peter smiled at Anna, then tilted his head with a thoughtful look at his bride-to-be. "I've planned for us to be married at three o'clock this afternoon. If that seems suitable for you, Catharine. My good friend Mario Cristini and his wife, Angelina, will act as our witnesses."

Catharine's heart thudded under her ribs, and she moistened her dry lips. "What about my sisters? Couldn't they be our witnesses?"

"Of course," Peter said quickly, "but at the time that I asked my friends, I didn't know your sisters would be coming with you."

An awkward silence fell over their conversation for a brief moment, and Catharine blinked nervously.

"I'm . . . I should have told you in my letters. Forgive me."

"There's nothing to forgive. The more the merrier for our ceremony . . . that is, if you're in agreement with doing it today."

Catharine flashed Peter the warmest smile she could muster. "Yes, you're right, but my sisters will be coming with me to the farm." She saw his eyebrow quirk and a slight frown seep into his handsome face. Now she'd done it. He would have no part of a mail-order bride dragging her two sisters along. She steeled her heart for what she knew he was about to say.

Peter cleared his throat and locked eyes with her. "Perhaps we can talk about this later?" Lifting his water glass, he quickly gulped down the entire contents.

Catharine looked down at her plate. *This will not be easy, Lord. I should've told him. I'm full of lies and deceit.*

Anna reached across to touch Catharine's hand with an affectionate pat. "Don't worry, Cath. I'll press your dress while you tend to your toilette."

The waiter came, and they all ordered the roast with potatoes and succotash. Throughout the meal, Catharine plied Peter about his farm, genuinely interested about her new home.

Over dessert of Apple Brown Betty and rich coffee, Peter tried to answer all the questions concerning his farm and Cheyenne.

The round table afforded him the perfect view of each of the ladies. It hadn't taken him long to discern that Greta was the voice for her sisters, asking questions when Anna and Catharine were probably thinking them but staying quiet. Anna appeared to be a sweet, pretty, but dreamy blonde with enormous blue eyes, much like Greta. One could definitely tell they were sisters. But Catharine? The complete opposite, with her shocking crimson hair and green eyes holding a hint of mystery—or was it sadness?

"To answer your question about my farm, you'll be helping with the fall wheat I planted, which we'll harvest in the summer. That reminds me . . . we'll stop off at Warren's Emporium before our ceremony and purchase proper clothing to wear on the farm." While Peter loved the soft blue gown Catharine was wearing, it wouldn't be appropriate for farm life. "Mrs. Moody, one of my favorite clerks there, will take your sizes and put together what you'll need."

"Why would we need other clothing?" Catharine blinked, her eyes warm but unwavering.

Peter cleared his throat. "I need to get you ladies some appropriate work clothes." He saw her swallow hard before speaking.

"What about the servants? You *do* have one or two, *ja*?"

Her pretty face held a tinge of pink, and Peter thought she was utterly stunning. Red hair or no. He looked down at his plate and cut his meat into bite-size pieces before answering. "Sorry to say, but the only help I have is when we plant or harvest the wheat."

Peter watched Catharine chew on her bottom lip, making him wonder now if she'd been used to having servants. There had been no mention of it in any of her letters. However, she hadn't said anything about her two sisters either. He felt as though he'd let her down by the disheartened look on her face. Maybe it was just the opposite—perhaps she'd been hoping to improve her life. He didn't think he'd led her to believe he was wealthy. The truth was just the opposite. His mother's family had been well-to-do, but his father had been only a hard-working farmer.

Changing the subject, Peter said, "I can hardly wait until you're settled and can tell me all about Amsterdam." He caught the sparkle in Catharine's eyes. "Who knows? Maybe one day I can take you back there for a visit."

"I'd like that very much," she said quietly.

"Which? A visit or describing your homeland?" he teased.

She gave a soft laugh. "Both. I think you might enjoy it." She dabbed her mouth with her napkin and laid her fork and knife across her plate.

"Do you ladies intend to live in Cheyenne?" Peter asked, looking across the table at Catharine's sisters.

Greta and Anna exchanged looks, then Greta answered, "Didn't Catharine tell you that we were going to the farm with both of you?" Greta threw an annoyed look at Catharine, who shifted nervously in her seat, not meeting Peter's confused look.

He shoved his chair back, the legs scraping against the

hardwood with a grating sound. "I . . . I guess I assumed the two of you would be staying in town." He didn't want to reveal his complete ignorance of the situation at hand. Why hadn't she told him? He held his tongue so as not to say what he really wanted to.

Anna giggled. "I fear our sister left out—"

Greta quickly butted in. "Don't worry, Peter. Anna and I will not be in the way and plan to help with the farm work in whatever way we can, but I have to warn you, none of us have any experience in that area." She laughed. "But we don't want to be a burden to you or our sister."

Anna nodded. "We'd better go shopping then. I think I might like a pair of farmer's overalls to wear, like I've seen in a catalog."

"I'll see what I can do, Anna." He suddenly felt very irritated and stood to leave when he heard voices arguing with the maître d'. Peter briefly shut his eyes. *Please, Lord . . . don't let it be . . .* is that woman ever satisfied?

Catharine and the others stood as well, following his lead. The raised voices near the front caused the diners to stop eating to see what the commotion was all about.

Peter slowly turned, and it was just as he thought. His mother, arguing about wanting the best table in the restaurant, naturally. Didn't she see that it was packed?

Another lady with her whom he knew as Mrs. Warren touched his mother's arm lightly and said something he couldn't hear. But he knew Mrs. Warren well enough to guess that she would smooth things over. He'd never met a sweeter soul.

"That lady is really impatient, isn't she?" Greta said, nodding in his mother's direction.

"Shush," Catharine warned.

By now, everyone in the restaurant was glued to the small group's discussion at the front door. Peter drew in a deep breath and said. "That . . . that is my mother."

"Ooh . . ." Anna said in a hushed voice, and she and Greta exchanged glances.

Peter watched the expression on Catharine's face, but she made no comment, and he felt relieved. At that moment, his mother sashayed in his direction, with Mrs. Warren trailing behind. He groaned but managed to smile as she came closer.

Mrs. Andersen's gloved hands held up her dress, and with her handbag swinging on one arm, she eased her slim form between the tables and chairs, walking toward them with determined steps. She wore a deep blue skirt, its hem edged in brown velvet trim, which matched the ribbons of the bonnet tied securely under her chin. Catharine could tell by the way her face softened when she glanced at Peter that she adored her son.

"Well, Peter. I had no idea that you were coming to town or I would have made sure we could have lunch together." Mrs. Andersen drew her shoulders up sharply, crossing her hands over her waist. Before Peter could respond, she eyed Catharine and her sisters with one eyebrow cocked. "And who might you be?"

Catharine felt intimidated by the older lady, who stood a little taller than herself with a face that reflected the same unfriendliness as her question. She might be someone to reckon with if given half the chance. Catharine was hoping her own demeanor appeared stronger than she felt at this moment. "I'm Catharine Olsen, and these are my sisters, Greta and Anna."

"How do you do?" Mrs. Andersen pulled her friend forward. "I'm Clara Anderson, and this is my good friend and the first lady, Mrs. Helen Warren. Her husband, Francis, is the ex-governor of our great Wyoming territory. She and her husband are exemplary leaders in Cheyenne's society and are charter members of the First Baptist Church." Mrs. Andersen beamed.

Helen gave a sweet smile and Catharine immediately liked her.

"I'm so happy to meet you. Have you just arrived in Cheyenne?" Helen asked.

"We arrived just yesterday," she said, clasping Helen's outstretched hand.

"Welcome to Cheyenne. I hope you'll be staying awhile."

Catharine noticed the bright twinkle in her eyes and the warmth in her countenance. "Thank you for welcoming us. We've been so blessed by Peter's ad." Immediately a dead silence fell on the group, and Catharine wondered what she had said wrong. "I'm sure we'll enjoy getting to know Cheyenne."

Peter looked at his pocket watch. "If you'll excuse us, we were just about to leave. Helen, it's nice to see you again," he said, then touched Catharine on the elbow.

"Ad? What ad?" Mrs. Andersen asked. "I'm confused. Peter, maybe you'd better explain." She glared at her son, blocking their way, then turned to Catharine. "Where will you be staying?" The edges around her mouth grew more pronounced as her lips formed a disapproving line, harboring a slight frown.

Catharine cast an anxious glance at Peter. So he hadn't told his mother that he was about to marry a mail-order bride? *Seems like I'm not the only one with secrets*, she thought with a momentary bit of smugness.

3

Clara nearly tripped over her own sleek high-buttoned heels, streaking past the wide-eyed patrons. They paused with their forks midair to watch her hasty pursuit of the man with three ladies in tow leaving the restaurant. No matter, she ran out onto the boardwalk and saw them walking up the street as if there wasn't a moment to delay. Maybe there wasn't, but she intended to find out. Passersby gave her wide berth and several nodded in her direction, but she barely even saw them.

"Peter! Wait!" Clara huffed and puffed and ran as fast as her legs could carry her. Peter turned and frowned when he saw her following them. She paused and expelled a breath, then held her hand to her side, bending slightly to quell the stitch there. The three young women waited at Peter's side, saying nothing.

Drawing closer, Clara adjusted her fancy hat, which had tilted sideways, forced back a stray gray curl, and patted her flushed face with a hanky she took from her reticule. "You didn't answer my question, and that's not like you, Peter. Just what did Catharine mean about an ad?" She hadn't meant to raise her voice. Now people were staring at her, and she was a dignified lady. She knew how unseemly this was, but she must get the answer to her question.

"Mother, I really can't discuss this now. We're on our way to Warren's Emporium for supplies." He rocked back on his heels impatiently.

Clara didn't care for his evasive answer. "Whatever for?"

Peter touched her arm, nudging her back in the direction she came from. "Why don't you just go on back and have a nice lunch with Mrs. Warren? We'll talk later on in the week."

"Peter, I am not budging until you tell me what you're up to. I am your mother, in case you've forgotten." Clara struggled to keep her temper in check. She loved Peter more than anything the world had to offer. She couldn't understand why he would shut her out like this. And who in the world were these ladies with their strange accent, and why were they with Peter anyway? "I'm waiting for an answer, Peter," she said, hands on her hips.

Peter blurted out, "I'm getting married at three o'clock today to Catharine Olsen."

Suddenly the world around her stood still and the street sounds became distant. All Clara heard was the pounding of her heart in her ears. She pursed her lips, trying to gain composure. "*What?* Whatever do you mean, getting married?"

Peter took her arm and walked her in the direction of the restaurant, and Clara took a deep breath and shut her eyes briefly when he stopped and spoke.

"I know I should have told you, Mother—"

"Of course you should have talked to me—"

Peter held his hand up. "Stop right there, Mother. My decision has been made, and I'm not going to stand out here and quibble about our private business for all of Cheyenne to see. Catharine has agreed to be my bride."

Had he lost his senses? "But what about Dorothy? You seemed interested in her, and she has taken quite a fancy to you." Clara blinked at her son in disbelief.

"I knew you would say that, Mother. But it's you who decided whom I should marry. I don't wish to discuss this any further."

Clara yanked her arm away and said through gritted teeth, "Was I not even going to be invited to this hasty marriage?"

Peter shifted and took a step away from his mother. "I was going to tell you all about it after Catharine and I were married. I knew how you'd feel, and from what you've just said, I was right. You would never have approved." Peter glanced over his shoulder at the three ladies waiting for him on the sidewalk and started backing away. "I'm sorry, Mother, but I must run along now or we'll all be late. You can meet us at Judge Carey's office at three, if you are so inclined."

"Peter, I'm so hurt that you would leave me out of your plans, especially your marriage! Have you no consideration for your mother at all? What about a wedding?" Clara could hardly speak and was shaking inside. Good thing his father wasn't here to witness this outrageous behavior!

"I'm sorry, Mother, but I knew you would just try to change my mind. Go on back now and have your lunch with Mrs. Warren. I'll see you at three, all right?" His eyes pleaded with hers and Clara felt the pull in her heart, but she was furious with him. "I don't know, Peter." She sniffed into her handkerchief. "I just don't know." Clara's voice cracked, then she walked away.

Peter's heart felt tight. He did love his mother and he regretted that he hadn't told her about his correspondence with

Catharine. He had been so busy on the farm, and when he was in town to see her, he really hadn't had much chance to tell her about his life because she was too busy planning it. She wouldn't have approved in the first place, but now, seeing the slump in her shoulders as she walked away, he knew he'd hurt her. Well, once she saw how wonderful Catharine was, she'd come around.

He forced a smile as he walked toward Catharine. His heart lurched when he looked into her pretty face. "I'm sorry for what just happened, but Mother will come around," he said with more assurance than he felt.

Catharine's face was lined with concern. "Peter, you never told your mother about me? I'm not sure what to think. I'd prefer not to be kept in the dark." Her eyebrows arched on her forehead.

"If my mother had her way in the matter, I would have been a lawyer or statesman instead of a wheat farmer. She wanted to see me marry someone else, but that just couldn't work." Peter took Catharine's arm. "Now, if you please, ladies, follow me. I'm going to get you outfitted for the rugged West, starting at the mercantile."

"I can hardly wait," Greta said with teasing sarcasm. "I don't believe I've ever donned farmers' clothing before."

Peter chuckled, but Catharine hung back. Greta and Anna slowed their steps, not sure whether to follow him or not. "Are you sure your mother will be all right, Peter?" Catharine asked.

"I believe everything will be fine. We really have no more time to waste since the ceremony is at three," he said.

Warren's Emporium sat diagonally across from the Inter Ocean Hotel. The sprawling three-story structure of stone and brick was the largest downtown structure on Sixteenth Street and covered most of the block just north of the Union Pacific depot.

Following Peter up to the massive entrance doors, Catharine was sure that Mr. Warren had spared no expense on its continuous line of plate-glass show windows to house the displays, which were made even more appealing by the sixty-foot-long skylight. Shopping here would certainly be an adventure, and she felt a tinge of excitement.

Once Peter ushered the ladies inside Warren's Emporium, he turned at the sharp intake of breath from Greta and Anna. All of them were impressed. Catharine noticed how proud he seemed and enjoyed the looks given them as he escorted them down the aisle.

Catharine paused, openly amazed at the modern store. She'd never seen anything quite like this. Peter went to find someone to assist them, promising that he would return in a flash. Anna and Greta seemed to be equally surprised, and Anna motioned with a wave of her hand for Catharine to hurry to where she stood admiring fine linens.

"Sis, have you ever seen anything as fine as this?" Anna asked, fingering a fluffy towel.

"I don't believe so, but I have a feeling that Peter didn't bring us here to check out the home goods today," Catharine said. She too ran her fingers across the towel wistfully. "Where did your sister go?" Catharine looked around, but it seemed her sister had disappeared.

"I have no idea. You know Greta, she's got to see everything there is to see."

Catharine shook her head. "Well, she'll have to do that another time, I'm afraid. We're a little pressed for time today. Let's see if we can find her before Peter comes back."

Moments later they spotted her talking to a soldier. Was he the same one they'd met when they'd arrived? He looked awfully familiar. Catharine bit her lip, hating to interrupt what seemed to be a pleasant conversation, but Greta was so gullible. She could easily be taken in by a man's charm, even if she barely knew him.

Catharine cleared her throat, and they both looked her way. "Greta, excuse me, but you must come with me and Anna. We have shopping to do." Catharine decided that she must sound like a nagging mother. The handsome soldier in his stiff army uniform gazed at her through dark, brooding eyes when she spoke, making her feel like an old maid indeed.

The soldier bowed slightly. "How do you do? I'm Staff Sergeant Bryan Gifford at your service, ma'am." He smiled at Anna with an admiring sweep of his eyes.

"These are my sisters, Catharine and Anna." Greta gestured with her hand. "Bryan was the one who offered to help us at the train station, remember."

Mmm, so they're already on a first-name basis . . . Catharine nodded at him and said, "Yes, I do remember." He seemed to be a flirt, and she stiffened, realizing that she didn't know anything about him. It was hard to trust anyone, and even though they were new to America, she was not accustomed to his open friendliness. But being tall and handsome would appeal to Greta. Especially tall, handsome, and in uniform.

"I'd like to invite you all for ice cream, if you have the time."

"That would be wonderful, wouldn't it?" Greta looked to

her oldest sister for her answer. "Bryan says the emporium has a café."

"We can't," Anna said. "The ceremony is in less than an hour, Greta. You know that."

"Perhaps another time, Bryan. We have things to tend to—" Catharine never finished as Peter walked up, along with a woman neatly dressed in a black skirt and crisp white blouse.

"Mrs. Moody is going to assist us in outfitting all of you for the farm," Peter said.

"You must be Catharine," she said, holding out her hand. "Peter's been telling me all about you throughout his correspondence, and you're every bit as beautiful as he said you would be!"

Catharine smiled back at the middle-aged lady, surprised that she might have been the topic of anyone's conversation. "*Dank U wel*," she told her, not knowing what else to say.

Bryan interrupted. "If you ladies will excuse me, I'll let Mrs. Moody help you with supplies. I hope we meet again soon," he said, turning hooded eyes on Greta. Greta blushed and waved as he strode to the front door.

Greta turned her attention to the list that Peter held in his hands. "Do we really need everything on that list, Peter?"

Mrs. Moody's face held a questioning expression as she looked from Greta to Anna and then back to Peter.

"Mrs. Moody, these are Catharine's sisters, Greta and Anna. They'll be staying with us for a while once we're married."

Mrs. Moody's face softened. "I see . . ." Catharine knew from the sound of her voice that she *didn't* see. "Please, ladies, follow me to the apparel department and you'll be out of here in no time."

"I'll be close by if you need me for anything." Peter gave Catharine a slight nudge and handed the list to Mrs. Moody.

Mrs. Moody turned out to be quite delightful, taking them under her wing. With one discerning look, she chose the correct sizes for each of them. A pile of various pants, hats, and boots was collected within minutes. She carried the items to the counter to have them wrapped and rechecked the list Peter had given her. Catharine watched as the clerk folded the garments and wrapped them separately from the boots.

"Ladies, I think that'll take care of the list. Next time you're in town, I hope you'll stop by and see our newest selections—they should be arriving any day. And later, when you start a family of your own, we'll have everything you need for a baby," Mrs. Moody said.

She couldn't have known that Catharine's heart ached at the mention of a baby. Anna patted her sister on the arm, and Catharine felt heat rising in her face as she stared down at Anna's hand.

Peter's face turned bright pink, but he smiled and said, "No doubt you'll be consulted in that possibility, Mrs. Moody." He paid for the purchases and handed Greta and Anna a few parcels to carry. He carried the boots and gave Catharine the hats to hold.

"*Dank U wel*, Peter. This feels like Christmas morning," Anna commented as she took the packages from him.

Greta giggled. "Not exactly, Anna. Remember, these are work clothes for life on a farm."

"Maybe so, but I for one am looking forward to spending time outdoors," Anna answered.

"Well . . . let's hope you'll still be able to say that after a few weeks of the constant wind and heat we'll have this summer."

Peter guided the sisters back to where he'd left the carriage. He squeezed Catharine's arm affectionately on their walk back, moving rather quickly, Catharine thought, probably in order to keep the ceremony time. She was filled with a mixture of excitement and nervousness and wondered if his mother would come and be a part of this. She was surprised that he hadn't told his mother, and she knew it wouldn't bode well to start a marriage off on the wrong side of the fence with one's mother-in-law.

Which made her wonder . . . what other surprises might Peter have, and how on earth was she going to tell him her own secret?

4

After storing all their packages, everyone got settled inside the carriage and headed to the courthouse. Catharine was disappointed that there hadn't been time to change her dress, but then again, so many things in her life hadn't gone according to plan. Anna and Greta sat in the back while Catharine shared the front seat with Peter. At least the cover helped a little to deflect the sun's afternoon rays.

Peter seemed in high spirits as he guided the carriage through the throng of people, buggies, and horses around the city streets. "Peter, what do you know of Bryan Gifford?" Catharine kept her voice low, not wanting Greta to hear.

Peter glanced sideways at her. "Not much, I'm afraid. We have an army post here named Fort Russell. Many soldiers come and go, so I'm only acquainted with a few of them." He cocked an eyebrow. "Why? Are you worried about Greta being friends with him?"

Catharine shrugged. "I suppose I am. Her care and Anna's was entrusted to me after my mother and father died. I need to protect them, and Bryan did seem rather flirtatious, in my opinion."

Peter chuckled and covered her hand with his, still holding the reins in his left hand. "Don't worry your pretty little head about the soldiers. If Greta and Anna decide to stay, I'll introduce them right proper to some eligible men. There are plenty in Cheyenne. Men outnumber women here and perhaps in most places in the West."

His reference to her "pretty little head" flattered her. She'd never considered herself pretty with her freckled complexion and auburn hair. And she wished she wasn't so tall. Catharine had inherited her father's coloring, but secretly she envied her two younger sisters, who took after their beautiful mother with their blue eyes and flaxen hair.

"Oh, I can't see them leaving me." *Did he just wince?* "But if you can help them find suitable jobs, I would be most grateful, Peter." She looked over at him, and his eyes were full of optimism.

"Anything I can do to help, Catharine, I will."

She loved how her name sounded when he spoke it. Softly, almost reverently, which she certainly didn't deserve.

Laramie County Courthouse was on Eighteenth Street and Ferguson Street, just a couple of blocks from the railroad depot. It was a two-story building with an adjoining structure at the rear. Catharine surveyed the area. "It's such a large building for a courthouse. Is this where we're to be married?"

"Yes. Those attached buildings are the jailhouse and the sheriff's office." Peter hopped down and set the brake, then turned to help Catharine down. His hand was warm and strong, and their eyes locked briefly, his crinkling at the corners with delight. Catharine smiled at him, feeling her pulse leap at the touch of his hands on her fingers.

"It won't be long now and you'll be my very own. You make me very happy, Catharine," he said softly. His eyes were sincere and filled with longing, and Catharine felt a strange quiver in the pit of her stomach.

"I surely hope so, Peter," she whispered in his ear. His aftershave lotion smelled good and tickled her nostrils.

Peter assisted her sisters, then ushered them through the heavy doors and down the hallway, stopping in front of the door that read JUSTICE OF THE PEACE, THE HONORABLE JOSEPH M. CAREY.

"Are you ready to become Mrs. Andersen, Catharine? Are you certain?" Peter stammered, doubt reflected on his handsome face.

Catharine heard Greta and Anna giggle, but she ignored them and looped her arm through his. "Peter, I'm very sure. Otherwise I wouldn't be standing here."

"Very well then." He swallowed hard and his Adam's apple bobbed. He swung open the door, and Catharine saw another young couple standing near the front of the room.

"There you are!" A heavyset man with an Italian accent and a curling mustache strode toward them. "Right on time, I see. And this has to be your wonderful Catharine." He stuck out his hand and shook hers enthusiastically. "I'm Mario Cristini, a good friend of Peter's. He talks incessantly about you."

"*Hallo*. Is that right? I know from his letters that Peter holds you in high regard," Catharine said.

Mario laughed. "Is that so? Well, good friend or not, if he gives you the least bit of trouble, you're to let me know." He pulled a dark-haired, pretty lady to his side, though she barely reached his shoulder. "Catharine, this is my wife, Angelina."

Angelina had a wide smile with friendly, dark brown eyes. "How are you? I'm so glad to meet you. I hope we'll become good friends, Catharine. Welcome to Cheyenne." She too had a rich accent, and it intrigued Catharine.

"*Hoe maakt U het?* How are you? Thank you so much for your warm welcome." Catharine turned to introduce her sisters, but Peter beat her to it.

"And these are her sisters, Greta and Anna," he said, leading them forward. "They'll be living with us."

"Oh . . . how . . . interesting. You never told us that Catharine had any family." Mario looked at them squarely, assessing the couple, and Catharine saw Peter shift uncomfortably. Angelina cleared her throat and gave her husband a "don't say another word" look, then clasped Greta's and Anna's hands in friendship.

The girls seemed uncomfortable but murmured a greeting to the Cristinis. Catharine felt their embarrassment. She knew they probably felt like they were a bother. Later she would reassure them that it would all work out. She was determined not to let anything get in the way of taking care of her sisters until they were old enough to find either suitable husbands or jobs, if at all possible. She intended to be completely devoted to their welfare because she had promised herself to do all she could for Greta and Anna. Now if she could just convince Peter of that. She would tell him again that she was sorry she hadn't brought up the fact that they would be coming with her.

The sound of heels against the walnut floor caused the group to turn as the judge entered the room. Catharine was shocked that the judge was a woman who stood about six feet tall. *And I thought I was tall.* She looked to be in her early seventies and walked with regal dignity and a no-nonsense attitude as she made her way to the small group. Her hair was stacked high on her head, and prominent cheekbones etched her weathered face.

"Good afternoon, ladies and gentlemen. I'm Judge Ester Morris, presiding in Judge Carey's absence today." Her piercing blue eyes looked over their group as she asked, "Who's the lucky couple getting married today?"

Peter stepped forward and pulled Catharine with him, a big grin on his face. "We are, Judge Morris," he said, handing her the marriage license.

She opened the folded paper. "I see you have the proper paperwork, Mr. Andersen." She looked at Catharine and smiled. "You are Catharine then?"

Catharine finally found her tongue. "*Ja*. I'm Catharine Olsen."

"Ah . . . first marriage for both of you, I take it?" Judge Morris adjusted the lacy collar of her black robe.

Catharine's heart pounded, and suddenly the room felt warm and stuffy, making her light-headed.

Without waiting for an answer, the judge continued. "I love seeing the first blush of love on a bride's face. Well, congratulations to you both! What are we waiting for? Who are your witnesses? I see you've brought more than enough." She cackled loudly.

"Mario Cristini and his wife, Angelina, Your Honor," Peter answered. "They're my best friends. And these ladies are Greta and Anna, Catharine's sisters."

"How do you do, young ladies? I believe I detect a foreign accent?"

"*Ja*. We are from Amsterdam," Greta was quick to answer.

"I've never met a female judge before," she said, unabashedly staring at the judge.

Judge Morris laughed again and crossed her arms across her tall frame. "I was somewhat of a rebel in my younger days. Maybe somewhat like yourself," she answered, her eyes twinkling in merriment.

"You have that correct, Your Honor." Anna poked her sister in the side and squinted affectionately at her.

"Follow me to the front and we'll get started. I have another matter at 3:30."

Moments later, all the joking aside, Judge Morris began commencing the vows. It all seemed so rushed. *But I don't deserve anything else for not being totally honest with Peter,* Catharine thought. How she wished she had. But it was too late now. If Peter knew the truth, she was sure he would change his mind about marrying her.

She heard the judge ask if Peter had a ring, when suddenly the door swung open and Peter's mother came charging down the aisle, waving her hand. "Wait, Peter! I have your grandmother's ring right here—the one that you were planning on giving to Dorothy!"

Peter's face drained of all color as Clara stepped up to him and pressed the ring into his palm. Anna and Greta gasped, and Angelina whispered something to Mario.

Who was Dorothy?

"Peter, what is she talking about?" Catharine managed to speak as the color returned to his face.

"No one, Catharine."

"Humph! No one? No one? He intended to marry Dorothy Miller before *you* came!" Clara's voice rose slightly, her nostrils flaring.

Catharine felt all of her earlier joy drain from her being, and the old familiar ache followed and burned in its place. Greta and Anna hurried to her side.

"Peter, *alstublieft*, is this true?" Catharine asked, but he was staring with shock at his mother.

"Mother, what are you doing?" Peter said through clenched teeth.

Clara gasped and took a deep breath. "You know perfectly well, Son."

"I had no such plans—"

Judge Morris interrupted, clearing her throat loudly. "Mrs. Andersen, will you please step aside and observe the ceremony or remove yourself from my courtroom? You have interrupted a holy matrimony, and the last time I looked, there were two consenting adults."

Clara sputtered as everyone watched the judge staring her down. Catharine was shaking now, though Anna held her hand. When she looked at Peter, his eyes were pleading.

"Well . . . I . . . only wanted to be certain Peter was ready to marry someone he'd never even met until today—"

"Madam, I won't ask you again. Either stand back while we proceed or leave *now*."

Clara harrumphed and took a step off to the side, apparently intending to stay for the ceremony. Peter took a thin gold band out of his coat pocket.

Judge Morris whispered under her breath to Catharine, "Do you wish to have a few moments alone to confer with your groom?"

"Catharine, believe me, I haven't been courting anyone but you these last months. My mother had plans, but they were not mine! Please listen to me and trust me." Peter's look was genuine, and his mother did seem to be a smidgen of a busybody. He squeezed Catharine's hand so tightly that her fingers were beginning to hurt.

Could she trust him? All through their correspondence, he'd professed his desire to take care of her and be a good husband to her. She looked over at Mario, who was nodding his head as though to vouch for his friend's faithfulness, and Angelina gave her a sweet smile of confirmation.

Catharine finally answered, "*Goed*. Okay, Peter." She gave him a feeble smile, and Peter's eyes softened as he squeezed her hands.

Judge Morris looked at the watch pinned to her black robe. "Shall we get on with it?"

"Your Honor, would you indulge me? It'll only take a moment. I have something I want to read before the ceremony," Peter said.

Judge Morris nodded. "Yes, Mr. Andersen. What would you like to say?"

Peter removed a piece of paper from his coat pocket and turned to face Catharine. "I want to read a letter that I penned for you but didn't mail before you left Holland." Peter's eyes caressed hers, and Catharine felt her face flush.

For my bride-to-be,

It's with great excitement that I look forward to meeting you face-to-face. Your loveliness comes through your letters, overshadowing any doubts I could have because of never meeting you before. We are destined to be together. You see, dear Catharine, I've prayed for someone like you in my life. Someone to share my heart's desire for children to fill the home with happiness and

teach them our values, and to work side by side with to
bring our dreams about. My heart is pounding with
anticipation that you might be feeling the same way as
I, and my fingers tremble as I struggle to hold my pen.
Soon my dreams will be reality, and I believe the best is
yet to come the day you're mine.

Peter folded the letter and handed it to her, and she felt the warmth of his hands on hers. She could barely see his face through her tears. Speechless, she squeezed his hand. She hoped she could live up to his expectations. She heard Clara snicker, but Greta and Anna were sniffling into their hankies, and Mario and Angelina smiled at Catharine and Peter. Another couple was waiting their turn in the back of the room, and the young lady turned to her groom and said, "Why haven't you ever written me anything like that?"

"Well, I've never had that in a ceremony before," Judge Morris commented, "but I declare you may have started something new, Mr. Andersen." She gave Peter a smile of approval. "Is there anything you want to say?" she said to Catharine.

Catharine shook her head, and her sisters breathed a sigh of relief, then moved away and stood next to the Cristinis. The judge began speaking once again.

Within ten minutes the ceremony was over, and Peter shyly leaned in to plant a kiss on Catharine's cheek. Her sisters and the Cristinis surrounded them with congratulations. No turning back—the ink was dry. She was Mrs. Catharine Andersen now.

5

"I wish you had told me about your sisters coming with you, Catharine," Peter said for her ears only, leaning closer to her on the buggy seat.

Catharine swallowed hard, focusing on his strong hands holding the reins. Without looking at him, she answered. "I was afraid that you might not let them come, Peter. If you'd said no, I'm not sure what I would've done. I just couldn't leave them behind to fend for themselves." She looked over and caught his level gaze. "Can you forgive me for not telling you beforehand?"

Peter looked away, then made a clicking sound to the horse to step up the pace. "I don't see how I have a choice now, but somehow we'll work it out."

Figuring there was little else to say about the matter, Catharine stared off at the rolling prairie grasses, praying she wouldn't be a big disappointment to her new groom.

As Peter's farmhouse came into view over the gently sloping hill, Catharine was not disappointed. It was larger than she expected, and she hoped that meant there would be plenty of room for Greta and Anna. The white clapboard Victorian home with a wraparound porch was trimmed in delicate fretwork along the porches, columns, and windows. The front door had a beautiful insert of beveled glass. The shutters stood out with deep green against the stark white clapboards. Huge trees lined the drive leading up to the house, offering plenty of shade for enjoyment on the porch. A spacious red barn with surrounding corrals stood at a distance from the house. She thought it all utterly charming. The only thing missing was flowers. She'd have to do something about that, wouldn't she?

"Peter, your home is nice," she said. "I like the trees."

"*Our* home now." He grinned, watching her take it all in. "Those trees are elm trees, and over yonder"—he pointed to trees that led down a path to a well made of stone—"are box elders. Fortunately, the elm trees help give shade out here on the prairie in the summer. In the winter, they offer protection from the constant wind." Peter stopped the carriage in front of the white picket fence. "We're here, ladies. Make yourselves at home." He helped Catharine down, and Greta and Anna scrambled down behind them.

He carried the first pieces of luggage to the porch, then put his hands on his hips, shoved his hat back, and looked around at the surrounding land. "So what do you think?" he said to his bride. "I know it's probably not what you all were used to in Holland, but I think you'll be comfortable here once you're settled."

"You have a lot of land. Is that the wheat you've planted?" It seemed to go as far as her eye could see. The wind blew gently through the field, bending the short blades.

"You're right. I have a hundred acres of wheat planted and will start harvesting in about three months. It'll be waist high by then."

Greta lugged her suitcase to the porch and heaved a breath of air. "I think you were right, Sis, my bag's pretty heavy."

Peter scooted over to take Greta's bag. "Here, let me help you and Anna. Why don't you just get the things we bought and I'll take care of the rest? We'll have a light supper since I'm sure you're tuckered out, and then you can retire."

Anna fairly skipped up the porch steps, headed directly for the porch swing, and plopped down. "Ooh, this is a perfect place to enjoy the outdoors. I think I'm going to be very happy here."

Catharine and Peter exchanged glances and Catharine could only wonder what he was thinking. Before she had time to think about it, Peter swept her up into his arms and, with a slight kick of his boot, swung open the front door. She squealed and he laughed, then he carried her across the threshold. Anna and Greta cheered him on and followed them into the large foyer.

He set Catharine down and gave her a quick kiss. "Welcome home, my beautiful bride. Have a look around. If there's anything you don't like or would like to change with the furnishings, let me know. This used to be my parents' home and I just never changed anything." Peter stood back and observed her with an adoring look that made Catharine smile.

Catharine stepped into the sitting room furnished with floral chintz-covered chairs and cherrywood tables. A light, fresh, lemon smell lingered in the room, telling her it had been recently dusted. The room was delightfully inviting, and she could see herself at the small lady's writing desk drinking tea out of her Blue Willow china. She clasped her hands together. "Oh, Peter, it's very lovely," she said, running her hand across the smooth desk.

He beamed. "And here I was worried . . . but just the same, you can add your own personal touch, Catharine. It's all yours."

"*Ja*. It's all very nice." Anna had followed them and openly admired the cozy room.

"Can you show us to our room, Peter?" Greta asked with one eyebrow quirked upward as she peered into the sitting room. "Mmm . . . nice." She looked about with a decisive eye.

"Yes, come with me and I'll show you the upstairs." At the second floor landing, he swung open the first door and swept his arm aside for them to enter the room they'd be sharing. "If you want to freshen up, I'll bring your things up once I get Catharine's luggage."

Greta touched his arm. "Oh, I can get mine and Anna can get hers. It's those big trunks that will be heavy." The two sisters headed back down the stairs, leaving them alone.

"You can just leave it downstairs for now, Peter. We'll go through it this week and unpack," Catharine told him. "But I'd like that smaller brown bag if you don't mind. It has most of what I need."

"Will do, but first let me take you to our bedroom." He took her hand and walked to the end of the hall.

Catharine felt a shiver slide down her spine but wasn't sure if it was excitement or tension. The bedroom had its own fireplace in the corner and a cherrywood tester bed with a canopy of white tatted lace draping its sides. The windows boasted creamy sheers that crisscrossed with a pleasing effect as late afternoon sunlight filtered through. Next to the bed, a crystal vase was chock-full of pink roses. They looked like climbing roses. Had Peter placed them there? She hadn't seen a maid and Peter hadn't mentioned one.

Silly, of course, she chided herself, *there wasn't help or he wouldn't have bought the items he said we need on the farm. Ladies of leisure have no reason to wear work clothes.* This might be quite a challenge for them, especially her younger sister.

Peter stood at the doorway, watching her response. "Do you like it, Catharine?"

Catharine dragged her eyes from the thick matelessé covering the bed and felt her face go pink. "I do, Peter."

He closed the door, flung his hat on the bedpost, and kissed her hands. "I intend to make you very happy, my beautiful Catharine. It's my greatest desire that I can be all that you expected of me."

His intense gaze caused her heart to thump against her ribs. She was nervous about how she'd feel tonight after the lights were out. She did want him to hold her, that was for certain, but it had been a long time since someone had done so. She tried to cover her apprehension with a soft laugh. "And I you, Peter. I hope I can be the wife that you've been searching for all these years."

He drew her closer to him until she could feel the outline of his firm legs through her skirt. He slowly untied the satin ribbons of her bonnet, removed it, and tossed it onto the bed, allowing her hair to fall around her face. He lifted a curl, breathing in its scent between his fingers, looked into her eyes with a frank look of delight, then kissed her mouth softly, lingering a moment. She could feel the tenseness of his body against hers and his strong arms encircling her waist as he nearly lifted her off the floor to kiss her again and again. Someone rapped loudly on the door and they sprang apart, forgetting for a moment they were married.

Catharine looked at Peter and he nodded, still holding one arm about her waist. "Come on in," she said.

Greta and Anna stood at the doorway taking in the two lovebirds and the nicely furnished bedroom. Greta cleared her throat. "We didn't mean to interrupt but wanted to ask about supper." Both of them were wide-eyed at the embarrassed couple.

Catharine knew her freckled face and neck were flushed, but she had nothing to be embarrassed about. Peter was her husband now. She wished she could wipe those grins off her sisters' faces.

"It's no matter. I believe there's ham to make sandwiches and we can have fruit to go along with that. I've never had a cook. Between the four of us, we should be able to handle the cooking." Peter let go of Catharine's waist and turned to her. "We could fix a bite to eat now. What do you say, ladies?"

Catharine was afraid of that very thing . . . no servants. Her father, who had been a wealthy shipping magnate, had a cook and a housemaid, so she knew very little of running a household. But she was determined to learn. She did not want to disappoint him.

"I'll be glad to help, Peter." Anna smiled at him, and her sisters laughed out loud.

"*Ach!* I do know how to make a sandwich!" Anna said.

"Uh . . . until something distracts you and you forget what you're doing." Greta chuckled.

Catharine took her sister's arm affectionately. "She's teasing you, Anna. Come with me and we'll show her." They started down the stairs, and Peter and Greta followed. Catharine swore she heard Greta say she wanted to learn to cook. Unbelievable. She'd never shown the first bit of interest in that sort of thing. *Well, looks like it'll be a much-needed necessity for all of us, or Peter may send us all packing back to Holland.* One place she did *not* want to return to—at least not now.

Supper was whipped up with little problem as Peter gave instructions about the kitchen, telling them where staples were stored and how to work the stove. The kitchen boasted a porcelain sink with a pump for running water from the outdoor well. Peter was very patient and allowed Anna to butter thick slices of bread while he sliced the ham. Greta set the table as Catharine made tea then quartered apples to go with the sandwiches. They had a cozy supper, followed by hot tea with sugar cookies Peter had made for dessert, impressing them with his culinary skills. How like a family they already seemed to be with their lighthearted bantering and talk of the Olsens' homeland and Wyoming, Catharine thought. Soon dusk crept into the kitchen and Peter left to feed and water the livestock.

"I won't be long," he whispered to Catharine out of earshot from her two sisters. "Why don't you go on upstairs and get comfortable?" She could feel his warm breath tickling her ear. His cerulean eyes lingered on hers, then he slipped out into the dusk, the screen door squeaking behind him.

Catharine was pleased that her sisters shooed her out of the kitchen. They promised they'd clean up the supper dishes, telling her this was her wedding night, after all. She slipped up the stairs, and by the time the sky was dark, she had bathed and changed into a fine lawn gown trimmed in delicate lace at the throat and sleeves, with blue ribbon that Greta and Anna had insisted on buying for her before they left their homeland. She looked at her reflection in the mirror, and with a resigned sigh she crawled beneath the covers. She was indeed more tired than she first thought as she lay there thinking about Peter. Though she tried to wait for his return, she drifted off to sleep.

Colorful tulips and lush meadows became a pleasant dream as Catharine walked in her garden, breathing in the cool night air . . . waiting for him—again. In the distance she heard the baby crying. She hurried back to the house and flung open the door. In the dim light she made out the outline of him holding the baby at arm's length, and then all was quiet . . .

Catharine awoke suddenly from her sleep, sobbing, as Peter gently touched her head. "Shush, sweet one . . . you've had a bad dream," he said. He continued to stroke her arms until she turned around, her tears wetting her cheeks. "It'll be okay."

Catharine didn't remember falling asleep and certainly didn't remember Peter climbing into bed. She sat up, wiping her tears with the back of her hand. "I'm sorry, Peter. I must've fallen asleep." She flung the covers off, unsure of what else to say or do, and walked to the window. She pulled back the curtain to gaze at the twinkling stars against the black sky. "I must've slept for a long time too. Forgive me." She looked over her shoulder at him.

"You were tired, my dear. Do you want to tell me about your dream?" Peter, looking sleepy-eyed, got out of bed, padding to her in his bare feet and nightshirt. Catharine smiled weakly, then realized she was clad in only her nightgown.

She suddenly felt very shy and awkward, not to mention her embarrassment at having red, swollen eyes. What a sight she must look!

"I'd rather not. It was just a dream." How could she tell him what that dream meant? She couldn't . . . she simply couldn't. She shuddered and folded her arms across her chest.

Peter pulled her to him. "You're shivering. Let me warm you up."

She breathed in his manly smell, a mix of soap and aftershave lotion. He had bathed for her before coming back to the house. She wondered where. Outside? In a creek?

He kissed the curve of her neck and nuzzled her ear, and she returned his kisses. He pulled her gently in the direction of their bed, and she lay back down as he removed his nightshirt. His chest was lean and tanned—she supposed from working outdoors—but bare of chest hair. He looked down at her with hungry eyes, and she allowed him to untie her gown. She kept her eyes on his face as he caressed her with his eyes.

"You're more beautiful than I have words for, I'm afraid," he said in a husky voice that made her tremble. "Your skin is like silk to the touch."

She smiled back at him. "Mmm . . . thank you," she murmured.

He lay down next to her, lovingly stroking her back, whispering sweet things in her ear until she'd almost forgotten about the bad dream . . . almost. Nestled in his arms was where she wanted to be, wasn't it? His touch was comforting, but why wasn't her heart racing the way his was?

6

Peter was glad to be doing chores the next morning and away from the house so he could ponder his thoughts. He'd left the womenfolk after a breakfast of oatmeal, bacon, and coffee. Certainly not their usual fare—he could tell by the way their stared at their dishes. He could cook well enough to keep from starving, but fancy he was not. He'd hoped that between Catharine and Greta, one of them would turn out to be a fair, if not good, cook.

When he finished milking the cow and putting the horses out to pasture, he turned to mucking out the stalls. He loved working with his hands and liked the sense of accomplishment he felt when he'd completed his work at the end of a long day or after a successful harvest.

While he'd admired Catharine from the first time he'd clapped eyes on her, something had seemed amiss last night. Memories of her in his arms last night brought renewed pounding in his veins, and he sighed heavily. Though she'd been willing, it seemed she was holding back something from him—something important. But then he was no expert where women were concerned. He only knew that something hadn't felt quite right.

He paused his raking and swept his hand across his brow. Maybe he'd rushed her or should have let her have more time to rest up from the trip. That's why he hadn't awakened her when he came back—she was sleeping peacefully, until the dream. Was that what had upset her, or was she upset with him? *Lord, you're gonna have to lead me in handling my new bride. Show me what to do or what to say to make her comfortable.*

Peter felt he'd been as gentle and as romantic as he knew how to be. But he had no experience with the art of lovemaking. Maybe he'd talk to Mario. He and Angelina were affectionate and deliriously in love. He wanted that too—was it too much to ask? But how in the world would they get to that point?

Catharine and Greta dragged one of their trunks to the sitting room and began unpacking their personal belongings. Catharine lifted out her most prized possession. Only a few pieces of Blue Willow china had been salvaged after the trunk was damaged during a storm on the ship. She treasured the beautiful teapot, cups, saucers, and sugar and creamer, but the rest had been broken into a million pieces.

"Why don't you set it on the tea cart, Cath?" Anna suggested when tears filled her sister's eyes.

Catharine looked around. "But there's a rose teapot there already."

"So?" Greta said, her hands on her hips. "This is *your* home now. You can do as you please, Sis."

Catharine chewed her bottom lip. "I suppose you're right." She carried her tea set over to the cart near the settee, and Anna picked up the rose teapot and cups and carried them to the dining room.

After several trips up and down the stairs, carrying their clothing and other personal items, they were hot and thirsty. "I could use something cold to drink." Catharine wiped her hands on her apron. "Then we'll need to carry this trunk to the attic. Peter has enough to take care of."

"I'll fetch us some water," Greta said. "We can take a short break first." She strode to the kitchen in search of glasses.

Anna sat down and leaned back on the settee. "Whew, I'm tired. I think I'll take a walk outside. It's stuffy in here."

Catharine pulled back the chintz drapery and shoved open the windows, allowing a breeze to circulate in the room. She wondered what she would put together for lunch and what time Peter would return. She'd have to come up with something. She didn't even own a cookbook, but maybe there was one in the kitchen somewhere.

Greta returned with a pitcher of water and three glasses. They gulped the water down and then had another glass. "The dry weather here is making me so thirsty!" Greta said, setting down her empty glass.

"I have to agree with you, but one good thing—water is good for you, and it hits the spot."

Anna laughed. "I've never seen you choose water over hot tea!"

"Never fear, dear sister, when I've had a chance to get this trunk upstairs and cool off, my tea will be made," Catharine said.

Anna chuckled, and Greta just shook her head and smiled at her.

"Okay, let's see if we can haul this trunk to the attic and get it out of the way." Catharine grabbed one of the leather straps on the end. "It's heavy, but not nearly like it was before we emptied it." Out of the corner of her eye, she noticed Anna slip out the door. She knew her sister was itching to explore the surrounding area. Catharine understood her free spirit, but she was trying hard to instill the importance of having responsibility in Anna's life. How did you teach a fifteen-year-old how to do that when her head was in the clouds most of the time? She sighed. Sometimes the responsibility of being mother and father to her sisters was a struggle, and she felt the weight of it on her shoulders.

"Are you all right? You sure are doing a lot of sighing," Greta said, taking her end of the trunk.

"*Ja*, I'm fine . . . just thinking." They started up the stairs with the trunk, Catharine in the back to bolster most of the weight.

"Oh? About Peter . . . your wedding night?" Greta teased.

Catharine bristled and said, "I wasn't thinking anything of the kind!" She realized that her protest sounded defensive and hurriedly added, "I was just thinking about Anna. She's such a dreamer."

"What you really mean is she's lazy!" Greta laughed.

Catharine paused halfway up the stairs to look at Greta. "In her defense, I doubt that's true. She just sees things through a different eye."

"Meaning she marches to the beat of a different drummer?" Greta raised an eyebrow.

"Mmm . . . you could say that." They both laughed. She continued on up the stairs, pushing the trunk as Greta pulled.

When they finally reached the attic door, they were tuckered out and paused to catch their breath on the landing. "I'll help you drag it into the attic space, but I don't like dusty, spider-filled rooms, so let's hurry," Greta said, breathing heavily.

"All right. Then I'll have to go start lunch."

Greta snorted. "Then count me out unless you *really* need me. I want to straighten our room and put our things away. You know Anna will only leave things right where she left them, and I can't stand clutter."

They continued up the last of the stairs that led up into the attic, and it turned out Greta was right. It looked as though no one had been in there for quite some time.

"We can just leave it right here by the door, Greta."

"Good. Now let's go." She turned back to the short flight of stairs.

"You go on ahead. I want to see if there's anything usable up here."

"Suit yourself, if you can find them under the dust and dirty cloths."

Catharine didn't mind being alone in the attic to explore. As a child, she had frequented her parents' attic, enjoying the history there. She lifted a cloth and found a stack of old books that she and Anna might like, then proceeded to the other items draped with the dusty cloths. There was a charming lady's dressing table and chair, whose now faded fabric had a tear in the seat. She might be able to repair it. It would be a good reading chair in the alcove under the window in her sisters' room. She'd think about it before asking Peter to carry it down.

The dust caused her to sneeze, and as she turned to go, something next to a rusty birdcage caught her eye. She slowly drew the cloth back so as not to disturb any more dust, and her breath caught in her throat. An exquisitely carved cradle of fine cherrywood sat vacant. She timidly touched the smooth wood, which caused it to rock slightly . . . almost eerily. Whose cradle was this? Peter's? How wonderful it would be if their own baby could lie in it next to their bed. She blushed, thinking of the previous night and Peter's gentleness as he wooed and touched her with his love. A tear started at the corner of her eye, and she knelt down next to the cradle. Maybe they wouldn't be able to have a child. *Maybe God won't entrust me with one.* She buried her face in her hands, struggling with emotions she'd tried to push deep inside.

"You're still up here?" Greta called out as she came up the stairs. She knelt beside Catharine and placed her arm around her sister's shoulder, giving it a tight squeeze. "Cath, it'll be all right . . . you've had a lot to bear. Don't torture yourself. Come on, let's get you back downstairs." Greta stood and draped the cover back over the cradle. She held out her hand and Catharine reluctantly took it. With a heavy heart she struggled to her feet to go prepare lunch.

After scouring the cupboards, Catharine found green beans and a jar of peaches. She sliced what was left of the bread and added leftover bacon from breakfast. Pretty sorry fare, she concluded. She hoped she'd be able to come up with something better for supper and wished there was some soup. She would have to figure out how to make it. Come winter, a hot bowl of soup would be a hearty dish to serve.

"Do you suppose we'll ever eat in the fancy dining room, Cath?" Greta said, placing the forks and spoons next to the plates.

Catharine muttered, "Maybe when I learn to cook something edible or special." She paused, looking at the food she'd placed on the kitchen table. "Though I have little appetite right now, I'm sure Peter will be hungry when he gets home for lunch."

"He's been gone for hours." Putting the glasses on the table, Greta turned to glance out the window. "What do you suppose he does all day long?"

"Plenty, I'm sure. I think I'll ask him what chores we're expected to do. Without help, I don't see how he gets it all done." For some moments Catharine watched as her sister gazed out the window with longing in her pretty face, far removed from the little kitchen. *What beautiful innocence.* "Are you longing for home?" Catharine asked.

Greta jumped at her question and turned to face her sister. "No . . . not at all. I was just thinking . . ."

"Something bothering you?" Catharine knew that Greta was never one to be quiet for long.

Greta moved to fill the glasses with water but kept her eyes lowered. "Oh . . . it's nothing, really."

Catharine didn't feel reassured. Ever since Greta had met the soldier in town, Catharine had caught her daydreaming at odd times. That was more in character for Anna than Greta. Catharine shook the worry away when she heard Peter swing open the back door.

Smiling, he walked over to where she was standing and kissed her cheek, then hung his hat over the rung of the kitchen chair. "Hello, beautiful!"

Before she could answer, he glanced over at the table with a puzzled look on his face, but if he thought the fare was bare, he made no comment. Instead he headed to the sink to wash his hands.

"There wasn't much that I could fix, Peter, but I hope this will do. Is there some meat I could use for dinner?" She felt her face flush as his gaze softened. *Probably regrets his decision to make me his wife.* "Greta, can you go call Anna and tell her lunch is ready? I don't know where she got off to."

Greta set the water pitcher down on the table. "I'll go find her," she said with exasperation in her tone.

As soon as she'd left the room, Peter pulled Catharine to him and gave her a long, delicious kiss that left her breathless. "Things would be different if we lived alone, you know." He gave her waist a tight squeeze, and his hand felt warm through the fabric of her dress.

She winced. "If you're regretting your decision, Peter—"

"I didn't say that," he said. "I'm just saying I might not have even left our bed this morning. I'd have you snuggled close to me until I *had* to go take care of the animals." He grinned mischievously and his lips twitched when she leaned back to flash him a smile. He reached up to tuck a loose curl behind her ear. "You smell so good."

"Oh. If you say so."

"I say so, and since I'm the master of the house, what I say is a fact," he teased. He kissed her brow before releasing her. "Will the girls be back soon?"

"We're here now, Peter," Greta said as she came through the kitchen door. Anna traipsed in behind her with grass stains on her dress and her blonde hair wild and loose.

"Anna, what happened to you?" Catharine stepped toward her sister.

"What?" Anna looked down at the marks on her dress. "Oh, that . . . well, *ja*, I suppose it's from sitting in the grass by the creek. It'll wash out, won't it?"

Catharine just shook her head, "*Ja*, but you'll be the one to scrub it."

Peter pulled out the chairs for them, then took his seat. "I'll bless the food." After he said "Amen," he dished a helping of green beans onto his plate, then passed the bowl to Anna. She wrinkled her nose at the dish, passed it to Greta, then reached for the bread.

Catharine waited until there was a lull in the conversation, then asked, "Peter, do you think you could make out a list tonight of certain chores you could assign to us?" She filled his water glass again.

Peter blotted his mouth before answering. "Well . . . let's see now, there's milking to be done, meals to prepare, taking care of the house and laundry, gardening, cleaning the stables, caring for the livestock, wheat harvest—" He paused when Catharine squirmed in her chair. "But we can divide some of the chores between you three. I'll be in charge of taking care of the wheat since it's already planted, but I may need some help with that later on."

"Well, I was counting on finding a job soon, but there's more than enough work around here," Greta said.

"Are you ever going to hire some help for the house?" Anna asked innocently.

"Anna!" Catharine snapped. "I believe that will be left up to me and Peter."

"To tell you the truth, my mother had some help when she lived here, but I've not felt the need to. I'm sorry if that disappoints all of you." Peter's jaw tightened, causing his mustache to flatten across his upper lip.

Catharine straightened her shoulders and passed the bread around. "We'll be fine, Peter, but there may be a few things you'll have to teach us."

"Nothing I do around here is hard to learn, really. Anything you want to know, just ask, and I'll be more than happy to show you how it's done." He shoved his chair back. "I'd better get on back to work. I'm going to ride out to the fields and make sure there's no break in the fence line. I'll be back by supper. Thanks for lunch." He clapped his hat back on but stopped when he got to the back door and came back to kiss Catharine on the top of her head. "By the way, there's meat hanging out in the smokehouse that you can cook or make a stew with. It's up to you. See you ladies later." Then he was gone.

"If I only knew how . . ." Catharine muttered, then she turned to face Anna, placing her hands on her hips. "You are so lucky to have a home and food in your belly! We need to do what we can here to show our gratefulness!" Catharine's voice rose in irritation. "Anna, why would you have the nerve to ask for help? There are three of us and we *will* make do!"

Anna's lips trembled. "But we've always had servants. I should think you'd want them since you know absolutely nothing about farming."

Greta smothered a laugh, and Catharine faced her with a look of displeasure. "How do you intend to do all those things he listed?" Greta asked.

Anna slipped in the middle of her sisters, her hands out to each side. "Please, let's not argue, sisters. We can split the list. I could help Peter with the livestock."

Catharine nodded. "*Ja.* That's the attitude that I'm looking for, Anna." She gave her a pat on the cheek. Anna was a nature lover, and she'd naturally want to do anything that wasn't related to being indoors.

Greta harrumphed. "You may say that now, but when winter settles in, you won't be so compliant, little sister."

Anna stuck her tongue out at Greta. "Catharine, is it all right if I take my pencils and go do some sketching this afternoon before you list our assignments?" she asked, smiling up at Catharine.

Catharine noted the enthusiasm in Anna's eyes. Youth and innocence were a dear thing. "Yes, you may. But first let's open the packages that Peter bought for us and see what he thought we needed so badly in order to work on the farm."

"They're right here where he left them." Greta grumbled under her breath as she picked up the brown paper packages on the counter, then placed them on the kitchen table. Catharine found the scissors in a kitchen drawer, and Greta quickly cut the string on the packages.

Complete silence followed as the three of them stared down. There were several serviceable, heavy dresses in various drab colors for each of them, complete with aprons. The sight of heavy-duty brogans brought a frown to Greta's face, making Catharine and Anna giggle.

"What in the world . . . ?" Catharine shook her head.

"Are these really for us? Is this what that clerk wrapped up?"

"Oh, look, there's overalls like our stable boy wore back home." Anna grinned. "I might like these."

Catharine held up the overalls in disbelief. "I'm not really sure why we would need these."

"Peter did say that we would be doing outdoor work, and working in a dress would be difficult in the wheat fields," Greta said. "These dresses are made of such rough material that I can only guess that's why they're for work—they won't tear easily."

Anna stripped off her skirt to don her new overalls. "Cath, could you manage the hooks, please?"

Catharine obliged and stood back with approval. "You look adorable in them, Anna!"

Anna slipped on the brogans and spun around. "I think I like these," she said, then turned to Greta. "Would you mind taking my skirt upstairs when you go? I'll be back early, Catharine."

"You know, I can see how it would be easier to do gardening in this than in a skirt with a lot of petticoats, can't you?" Catharine asked Greta, who was holding a dress up to see if it was the right fit.

"Well . . . you could be right. They seem to be the right sizes. But those shoes are hideous. I can't see myself in those." Greta groaned.

Catharine slipped off her shoes and put on one of the brogans. "They're really not that bad, honestly." She twisted sideways, hiked up her petticoats, and looked down at her feet. "They'll give me sure footing while I'm planting a garden. I intend to have a flower garden and a vegetable garden." She bent down and put the other shoe on and laced them both up. Straightening up, she decided that the shoes would serve their purpose.

"Greta, could you finish the dishes? I'm going to take a walk around the place, unless you'd like to come with me. Fresh air would do us both some good."

"Maybe another time. You go on ahead and see if you can locate a vegetable garden." Greta started stacking dishes in the heavy sink. "Guess there's no time like the present to get my hands wet!" She held up her slender hands, admiring them. "I have a feeling my hands won't look this good as long as I'm at this farm."

"Oh, don't be so self-centered. Your hands will survive." Catharine tsked. As she slipped out the door and down the porch steps into the warm afternoon sun, guilt pressed in about how she'd chided Greta, but she wondered how she herself would survive this complete change of lifestyle. Would the love between her and Peter grow to be enough?

7

Peter climbed down from the buckboard and tied his horse to the hitching post in front of Mario's Ristorante. On his drive to town for necessary supplies, he'd thought constantly about Catharine. The beautiful image of her face kept floating in and out of his mind like the moving clouds across the Wyoming prairie. He was beginning to like the tumble of auburn hair that had a mind of its own. It was hard for him to resist touching the silky curls, which surprised him because he never thought he'd be attracted to a redhead. *I'm such a lucky man!*

"Peter! You're back so soon." Mario gave Peter a puzzled look when he strode through the door of the restaurant. Delicious garlic and onion smells wafted throughout, reminding Peter of his meager lunch, and his stomach rumbled. The lunch crowd had already dispersed, and Mario and Angelina were cleaning the tables for the dinner hour.

"Have you had lunch yet?" Mario said, clapping Peter on the back.

"I have, such as it was. I wanted to stop in and thank you for standing up for me at the wedding ceremony. I'm sorry about the way my mother acted." Peter smiled at his best friend.

"Mmm." Mario fingered his mustache. "You're welcome, of course, but you needn't have made a special trip into town just to tell us that."

Peter shifted from one boot heel to the other, then cast a glance at Angelina, who smiled and waved from the corner of the dining room, then continued with her work. He really liked Angelina. She was sweet and kind, and Peter hoped that she and Catharine would become good friends. But today he wanted to have a word with just Mario.

Seeming to notice Peter's uneasiness, Mario pulled him to the side of the gleaming wood counter, where water glasses and starched white linen napkins were stacked. He leaned toward his friend. "Is there something on your mind, Peter?"

"Well . . . uh . . ." He shot another look in Angelina's direction.

That's all it took for Mario. "Angelina!" he yelled.

Angelina turned her head in their direction. "What *ees* it? You need me, Mario?"

"I'm stepping to the back for a moment. Will you watch for customers?"

"*Sí.*" She smiled and motioned him to go with a wave of her cleaning cloth.

Mario pushed back the swinging doors that led to the kitchen prep area, where row upon rows of staples and canned goods lined an entire wall. He wiped his hands on his apron and crossed his arms. "So, what's on your mind, my friend?"

Peter shrugged. "I'm not sure anything's the matter. It's just . . . I'm not sure . . . last night, Catharine—"

"Ah, I see . . . matters of the heart." Mario uncrossed his arms and smiled at his friend. "Barely newlywed, and yet . . ." His voice trailed off.

"I think I know nothing about the art of love . . . or maybe women for that matter." Peter stared past Mario's shoulder, looking at the big pots on the stove. "I want to make her happy, and I do care for her. She's . . . she's beautiful," he said in a hushed voice. He raised his eyes to meet Mario's.

His friend tore off a chunk of the fresh bread that was cooling on the table and shoved a piece at him. "Then that's what really counts! Ahh . . . I'm remembering me and Angelina before Alfredo and Angelo came along. It was bliss, I tell you!" A broad smile lit his face. "Come, sit down." He patted the chair next to a small table and sat down. "Let me tell you, my friend, the art of love and making a woman happy is not a hard thing to do. You find out what makes her tick. If it's flowers, then you give her those, or better yet, plant them for her. Do extra small things for her, like draw her bath, brush her hair. Or bring her a cup of hot coffee or tea—whichever she prefers when she least expects it." He paused a moment. "Don't rush her, but hold her and tell her sweet and wonderful things you've observed about her."

Peter winced. "That may take some time, but I can try. Our affection grew through our correspondence, you know," he said, biting into the crusty piece of bread.

"Yes, yes, I do. Sometime I want you to bring her to town for a little honeymoon. Bring her here for dinner, then spend the night at the Inter Ocean. I will prepare the most delicious pasta for you that will melt in your mouth." Mario pressed his fingers to his lips and kissed them. "*Bellissimo!* It will be so romantic, I assure you." Mario stood with his hands on his hips.

Peter hesitated, scratching the stubble of hair now sprouting on his chin. "I don't know . . . maybe. I'll have to give it some thought."

Mario's two young sons came running through the kitchen and chased each other around the table, their dark hair flying and heavy shoes pounding the hardwood floor.

"Alfredo! Angelo! Stop that! Can't you see we are having a private conversation here?" Mario put his arm out and grabbed Alfredo by the arm.

"Sorry, Father, but Angelo started it," Alfredo said, breathing hard.

"I did not!" Angelo glared at his brother as he slid to a stop, nearly upending the table.

"No matter, apologize to Mr. Andersen, and then take yourselves outside and run all you like."

Both of the boys muttered "sorry" to Peter, and off they went racing through the dining room. Peter could hear Angelina yelling something in Italian at them as they went weaving through the tables.

Peter laughed, and Mario raised both arms above his head in exasperation and shrugged. "Sorry, sometimes they can be a handful. But you'll find out for yourself soon enough." He chuckled.

"I look forward to that. I'd better get on back home before supper—whatever Catharine will come up with." Peter chuckled. "Thanks for the advice, Mario." He moved to the swinging door. "I'll be in touch."

"Ciao!"

Peter said goodbye to Angelina, promising to bring Catharine the next time, then hurried out to where he'd hitched the wagon. On the ride home, he pondered what Mario had told him. A honeymoon weekend might be just the thing to make Catharine feel more at ease. He could surprise her, but he wasn't sure if it was safe to leave her sisters alone out on the farm. He didn't want to bring them too—that would defeat the whole purpose.

To tell the truth, if her sisters hadn't tagged along in the first place, things could have been so much more romantic, but his plans had been squashed when Catharine brought them. He sighed wearily, knowing that if he'd had two brothers to raise, they would've come as a package too. It was only the right thing to do, but it just didn't seem fair. *Well, Lord, I'll just have to figure out how to make it up to her and myself, since she's devoted to her family. But it'd be nice if she'd be devoted to me someday.*

Catharine pulled the three-legged stool next to the cow, Bessie, who swung her head around at the sound of Catharine's movements and looked at her with large brown eyes. She patted the cow's rump and murmured a greeting. "Now see here, Bessie. I know I'm not very good at milking, so please be patient with me."

Bessie went on chewing her cud. Catharine plopped down on the stool, pushed her skirts between her legs, and reached for Bessie's udders to wash them gently with warm water before starting to milk her. "I've seen milking done before. I might be a complete flop at it, but I'm determined to give it a try, my dear cow." She giggled, thinking that if someone heard her now, they might be concerned about her sanity.

She placed a milk pail under Bessie and pulled down on one teat. Nothing. Catharine tried again, but no stream of milk appeared. After a few minutes of frustration, she wiped her brow and blew a dangling curl away from her eyes.

The barn door opened and Greta and Anna strode in.

"Catharine, we've been looking all over for you!" Greta's eyes glanced over at the empty pail. "No luck, huh?"

Catharine groaned. "Not yet. It looked simple with Peter's help. But I didn't learn well enough, I guess." She sat back, giving her lower back a rub.

"Move, Cath. I think I can wring some milk out of that ol' cow." Anna pushed Catharine's shoulder, then knelt in the straw next to her. "Peter said I'm good at it. I'll show you how."

Greta stood by to watch, her arms folded. Catharine knew Anna wasn't afraid of anything and remembered she'd gotten the hang of milking with the first try.

"See how I kind of roll Bessie's teat in the palm of my hand?"

Catharine nodded. Anna's blue eyes sparkled up at her, and she gave Catharine a grin. "Good. After you do that, you pull. Just roll and pull the teat in the palm of your hand in one movement." Anna demonstrated, and the milky stream hit the empty pail with a loud splash. "Here . . . try again."

Catharine eyed her sister and pursed her lips with determination. If Anna could do it, surely it couldn't be that hard. She grabbed another teat and mimicked Anna's motion. With the first attempt, milk appeared and Greta clapped her hands together.

"You did it, Cath! Good for you. Now you can do *all* the milking while Anna and I explore fun chores more to our liking." Her lips turned up as she leaned down to look in the pail.

"Oh no you don't! You'll help me."

"But you're doing so well without our—" Suddenly a squirt of Bessie's milk hit Greta's cheek as Catharine directed the teat in her hand right at Greta. Anna laughed so hard she had to hold her stomach. Bessie mooed her sentiments with a loud bellow, making the bell around her neck clang loudly.

After her initial surprise, Greta wiped her cheek with the corner of her apron and pretended to be miffed at her sisters' laughter, but she giggled good-naturedly. "All right. I guess I deserved that, didn't I?"

"You certainly did. In fact, I think tomorrow's your day." Catharine laughed. "But I think you need to try your hand at it to see if you've forgotten how." She continued to milk Bessie using both hands, now feeling much more confident.

Greta cocked an eyebrow in disdain. "Oh, all right. You win this time. But watch out. Milk could go flying again, you know!"

Catharine shrugged her shoulders playfully, then dried Bessie's udders with a clean cloth. She breathed a sigh that the chore was done. "You get to milk her tonight."

Anna clapped her hands. "Oh, this should be fun. I don't want to miss it!"

Catharine fanned herself with her apron after standing over the hot stove for hours. She couldn't remember when she'd been this warm, and it made her long for Holland. She opened all the windows and a door to get a cross breeze to cool down the kitchen and was grateful that Wyoming was a windy place.

After finding what looked like a side of roast beef from the smokehouse, she'd sprinkled it with salt and a dash of pepper and shoved it into the oven. The potatoes and carrots she'd found in the cellar simmered on the stove. A lump resembling a loaf of bread sat on the counter, ready to be baked after the roast was done. She'd seen their cook back home knead dough before but wasn't sure of the ingredients except for flour and eggs. Was she supposed to sift the flour? Hopefully the bread would rise up in time to bake for supper.

She was feeling pretty good about what she'd thrown together after shooing her sisters out of the kitchen. They were only making matters worse, especially Greta. She could be doggedly stubborn sometimes.

Am I really going to have to do this every day? How in the world can I manage it all—especially if we have children? There'd never be time to read or sew, not with vegetables to can, the wash to do, and the house to care for. One would have to get up at dawn and drop like the sun on the horizon just to get it all finished. She was ready to drop now. But oh, how she wanted to make Peter proud.

Catharine glanced over at the dough and decided that it certainly hadn't risen much. Maybe that happened after it went in the hot oven. She looked around with a critical eye. The table was set and even had a vase of yellow bearded irises that Anna had picked earlier, which added a nice touch. She wished her mother's Blue Willow china graced their table. If it hadn't been for the unfortunate storm at sea, it would have. No use crying about it now. She wondered if she should be using the dining room but thought maybe that was only for company or special holidays.

The apples had been sliced and soaked and were now waiting off to the side for a pie. Catharine moved the rolling pin back and forth across the leftover dough to make a piecrust, as she'd seen Cook do when she was a child, and flour flew every which way. She wanted to see if she could flute the sides like Cook always

75

did, but when she tried to lift the crust up, it wouldn't budge. It was stuck to the countertop! She tried peeling it up with her fingertips, but it only continued to tear and was gooey, sticking to her fingers like syrup. The more she handled the crust, the more frustrated she became. She was getting nowhere with the wad of dough, and it seemed to laugh at her attempts.

After the third try, she jammed the dough into a wad, then threw the entire thing on the floor and stomped on it. *There! Now you're flat and of no use to me*, she thought, clamping her jaw. Heaving a big sigh, she bent down and began to clean up the mess she'd made, then lifted her shoe to wipe the goo off the bottom.

Her nose twitched as the smell of the roast beef filled the kitchen. Good, it was cooking nicely. She added more wood to keep the fire hot, and suddenly the foam from the potatoes rose up and boiled over, making a complete mess all over the stove. Quickly she grabbed a dishcloth, and as she moved the pot of potatoes off to the side, she saw that the cloth was scorched from the flame. There was smoke coming from the oven, so she bent down and yanked the oven door open to discover a thoroughly burned roast stuck to the pan. She let out a cry of anguish and covered her face with her hands, sinking to the floor with tears of defeat. Her dinner was ruined!

It was at that very moment that Peter strode in through the back door to find his discouraged bride in a heap on the floor, sobbing in front of the stove. Her hair had come loose from its pins and now fell across her face, and splats of flour covered her chin and one cheek where she swiped her hair back with her hands. It was quite a different look for her in her homespun dress, apron, and brogans. One quick look around revealed a burnt pan of meat teetering on the edge of the oven door and something resembling vegetables still bubbling in a nearby pot. A somewhat strange-looking concoction sat in a bowl next to a pie pan.

Peter's laughter reverberated through the farmhouse, and he clapped his thigh in amazement. Catharine shot him a glance, and he immediately clamped his mouth shut and dropped to the floor next to her. Lifting her sticky hands in his, he whispered, "Don't cry, Catharine. I'll help you clean this up and we'll have something simple." Touching her chin, he lifted her head until she met his gaze through tear-filled eyes, but she quickly glanced away.

"Oh, Peter, I've made a mess of everything and I still haven't even baked the bread. I'm sorry."

"Hush, it'll be all right." Peter pulled her to his chest until she was in his lap, and she nuzzled her face in his neck. The sweet scent of her made him groan. With her body snuggled close to his, he was of a mind to sweep her off the floor and take her to their bedroom. But instead he said, "I had forgotten that you were used to having servants wait on you. Perhaps Angelina could spend an afternoon teaching you to cook and clean."

She drew back, pushing her palms against his chest. She struggled to her feet, but the flour on the floor made her slip, and she fell hard against the table. He tried to grab her from his seated position but missed, and she winced in pain, then turned to glare at him. "I'm all right. Just leave me alone while I clean this up. Servants or not, I *will* learn to make do!" she snapped, then muttered something unintelligible under her breath.

What had he done now? "I'll help you. I didn't mean that to sound the way it did."

"Really?" She swung around, her green eyes ablaze. "You

expect me to take care of the house, cook, and tend the garden, all in the first day of our marriage?" Her voice was starting to screech, and her freckles stood out pink and bright on her white skin. "How can that be?" She wiped her hands on her apron, picked up the roasting pan, and stuck it in the sink.

Peter wasn't sure what to say. After a long moment of silence, he walked over to her where she stood with her back to him, shoulders slumped. "I'm sorry if this isn't what you thought married life would be." She turned around to face him. She blinked, but he couldn't read what she must be thinking. "Where are your sisters? Couldn't they help?"

"I didn't want their help. I'm your wife." With a catch in her voice, she said, "I just wanted . . . to please you, Peter, not make you laugh at me as if I were an incompetent child." Catharine stared down at her feet with a pout.

Peter surely didn't understand how a woman could be sweet and sassy all in the space of a split second. He had a lot to learn about the opposite sex. He reached out and stroked the side of her cheek with his thumb, wiping the flour away. "I said I was sorry. I don't know what else to say, except I'm here to help you. Let's clean this up, then you can put the bread in to bake while the oven's hot, and I'll go fetch more wood. I'll show you how to whip up stew with what we can salvage from the roast. Deal? Besides, you look mighty cute in that apron and flour in your hair." He smiled and tucked a loose curl behind her ear.

Her face softened, and he could tell he'd struck a chord with her. "Okay. But do you think we can do all this before Greta and Anna come in? I'm embarrassed enough for one day, I think."

Peter leaned over and kissed her brow. "If we hurry, they'll be none the wiser." He took the dishcloth from her hand as she gave him a weak smile. He briefly touched her mouth with his, and though she quivered, she didn't push him away. *Mmm . . . maybe I'm making some headway, Mario.*

After supper, Peter left, saying he had a few things to attend to in the tack room. Catharine was grateful for a little time alone while Greta and Anna cleaned up the kitchen. Greta had told her at supper that she wanted to do some of the cooking, and Catharine was only too happy to share the chore with her sister. Between the two of them and the cookbook, it wouldn't be too bad. Peter had given her a few tips and was eager to help her learn.

In the parlor, she picked up her Bible, settling in Peter's chair to read. Noting that it smelled like him, she snuggled in, tucking her legs under her skirt. Holding her mother's Bible in her lap reminded her of all the times she and her sisters would gather around her mother's chair as she read the Christmas story. Someday Catharine hoped to have children so she could share the greatest gift of all with them.

She could hear the pleasant chatter of her sisters, and she was beginning to feel a rhythm to the Andersen household. The feeling made her content, so she took a moment to thank God for all that she had. When she finished her reading, Catharine moved to the desk, pulled out the chair, and looked for a fresh sheet of stationery.

Catharine was already in bed by the time Peter was ready for bed after tending to the cow and feeding the horses. What a pretty picture she made as she lay against the white linen sheets, her red hair fanned out against the pillow top. His gaze slid to his pillow, where a folded piece of paper was propped. He picked it up, then glanced over at Catharine.

"What's this?" Peter asked quietly, but receiving no answer from her, he opened the folded paper and saw Catharine's feminine handwriting.

> Peter,
>
> My greatest desire is to be your helpmeet and make a home for us. I'm sorry if I disappoint you with my skills in the kitchen particularly. Thank you for your help. I will get better at this, I promise. I want you to know how grateful I am that you accepted my sisters into our home. Your patience with me is what I most need now. I forgot to tell you how much your letter the day of our wedding meant to me. I'll treasure it always.
>
> Proud to be your wife,
> Catharine

Peter climbed into bed, still holding the letter, and reached for Catharine, who he knew feigned sleep. Pulling her against his chest, he whispered against her brow, "My sweet one, ahh . . ."

Catharine lifted her head and her lips met his.

8

Clara glanced at her reflection through the clear glass front of the door labeled Private Investigator in bold black lettering. Satisfied with how her new hat looked perched to one side, she swung open the door. She knew if she wanted to uncover personal information about her daughter-in-law, it wouldn't come from Peter. What if this woman was a gold digger? Why Peter hadn't asked Dorothy Miller to marry him was simply beyond her. Dorothy's family was respected, and her father was their beloved family attorney. It made no sense at all. Dorothy, a schoolteacher, was kindhearted and comely. She and Peter would have made a nice match with her blonde hair and blue eyes, and their children would have reflected their good looks. Not like that brazen redheaded Catharine, with the strange accent and brooding eyes.

Clara squared her shoulders and smiled at the man hunched over a sheaf of papers at a battered wooden desk. He stood as she walked toward him. Stretching out her gloved hand, she greeted him with a smile. "I'm Clara Andersen." She took a step back and let go of his hand.

"I'm Mac Foster. Nice to meet you." He pushed his coat

back, his hands on his hips, and looked intently at her. "What can I help you with, Mrs. Andersen?"

She leveled a steady look at him, but inside she was trembling. She'd never done anything like this in her life. "I need to have a background check done . . . er . . . on a certain individual." She paused nervously, fingering the collar of her jabot blouse. "It needs to be done with utmost haste. Can you help me with that?"

"I can most certainly." He paused and pushed back a lock of dark hair touched with gray that fell over his eyes. "But it'll cost you, since I usually handle, shall we say . . . delicate situations." His mouth smiled, but his dark eyes narrowed as he looked her up and down. "Please, have a seat." He picked up a box of files from a chair next to his desk and gestured with his hand.

Clara's heart fluttered in her chest. Mac seemed a take-charge man with a direct approach. Good. It'd take a man like him to dig around to uncover any shred of evidence that she could use against her daughter-in-law. And boy, when she did have something—and she knew she would—Peter would thank his mother for saving him.

"I'll pour us a cup of coffee while we talk." Mac moved toward the coffeepot that sat simmering on the potbellied stove. Ignoring his offer of coffee, Clara squirmed in her chair, took a deep breath, and began.

"My son, whom I love very much, has hastily married a woman of unknown means and questionable character who came from Holland looking for a husband. *And* brought along her two sisters! I know nothing about her at all. My son lives on a wheat farm that my husband and I gave him. I believe her to be more interested in the land and becoming a citizen of our country than caring about my son. I want you to find out more about her." She looked him directly in the eyes to show that she was telling the truth.

Mac's eyes narrowed as he rubbed his chin with his thumb. "Let me get this straight—the son that you say you love so much is newly married, and you want to destroy that?" He cocked his head and waited for her reply.

Clara puffed out her chest. "I most certainly do not! I'm looking out for his own best interests."

Mac rolled his chair around to her side of the desk. "When was the last time someone looked out for *your* best interests, Mrs. Andersen?" Mac said with mischief in his twinkling eyes.

"That is none of your concern, Mr. Foster. Are you going to help me, or should I just leave now?" How dare he make a pass at her! Or was it that? It had been too many years since anyone had been directly concerned about her personally. Maybe too long for her to care . . .

Mac straddled his chair. "If you have the cash, then I can assure you I have the time, madam. But for starters, call me Mac." He sipped his coffee as he eyed her.

Clara wasn't sure if she should run for the door and drop the entire plan or continue. She was treading on shaky ground with this impertinent detective. Sweet-talking to his clients was definitely not in his repertoire. But she must know more about Catharine. She opened her handbag and gave him an envelope filled with bills. "Will this be enough, Mac?"

Mac peeked inside the envelope, quickly counted the bills, and gave her a steady gaze. "It's a start. Now, let's get down to brass tacks. I'll need you to answer some questions before

I get started with my contacts abroad." He took the pencil from behind his ear, then strode over to his desk for a tablet.

Clara breathed a sigh of relief as he started taking notes.

Catharine rolled over to the edge of the bed and groaned. The morning light was just beginning to peek through the slit in the curtains on the window. Even with the slightest movement, her back ached, her feet were sore, and she was sure she had just dropped into bed only moments before. She stretched her arm behind her and felt the mattress next to her. It was cool to her palm. The last several evenings, she'd been in bed before Peter but he'd been up before her the next morning. He had tilled a flower bed for her, and she spent her time between the kitchen and the garden, pulling out the grass and roots. By autumn she'd plant the tulips that she brought with her from Holland, and hopefully there'd be a dazzling array to brighten the yard and remind her of her homeland.

Might as well get up and start the fire for coffee. She moved slowly to stretch her aching back when the bedroom door opened a crack and Peter peeked in.

"I wasn't sure if you had awakened," he said, color staining his cheeks. "I made some of your favorite tea." He pushed the door open further with one elbow, balancing a tray complete with her Blue Willow tea set.

Catharine made a move to get out of bed, but he stayed her. "No, no. Don't get up. Sit right there and have your tea. You've been working from sunup to sundown every day for the last few weeks. But not today. I was hoping we could all go to church in town, now that you're finally settled in. You can meet some of the people of Cheyenne." He hesitated as he poured her tea. "If that's okay with you?"

Catharine scooted back against the giant headboard, touched by his simple act of kindness. He set the tray across her lap and whipped out a muslin napkin that was delicately embroidered with the initial A. "I'd like to go to church. I've missed it. Now if I can get the girls up . . ." she said, taking a sip of her tea.

Peter took a seat on the edge of the mattress, and the springs squeaked in protest. "Not to worry. I've already woken them up and they're getting dressed. I can't wait to show off my bride."

He smiled at her, his half-lidded eyes sliding down to gaze at her nightgown, and her heart lurched. Her fingers flitted at the ribbons of the gown's neckline as though he could see right through it, but she lifted her cup and took a sip of tea, hoping he hadn't noticed the effect he had on her. She liked the way his eyes flirted with her, and the blue shirt he was wearing set off his disarming eyes.

"I'm afraid I've been so busy taking care of the wheat crop that I haven't spent nearly as much time with you as I'd have liked since you arrived. But I intend to change some of that." He picked up her hand and rubbed his thumb back and forth over it. Her hand felt small in his large one, but his felt tender when he touched her this way. She remembered their first night together when he'd cuddled with her and given himself to her with total abandon. But she'd held back a part of herself because deep down inside she didn't feel worthy of his love.

"Thank you for the tea, but you didn't have to do this."

"But I wanted to do this for my sweet bride." Longing was reflected in his husky voice.

She picked at the nubby threads on the heavy quilt. "That was very sweet of you, Peter, really."

Giving her a tender smile, he stood, and with a sweep of his hand and a mock bow, he said, "Then I'll let you finish your tea and get dressed." Straightening, he beamed at her and she giggled. "I'll throw some bread in the oven to toast and scramble some eggs. Sound good?"

She smiled at him, enjoying his playfulness, and was amazed that she might have caused the zip in his step. "Sounds wonderful. I'll hurry and get dressed as soon as I finish my tea."

Peter gave her a wink. "Take your time . . . there's no rush." He backed out, shutting the door behind him.

Catharine slid down against her fluffy pillow and savored her second cup of tea. It was brewed to perfection. Though she liked coffee, Peter knew she enjoyed hot tea and had watched her make it. Knowing he was trying to please her filled her heart with joy. Maybe she was truly special to someone at last.

But even as she delighted in being his wife, her mind filled with darker thoughts. *If he really knew me, he would reject me. Totally—completely.*

Clara hurried down the boardwalk Sunday morning, missing her usual church service to meet Mac Foster, and as it was, she would be late. She'd spent more time on her toilette than usual, telling herself that it merely took longer at her age. Then she chided herself. It wasn't as if Mac Foster would notice her new dress . . . or would he?

Mac was leaning against the porch railing in front of the Prairie Café, his arms folded across his chest, and he smiled broadly as she walked up. "Good day, Miss Clara," he said, tipping his hat. "You're looking very well. That shade of blue suits you."

Clara felt her face go pink. "Thank you . . . I'll take that as a compliment." She gave a quick glance around to see if anyone she knew was there. A small pang of guilt pricked her conscience, but she pushed the nagging feeling aside. She shouldn't feel guilty for gathering information, should she?

"Shall we go in and have a seat?" Mac offered his arm, and she noticed that he had impeccable taste in clothing. She nodded, and he led her inside the cool restaurant and asked the waiter for a table in the back, apart from the crowded lunchgoers.

After the waiter had taken their order, Mac leaned back in his chair, his dark eyes staring admiringly at Clara until she squirmed in her chair. She felt unnerved by him and was trying to guess his age. She thought it to be close to hers, but it was hard to judge. Why hadn't she noticed him around town before?

"I thought it'd be nice to grab a little lunch before I tell you what facts I've uncovered."

"Mr. Foster, I'd rather you just skip all the formalities and get right to the heart of the matter. I really don't have time for frivolities." Clara gave him a level gaze, and his eyes held hers.

"Frivolities? I'd hardly call discussing business over lunch a frivolity. However, I may be able to set another time where you and I could have a taste of fun and frivolity." He gazed at her with hooded eyes.

"Mr. Foster—"

"Please, I'd like it much better if you'd call me Mac and

allow me to call you by your beautiful name, Clara. Less formal between friends, wouldn't you say?"

Clara cleared her throat. "I'd hardly call us friends. I don't know what you're implying anyway. We merely have a business relationship. One for which I'm paying you a large sum of money, I might add!" He was beginning to make her feel uncomfortable. Her mouth felt as dry as the Cheyenne dust, and she picked up her water glass and took a drink.

"I didn't mean to imply anything out of the ordinary, Clara. I like being around you, and however businesslike you pretend to be, we can be friends. A little fun never hurt anyone. All work and no play is not a particularly good way to live your life. You did tell me that you were widowed, correct?"

Clara sighed deeply. "Yes, I am."

"Good. Then there's no harm in two people getting to know each other better, is there?"

"Er . . . I haven't said that I wanted to . . . Mac." She glanced away, not daring to meet his gaze.

"Ah, there's the rub. You pretend not to be interested, but something tells me you might be persuaded to enjoy my company, if given the chance. That's all I'm asking for . . . a chance to get to know you better."

Clara couldn't believe her ears. Not one man had shown a passing interest in her, though she had been widowed five years. Not that she'd met anyone she wanted to know better. "Are you serious? Or just trying to flatter me so that you can find ways to charge me more?"

Mac laughed and banged his palm on the tabletop, drawing the attention of a few patrons. Once again, Clara felt embarrassed with everyone watching.

"You do have a way with words, don't you, Miss Clara?"

Clara lifted her chin. "And you, Mr. Mac, are a huge flirt."

"I think by the becoming blush on your cheeks that you somewhat like it. But have it your way for now." Mac pulled out an envelope from his breast pocket. "Here's what I do know. I'll have validation coming by wire as soon as it's available."

Clara's heart thumped with anticipation, and she hung on to every word Mac said.

Peter enjoyed Pastor Allen's sermon that morning—doing everything as though you're working for God. The message was taken from the book of Colossians, chapter three. When he glanced over at Catharine, he could tell the message hit home, and he hoped it made her feel somewhat better after how hard she'd thrown herself into the farm work. She caught on quick.

His heart swelled with pride. The sermon was a good reminder for him about who he'd placed his trust in. He closed his eyes and thanked the Lord for the good fortune to have found his lovely wife.

Catharine gave Peter a poke in the ribs as the congregation was dismissed. He stirred and glanced at her.

"For a moment I thought you'd gone to sleep. Are you tired this morning?" She gave his shoulder a gentle pat.

Peter stood. "No, not at all." He took her elbow and gently steered her into the aisle while Greta and Anna followed. "I want to say hello to Angelina and Mario. You haven't met their twin boys yet."

"Everyone has been so nice and—"

"Peter! Well, hello. It's been awhile since I've seen you."

Catharine turned in the direction of a lady's voice, and Peter suddenly stopped, causing Greta and Anna to bump into them and turning Catharine's straw hat askew. She reached up to adjust it as they all stared at the woman speaking to Peter, her hand touching his sleeve.

Peter stepped back onto Anna's toe and she groaned. "Anna, I'm so sorry." He turned to all three of them. "I'd like you to meet Dorothy Miller. She's one of our finest local schoolteachers."

Catharine blinked. Why was Dorothy clutching his arm? Didn't she know that he was married now?

Peter pulled his arm away from Dorothy and wrapped it around Catharine's waist. "Dorothy, this is my wife, Catharine, and these are her sisters."

Dorothy's posture stiffened, and she acknowledged them through cool blue eyes. "Really? Wherever did you two meet?" Her eyes passed over Catharine in one swift glance. But whether or not Catharine met with her approval was hard to guess.

It was an innocent question, but Peter heard the edge in Dorothy's words. She wasn't happy, he could tell. He knew that Dorothy had not given up on him, even though he'd made it perfectly clear they were nothing more than friends.

"Does it matter?" Peter shifted uncomfortably, guessing she was probing to provoke him . . . or Catharine.

Dorothy suddenly regained her composure. "Forgive me. Where are my manners? I'm glad to meet you."

Catharine murmured a hello and shook Dorothy's hand. "*Hallo*. This is my sister, Greta," she said with a touch on Greta's sleeve, "and this is my youngest sister, Anna."

"Ooh . . . do I detect an accent?"

"*Ja*. We traveled all the way from Amsterdam to America." Anna beamed.

"I see . . . how nice. I'd love to hear all about it and how you came to be in Wyoming. That's quite a long way." She tilted her head and stared at Catharine.

"We must move on, Peter." Greta urged them forward. "We're blocking the aisle."

Catharine slipped her arm through Peter's, taking a step toward the door. He was glad she did.

"Yes, let's move out of the way. Nice seeing you, Dorothy. Give my regards to your parents." Peter walked on past her, feeling awkward as she moved aside. He hoped she'd come to accept Catharine and not give her a hard time. He didn't want any bad feelings between him and Dorothy. He'd always thought highly of her, but she'd never touched that special place in his heart, even though he'd tried to care for her for his mother's sake. His feelings for her had never grown, but he was certain hers had for him.

While Catharine and Peter began preparing a quick lunch of cold cuts after church, the afternoon heat began to build. She unbuttoned the top of her blouse and fanned her chest. The girls strolled in to help, chattering about the new acquaintances they'd made at church. Catharine suggested they all take their plates to the porch to eat by the trees. At least they'd be cooler there, with the prairie breeze. Everyone agreed and began to gather their plates when the sound of a carriage coming up the drive caught their attention.

"Are you expecting someone, Peter?" Catharine glanced at her husband.

Peter froze. "It must be Mother. I believe I mentioned that she should come to lunch today after church. But since I didn't see her there, I assumed she wouldn't."

"What? Why didn't you tell me? I haven't cooked anything." Catharine's mind was whirling with what kind of impression that would make on her new mother-in-law. Now what was she supposed to do?

"She'll have cold cuts, just like us." Peter reached for another plate for his mother.

"We have potato salad," Greta said. "I'll get it while you answer the door, Anna."

Anna took off to the front door while Catharine quickly pulled out a tray and began filling it with their sandwiches. She dropped the forks in her haste and knocked over the pitcher of milk, which then soaked the sliced bread and made large splats across the floor. "Oh no!"

Peter reached out to steady her hands. "Catharine, she's not Queen Esther. Please don't fuss so."

"I'll get this cleaned up," Greta said and moved faster than Catharine had seen in a long time. "Do we have more milk?" She sopped up the milk while Peter dropped the ruined bread in the trash.

Catharine walked toward the pie safe for more bread. "Afraid not, but there's some lemonade that I made for later—"

"What's all the fuss about?"

Catharine halted and turned to see Clara standing in the doorway, hands on her hips, with Anna right behind her. Clara's eyes rested on Catharine's open buttons, and Catharine quickly buttoned her blouse.

Greta waved her hand. "Oh, it's nothing we can't handle. Just a little accident, that's all."

Clara stood looking at the mess, disapproval clearly reflected in her eyes. But then she removed her stylish black hat, took the mop propped next to the back door, and began to wipe the floor without a word. "I can see Peter forgot to tell you that I was coming, Catharine, from the looks of the lunch. I can come another time, if that suits you better." She paused and looked at Catharine.

"Nonsense, Mrs. Andersen. It's just simpler to have a cold lunch after church, you know. I don't remember seeing you there this morning." Catharine wrung the wet dishcloth out into the mop bucket and handed it to Greta. "We were just going to have lunch on the porch because of the heat, but I hope you'll stay."

Clara paused before answering, glancing over at Peter. "I guess I could stay for a little while." It seemed Clara wanted Peter to feel sorry for her and beg her to stay.

"Mother, I wouldn't have asked you if I hadn't wanted you to come," Peter said. "Now grab a plate and help yourself while Catharine slices the bread."

Peter proceeded to slice enough ham for all of them. Catharine shot him a look of agitation. She was irritated that he'd forgotten to tell her about his mother. Clearly they'd have to start communicating better, especially where his mother was concerned.

9

Catharine didn't know when she'd been more unnerved. Her mother-in-law arrived for a lavish Sunday dinner only to find cold cuts and Catharine totally unprepared for company. She was shaking inside and tried not to let her hands show it as she poured the lemonade. *How in the world could Peter forget to tell me something like that? I'm sure I looked like a bumbling bride in the kitchen.* He should've known she would want to fix a special dinner for her mother-in-law's first time to the home of Mrs. Peter Andersen.

Catharine knew the bumbling was partly true. She was still learning how to fix a full meal by herself, but with Peter's patient teaching, she was beginning to feel a little more confident. Though not far enough along that she wanted to cook for Clara. Hardly!

A deep breath calmed her somewhat, and she plastered a smile on her face. Once they were settled in rockers and on the porch swing, she lifted the pitcher to fill Clara's glass, but Clara stopped her.

"If you wouldn't mind, I'd love to have some of your

English tea that Peter's told me about." Clara's dark eyes glinted, but there was no hint of a smile in them.

"It's no problem at all, Mrs. Andersen. I'll just go boil the water. Are you sure you don't want a refreshing glass of lemonade while you wait?"

Clara shifted in the rocker, balancing her plate on her lap. "I guess I could, but I'm not used to holding my eating utensils on my lap. What do you suggest I use for a table?"

"Mother, you can set your glass on the floor like the rest of us. This is not like having a formal dinner, you know." Peter's voice seemed a little on edge to Catharine.

Clara harrumphed. "Well, I can tell that, Son."

"Is that a yes, then?" Greta took the pitcher from Catharine, shooing her toward the kitchen to make the tea.

"Yes, I will have a bit while I wait for the tea." Clara watched as Greta poured her a glass of lemonade.

Catharine scooted back inside, set the kettle to boil, and ran to the sitting room for her pretty tea set and tray. *At least I can make good tea and present it nicely at the same time.*

"Greta, what do you intend to do now that you're here in Wyoming?" Clara asked with a clipped tone, eyeing the girl. She bit into the thick sandwich, touching the napkin to her lips as though she were in a fine dining room.

Greta laughed good-naturedly. "I have no idea presently. I'm helping Catharine right now, but I've given some thought to finding a job in time. I have a few clerical skills that I learned at my father's shipping company."

"Mmm. I see." She shifted her gaze to Anna. "And you, young lady, what do you do all day long?"

Anna swallowed the last bite of her lunch before answering,

gazing pensively over the porch's railing. "I'm really not much help, I'm afraid. With the farm work, I mean. I try, but then I get interested in nature and hiking, painting, and watching the wildlife more, much to my sisters' displeasure." She sighed.

Peter quickly inserted, "Ah, but you've been a big help to us without knowing it, little one." He patted her on the head. He began stacking their lunch plates on one arm and left them by the door for later.

Anna turned and smiled at Peter. "*Dank U*, Peter. You make me feel at home. Since I've never had a brother, I think I'll adopt you."

"I'm honored, Anna."

When Peter bent to take his mother's plate, she leaned close to his ear and muttered under her breath, "I must have a private word with you after lunch, dear."

Catharine, her dress now sticking to her from the hot kitchen and her unruly hair curling out of its braids, stood at the doorway with the tray of tea and caught Clara whispering to Peter. Greta sprung up and held the door open for her. Giving her brightest smile, Catharine held the tray out toward her mother-in-law. "I'm sorry there's no dessert this time."

"What have we here? Where's the rose tea set that I left for you to use, Peter?" Clara frowned but took a cup of tea, then helped herself to two sugar cubes and lemon. "It's Royal Doulton, you know. Straight from England and very expensive."

Catharine felt heat rising up from her neck to her face. "This is what's left of my mother's Blue Willow tea set, and I treasure it. Isn't it pretty?" Catharine was determined not to let Clara's barb bother her. After pouring her sisters and herself some tea, she took a seat next to Peter on the swing. Peter passed on the tea, preferring his lemonade.

"We are fortunate to have any pieces left at all," Anna added. "Catharine is quite fond of it. We had a terrible storm at sea that broke most of it."

"I see," Clara said, sipping her tea. "It's good. I'm surprised."

"Why would you be surprised, Mother?" Peter's voice still seemed a little too sharp, but he looked at Catharine and flashed her a broad smile.

"No reason, dear." Changing the subject, she dabbed her lips with her napkin. "Greta mentioned your father was in the shipping industry, Catharine. I would've thought you'd want to stay in Holland to inherit it at some point, if you have no brothers."

Catharine swallowed a lump in her throat. "Our parents died at sea while on a mission for one of his shipping ventures. After they died, we thought it best to leave and start over."

If Clara was surprised, she didn't show it outwardly.

Peter reached over and stroked Catharine's shoulder. She looked down at her teacup and took a sip with trembling hands. *Please, Lord, don't let her ask any more personal questions.*

To her relief, Clara stood and set her cup and saucer back on the tray. "Thank you for lunch and the tea. Peter, would you walk me to my buggy?"

"Please come again, Mrs. Andersen," Catharine said, and her sisters waved goodbye. Now she could breathe a sigh of relief and enjoy what was left of their Sunday afternoon.

"So what did you think of our new pastor?" Greta kicked off her shoes and tucked her feet up under her, getting comfortable in the rocking chair.

"He seems nice enough. With a name like Culpepper, I'm sure he gets a few jokes." Catharine laughed. "I really took a liking to Cora Jenkins, the librarian. We need to go visit the library sometime."

"Me too!" Anna sat up at the mention of a library. "I wonder if they'd loan me some books."

Greta shook her head. "*Ja*, silly. That's why it's called a library."

Anna stuck her tongue out at her. "I'm not familiar with the ways of Wyoming, and neither are you."

"We'll do that soon. I promise." Catharine leaned her head back and closed her eyes, wondering what was keeping Peter. She was soon asleep in the afternoon breeze.

Peter had followed his mother down the steps into the yard at the end of the drive where Clara's buggy was parked underneath one of the spreading elm trees.

As soon as they were out of earshot, Clara started her chattering. Pausing next to the buggy, she pulled on her gloves. "Peter, I believe that I have bad news to tell you, and I know of no other way than to just say it."

"Mother, for heaven's sake, why do you have to make a big secret of everything? Whatever you have to say could be said in front of my wife. We're a married couple, and couples share everything."

"*Everything?*"

"Yes, mother, *everything*."

"Well . . . maybe not for long." Clara avoided his gaze.

"What are you talking about—what's on your mind?"

"Very well . . . I hired a private investigator to look into Catharine's background—"

"What did you say?" Peter was sure he hadn't heard her right.

"You heard me. Now don't be angry with me," she said.

Peter stood with his hands on his hips. "Mother, so help me—"

"Just listen to me, Peter. I was worried about you, and since you never told me one whit about her, I thought it best. You have too much at stake to lose to a conniving foreigner."

The muscle in his jaw twitched as he clenched his fists at his sides. *If she wasn't my mother, I'd make a scene right here and now.* "Are you calling my wife a conniving foreigner?" he said through gritted teeth.

She touched his arm. "Peter, if you will just listen for one moment—"

"I've heard enough!" He flung her arm away and spun around to leave. "I know everything about Catharine that I need to know!" He started to walk away.

"Do you need to know that she was married?" Clara spat out.

Peter froze, a flash of pain hitting him in the gut. His mouth suddenly felt dry and he licked his lips.

Clara continued. "But not divorced!"

"Mother, I don't know why you'd tell me a story like that. But stop right where you are." Was this the same sweet mother who had raised him, sang to him, and baked cookies when he was a child, but now thought she needed to continue orchestrating every detail of his life? *Lord, help me. I don't want to say anything to hurt my mother.*

Clara groaned. "Sooo, you didn't know then. It's just as I feared."

Peter walked back toward her. "Why did you do this?"

Clara shrank back. "I should think you'd be happy to find out the truth now, before children come along."

Through gritted teeth, he said, "I asked you a question, Mother. Why?"

"I was trying to protect you. You're my son and I'm devoted to you, and I have only your best interests at heart."

"I don't believe it, and frankly, I'm saddened by what you call your 'devotion' to me. And I'll ask you to never talk about Catharine that way again!" It was all Peter could do to keep his voice down. "And I don't want that kind of devotion!" He strode back toward the house, never looking back, his fury so thick he thought he'd choke.

"You'll thank me later," Clara called after him as she climbed into the buggy.

Anna, wearing Clara's fancy hat on her head, came down the steps and passed Peter, but he never gave her so much as the time of day. He flew past her, thundering up the steps and into the house. He looked through the screen door and saw Anna waving at his mother.

"*Hallo*, Mrs. Andersen . . . you left your hat!" Anna called out as the buggy rumbled down the road. But Clara didn't stop. She whipped the horse into a trot away from the Andersen farm.

10

The sound of the slamming screen door startled Catharine from her pleasant, dreamless doze. When she sat up and looked around, both Greta and Anna were gone. Hadn't she told Anna not to slam that screen door? She sighed, then dragged herself up from the comfort of the old porch swing and began to gather the remnants of the lunch dishes. The house seemed quiet, which meant the girls must be relaxing in their own way.

Wondering where Peter was, Catharine placed the dishes in the sink, then set the teakettle to boil water to wash them. When the kettle began to sing, she covered the dirty dishes with the warm water. As she washed them, she smiled to herself, curious as to what her mother would think if she could see her becoming so domesticated—happily married in her homespun dress and apron. She realized being at peace didn't necessarily mean having servants wait on her and living in an opulent home and reaching a certain social status in the community. She felt at peace on Peter's farm even with a dozen newly acquired responsibilities as his wife. In fact, she rather liked it.

Looking down at her hands, she frowned. They were rough despite the lotion Peter gave her to apply every night before bed. She blushed when she remembered how he'd lovingly lifted her hands to his lips, kissed them, and declared they were all better before he tucked her into bed.

Drying the last plate, Catharine heard a sound overhead. Was one of the girls in the attic? Hardly. They hadn't liked going up there from the first day. That left only Peter. She carried the clean dishes to the cabinet and wiped the crumbs off the table just as he came down the stairs carrying the small lady's chair.

He paused at the doorway, holding the chair between his well-muscled forearms. She couldn't help but notice the thick curling hair that stopped at his wrist.

"Where do you want this?" His voice was flat, and his usual smile was replaced with a sober look that Catharine interpreted as weary. Gone were the dancing, teasing eyes that she'd grown fond of.

"Why don't you put it in the corner of the kitchen since I'm in this room most of the time? I can work on fixing it when I get time between chores, but first I'll need to purchase fabric and upholstery tacks." She wiped her hands on her apron and stepped aside for him to pass.

"Have you ever done this sort of thing before?" Peter quirked an eyebrow.

She laughed. "No, but I can sew, and I think if I remove the chair's cover, I can make a pattern out of it to use as a guide for a new one. It can't be all that hard." Peter was close enough that she smelled his masculine scent, something between soap and the smell of outdoors—a familiar but endearing smell.

Peter placed the chair near the hearth but far enough away

102

from the table so it wasn't in their walking path in the kitchen. He looked up and regarded her with cool eyes and a cheerless look. "I'm going for a walk. I'll be back later." He turned away.

"Peter, is some—"

The kitchen door slammed behind him. Catharine was perplexed. He hadn't even asked if she wanted to come. Nothing. Why was he being so distant suddenly? Was he displeased because she hadn't fixed a nice lunch for his mother?

Catharine removed her apron and hung up the dish towel. She embraced the quiet that settled over the house since it was their only real day of rest. The work of a farmer's wife was never ending, she concluded. Tomorrow she would be doing the wash, which would take the better part of her day. Perhaps if she rose soon enough, she could get it finished early, then start working on the chair for Anna.

She wondered where her sisters might be as she wandered into the parlor, trying to decide what to do with her free time. She chose a book from the array lining the shelf, but after a few moments she felt restless with pent-up energy. She put the book back and wandered out into the grassy road leading away from the house. She'd be on the lookout for wildflowers to pick for their table.

The warm sunshine pressed in on her shoulders, but as usual the prairie wind blew across the road, sweeping wisps of hair across her eyes until she pushed the loose hair away.

She was becoming used to her new environment, which was so different from her life in Holland. The chirping of birds sang out their beautiful melody from the thick trees leading down to Crow Creek. The cool water would feel refreshing on a day like today, and Catharine decided to wade in once she reached its banks.

As she neared the creek, Catharine glimpsed a flash of white through the chokecherry bushes, and she slowed her pace. Prickles of fear crawled up her neck. Was someone out there? Catharine separated the branches of the bushes and peered through the leaves. When she saw Peter's back, she sucked in her breath in admiration. Though she had been his wife for weeks now, she'd never been able to admire him unobserved.

Peter was standing in the stream, arms akimbo as the water flowed over him in waist-deep, swirling water. His well-sculpted muscles rippled on his tanned torso in the afternoon sunlight. Wet hair just brushed the nape of his neck, where droplets of water clung. He bent down and splashed water across his face and arms in apparent delight.

She hadn't known he would be bathing. This must be where he'd come to bathe that first night he shared their bed. She shuddered at the thought of washing in the creek's icy water, but she admired his consideration of her in bringing pails of warm water for her bath that night. It brought a slow smile to her lips, but she dare not laugh out loud for fear he might hear her. And as much as she was enjoying the scene, it made her wonder why he hadn't invited her along. They were still newlyweds, after all!

Peter turned, and her gaze slid to just above where the water lapped gently at his trim waist. Desire flicked its way to her heart, spreading like warm honey through her, and she sighed. Her mouth became slack with surprise at what she was feeling . . . what she thought had been dead and buried forever. Then she remembered how cool he'd been toward her earlier. Something was on his mind, she was sure of that.

Peter started making his way toward where he'd left his clothing on a rock near the creek's bank. At first she thought he'd seen her, so she quickly let the branches fall back into place, but not until one had smacked her across the cheek, stinging her. He neared the creek bank, arms pushing the water aside, and came fully out of the water. She quickly turned away in modesty, her cheeks flaming hot, and was glad he couldn't see her spying on him.

This was the same incredible man who had held her that first night, wooing her with love, convincing her throughout the night to trust him fully, while he held her tightly against him until they'd become one. Catharine's heart beat wildly in her chest. She knew she had come to care for him through their correspondence and mutual interests and love of God, and they had become good friends, but abruptly another thought hit her full center—she desired him as never before.

She quickly turned, lifting the hem of her skirt in her hands to keep from stumbling, and made her way back to the house, determined to show him tonight that he did own her heart. She could hardly wait!

The bracing dip in the creek invigorated Peter as he tried to turn his thoughts away from his conversation with his mother. Why would she try to discredit Catharine? Didn't she think he was old enough to handle his own life since his father died? The farm was his now and he'd run it single-handedly, and so far he'd been able to continue making a profit. His mother lived in the modest home inherited from her parents in Cheyenne's nicer neighborhood. What was she afraid of? Losing his love? Ridiculous!

Then his thoughts turned back to the knowledge that Catharine might have already been married and possibly not divorced. That opened up a whole new batch of concerns. But how could that be possible? Had she duped him into marrying? *Lord, say it isn't so . . . but then . . .*

Peter wiped the water from his hair until it was slicked down. When he'd retrieved the chair from the attic for Catharine, curiosity about her trunk had made him stop and lift the lid. He never would have looked inside if his mother hadn't shared her shocking news earlier. And what he saw surprised him. Lying near the top was a delicate christening gown. Had it been hers as a child, or one of her sisters'? *Or could it be . . . ?* No, he wouldn't let his mind go there. No need to make that assumption, but what if his mother had told him the truth? But why would Catharine lie—if she did?

His mind strayed to Catharine's lovely oval face, her red hair tumbling about her nightgown, tantalizing his mind with thoughts of what lie beneath, and of the love they'd shared. His gut twisted in agony. Was it all going to be for naught? He'd made so many plans that he wanted to share with her. And he wanted her to have his children. Now . . . well, now all was changed in one brief moment of distrust.

Angrily he started toward the creek bank for his clothes. Instead of the water cooling his temperament, he'd only wound up dwelling on Catharine's past. He paused a moment, thinking he saw movement in the brush. Probably just a deer. He needed to get on back before his wife came looking for him. He wouldn't speak of this news until he knew it was the absolute truth and his mother produced documentation.

Her mind full of excitement, Catharine fairly ran up to the house. Both Greta and Anna were sitting on the porch and gave her curious looks as she hurried up the steps.

"Where's the fire?" Greta chuckled.

"What?" Catharine paused, catching her breath.

"You just seem to be in a terrific hurry. That's all."

Catharine didn't respond to that. "Where have you two been all afternoon? I cleaned the kitchen by myself, and you were nowhere to be found."

Anna threw Greta an anxious look. "I was just out walking and sketched a curious prairie dog. Want to see?" She held up her drawing.

"Yes, that's nice, Anna. Cute little creature." Catharine patted her on the shoulder, then asked Greta, "And you? Where did you get off to?" Catharine couldn't help but notice the reticence in her manner and the fact that Greta didn't look her in the eye.

Greta twirled a strand of hair. "I, uh . . . nothing really . . . just wanted time alone."

"Ha! You? Time alone? Anna maybe, but you're not one to be alone unless you're sleeping." Catharine chuckled. "Next time I'd appreciate it if you'd tell me when either of you will be gone from the house for more than an hour, as well as where you'll be. I can't stress enough the dangers out here on the prairie. Peter told me that the elk and moose can be aggressive during rutting season if humans are around. Catharine pressed her hands together. "Besides, who knows when you might come across a mother bear and her cubs? From now on you both need to inform me of your whereabouts. Understand?"

"Sure, Cath. We didn't mean to worry you."

"It's getting dark. Why don't you two have a snack before bed? I'm going to heat water for a bath." Catharine pretended that her bath was a typical Sunday evening event and scurried on into the house before either of them could tease her. She wanted to be ready before Peter returned.

"I promise we'll be in directly," Greta said. "Need any help with the water pails?"

Catharine paused and answered over her shoulder. "Thanks, but I can manage. Clean up after yourself in the kitchen."

As quickly as she could, Catharine lugged several pails of warm water from the stove to the large claw-foot tub in their bathroom. She would ask Peter if it would be possible to get hot water run upstairs. She wished it was cool enough for a fire in order to make the room more romantic, but instead she lit candles that she'd found in the dining room and placed them on the bureau. She turned back the quilt, fluffed their pillows, and scattered rose petals that she'd collected from a wild rose growing along the path to the house. Next she laid out her finest lawn nightgown that Peter liked. Quickly pulling her hair up to the top of her head, she finally stripped off her clothing and slid into the lavender-scented water.

She felt flushed with anticipation. Tonight she would let Peter see how much she loved him and was so proud that he'd chosen her to be his wife. Why, he was so handsome, he could have any woman in Cheyenne instead of her with her funny accent, red hair, and two sisters! Of that she had no doubt. She heard footsteps coming to pause near the door and slid further into the water.

Someone tapped at the door. "Just wanted to let you know we're off to bed now," Greta said. "Everything all right?"

Catharine called out, "Everything is just perfect! See you in the morning then." She breathed a sigh of relief as she heard Greta's footsteps down the hallway. She knew Greta was being discreet by making sure she and Anna were out of the way for the evening and was glad she hadn't said anything. Now if Peter would just show up before she became waterlogged.

She smiled lazily as a warm burst of love pierced her heart. She'd set the stage for a great romantic night and blushed in spite of herself.

11

Evening shadows enveloped the woods with only a sliver
of moonlight to light the pathway home from the creek.
His mind all in a jumble, Peter wondered how he'd be able
to look Catharine in the eye. Other times when he'd come
in for supper after seeing to the livestock, his steps would
quicken at the sight of the cheery glow from the windows
of the house, and he couldn't wait to see Catharine's sweet
face and embrace her. Then they'd all sit leisurely around the
kitchen table until it was dark.

Now his feet dragged with dread and his heart felt like
a stone at the bottom of the creek bed. He'd do his best to
appear normal, but his mind kept straying to the christening
gown in the trunk.

He was glad that the house was quiet when he entered.
He assumed everyone had already gone to bed. Good. He
wasn't in the mood to talk. He eased down the hallway, trying
not to make noise when he passed Greta and Anna's room.
Further down the hallway, a light under his bedroom door
told him that Catharine was still up. He took a deep breath
and turned the doorknob to face her.

Catharine, in the glow of numerous candles, was sitting in the bathtub with a sponge to her leg, which was dangling out of the tub. She sat up, looking startled, then realizing he stood staring, she quickly slumped back down under the bubbles.

Peter heard his own sharp intake of breath at the vision of loveliness submerged in a bubble bath before him. *His* wife. His tongue felt glued to the roof of his mouth until he finally said, "Excuse me. I had no idea you were bathing." He started to close the door. "I'll leave you alone."

"Don't do that. I'm nearly through. Perhaps you could wash the spot on my back that I can't seem to reach." She shot him a daring look.

Was she flirting with him? This was different from the reserved bride that he'd held in his arms for the last several weeks. Something must have changed. *But why now, Lord?*

"Please . . ." she purred as he stood hesitantly, shifting on his feet.

There was nothing he could do but fulfill her request, then he would head to bed. He knelt down on one knee, taking the sudsy sponge from her hand as she leaned forward. A more beautiful back could not exist, he concluded. He applied the sponge gently, admiring her shoulders and the way she narrowed delightfully at the waist. The water smelled like her, and the lavender scent was heady. She was all femininity . . . soft with wet, curling tendrils of hair dangling at the base of her slender neck, now tan, in contrast to her back.

"You can scrub a tad harder. I won't break, you know," she teased, looking over one shoulder at him with her usual smile. His eyes locked with hers until he forced himself back to the task at hand.

"Mmm . . . a little to the left." He heard her soft sigh. "I have a slight itch there. Ahh . . . that's it."

Peter's blood began to race, and the hand that held the sponge shook. He wanted to lift her out of the water and carry her to the bed and keep her there until morning, but he wouldn't—not this time.

"You're very quiet today. Anything wrong?"

He stood and dropped the sponge with a plop in the tub. "Nope. Will that do? I think I'm kinda tired. It's been a long day." It was a blatant lie, he knew, but he was not inclined to hold someone else's wife in his arms tonight—or any other night. *You don't know if that's true. But better to be on the safe side*, he thought.

"Could you hand me the towel then?" Her hands clutched the side of the tub. He watched her brows knit together in a deep frown.

Peter lifted the towel and tossed it to her, then turned his back discreetly as she stood. That's when his eye caught the rose petals on the bed and her filmy nightgown lying in wait. *I can't believe she's tempting me while she's married to someone else!* Hot anger flashed over him, and he turned, stalked out of the bedroom, and left her standing in her bare feet, clutching the towel. Any other time he would have been flattered, but tonight his blood boiled. The desire that he'd had earlier fled like geese on a cloudy November day.

Clutching the towel to her chest, water pooling at her feet, Catharine felt numb. Had he just stalked out of the room without a word as to where he was going? Had she done something to deserve his anger? Hot tears formed, threatening to spill over. She looked over at the bed strewn with rose

112

petals and candles burning nearby. Suddenly she felt morti-
fied. Maybe Peter wanted to be the one to initiate romance
in the bedroom. She realized with a sobering thought that
she knew very little about the ways of men, but by now she
should have learned something from her past.

Wiping her tears with the back of her hand, she patted
her skin dry, donned a nondescript cotton gown, and placed
the delicate nightgown in the bottom of her bureau drawer,
totally out of sight. There would be no need for it now. With
one swift motion, she swept the rose petals into her palm and
deposited them in the trash basket. She blew out the candles
and climbed into bed, not sure what to think.

Her heart felt raw. The evening had not gone at all the
way she'd envisioned it. All she'd wanted was to feel Peter's
strong arms about her. Now she felt foolish. Maybe he'd had
a change of heart or maybe he expected something different.
Whatever the cause, she hoped she could get it out of him.
He was totally different than he'd been before he'd chatted
with Clara and taken a walk.

Catharine had gotten the distinct feeling that Clara dis-
liked her and her sisters. Though she'd never said anything
directly, her scrutinizing eyes told the truth.

Catharine wasn't even aware that she was crying until her
pillow became damp with her tears. She sniffed, then listened
for any sound that Peter was in the kitchen or parlor downstairs, hoping he would come to bed, but after what seemed
an eternity, she dropped off to sleep, a light smell of roses
still clinging to the sheets.

Peter took care not to wake Catharine while he removed his
clothes. He'd taken another walk to simmer down the turmoil

twisting in his mind, making it impossible to think clearly where she was concerned. Catharine was sleeping soundly now, so he moved closer to the edge and told himself it was so he wouldn't disturb her. Truth was he didn't trust himself laying this close to her. Maybe he should consider sleeping in the barn as an alternative, but then questions would surely be raised by her sisters. He listened to the even rise and fall of her breathing and felt guilty that he'd walked out when she had all but given herself to him.

But he thought the cost too high for now until he got clarity on the situation. Thoughts of her luscious skin and open innocence riled his aching heart, but he wouldn't want to use her that way.

He needed a way to turn his mind off, so he began to think about his wheat crop. The plants looked healthy, and though he was worried about getting rain, he felt sure it would come and the wheat would be ready for summer harvest. It made him smile when he thought of all the questions Catharine had first plied him with about growing wheat. He was so pleased that she was eager to learn about wheat farming and running the household in general. She was what the Lord called a true helpmeet.

He groaned deeply. *What am I to do, Lord? What if she isn't who she says she is?*

You'll stand by her . . . that's what you'll do.

Though his head heard the answer clearly, his heart wasn't feeling so inclined.

12

A deafening crack of thunder woke Catharine from her fitful sleep. Startled, she sat up halfway in bed and saw the entire room bathed in bright blue light as lightning flashed. Thunder crashed again, its rumble shaking the very foundations of the house. She glanced out the window as another flash of lightning illuminated the surrounding woods, and she shivered and scooted back under the covers. She hadn't heard a drop of rain, but the storm continued to rage. She wanted to move to Peter's protective arms, but she didn't dare. He'd rejected her once tonight, and once was enough.

The next clap of thunder caused her to shriek with fear, which awakened Peter. He rolled over and propped up on one elbow, squinting through half-closed eyes to ask her what was wrong. Before she could answer, another jagged flash of blue light struck a tree nearby, and she jumped, yanking the covers over her head. Never had she witnessed such a lightning storm. She was thankful she was safe at home in her own bed.

Peter patted her arm through the sheet. "It's okay. It's just a lightning storm moving across the prairie." The wind rose, banging the shutters against the windows. He hopped out and quickly closed them, then returned to bed. "They usually create more racket than damage, but they do put on a spectacular light show against the sky." He tentatively reached out to reassure her. She took that as a signal to move closer to his side, and she snuggled next to him so she couldn't see the jagged bolts of lightning. After a long moment, he placed an arm about her shoulders.

Catharine sighed, enjoying the feel of his strong arms. She felt safe and cared for, though she wasn't sure she should've snuggled up against his unwilling body. He smelled so manly that she almost forgot there was a storm raging. She never wanted to move back to her side of the bed. How could she understand him if he wouldn't tell her what was wrong? She was afraid to speak and said nothing, not wanting to break the intimate moment.

A sharp pounding on their bedroom door caused them both to separate and spring up. "What is it?" Catharine called out.

The bedroom door swung open, and Anna nearly tripped on her nightgown in her haste. "I'm sorry, Catharine, but the noise woke me and scared me. I yelled out to Greta, but she's not in her bed, and she's not anywhere to be found." Anna's eyes were wide with anxiety.

Peter grabbed his pants next to the bed. "Give me just a moment to get dressed, Anna. I'll find her."

Anna turned her back to them and waited.

"Where do you think she went, Anna? Was she in bed when you retired?" Catharine tried not to allow panic into her voice. Anna was already upset. Where in the world would Greta be this time of the night?

"We both went to bed at the same time." Anna fingered her cotton nightgown nervously. "It's not like her to take off."

Peter, dressed now, strode over to Anna's side. "I'll check around outside. Maybe she couldn't sleep and then the storm came up. She's probably in the barn waiting for it to pass." He glanced over at Catharine. "I'll be back. You two stay put." He strode down the stairs, taking them two at a time, his boot heels pounding against the hardwood. Catharine and Anna followed.

Catharine called out, "I'll make us a pot of coffee. Please be careful!" When he opened the front door, there was still not a drop of rain to be seen. After he disappeared into the darkness, she quickly shut the door. "Anna, go get your robe and I'll do the same, then I'll make some coffee."

Anna answered as she moved to the stairs. "I'll get both our robes and be right back down."

"*Goed.* I'll be in the kitchen." Catharine hurried over to the stove to start the coffee and jumped when a loud clap of thunder roared. *Lord, let Greta be safe from this lightning, and help Peter find her and bring her back to us.* Her eyes were wide open now, and she knew they were swollen from last night's tears. She hoped Anna wouldn't notice they were red and purposely kept her head down to avoid being asked questions. She filled the coffeepot with water and scoops of coffee as she'd seen Peter do every morning, and placed it on the stove to boil. Then she sat down at the table and waited.

Anna burst into the kitchen. "Catharine, look what I found on the floor next to her bed!" Anna held out a wrinkled note.

Catharine briefly scanned it. The note from Bryan, asking Greta to meet him out at the line shack at midnight. Catharine dropped her hands to her lap, still clutching the note. "I wish I'd seen this before Peter left. I just heard him streak out of the yard on horseback."

117

"I'm sure he'll head that way. At least we know she's not alone." Anna hugged her robe tighter. "Maybe not alone, but safe? That's what I'm worried about."

One quick glance around the house and porch, and Peter knew that Greta wasn't nearby. He hurried into the barn and was greeted with a brief snort from Star. Misty's stall was empty, indicating Greta had taken her. He quickly threw a saddle across Star's back, not wanting to waste time.

He wondered where Greta might have gone this late at night. She seemed happy enough living here, so he didn't think she'd run away. What then? By the time he straddled Star's back, he thought he knew the answer to his question. She must be meeting someone, and he had a sneaking suspicion that it might be Bryan Gifford. He'd seen the way Bryan flirted with Greta when they were in town and at church when he'd sat with her.

He gave his horse a tap with his boots as he clicked his tongue, and soon they were trotting down the lane that led away from the house and out along the edge of the road. He held the horse's reins tightly, his knees firmly against the horse's sides since the lightning might cause Star to bolt.

Peter knew that Catharine was fiercely protective of her sisters and felt responsible for them. Something to do about a promise she'd made to her father before that fatal shipping accident when she'd lost both her parents. He'd bring Greta back, providing he could find her. He owed Catharine that much.

He hadn't gone but a couple of miles when he saw the line shack illuminated by a flash of lightning. Used by cowboys during the winter to mend fences and keep track of strays, it could be a safe haven away from a sudden snowfall—or downpour. He urged his mount in that direction, and as he drew closer, a light through the window told him someone was there. He slid off his horse and wrapped the reins around the hitching post, next to Misty and a second horse.

He called out, "Anyone there?" but didn't hear a sound. So he pounded on the door, and Bryan opened it. Peter saw Greta behind him, clutching his sleeve with a look of fright. It was hard to see with only the kerosene lantern that sat on a makeshift table in the center of the room.

"Peter, what are you doing here?" Greta lifted her chin.

"I could ask you the same question." Peter's jaw clenched as he tried to control his temper. He wasn't her father, and he'd have to be careful of what he said. "Greta, go outside and wait for me by my horse."

"But I'm afraid of the lightning." She chewed her bottom lip.

"Well, you weren't too afraid to be out in it! I want to have a word with Bryan."

Bryan's lips twitched in annoyance, but he gave Greta a brief hug, then grazed her brow with a kiss. "Do as he says. I'll see you soon." She reluctantly let go of his hand, tears filling her blue eyes.

Not if I have anything to do with it. Peter stepped aside to let Greta pass.

When she was out of earshot, Peter's gaze focused on Bryan. "The next time you want to court a lady, you should do it the proper way instead of sneaking around. I doubt there will be a next time with Greta, once Catharine hears about this."

119

"Greta and I will see each other, and there's nothing you can do about it. You're not her father." Bryan held Peter's gaze through narrowed eyes.

"No, but I'm her guardian as long as she lives in my home." Peter turned to leave, but Bryan stayed him with a hand on his arm.

"She's almost eighteen, and you can't tell her what to do then."

Peter looked down at his arm. "Take your hand off me." Bryan dropped his hand to his side. "I'll give you just one piece of advice my father told me. 'A man don't have thoughts about women till he's thirty-five. Before that, all he's got is feelin's.' So, Bryan, don't you dare consider taking your *feelin's* out on Greta. Do you get my drift?"

Bryan nodded, a sneer forming on his lips. "What I hear is someone trying to tell me how to run my life. The army already does that, so I don't need an old farmer's useless advice."

Peter flinched. He'd never been called *old* before. "You'd best consider what I said."

"I consider that a threat," Bryan hissed, hands on his hips.

"Take it however you want."

Lightning popped again. The conversation was over, so Peter stepped back to his horse and pulled himself into the saddle. Greta did likewise while Bryan stood glaring at Peter.

Peter and Greta rode in complete silence until they were in sight of the house. Greta twisted in her saddle to face Peter. "Catharine will be very upset with me . . . Maybe you could persuade her to go easy on me." She gave him a hopeful look.

"I tend to stay out of other people's business until it affects my own." As they neared the barn, Peter paused. "I'll

120

put the horses away, but next time you want to take one of them, you'd best let me know first." He slid off Star's back and grabbed the reins from Greta.

Visibly angry, Greta dismounted. "Somehow I thought I could count on you," she said. "Haven't you ever been in love, Peter?"

Her turned and fastened his eyes on her. "I *am* in love—with your sister—but I'm not sure if Bryan has love or lust for you. There is a difference, you know," Peter said through tight lips.

Greta clenched her fists at her sides, flashing him an irritated look. "I'm almost eighteen, and I assure you that I know the difference!"

"Just be careful, Greta, and listen to your sister. You and Anna are her main concerns." Peter led the horses inside the barn for a quick rubdown before going inside. It was time for Greta to face the music.

The lightning storm had all but subsided while Catharine paced the floor in concern for her sister, but she abruptly stopped wringing her hands when Greta entered the living room. She wrapped her arms around Greta's shoulders. "Oh, thank God you're safe!" Then she pushed Greta away. "How could you worry me like this? Have you no consideration for anyone but yourself, Greta?" Her voice quivered with anger, which had only mounted as she'd thought of every possible scenario while at the same time prayed for her sister's safety. "You could have been struck by lightning. What do you have to say for yourself?"

Greta stood with her arms hanging limp at her sides, staring at the kitchen wall as if the answer would be found there.

Anna moved toward her sister. "Are you all right, Greta?" Concern reflected in Anna's face as she lifted Greta's hand to her cheek.

Greta shrugged. "Don't worry, Sis." She smiled at her and dropped her hand. "I'm perfectly fine, in spite of Catharine's worries." She turned to Catharine. "I'm almost eighteen, Cath, and you need to remember that."

"I don't need you to remind me, young lady. I've been your guardian for six months now." Catharine shook her head in frustration and disbelief. How could she act so nonchalantly?

"Then you shouldn't jump to conclusions," Greta said. She bent down to remove her shoes, then wiggled her toes with a resounding "ahh." She started for the stairs, dismissing the conversation.

Catharine scurried to her with Anna right on her heels, then grabbed Greta's arm and spun her around. "Where do you think you're going? I'm not through talking with you."

The front door opened and closed, and Peter walked in. Catharine ignored the warning he cast her with his eyes and continued. "Tell me where you were and who you were with." She turned to Anna. "Anna, go on up to bed. This is between me and Greta."

Anna hung back. "But I just want—"

"Upstairs, now!" Catharine's stern tone sent Anna scurrying up the stairs, and Catharine waited until she heard the bedroom door slam before continuing. "Greta, I want some answers." She knew she was raising her voice, but now she was thoroughly aggravated with Greta's attitude.

"Please, Cath, you don't have to yell," she snapped back. "Can't we talk about this in the morning? I'm feeling tired—"

"Tired!" Catharine shrieked. "You're tired? How dare you

pretend this is a usual outing in the middle of the night. You'll talk to me now—"

Peter placed a heavy hand upon Catharine's shoulder. "Maybe it would be better if you both slept on this and talked when you're calmer."

His hand had a calming effect on her, and Catharine sighed in exasperation, but Greta only glared at her, crossing her arms. "Okay . . . but after breakfast you and I are going to have a heart-to-heart talk. Is that clear?"

Through gritted teeth, Greta answered, "Yes. Good night." She slipped quickly up the stairs, her shoes in her hands.

"Let's go have that cup of coffee since it's already made. We can talk in the kitchen," Peter suggested.

He led her to the table, and after he'd poured the coffee, Catharine said, "Peter, I don't know what to think. What happened?"

"Greta was at a line shack a couple of miles from here, with Bryan Gifford." His face was sober.

"Yes, I know. Anna found a note in Greta's room. I knew she was acting strange the last couple of days, but I had no idea she would sneak away." Catharine stared into the dark liquid, wondering what she would do to rein in her sister.

"I had a little talk with him, but he didn't back down. He spells trouble, and Greta is ripe for the pickin'."

Catharine's heart skipped a beat. "Oh, Peter . . . you don't think they . . ."

Peter pursed his lips. "I don't know. You'll have to ask her. But I will say if there's no intervention, it'll only be a matter of time. I don't trust him. He's cocky and unreliable." Peter lifted the mug and drained it. "I need to get to bed." He rose and took their mugs to the sink.

Catharine dragged herself to her feet and touched his sleeve. "Peter, I want to thank you for going out in that storm and bringing her back . . . and I'm sorry if I made you feel uncomfortable earlier tonight. It won't happen again." Her voice trailed off.

He gave her a halfhearted smile. "You're welcome. You know that I wouldn't want anything to happen to your sisters on my watch."

She waited for him to say something about his rejection of her, but after a few moments, Catharine knew he either chose to ignore it or had already put it out of his mind. But her feelings were hurt all the same. She'd apologized, but for what? She wasn't sure. He'd always seemed eager to make love to her, even when she had been distant. But that suddenly ceased with Clara's surprise visit. Now that she felt true desire for him, it wasn't reciprocated.

She turned down the wick on the kerosene lantern and followed him upstairs, her heart aching and confused.

13

Clear blue skies as far as the eye could see greeted Catharine when she set out with a rake she'd retrieved from the barn to work in her flower bed. From her apron pocket she pulled out a pair of soft leather gloves. Peter had purchased a pair for each of them when he'd outfitted them at the mercantile. She slipped them on her hands to keep from getting blisters while she worked. She would clear out the rest of the weeds and prepare the ground so that the next time they went to town, she'd purchase flower seeds from the mercantile, or plants if they were available.

She was glad to be outdoors with a task to focus on. When something was on her mind, her best thinking came while she was outdoors. Wyoming was as far from Amsterdam as possible in every way, but she was beginning to appreciate the vast silence and the constant wind. She was used to the hustle and bustle of city life, and now there was no one for miles around. Since her father had been a shipping magnate, most of her life had been spent in their home nestled downtown, surrounded by glorious fountains and beautiful parks in vast array. Occasionally, for respite from the city, they would travel to the countryside where her uncle lived, which was an added pleasure that she'd looked forward to as a child. She closed her eyes and remembered the gentle rains of Holland and wished rain would come to the prairie, especially once she had her flower bed planted.

Greta hadn't come down for breakfast. She had told Anna she wasn't hungry and would be down later. That gave Catharine time to ruminate on last night's situation, so she left Anna doing the dishes. She needed to get the ground worked before the sun was high in the sky.

The wind blew, causing her apron and skirts to flap. She held the rake against her skirt to keep it from flying upward when the next gust came along. Not that anyone would be around to see her undergarments. Glad for the protective bonnet covering her head, she feverishly worked out her frustrations, dragging the rake across the tilled ground, yanking away any unwanted grass or roots that she'd missed the first time.

She was quite sure that Greta was smitten by Bryan just by the way she'd talked last night. *Lord, please help me to control my temper and say the words to Greta that You'd have me say. I don't want her to distance herself from me, but I must protect her. Make my words graceful and not accusing so that she'd consider what I have to say. Amen.*

It wasn't long before she heard the screen door squeak open. Catharine watched as Greta bounded down the steps and strolled toward her. "Morning, Greta. I see you finally got up. I'm afraid breakfast has long been over." Catharine paused and leaned on the rake to catch her breath.

Greta met her gaze warily, then folded her arms across her chest. "I wasn't hungry. Do you need help with that?"

Was that her way of making peace? It would take more than that.

"I'm nearly finished. But you can help me pile up the debris on this tarp so I can drag it over to the burn pile." Catharine got down on her knees and started working again. She watched out of the corner of her eye as Greta followed suit and waited anxiously for her to break the silence.

They worked quietly until Catharine started to speak, but Greta touched her hand. "Cath . . . I just want to say . . . I'm sorry if I worried you needlessly. Truly I am."

Catharine sat back, clasping her arms around her legs. Greta did seem genuine in her apology. "*Goed!* Apology accepted. But we need to discuss this and consider your actions."

Greta looked away but continued on her hands and knees, gathering the discarded weeds. "What is there to talk about? You know that Bryan likes me—"

Catharine interrupted, shaking her head. "Then he should court you in the proper way by coming to the house and asking to see you. That's how it's done, Greta. I don't need to tell you that!" She was desperately trying to keep her tone even but felt it was a losing battle.

Greta turned back to stare at her sister, her face a mottled pink. "In a few weeks, I'll be eighteen. I thought that was old enough to make my own decisions."

Catharine took a deep breath to control her emotions. "You are old enough and I expect you to, but with guidance from someone who knows more than you do. I'm just afraid you don't see the danger there. A gentleman would have asked to call on you and be proud to escort you out in the daylight, not sneak around after midnight like a thief. He needs to be honorable in his actions toward you. I'm scared that you don't see him for who he is. How could you, in such a short time?"

Greta tossed her head, pushing a loose strand of her silky hair behind her ear, then shrugged. "I don't know . . . we just liked each other from the moment we spoke at the depot."

Catharine's lips formed a thin line, and she looked at her innocent and gullible sister. "Are you sure it's not attraction instead of mutual admiration? Would you know the difference? Men who are transients, like those in the army, don't always form strong attachments before they're assigned to another post." She knelt down in the dirt and filled her apron with more roots.

"What are you saying?" Lines formed across Greta's forehead.

"Greta, did Bryan touch you in an unfamiliar way?"

A silvery laugh escaped Greta's lips. "Please, he's not like that."

"I'm afraid, my dear sister, that you don't know that. Do you understand how babies are made?"

"What?" Greta's eyes were wide as she stopped and brushed the dirt from her hands.

Catharine did not like bringing this topic up but knew she must. "My devotion to you and Anna extends much farther than you having a roof over your heads. I don't want to see you hurt or someone take advantage of you, that's all. I think you're blinded with infatuation, and I want more for you and Anna than that."

Greta grabbed Catharine's hands. "Sweet Cath, I know you worry about us. I know your experience with Karl brought you so much pain, and I'm sorry for that."

Catharine stiffened at the reminder. She had tried to put

away those thoughts that would creep into her mind. "You were a big help to my healing, Greta. I owe you."

"*Nee*, you don't owe me, but you can't compare my experience to what you went through. I see the pain behind your eyes, except when you look at Peter. I can tell you love him." She gave Catharine a tight squeeze, tears glistening in her crystal-blue eyes. "Worry about Peter and let me worry about me."

"Well then, while you are living here, Bryan will come calling on you in the proper way, and you'll come to me if you need to talk or have any concerns. The ways of the heart can be hurtful. I don't want that to happen to you."

"You're worrying too much. You know I'll talk to you if the need arises, but I can take care of myself."

Catharine wasn't exactly reassured, but she could pray it was so. "Shall we drag this pile over to be burned? I appreciate your help. I know how you hate yard work—you never even went in the garden at home." She bent down and picked up a clump of dirt. "Now if I can just get some flowers to plant . . ." She allowed the rich dirt to sift through her fingers. When she looked up, she could see the relief on Greta's face and knew that there was nothing more to be said about what they'd discussed.

Greta hooked her arm through Catharine's. "Let's go get something cool to drink. This spring weather is warming up quickly." They turned around in time to see Peter striding across the lawn to the barn.

Catharine lifted her arm in a wave, so Peter paused midstride, a hand on one hip. "I'm heading into town on a business matter, but I shouldn't be long," he said.

He was about to continue on when Catharine called out to him. "Do you mind if I tag along? I want to buy some seeds for my flower bed." She and Greta walked closer to him.

Peter looked at her apron and fingernails full of dirt, her smudged face, and her bright green eyes, and he felt a tug in his heart. Greta's arm was linked through hers, and it looked as though they'd made some sort of peace about last night's episode. Looking at Catharine now, he felt guilty that he'd judged her so quickly. "'Course you can come. I can drop you off at the mercantile, but you might want to change your apron and wash the dirt off your cheek fist." He grinned and watched as her face lit up. Her smile was so infectious, and the blush on her cheeks was charming and hard to resist. This was the side of her he liked, not the sad, brooding face of last night. *But you were part of the problem*, he reminded himself. He swallowed hard.

Catharine spun around, releasing Greta's hold on her. "Greta, you and Anna can fix your own lunch today. I'll be back in time to fix supper. I'll only be a minute, Peter." She crossed the yard to the house.

He had never seen her move so quickly before and called after her, "Take your time. I have to hitch up the wagon now that you're going."

"Just make sure you're back before supper, Peter. You don't want to have to try to eat anything I'd fix," Greta said.

"That's for sure." He smiled. "I'm glad to see that you and Catharine talked."

"It was a good talk. I think she forgets sometimes that I'm a grown woman."

Peter scratched his chin, then looked her squarely in the eye. "I don't think it's that. I think she just doesn't trust a

130

man a couple years older who's convincing you to sneak out of the house late at night."

"I see her point, really, I do," Greta said in a somewhat patronizing tone.

"Then listen to her. She knows what's best."

"Not always." She flipped her blonde hair back over her shoulder and walked back to the house. She definitely had a strong will, heaven help her. Catharine would have to keep a close eye on her—he was certain of that.

14

Giving a short whistle, Peter tapped the reins against Star's back. Star lunged forward, his harness making a jangling noise along with the clatter of the wagon wheels as they headed down the drive toward Cheyenne. Peter had been surprised when Catharine emerged from the house with Greta and Anna, who wanted to go to town too. Not exactly what he had in mind. He'd been looking forward to spending time alone with Catharine on the ride. Now he'd have to endure their chatter the entire way to town.

He bit the inside of his jaw rather than protest, acknowledging that females didn't need any excuse to go to town. Perhaps they'd been out here away from other people too long. Catharine had written to him about how active they were in their community in Amsterdam.

Hopefully her sisters would keep Catharine occupied while he visited his mother. He had questions that had plagued him since their talk. And he didn't think he could let another day roll by until he talked with her, or he wouldn't get any sleep tonight. He'd had enough of tossing and turning and staying on his side of the bed.

Clara pulled aside the lace sheers to look out of the upstairs window of her fashionable Terrace Row house, swallowing the lump in her throat. Ever since she'd talked to Peter, she'd anguished over their conversation. Would he ever speak to her again? Then she chided herself for thinking such incongruous thoughts. *He'll come around,* she thought, *once Mac produces evidence that Catharine was married before.*

When she thought of Mac, her heart gave a flutter. He'd sent an invitation by messenger yesterday, asking her to dinner tonight at the Tivoli restaurant. Maybe he had the proof she needed. Or wanted to spend time alone in her company. *Hardly, you old fool!*

Deep in her heart, Clara knew she shouldn't entertain such thoughts or read anything into the invitation, but she was lonely. Other than her volunteer work at the church and tea with the ladies' social club, her life held few amusements. Widowhood was lonely . . . very lonely indeed. And now that Peter was married with an instant houseful, he didn't need her. The Lord had not seen fit to bless her with any other children, so after several miscarriages, Clara had given up hope for a baby sister or brother for Peter. It had been her dream that he would marry Dorothy and have a brood of children she could dote on.

She dropped the curtain back in place and headed downstairs to her favorite chair to sew. Taking care of a town house for one person required little work at all, so she hadn't hired a maid, preferring to keep up her own house to help fill the hours. It was a distraction for a while, until everything seemed to become mundane and repetitious. She reckoned that was the reason for being flattered by Mac so quickly. *Well, I'll enjoy it while it lasts.*

Only moments had passed since she'd picked up her

embroidery when the doorbell chimed. She nudged the sleeping calico off her lap, and the cat landed on her feet with a whimper and stared up at her. "Amelia, you are the laziest cat in town. Why, you never even catch me a mouse," Clara complained. The cat scampered away to bask in the shaft of sunlight dancing on the floor beneath the window.

She opened the door to find Peter with a somber look on his face. "Peter, I must say I'm very pleased to see you. Come in." She swung open the door for him to enter.

"You may not think so later, Mother."

"I was just doing some needlework," she said, ignoring his comment. She walked to the parlor. "May I get you something to eat or drink?"

"No thank you," he said, taking a seat opposite her.

"Where is Catharine? I would've thought she'd be with you." She gazed at her handsome son, aware of the chasm between them.

Peter removed his hat, placing it to rest on one knee. "I've been thinking about our little talk and going over it in my mind. I'm sorry if I was in any way disrespectful to you, and I know my temper kept me from thinking clearly or asking you any questions."

He paused as if thinking of what to say next, and Clara felt her mouth go dry. She didn't like confrontation, but she should've been expecting this. "Peter, I didn't want to upset you. But what was I supposed to do? Not share my information with you?" She squirmed in her chair and shifted, trying to stifle the sudden heat she felt rise to her face.

"Matter of fact, Catharine is in town. I dropped her off at the mercantile with her sisters. I want to know who you hired to find out that *supposedly* Catharine was once married."

"I told you. He's a private investigator whose name I got from a reliable source. It's Mac Foster, and he's very good at his job."

"Mac Foster?" Peter's eyebrows elevated as he raised his voice. "From what I heard, I wouldn't trust him as far as I could toss my hat!"

Clara puffed out her chest, taking a deep breath before speaking. "Son, I don't know who told you that, but he's very kind and very professional toward me. He even asked me to dinner tonight."

Peter groaned—not exactly the reaction she was expecting. "Oh, Mother! Professional? Then why is he taking you to dinner?"

"I don't know," Clara stuttered. "Maybe he has more information to share with me."

Peter ran his hand through his hair. "He could do that in his office. I'm warning you, Mother—don't trust that man. I don't know why I ever gave any thought to your story in the first place!" Peter stood. "That settles it. I treated Catharine badly after listening to you, and I need to apologize to her."

Clara jumped up and grabbed Peter's arm. "Son, I already told you. I thought it was best that we look into her background for your own protection. A mail-order bride—really, Peter. You could've done so much better with Dorothy."

Peter clapped his hat back on his head. "Think whatever you like, Mother. You don't really know Catharine at all. If you weren't being so unreasonable, you could get to know what a wonderful person she is instead of making her your enemy." He pulled away to leave, then turned around and leveled a brooding look at her. "And you can forget about

Dorothy. Just be glad I didn't share this with Catharine. Now I'm going to go spend the rest of the day with my wife!"

The door slammed shut, rattling the beveled glass, but Clara stood rooted to the spot long after she heard Peter hurry down the steps. *He's wrong . . . I just know he is.* Mac wouldn't take advantage of her. He simply couldn't. Not after the way he'd looked at her the last time they'd met.

She turned her thoughts to what she'd wear to dinner while she sat down, then continued to embroider a pillowcase. The pattern of bluebirds and hearts on the cotton brought to mind two lovers in springtime. The thought brought a smile to her lips in spite of the angry outburst from Peter.

A knock on the door startled her. Peter! But when she peeked out to open the door, it was Anna. Not at all whom she expected.

"Mrs. Andersen, may I please come in?" Anna's large blue eyes were warm and friendly.

"Well, I . . . er . . . yes, yes, of course. Where are my manners? Are you looking for Peter? He's just left, though I didn't see which direction he was headed." Clara stared back at the slip of a girl with striking Dutch looks.

Anna smiled. "Oh, I'm not here to see Peter," she said, stepping across the threshold. "I followed Peter and saw your name on the brass plate by the door. I just came to bring you your hat." She pulled the hat from behind her back and held it out to Clara.

Clara, somewhat surprised, took it and gestured for her to come in. "Why, thank you, Anna. What a sweet thing for you to do."

Anna strolled into the parlor, looking around with interest. "It's the least I could do since you seemed to be very upset about something," she said as she picked up a silver picture frame from the table. "Was this your husband?"

Clara was grateful that she hadn't asked what had upset her so much. "Yes, it was. Mr. Andersen, God rest his soul." Clara watched as Anna moved her finger over the dress in the picture.

"My, that's a beautiful wedding dress you wore."

"Yes, dear. It was made from the finest Belgium linen and lace. My family was well-to-do, and my mother spared no expense on her only daughter," she said, remembering how she'd cherished it.

"I don't know if I ever will marry, but if I do, I hope my wedding dress will be as beautiful as this one." Anna placed the picture back onto the table. Her wistful look softened her face, which reflected promise and hope.

What a lovely young girl. Ahh . . . to be so young again. How Clara wished she'd been able to have more children. Somewhere along the way she'd learned to accept the fact, but deep in her heart she knew she'd been angry at God.

"Anna, would you like to stay for tea? I was just about to have some."

"If it's no trouble, yes, Mrs. Andersen. I'd like that, but I can't stay long. I have to meet my sisters soon. Maybe you can tell me about your husband. He had a nice face."

Kindliness flooded Clara's heart, quite by surprise. "I'll only be a few minutes. Make yourself right at home."

Anna took a seat, and Amelia hopped onto her lap and curled up. Anna and Clara both laughed, and Anna stroked the cat under the chin.

"Anna, I hope you like cats. Seems as though Amelia has taken to you."

"I love animals, Mrs. Andersen. I wasn't able to persuade my parents to get any, but I've always longed to have a pet."

"Then you should." Clara scurried off in the direction of the kitchen, happy to have a guest for tea to break the monotony of her day.

15

Peter hurried away without saying where he was going, leaving Catharine to select her seeds on her own at the general store. Anna and Greta begged to take a walk through town, with strict orders to return within the hour. Catharine watched Peter walk down the sidewalk and get lost in the crowd, then she turned to walk across the street to the post office. A young man smiled as she approached the counter.

"I'm Mrs. Catharine Andersen. Would you check our box and see if we have any mail?"

"Sure thing, Mrs. Andersen." He walked over to the wall of mail slots behind him, then returned. "Nothing today, ma'am."

Catharine sighed. "Thank you." She thought surely she would have her copy of the divorce paper by now. It had been months since the solicitor had said he had them and they would be forwarded on to Peter's address. She wasn't sure what she would say when they did arrive. Her heart started pounding. *I'll have to tell him the truth then. Maybe he'll still care for me and understand when he knows what I've been through.* A knot formed in her stomach at the thought.

She hurried back over to the general store. When she was satisfied that she had enough seeds to complete the small patch of ground, the young clerk measured seeds into small envelopes. The snapdragons and cockscombs would render nice, tall flowers that she could surround with marigolds, impatiens, dusty miller, and sweet alyssum for a border. She placed the order on Peter's account, and as she turned to go in search of her sisters, she saw a familiar face. Angelina was shopping with her twin sons in tow.

"Angelina!" Catharine called to her. The petite beauty turned around with her purchases in hand. She caught Catharine's gaze and hurried across the room, pulling on each of the protesting twins, who, from the looks of it, would rather be outside or back at home.

"*Buongiorno*, Catharine! It's so good to see you. How have you been? Seems the only time I get to see you is at church. I hope that doesn't mean Peter is working you too hard."

It was hard not to be struck by Angelina's smile and Italian looks. "*Hallo*. No, I'm adjusting, so he hasn't been too much of a taskmaster. I think being a farmer's wife is a never-ending job, however."

"Mama, can we wait for you outside?" Angelo pleaded while he yanked on his mother's arm.

"Don't interrupt, Angelo. I'm talking with Mrs. Andersen."

"Please, Mama, we'll stay close by, I promise." Alfredo took up the cause.

Angelina rolled her eyes. "Excuse me," she said to Catharine, the turned to the twins. "When I'm through talking, both of you had better be sitting on the porch waiting. Do you hear me?"

"Yes, Mama," they answered in unison, then tore out of the store before she had time to change her mind.

Angelina gave Catharine a quick kiss on the cheek, which surprised her. "Ah, my boys forget to use their manners now and again." She laughed. "But I have to keep a close eye on them so they won't get into any trouble. What brings you to town?"

Catharine held up her sack. "I wanted to buy seeds for my flower bed. Peter helped me till a garden space. I wasn't sure what sort of flowers grow here, but the clerk seemed to know quite a lot about what I should plant."

"I see. Well, next time perhaps I can share with you some plants that I've learned to propagate. I've heard about the beautiful tulips in Holland. I wonder if they'll grow here."

Catharine tucked the package under her arm. "I intend to find out. I brought some bulbs in my trunk to plant this fall. If they come up and do well, then I'll be most happy to share them with you."

Angelina's dark eyes twinkled as she crooked her arm around Catharine. "You and I will become good friends. I can feel it." She guided them toward the door. "I have an idea. Why don't you come back to the ristorante and we can have coffee and biscotti? That is, if you're finished with your shopping."

"I am done, but, Angelina, what is bis . . . co . . . ."

"Biscotti," Angelina repeated. "It's a type of Italian cookie. I think you'll like it." Her full lips curved in a smile. "You'll have to teach me some of your native language."

"Okay. Maybe we'll see my sisters and Peter along the way. I'm not really sure where they got off to, but none of them seemed interested in picking out seeds for a garden. My sisters were more interested in exploring Cheyenne."

Angelina giggled softly. "The town is not so big that they won't be able to find you, my dear."

As they stepped out onto the sidewalk, Catharine noticed clouds blocking out the sun's earlier rays, making the air cooler. She was glad she had brought her shawl along. She gathered it around her shoulders and let Angelina lead the way.

Angelina called to Alfredo and Angelo, who ran up to them. She paused, looking up at the sky. "Mmm, looks like a spring storm might be brewing."

After last night's lightning storm without a drop of rain, Peter had told Catharine that storms on the plains could pop up without warning. Would they be able to make it home before any rain or lightning developed? Maybe it wouldn't rain at all. She shuddered. She had no desire to see that kind of lightning again.

Angelina's boys ran on ahead while the two women scooted on down the sidewalk in the direction of the restaurant. Angelina stopped underneath a sign hanging overhead that read MARIO'S RISTORANTE. She pushed open the door and they hurried inside.

The mixed smell of garlic, onions, and something else Catharine couldn't identify tickled her nostrils. Angelina led her to a table and called out to her husband in a cheery voice. She seated Catharine next to the window overlooking the busy streets of Cheyenne.

"Next to the window we'll have a perfect view. You'll be able to see your family coming in either direction. I'll go get our cups of coffee and be right back."

Catharine settled back in her chair and gazed around the restaurant, enjoying the warm, cozy atmosphere. The smells were tantalizing, and she watched as Mario served several tables, then paused with a nod of greeting in her direction. She supposed the patrons were in between a late lunch and supper, which made her consider what she could prepare quickly once they were home. Peter ate what she prepared, but Catharine knew sometimes he was simply being polite, and last night . . . well, he'd hardly touched his food at all. The thought pierced her heart, but she was at a loss as to what to say or do to fix the ever-widening gulf they seemed to have. A lone tear rolled down her cheeks, but she quickly wiped it away before Angelina returned.

She heard Angelina's heels *tap*, *tap*, *tap* across the hardwood floor. She carried over a tray with steaming cups of coffee and the biscotti, and Catharine savored the aroma that came from the cup in front of her. Angelina placed the tray on a nearby empty table, then pulled out a chair directly across from Catharine.

"My friend, why the long face?" Angelina leaned forward, her forehead wrinkled with concern.

Catharine tensed and opened her mouth to protest, but smiled instead. "Oh . . . I was only thinking of the chores that didn't get done today that will have to be made up. That's all."

"Don't concern yourself with that. Just enjoy the moment that we have right now. I've learned that all things fall into place whether we fret or not, it seems."

Angelina's effervescent personality was good for her, Catharine decided. Peter was right, it would be nice to have such a warm person as a friend. She took a bite of the biscotti as Angelina watched her reaction.

"Well . . . what do you think?"

"I like it. It's a little hard, though."

Angelina grinned. "Try dipping the tip of the cookie in your coffee for a second. My husband calls it dunkin' his biscotti." She demonstrated with her cookie, then popped the piece into her mouth.

Catharine did the same and, to her delight, found that the coffee enhanced its flavor. "It's *goed!*" Catharine dabbed her napkin on the coffee that dribbled down her chin. The women giggled like two schoolgirls.

"What is it like to be a mail-order bride?" Angelina's eyes were wide with genuine interest.

Catharine sipped the strong coffee before answering. "Well . . . it was a big decision for me to even consider such an ad, but after my parents died, I was ready to change everything about my life and start over completely." She gazed out the window before continuing. "Peter and I began to care for each other through our correspondence, and now that I think about it, maybe it's one of the best ways to find a mate, *after* you become friends."

"Mmm . . . maybe so, but with Mario . . ." Angelina pressed her fingers to her lips and flung a kiss. "It was *bellissimo*, I tell you!"

"And that means?"

"Italian for *lovely*, *wonderful*. So the marriage is working out wonderfully, no?"

"Er . . . yes . . . most of the time." Catharine swallowed hard. She hadn't meant to let that slip.

Angelina quirked an eyebrow upward. "What does that mean? Most of the—" She stopped when Catharine squirmed and looked down at her hands. "Excuse me, Catharine. I have no right to pry. It's just that you looked so unhappy."

Catharine waved her hand. "No, it's all right. It's just that he's been upset with me, and I'm not sure what to do." She shrugged.

Angelina made a clicking noise with her tongue. "Ah, my friend, you have come to the right place for advice. I should know. I've been married eight years now. Perhaps I can help if you'd care to share with me. I will not break your confidence, I assure you."

Catharine glanced out the window and sighed, then began to talk in a hushed voice. She told her how at first she was unable to respond to Peter, but after a few weeks she began to feel real desire for her husband. Angelina's face reflected sympathy. Catharine finished by telling her about the special night she'd planned and Peter's rejection of her, and just then Mario strolled up to the table with the coffeepot.

"Catharine, it is so good to see you again. Is Peter with you?" He refilled their cups with a smile, showing even white teeth.

"*Dank U wel*, Mario. Peter is in town and my sisters are with us too."

"I hope he stops by then. I'd like to see your sisters as well. How did you like the biscotti?"

"It's very good and goes well with the coffee," Catharine said.

Mario bellowed loudly, his voice carrying across the room, "I make the coffee and Angelina bakes the biscotti . . . among other things, right, my sweet?" He leaned over to give her a peck on her temple. "I'll leave you ladies alone to talk for now. I must go stir my sauce for tonight's dinner." Mario bowed, then moved away quickly for such a large man.

"I think I see one of your sisters coming down the walk, and not a moment too soon," Angelina said.

Catharine looked out the window once more and saw huge raindrops pelt the dry, dusty streets of Cheyenne. She pressed next to the window and motioned to Greta, then met her at the door with Angelina right behind her.

"Have you seen Peter? And where's Anna?" she asked.

"No, I thought he was with you. Anna took off on her own." Greta turned to Angelina. "*Hallo* again." She wiggled her nose. "Something smells delicious!"

"Do come in. Your sister and I were just having a snack. Would you care to join us?" Angelina asked.

"Greta, you let Anna go off alone? She doesn't know anything about the town at all!" Catharine tried to squelch her fear. Where was Anna? Catharine looked at the watch pinned to her blouse. The hour had long since passed. "We have to find her." She moved to the door, but Angelina stopped her.

"Let's wait a few minutes. She probably ducked into a shop when the rain started."

Greta nodded. "You're probably right. I'm sure she'll look for our wagon in front of the general store and wait for us."

Catharine wasn't convinced. She twisted the edge of her shawl between her fingers. "I hope you're right. When the rain stops, if she's not here, we'll go look for her. Maybe she and Peter are at the store now."

Greta moved toward the table that Angelina indicated. "I could use a good cup of coffee," she said with a laugh. "Peter has spoiled me with his, and I almost prefer it to tea."

"Mmm. We shall see what you think of Mario's coffee." Angelina went to get another cup and winked at Catharine, who reluctantly took her seat again.

"Where did you go, Greta?" Catharine asked.

"Oh, nowhere in particular." She shrugged. Catharine

thought Greta seemed a little uneasy. "Just walking. I looked in a millinery shop. You'll have to go sometime yourself. Did you find what you needed for your garden?"

"*Ja*. I did. But I'm not sure what happened to Peter. He was to meet us in an hour."

They sipped their coffee while they watched the steady rain, enjoying their visit with Angelina, who pelted them with questions about their homeland. It wasn't long before Peter strode in, stomped his feet at the door, and hung his hat on a peg nearby. His face wore a crooked half smile that Catharine had come to know but hadn't seen much of lately.

"I see you ladies are getting to know one another."

Angelina stood to give him a peck on the cheek. "My dear Peter, you're drenched. Here, you can use this napkin to blot your face. A spring rain is good, no?"

"Yes, ma'am, it is. Now, if it'll just do this throughout the summer, it'll be good for the wheat." He looked around the table. "Where's Anna?"

"We don't really know. We're going to go look for her as soon as the rain stops. I'd hoped you'd have passed her on the street," Catharine said, cocking her head with narrowed eyes at Greta. "I thought she was with Greta, but it seems they went different ways."

Mario walked up to the group, tying his apron about his waist. "Is something the matter?"

"They don't know where Anna is. I'm sure she's just fine, holed up in a shop waiting for the rain to stop. It never lasts long out here." Angelina glanced over at her husband.

Mario's face twisted into a frown, and he rubbed his chin, bending down to peer out the window. "Mmm . . . I don't know. Looks like the rain will continue awhile."

Straightening up, he asked Peter, "Want me to go with you to find her?"

"I appreciate it, but I'll go now. No sense waiting for it to stop raining. She doesn't know her way around—"

The door flew open, and a drenched Anna, looking like a little waif, hurried inside, searching the dining room for a familiar face.

Catharine rushed over to where she stood. "Anna! Wherever in the world have you been?" She guided her sister over to their table and sat her down.

Anna sneezed and wiped her face with her sleeve, then sneezed again.

"*Gezondheid!* Bless you!" Greta said. "What happened to you?"

"I was having a nice visit with your mother, Peter," Anna answered, then covered her mouth to sneeze again.

Peter looked dumbfounded "*My* mother? Whatever for?"

"I wanted to return her hat," Anna said with an angelic face. "We had a nice chat."

Catharine saw Peter's surprised look and wondered why he would be shocked.

Angelina took Anna by the hand. "Sweet one, let me get you out of those wet clothes. You could catch a cold. Since I'm not very tall, I'll bet you could wear one of my dresses. You can't ride home like this. Come with me."

Catharine just shook her head at Anna. Angelina passed them with a look at Catharine that said she wasn't through talking with her. "Don't take long. We've dallied long enough," Catharine said to Anna.

Mario threw his hands up. "I have a wonderful notion. Why don't you all stay for supper and have a bowl of my

148

famous spaghetti? After all, it's pouring rain and you don't want to travel in this kind of weather if you're in your wagon, do you, Peter?"

Angelina clapped her hands. "I don't know why I didn't think of that. What do you say, Peter?"

Peter glanced at his wife, who shrugged her shoulders slightly. Greta looked over at Peter. "Oh, wouldn't that be a wonderful break from Catharine's cooking—" She put her hand over her mouth with a giggle after Catharine's disapproving look. "I didn't mean anything by that, Cath. But it would be a nice change, don't you think?"

"Well . . . I think it's up to Peter." She looked back at her husband, who smiled.

"Okay, Mario." Peter winked at Mario. "It's time the girls tasted some of your fine Italian cooking."

"Then it's settled. While Angelina gets Anna a fresh set of clothes, you all can get cleaned up for one of my best meals . . . not to brag," he said, tweaking his mustache. Angelina and Anna left in search of dry clothing.

Peter clapped Mario on the back. "It's not called bragging when it's the truth, my friend." They both laughed, and Catharine thought how different Peter and her first husband were. Peter was amicable and thoughtful, and her first husband had been dark and brooding. "Is there a way Greta or I can help? Maybe serve your customers at supper?"

Mario's face was incredulous. "Absolutely not! You will be *my* guests tonight."

Catharine was beginning to see that Peter had a very romantic side to him, and she liked it. She liked it a lot.

Peter gazed down at Catharine's face as Greta teased, "Aww, cut it out, you two!"

16

While the rain continued to fall, inside Mario's Ristorante the dim lights cast a cozy ambience to the round table set especially for the Andersens. Angelina had cut some of her climbing roses for a centerpiece and lit candles. Between mounds of spaghetti and meatballs heaped high in large bowls, laughter was shared while the troubles of the farm work were left behind. Between serving them and their patrons, Mario and Angelina, along with the twins, continued to fill their water glasses and bring them piping hot, crusty bread with slabs of butter. Just when Peter was sure none of them could eat another bite, the twins removed their bowls and Mario delivered a creamed dessert swirled in clear parfait glasses. Peter smacked his lips, enjoying the delicacy that held just a hint of lemon.

Glancing over to Catharine, he saw her close her eyes in sheer delight as she filled her spoon again and again until she reached the bottom of the glass. She caught him watching her, so he smiled, capturing her eyes for a long moment until she looked away shyly.

"Peter, your mother asked me about registering for high

school in Cheyenne in the fall." Anna looked over at Catharine. "Do you think I could?"

"I'm not sure how that would work, Anna. It would be quite a long drive every day, wouldn't it, Peter?"

Peter dragged his eyes away from Catharine's lovely face and the thoughts that were swirling in his mind and turned to Anna. "You'd be riding nearly an hour each way, and I don't know if we can spare the time it would take for me to get you back and forth to Cheyenne every day. Maybe Catharine can teach you at home."

Anna shook her head, excitement in her voice. "You wouldn't have to. During the school months, Mrs. Andersen said that I might be able to stay with her, sort of like a companion to her. She seems so lonely."

Peter was baffled. Why would his mother suggest such a thing when she was trying to uncover Catharine's past? Was this one of her ploys? He let out a huff. "With my mother . . . I'm not so sure that would be a good idea, Anna. Catharine might need you at home." He grimaced. Catharine shot him a sideways look.

"*Ach!* I could come home every weekend, to be sure," Anna stammered. She sneezed and tried to cover her mouth quickly.

"We'll have to talk about this and consider what to do. Mrs. Andersen hardly knows you." Catharine finished off her dessert and set her spoon next to her plate.

"But I know her now! I spent the afternoon with her."

"Anna, please . . . Peter and I need to talk about it. But for now finish your dessert. It's getting so late. We should be going soon, don't you think, Peter?"

"That would be wise." *If only you knew.*

Greta pushed her empty glass away. "I'm so full that I'm

sure I won't be able to move from the table. I have to say that was a delicious meal and I love Mario's cooking!"

"Me too!" Anna patted her tummy. "But I can't eat another bite."

Peter thought Anna looked a little older now that she was wearing one of Angelina's frocks. Suddenly he realized how much like Catharine Anna was, except for their coloring. He gazed again at Catharine, whose face, illuminated through the flickering candlelight, couldn't have looked more fetching and soft than it did at this moment. He truly desired her, but how did she really feel about him now? He would try to put away his mother's accusations and give Catharine the benefit of the doubt. *She's my wife, for heaven's sake, and I can trust my instincts. Have I been wrong before?*

With one last swipe of his spoon, Peter finished off the delicious cream dessert, and Mario stepped back up to the table to clear the dessert glasses. "My friends, I don't know if you realize it or not, but the rain is continuing to fall. Perhaps it would be wise to spend the night in town rather than drag yourselves through the rain to get home. It'd be so late anyway that you wouldn't get anything done before morning." He looked Peter in the eye, giving him a wink.

Peter squirmed. What was Mario thinking? Playing matchmaker again? This time there was no matchmaking to be made—more like patch making, Peter decided. "Let me take a look outside," he said, pushing his chair back.

When he and Mario walked to the door to look out at the steady rainfall turning the streets of Cheyenne to mud, Mario nudged him.

"It appears that it'll continue through evening," Peter said. "We could still make it home. Too bad I didn't bring the carriage, although . . ." Peter grinned at his friend. "To tell the truth, I've sort of been planning something like this all along."

"Ah, Peter, tonight is the perfect time to have that private time with your bride that we talked about. The girls can stay with me and Angelina in the guest room. What do you say? Unless you'd rather ask your mother."

Peter threw Mario an annoyed look and then thought for a minute. He wondered what Catharine would think. He certainly wouldn't knock on his mother's door tonight. "I don't know . . ."

Mario clapped Peter on the back. "The chores can wait, and you can leave right after breakfast. From what Angelina told me, your sweet bride is down in the dumps."

Peter jerked his head around. "What did she say to Angelina?"

"I don't know the exact conversation, my friend, but she needs your attention. My advice to you is don't wait too long. The sooner the better."

"I'm sure I could get a room somewhere, but we'll get drenched just getting there. We don't have a change of clothes either."

Mario laughed. "That's more like it. Don't concern yourself with the clothes—we can spare an extra set, and you can borrow our umbrella. You can have Angelo run down to the Inter Ocean with a note to reserve a nice room for tonight. He'll consider the rain an adventure. Now, let's go tell the ladies."

"But, Peter, who'll milk the cow? Bessie will be fair to bursting before we get back home," Catharine asked when Peter suggested they stay overnight.

Mario gave a little cough and looked at Peter. Peter's lips twisted into a smile. "I must confess. I planned for us to stay overnight as a surprise. I didn't know about the rain though. Don't worry about Bessie. I stopped by earlier and asked our neighbor if he could do me a favor. We'll be home tomorrow before the evening milking time."

Catharine touched Peter on the arm, and he put his arm around her waist. "Seems you thought of everything, dear."

An hour later, using Mario's umbrella to ward off the steady drizzle, Catharine was whisked away under the protective arm of Peter to the hotel just down the block. Not many people were about, and Catharine was glad that this rain hadn't produced any lightning.

Angelina had been like an old mother hen with her chicks, shooing the children and Catharine's sisters upstairs for the rest of the evening. With a brief wave to her sisters and a lingering look at Angelina, who assured her Greta and Anna would be perfectly fine, Catharine and Peter had left them to have an evening alone . . . uninterrupted.

Catharine was giddy with anticipation and felt her heart racing. Peter must have gotten over whatever he was upset about in order to take a night away from home. Perhaps he would tell her later. He'd said this could be a little bit of a honeymoon they'd never gotten a chance to have. Had the overnight trip been planned, she would've packed her wedding nightgown. The thought made her blush, and she was grateful her head was down to ward off the rain.

Peter's arm was tight about her waist, and he picked up their pace. In eagerness? She hoped so. As they were about to cross the street, a fast-moving brougham hit a mud puddle. Though they jumped back, both of them were thoroughly splattered when its wheels flung clods of mud directly on them. They started to cross the street but stopped in the middle as Peter lost control of the umbrella, which turned inside out with a gust of wind. Catharine gasped. So much for the umbrella.

She wiped the cold mud off her face with her hands, then felt more mud clinging to the hair escaping from her bonnet. She giggled, then turned her face to the sky and let the rain wash over her. She was sure Peter thought she'd lost her mind, but she hadn't seen rain since she left Holland, and it felt good. One look at Peter, mud splattered across his shirt, and she started to cackle, pointing at him.

"You're no sight to behold either, my lady," he bellowed. His laughter rang out as his eyes took her in from top to bottom.

As the rain pelted them, she leaned forward and saw her high-top boots sinking into a muddy hole. She lost her balance and fell over on her hands and knees in the squishy street. "*Ja*, but not near as bad as you are going to look!" She flashed him a mischievous smile. Peter reached out his hand to assist her with an impish look on his face. She gave a hard yank, catching him off guard, and he tumbled down in a heap. Before he knew what hit him, Catharine had scooped up a handful of mud and wiped it across his nose and face. "That'll teach you to laugh at a helpless, wet female."

He looked at her with shock, sending them into fits of laughter. They drew themselves upright, and Catharine was laughing so hard that she leaned over, a hand to her stomach, as tears streamed down her mud-streaked face.

Peter grabbed her wrist, chuckling the entire time, and held her close to his body, mud and all, unmindful of the passersby. "It's so good to hear your laughter. I've missed it."

His eyes glistened with amusement. "You look rather cute with the embellishment of mud to enhance your outfit, even if your feet are sinking!"

Catharine gazed up at him, and their eyes locked. She liked the feel of his strong arms about her. "Is that so?"

His lips curved into a broad smile, the brim of his hat dripping water down her shoulder. "I have just the cure for being splattered with mud on a rainy night." His eyes teased her, and he leaned down to kiss her. "A nice hot bath where we can both peel off these wet things and soak to our hearts' content. What do you say? Shall we get out of this rain?"

Catharine's answer was a slow, lingering kiss while they stood in a tight embrace, ignoring the rain. A harrumph came from a person walking by, and they slowly pulled apart. Peter grabbed her hand tightly, and laughing and gasping for breath, they sprinted the rest of the way to the hotel.

Clara and Mac inched their way through the crowded room at the Tivoli filled with laughing couples. She admired the dark polished wood of the bar where waiters ran to and fro with their orders. She'd heard that certain kinds of women occupied the third floor above the restaurant, but she wouldn't think of that now. She'd rather remember that the ladies of Cheyenne gathered for tea here in the afternoons. A much more pleasant thought.

She'd taken a long time with her toilette, hoping to impress Mac. When he'd picked her up in the brougham tonight, she'd caught his appraising look as he handed her into the carriage with orders to the driver, then took his seat next to her rather than across from her.

As they continued to make their way across the room following the maître d', Clara caught sight of a pretty blonde coming toward them on the arm of a soldier. No, it couldn't be . . . It was Greta! She got the distinct feeling that Greta didn't wish to be seen, but Clara stopped and spoke as they drew nearer. "One moment please, Mac. I want to say hello to someone."

The look on Greta's face showed her unease, but she quickly recovered as Clara spoke. "Greta, what are you doing in town tonight?"

The soldier holding Greta's arm coughed and looked at Greta to say something. "I . . . we . . . er . . . I was just having a cup of coffee with my friend here. Bryan, this is Clara Andersen, Peter's mother."

"How do you do?" he said with nod.

"This is Mac Foster." Clara indicated Mac at her side. "This is my daughter-in-law's sister, Greta."

Mac nodded and said, "I see. Hello."

Greta made a move to go, but Clara's hand stopped her. "Are you staying in Cheyenne tonight?"

"*Ja*, we are," she answered, not looking her in the eye. She offered no further explanation, to the disappointment of Clara.

Mac nudged Clara. "Our table is waiting."

"Well, have a nice evening then." The young couple hurried away, leaving Clara wondering as the waiter seated them at a cozy table away from the crowd.

17

"Do you have more information for me, Mac? I'm anxious to hear what you've found out," Clara said, folding her napkin after their delicious late-night dinner. She had eaten only half of her meal, suddenly mindful to watch her figure now that she had the attention of an eligible bachelor. Somehow her appetite had fled soon after Mac's invitation to dinner, and then when he'd asked for a table in the corner where it was more private, well . . .

Clara's stomach developed a severe case of the butterflies whenever she was in Mac's presence. His enigmatic persona swallowed her up. She hoped she didn't appear too eager to dine with her private investigator, but she couldn't help this growing feeling for him.

Mac pushed his empty plate away, leaned back in his chair in a comfortable pose, and stared at her through dark eyes. "Why are you in such a hurry to talk business? I thought I made it clear that this was a dinner date."

Clara felt flustered and fidgeted with her spoon as she stirred her coffee. "I . . . I'm just asking, that's all."

"Set your mind at ease. I hope to have confirmation on the

facts we discussed in a week or so. These things take time, you know. I'll be wired as soon as my contact has anything of substance." He took a sip of his coffee, then blotted his mouth with his napkin. She noticed he had long, slender fingers as he folded the napkin and deliberately placed it next to his plate. Hands that might play the piano? Or stroke a woman's cheek?

Now why was she thinking these thoughts? *What's wrong with me?*

"How about dessert? I may be able to make it worth your while." His eyes toyed with hers with a mischievous twinkle, crinkling at the corners.

Clara felt the heat rise in her face. "I don't think I could eat another bite, but thank you."

"So that was your daughter-in-law's sister that we met earlier? Is the soldier courting her? It must have been hard for him to get time away from Fort Russell to escort her to dinner." He tilted his head upward. "You know, the third floor here has been purported to be a lover's getaway, and . . . er . . . possibly other things go on as well."

Clara's heart pounded fast under her corset. Was he making reference to Greta or taunting her? She wasn't sure. Not at all sure. "I've heard stories . . . but it's all speculation. As to Greta, I know very little about Catharine or her sisters. That's why I'm paying you to find out." A nagging thought about Greta popped into Clara's mind. How old was she anyway? Was she safe with this soldier? Clara had a mind to go find them and check on her. She wouldn't want anything to happen to her, even if she was Catharine's sister.

"Ah . . . always the reminder for services rendered. Tell me, my lovely Clara, what have you been doing for enjoyment since your husband died?"

Clara squirmed in her seat and moistened her dry lips, remembering that he'd asked her this question before. "I attend church and volunteer for a variety of things there. Before Peter was married, we frequently got together for dinner. I read a lot."

"Sounds perfectly perfect, but boring and lonely. Are you lonely, Clara?" He paused, and when she didn't answer, he continued. "Allow me to add a little fun to your life. It'll be good for you." A charming grin split his face, and his eyes smoldered through lashes too thick for a man.

She sucked in air, then released a heavy sigh. Best to say what was on her mind so there would be no misunderstanding. "That depends on what kind of fun you propose. If you mean fun up on the third floor, then I'm not interested," she answered, compressing her lips. "That would be entirely wrong."

Mac laughed. "That was not what I meant. However, I'll admit the thought has crossed my mind. Not to worry, I'll respect your wishes and your morals, though mine may differ somewhat."

Clara blinked. What did he mean by that? She wasn't sure if she should be flattered or not. Mac's way of talking confused her, but she was drawn to him. "It's getting late—I should be getting home," she said, glancing at the watch fob dangling from her neck. She made a move to leave.

"What's the hurry? No one is home waiting, right?" He shoved his chair back and was at her side in a heartbeat. "Besides, I'd like to have more evenings like this with you." He leaned over to pull her chair out, and Clara could feel his warm breath along her neck.

She stood and he offered her his arm. "You're right. There's no one to answer to but a lonely house."

Mac patted her hand and pulled her close to his side as they left the Tivoli. Clara couldn't remember when she'd felt in such high spirits, and for a short while all her burdens lifted like clouds blown away by the prairie winds.

Sometime during the night, the rain stopped. Catharine was awakened with a kiss from Peter, who was shirtless but dressed in clean trousers that Angelo had delivered promptly at seven. They were too large, but Peter belted them tightly around his hips.

"Good morning, my sweet one." He took a seat on the side of the bed. "I hated to wake you, but if we're to have breakfast and pick up your sisters . . ." He smiled tenderly at her as he fingered a red curl lying on her shoulder. "Did I ever tell you that you're beautiful in the morning when you first wake up?"

Pulling the covers around her chest, Catharine sat up and stretched, then stifled a yawn. "I don't believe you have, but I'm sure I'll never tire of hearing it from you," she whispered. She gazed at his handsome jawline, remembering his delicious kisses and more during the night. Loving him was heaven on earth for her . . . like breathing fresh air. She'd never tire of him and didn't want to let him go.

"I had a breakfast tray delivered to our room." He indicated covered dishes on a nearby table. "I might let you share it with me, if you can drag your beautiful self from the bed to the table."

She flashed him a wicked look. "I'm afraid I'm too worn out from last night."

"You little tease. I might be tempted to get back into bed,

but instead you leave me no alternative!" He leaned down and flicked back the covers, leaving her just the sheet, then lifted her in his arms, showering her with kisses along her cheek and neck. She returned his kisses with fervor, wrapping her arms about his neck. "Peter, you're so good to me." She saw a flicker of desire in his blue eyes as a muscle twitched in his jaw.

"Nothing's too good for my bride. Let's have something to eat now. Then we can continue later tonight, the next night, and forevermore trying to make one another happy. Mmm . . . that might be nice."

The look he gave her melted her heart. He kissed her again, then he sat her in a chair at the small table and lifted the pot of tea he had steeping for her. "See if this meets with your satisfaction," he said, handing her the cup. Admiring his strong forearms as he lifted the covered domes from their plates, she reached up to push away a lock of sandy brown hair from his eyes.

Over toast, fresh blueberry jam, and scrambled eggs, they talked about the Cristinis' delightful supper and their frolic in the rain. Peter teased her lips with a piece of buttered toast. She caught his hands and kissed his knuckles, and finally he popped the toast into her mouth. Love was spilling over in her heart, and even more, a closer friendship with her husband was beginning. She marveled at how sweet and attentive he was to her. She didn't mention his attitude a couple days before, not wanting to spoil their brief honeymoon.

Finally she moved to get dressed while he donned a shirt and then went to retrieve the wagon. He'd tipped the bellboy the night before to settle Star at Abney's livery directly across from the hotel. That gave Catharine just enough time to spend on her toilette.

The dress Angelina loaned her was too short, but it was a pretty green and brown calico with a fetching row of tucks along the bodice that flared at the waist, complementing her hourglass figure. After braiding her unruly hair, she located her shoes by the door, the mud now hard and cracked and still sticking to them. They'd have to wait until she was home to be cleaned.

She laughed softly, amused by her new look. Her fingernails, usually neatly filed ovals, now had ragged edges. She hadn't had a lot of free time, and she had quickly found out that farm work was very physical indeed. Besides the cooking and cleaning, she assisted Peter whenever a fence needed mending or barns needed mucking or the cow needed milking. Hard to believe how much her entire life had changed in less than two months. What would her mother say if she could see her now?

I do fit the part of a farmer's wife. Would I change it for what I had before? Most definitely not!

She stared at her reflection in the cheval mirror and made a mental note to ask Peter about a new dress for church. Her clothes were showing wear, and she hoped to convince him to buy new ones for her sisters as well. They weren't his responsibility, but they were helping out around the farm the best they could.

She stuffed all their dirty clothes into a paper sack. She'd wash the borrowed clothes, then return them the next time Peter made a trip to town. To save time, Catharine decided to go downstairs to wait for Peter. The town was thoroughly awake now, with all kind of folks moving around in wagons and carriages, or merely walking down the sidewalk on their way to their various occupations or ventures. When she stepped out of the hotel, rays of bright sunlight lit the spacious blue skies, making her squint, so she shaded her eyes with her hand.

Peter was parked a few feet away and chatting away with the pretty blonde Dorothy Miller. Catharine watched as he leaned nonchalantly against the wagon, smiling with obvious interest in what Dorothy was saying. She knew she shouldn't stand here observing them, but she couldn't help herself. Peter looked so relaxed and in no hurry to come after her. Why was he looking at Dorothy that way? Like a bolt of lightning from their recent storm, jealousy shot through her.

Dorothy was dressed in a smart blue dress with matching bolero trimmed in black velvet. The hat that sat cocked to the side of her head was the latest fashion in black velvet adorned with a pretty feather. Catharine sighed. Here she was in a dress that was considerably too short for her, wearing mud-caked boots. Rooted to the spot, she waited for them to finish their conversation, hoping Dorothy would leave before she caught sight of her dressed in ill-fitting clothing with a sack in her hand.

Suddenly Peter caught sight of her and motioned to her. *Ach!* There was no way she could compete or escape the company of Miss Miller. Stiffly, Catharine strolled toward them, feeling like her leather boots had shrunk at least one shoe size from the rain . . . and feeling like an outsider. All the joy she'd felt earlier had somehow dwindled to a far-away spot in her heart.

"Catharine, you remember Dorothy from church," Peter said when she walked up to where they stood.

"*Ja*, I remember. Nice to see you again." Catharine saw Dorothy's eyes sweep critically over Catharine's appearance, as if she were comparing her or sizing her up. "Are we keeping you from something? You're out awfully early."

Dorothy smiled and said, "It's hardly early. It's nine o'clock by my watch."

Catharine felt the blood rush to her face. "You're right. I guess Peter and I were enjoying our time so much that we lost track of the hour." She looped her arm through Peter's possessively, and he gave her arm a squeeze.

Dorothy observed her with a cool look. "I was just telling Peter that he should bring you to the opera some evening. There's a divine actress by the name of Sarah Bernhardt coming to perform *Fedora*, and I've heard she's incredible, though she only speaks French."

"I may consider doing that, Dorothy, if Catharine wants to."

"I would. I'm sure I'd love it." She looked up adoringly at her husband.

"I can get us tickets as soon as they become available. Would that be all right? We could all sit together."

Not if I can help it! Catharine plastered on a fake smile for Peter's benefit.

"Sure. Guess we need to get going now." He turned to assist Catharine up to the wagon seat. "We have to go collect Greta and Anna."

"Oh?" Dorothy said, as if waiting for him to explain. "Yes, well then . . . I must be going too. I hope to see you soon."

Who does she hope to see soon, Peter or both of us? Catharine wondered, but she just replied, "Nice to see you again, Dorothy." Catharine adjusted her skirts, and Peter crawled up to the wagon seat beside her, then lifted the reins. With a wave of his hand and a shake of the reins, Peter headed the wagon toward Mario's.

Lush, rolling prairie hills undulated in the distance with every mile as Peter drove home. The rain was an unexpected treat in Cheyenne. Before long the wheat would be a foot tall. He loved how the wheat looked like rippling waves when it grew waist high. He'd walk through it, looking for any possible insect infestation that might be harmful, reveling in the bountiful harvest that would soon come from God's gift of grain. He was so blessed.

He glanced over at Catharine seated at his side, breathing in the scent of her until he thought his heart would burst with pride. She had more than responded to him last night, and he would forget any doubts of her love for him. It had been a very good decision to spend the night in town!

Catharine caught his gaze and smiled. "Peter, what are you smiling about? You look like the cat that just caught the mouse."

"I was thinking of you and what a lucky man I am." He watched her freckles become more prominent as her face colored at his words.

She blinked. "I'm happy if I've made you happy, Peter. That is my greatest desire," she said in a hushed tone so her sisters couldn't hear. But they were chattering away about the events of the Cristini household and the fun of staying with them.

"Why did you quit our game of checkers, Greta? We were having so much fun playing with the twins," Anna asked. "Then I played another game with Angelina."

"I . . . er . . . I had a headache," Greta answered quietly.

"Is your headache gone now?" Catharine turned on the wagon seat to look at her.

Greta licked her lips. "Matter of fact, it is."

"Well, you weren't in bed when I came up, so I didn't know where you were. I guess I fell asleep before you came to bed," Anna said.

"Silly girl." Greta fidgeted with her bonnet strings. "Of course you did."

"I'm so glad you girls enjoyed staying with the Cristinis. They were nice to offer their home . . ." Catharine's voice softened. "So we could have a night alone."

Peter cleared his throat, feeling heat in his face. He wasn't comfortable with them discussing this. "Well, we had a nice time despite the rain—"

"Don't be embarrassed, either of you!" Greta laughed. "You two deserved a little respite."

"Just the same, it all worked out so nicely. When we get home, there'll be plenty of chores waiting for us to attend to." Peter guided Star around a rut to keep from spilling them onto the road. "It appears that the rain barely fell here. I was hoping for a good drenching for the fields."

Catharine reached over and patted him on the arm. "Don't worry. There'll be another rain shower. How about apple dumplings after supper tonight?" That brought a loud cheer from the other three. "Then I expect someone to peel the apples while I attempt to roll out the dough."

"I hope it's better than your first attempt at making a pie," Peter teased.

"Oh, Peter!" Catharine poked his side with obvious embarrassment. "I admit that I'm still learning. But no one's died yet." They all laughed loudly. "Maybe Angelina can teach me how to make that cream dessert we all loved."

Anna clapped her hands. "Oh, yes! Please ask her, Cath."

"I will the next time we venture to town." Catharine turned

back to face the road ahead, anxious to be at home. Their home. Her heart swelled with pride at the thought. They would make a wonderful home, and Lord willing, children's laughter would someday ring throughout it.

"What do you think of me staying with your mother this fall, Peter?" Anna asked. "I think I could be a companion to her in the evenings after my studies are done. Besides, I'm really not a farmer's daughter." She sighed and twirled a lock of her long blonde hair around her finger.

Peter coughed. "I'm not sure that would work with my mother right now, even if she did suggest it. She probably doesn't know what she's getting into. She hasn't had a young person living with her in years, and she might get on your nerves." Peter knew he was just making excuses to avoid a decision until he could resolve the rift between him and his mother.

"Couldn't you at least consider the possibility? I do want to finish school."

"I think you should let her. Then she'll be out of your hair." Greta chuckled.

"We'll talk about it, Anna, but now is not the time. We're almost home."

Anna harrumphed. She folded her arms across her chest and stared out over the prairie.

18

Catharine and Peter worked side by side with a renewed close-
ness, planting seeds in the neatly laid-out rows in the flower
bed. When she looked up from where she knelt on her knees
in the soft earth, he grinned back at her as he sprinkled the
seeds, then lightly raked the soil over them.

"You wear the dirt well," he teased. "You've become a
farmer's dream."

She reached up, feeling the smudges on her face, then lifted
the edge of her apron to wipe the dirt away as best as she
could. "What I'll need is a good long soaking to get the dirt
out from under my nails." She flashed him a smile and leaned
back on her heels. She placed her hand behind her aching
back and stretched. "This is hard work, but the rewards will
be worth it in just a few short weeks."

Peter laid the rake down. "I'll go start filling the buckets
with water if you're through planting. You just take a break
for now."

She gave him a nod and didn't argue, then sat down to wait
until he returned to water the seeds in the freshly turned soil.
As usual, there was a nice breeze that cooled the dampness

under her arms. She liked the fecund smell of the earth and the buzz of insects and watched a fat earthworm digging his way back down into the cool earth. Enjoying nature on the prairie was a continual learning process and entirely different from Holland, where spring showers were abundant.

The thought of home caused deep pain in her heart. The last thing she'd planted were the tulip bulbs at the head of a little plot in her family's cemetery. The only way she'd survived the grief was with God's constant reminder that He was with her and would send the Comforter to soothe her anguish. She'd clung to that promise. She squeezed her eyes shut for a few moments and once again felt peace. Wiping her eyes, she dragged herself out of the dirt to help water the seeds.

Watching Peter carrying the two buckets filled with water made Catharine's heart swell with love. He didn't have to be out here helping her when he had other things that needed tending to, but he'd insisted. She had no idea where Anna was, and Greta was supposedly peeling vegetables for dinner. Catharine had a roast in the oven, and its delicious smell now wafted on the breeze from the open kitchen window.

"Supper sure does smell good!" Peter said when he reached her. He tilted the bucket so that the water would flow in a slow stream, pouring it slowly back and forth over the rows until he'd emptied the bucket. "My appetite is growing by the minute."

"I can help," Catharine said, reaching for the other bucket.

He pushed her hand away. "Oh no you don't. I can do this. Why don't you go on inside and clean up before you finish supper?"

Catharine shifted her gaze to movement across the yard

and saw Anna hurrying up the hill, her apron rolled up in a ball. "Here comes Anna. What has she gotten into now?" she said, her hands on her hips.

Peter chuckled. "I'll tell you one thing, that Anna is a free spirit with a big heart."

Her hair escaping her braids, looking flushed and out of breath, Anna nearly fell at Catharine's feet in her excitement. "Look, Cath, I've rescued a litter of puppies by the creek. Aren't they adorable? Can I keep them?" Her blue eyes sparkled with joy as she pulled her apron away to reveal four squirming balls of fluff.

"Whoa . . . slow down a minute. Where's their mama?" Peter asked, reaching down to scratch one of the puppies behind the ear. The puppy yawned, then looked into his face with large brown eyes.

Anna sat down in the grass and the puppies scrambled out of her apron to pounce on each other in play, but they didn't amble too far away, apparently preferring Anna's attention. "She was nowhere around," she said. "Can I keep them?"

Catharine knelt down, fondling the fuzzy heads of the puppies as their pink tongues licked her hand. "Mmm . . . I don't know. What do you think, Peter? Maybe just one?" She was already falling for the adorable little bundles. "What kind of puppies are they?"

Peter's expression was thoughtful. "After my last dog was bitten by a snake and died awhile back, I hadn't really considered it. Not sure I want to get attached to another dog just yet."

Catharine struggled to cover her laughter as she watched Anna's face crumple. "Don't look so serious, Sis. It's not the end of the world." Looking up at Peter, she said, "I'm sorry you lost your dog. I didn't know, but maybe we could use a dog around here to alert us to visitors or varmints."

"*Pleeease.* I'll take good care of the puppies until you decide which one we should keep."

Peter rolled his eyes heavenward in defeat. Shoving his hat back further on his head, he said, "Now how can I refuse when the two of you gang up on me?" He knelt next to them in the grass. The puppies hopped around and one of them chewed on Anna's shoelaces.

Anna clapped her hands, stepping over the puppies to give Peter a hug. "I knew you'd say yes. Thank you!" Peter started to say something but clamped his jaw shut and returned Anna's hug. "What kind of dogs are they, do you think?" she asked.

"They look like sheepdogs to me. Should be a right fine pet for you, Anna. Notice I said *pet*—singular. You'll have to find homes for the other three."

"Whatever you say." Anna's entire face lit up. "I'd better go find some bowls and give them some milk or something to eat."

"There should be two or three bowls I used in the barn near the tack room. You'll see 'em on the floor. Be sure and wash them up before you use them."

Anna scampered in the direction of the barn. "Keep an eye on the little fellows," she called over her shoulder.

As the puppies crawled all over Peter's legs, Catharine scooted over to where he knelt in the grass to give him a kiss.

"What's that for?" He leaned back to look at her.

"For being such a softie, that's what." She kissed him again and removed his hat to ruffle his damp hair. He grabbed her, wrapping his arms tightly around her waist. She swayed and their kiss deepened until Catharine pulled away. "Phew! We both need a dunk in the creek before supper!"

"I'll race you," he said, pulling her to her feet.

"But what about the puppies? We're supposed to watch them until Anna returns."

Peter's gaze softened. "They made it just fine before she found them, didn't they?"

Catharine arched an eyebrow, giving him a knowing look. Lifting her skirts, she whirled around and ran in the direction of the creek with Peter hot on her heels, her laughter ringing out across the meadow.

19

Vapors of heat rose in the distance throughout the surrounding landscapes, proof of a hot, dry summer to come. Every passing week, as temperatures climbed with no rain in sight, Catharine stood at the kitchen window and watched as Peter stood in the wheat field praying for rain. She knew he was worried, and all her reassurances that the rain would come didn't help. Even the flowers they'd planted hadn't grown as fast as she'd expected them to. Though she watered them every day from the well, the wind quickly dried the plants out.

Peter walked deeper into the field and further away from the house, so she didn't bother him. Catharine peeked at the chicken she had roasting, decided it was cooked, then replaced the lid and shoved the pan back in the oven to stay warm. It was early yet for supper, but at least everything was ready for her family. Walking out to the front porch, she was glad to be out of the warm kitchen and decided to head down the lane in search of the cool water that Crow Creek offered. She made a mental note to remember to apply lotion to her hands tonight before bedtime. The last few days she'd felt fatigued, and the heat of the kitchen made her stomach feel weak. Putting her feet in the cold stream would be refreshing and just the thing she needed before supper.

Trekking down to the creek, she was thinking about another short trip to town. Occasionally now Catharine rode into town by herself or with her sisters, since Peter felt confident that she knew the way and could do the trip in a couple of hours. Each time she looked expectantly for a letter at the post office, and each time she was disappointed when there wasn't one from Amsterdam, but she pretended indifference when the clerk handed her the mail. Amazingly, she hadn't run into Clara, though she did make the trip to town and back as quickly as possible.

After sliding off her brogans and socks, Catharine tucked her skirts into her waistband and waded into the creek. The water rushing over her feet and ankles cooled her instantly. Carefully, she stepped over rocks and downed tree limbs until she finally reached a nearly flat, smooth rock to lie on while allowing her feet to dangle in the water. Gazing up at the blue sky through overhanging tree limbs, she relaxed and listened to the sounds of buzzing insects along the creek bed and the stillness around her. Her eyes became heavy and she drifted off.

She heard a voice calling her, but her mind felt thick and her sight was foggy. She lifted the wrought-iron latch to the gate and stood in the warm rainy mist, pulling her cloak around her and staring down at the fresh mound of dirt. Each time she visited, the pain lessened a little. Would it ever leave? She pressed her hand to her mouth to quiet her sobs. *Why did this have to happen, Lord?*

The voice calling her name became louder. It took a moment before Catharine realized she'd been dreaming, and in reality Anna was calling her. She sat up, blinking, and looked over at the water's edge to where Anna stood, one puppy in her arm and the rest of them nipping at her heels.

"Didn't you hear me, Cath? You must have been in a deep sleep."

"I think I was. I just can't seem to get enough sleep these days and I'm always tired. This farming life is demanding." Catharine traipsed back through the creek to Anna, who held out her hand to assist her up the bank.

"Supper's ready. Peter's washing up and Greta sent me to look for you."

Catharine picked up one of the pups and snuggled it against her neck. "I do enjoy the pups, Anna, but soon we'll have to find homes for them. Peter's orders."

"I like them too," Anna replied when they started down the path to the house. "It will be hard to pick just one—Cath, have you been crying? Your eyes are red."

"*Nee.* It must be from the heat of the kitchen. I was in there most of the afternoon." She lowered her eyes and looked at the puppy with its innocent eyes. No need to burden Anna or make her worry. Once she'd been as carefree as her sister, but that was before Karl Johnsen.

The warmth of the morning sun filtered through the curtains billowing inside the bedroom, and by the time Catharine awoke, Peter's side of the bed was cold. She couldn't believe no one had awakened her. Wiping the sleep from her eyes, she struggled into her robe and hurried to the kitchen. Greta was already at the stove, struggling to scramble eggs in a skillet with a flame that was too hot, and Anna was just lifting what looked to be very toasty toast out of the oven.

"Morning, everyone! Why on earth didn't you wake me? Where's Peter?"

"Right here," he said, slipping through the back door. "Somethin' burning?"

"No, but nearly," Anna said. "I wanted to help out and give Catharine a break. She's been extra tired the last couple of mornings."

"Aren't you sweet!" Catharine gave her a quick hug. "Need help, Greta?"

Greta moved quickly, flipping bacon in the pan next to the eggs. "I think I've got it. Why don't you have a seat?"

Peter pulled a chair out for her and, with a wide sweep of his hat, bid her to sit down. He picked up the coffeepot to fill the Blue Willow cups, then took a chair himself.

After they were all seated and Peter said grace, he cleared his throat. "While you're all sitting here together, I just wanted to thank you for pitching in with the farm work. I know it's not what you're used to, and I apologize for that." He stared down at his untouched breakfast, then looked up and continued. "To tell you the truth, I would consider hiring some help when I sell the crop this fall, but I'm concerned because of our weather. It's drier than ever, and the temperatures are warmer than normal this time of year. I expect I'll plant winter wheat or alfalfa this year after the harvest."

"I didn't mean to complain if I did, Peter." Catharine placed her hand reassuringly on top of his.

"You didn't complain, Catharine. Each of you was thrown into a different way of life. Just the same, I wanted to express my thanks to all of you. You have made my life more than

DEEPLY DEVOTED

interesting." He smiled warmly at Greta and Anna. "I never had a brother or sister. I'll make it up to all of you somehow."

"I've learned a few things about how to run a home . . . not that I'd choose to," Greta said.

"It'll prepare you for your future as a wife." Catharine smiled at her sister.

Greta laughed. "*Nee*, I'm going to have servants to do the big chores when I get married."

Peter raised an eyebrow at her. "Then you'd better think twice about marrying a private in the army. They make little to nothing."

Greta bristled. "Oh, but he'll get promotions and have a future as a colonel or general in the army soon."

Catharine looked at Peter, indicating not to say more.

"I hope Bryan will do just that." Catharine had her doubts, but she would let Greta have her dreams. Besides, Bryan wasn't even courting her officially. No need to worry about that just yet.

Anna ate the last of her eggs, then sneaked a piece of bacon beneath her chair. "And I want to thank you for letting me have the puppies."

Catharine leaned down and peered under the table. "Did you let those puppies inside? You know they're only allowed on the porch."

Anna's face blanched. "Uh . . . I—"

Peter shook his head. "Anna, I'll have to ask you to remove the puppies and take them back to the porch." His tone held no nonsense.

Anna shoved her chair back and bent down to scoop the puppies up. They squirmed from her hands and ran in every direction, yapping playfully. One accidentally knocked

178

over the ash bucket by the hearth, and another walked right through the ashes, then ran out of the kitchen and down the hall, leaving footprints in his wake.

"Oh dear!" Anna shrieked, chasing the pup.

Greta popped up. "I'll get this one," she yelled as the runt of the litter bounded across the kitchen hardwood floor. The puppy slid directly into the sewing basket Catharine was using to re-cover the dressing table chair. It tipped over, spilling its contents, and the other two puppies gleefully hopped in, sending spools of thread and ribbon every direction. The runt held a piece of ribbon in his mouth and ran around the kitchen while the other two chased after the length of pink ribbon. Greta began to laugh, realizing her futile attempt to catch the little pups.

Catharine started to laugh too until she saw the I-told-you-so look plastered across Peter's face. "This was exactly what I feared would happen," he said with irritation.

Catharine shoved back her chair to help Greta as they hopelessly chased three furry balls of fluff. There went Anna's hope to keep all four puppies now. Of that Catharine had no doubt.

Days passed, and if possible, the weather became even drier with every passing day. The women were continually applying lotion to their itchy, flaky skin. Catharine went about picking up the dirty clothes since today was laundry day. Anna was out with Peter to help milk the cow. Greta was assigned to polishing the huge oak staircase, a job Catharine knew she detested. But as Catharine explained, it must be done, especially with the dust they were having now.

She gathered all the dirty clothes from her sisters' room and was just about to leave when something caught her eye in the corner of the closet. It looked like a wad of blue fabric. Was Greta making something? She pulled out the material and shook it to release the folds. To her surprise, it wasn't fabric at all but a pretty dress, suitable for evening. She didn't remember seeing it before, and none of them had been shopping yet. It was very enticing, with delicate lace that trimmed the cuffs and ran along the V of the décolletage. Where had Greta gotten this? When and how?

She didn't have long to wait to get her questions answered.

"Cath, I've finished the stairs—" Greta stopped in the center of the room with a stricken look on her face. "I . . . what are you doing in our closet?" She moved slowly toward Catharine.

"Where did you get this, Greta?" Catharine got right to the point. Greta's look of guilt didn't surprise her.

Greta twisted the polishing cloth in her hands. "I can explain."

"I'm waiting."

Greta reached over and took the dress out of Catharine's hands. "I bought it the day we spent the night in Cheyenne."

"With what? I wasn't aware you had any money of your own." Catharine thought back to that day but didn't remember seeing a package in Greta's possession.

"I put it on Peter's account at Warren's Emporium, then hid it in the wagon."

"You *what*? Without asking?" Catharine said through tight lips to keep from raising her voice.

Greta lowered her eyes and fingered the dress. "I wanted to look pretty for Bryan."

"Bryan? But you didn't see him then. You spent the night with the Cristinis."

"The truth is I did see him. He asked me to meet him and I slipped out." Greta's eyes flitted toward the window as if she wished she could fly away.

Stay calm, Catharine. "Greta . . . where did you meet him?" Catharine was getting all types of images, remembering how Peter had found them at the line shack. Suddenly she was feeling nauseated, and she backed up to the edge of the bed and sat down.

"Cath, are you all right? You look a little pale." Greta flung the dress on the bed and knelt in front Catharine. "Do you want some water?"

Catharine licked her lips and put a hand to her stomach. "No, I don't need water. I need you to tell me, where did you meet Bryan?" *Lord, I promised to guide and protect my sisters. I'm a failure in more ways than one.*

"Don't look so disgusted. We went to the Tivoli for a late-night dinner. That's all. Then he walked me back to the Cristinis'." Greta's bright blue eyes were beginning to fill with tears.

"I don't know . . . you sneaked out once before, and now this. How am I supposed to believe or trust you?" Catharine stared down at Greta, her eyes unwavering.

"I swear. That's the truth." Greta crossed her chest with her finger. "Cross my heart. If you don't believe me, you can ask Clara Andersen. She was at the Tivoli."

"Is that so?" Catharine felt weak. "Why didn't you tell us on the ride home then, Greta?"

Greta's pretty face mirrored remorse. "I know I should have . . . but I knew you'd be angry and I wanted to see Bryan again, so I just didn't. I'm sorry. But you have to believe me."

"I want to. Have you seen him since?"

"No, I haven't, but I'll be eighteen in a week. Please don't treat me like a child, Cath."

Blinking back tears, Catharine took Greta's hand, the nausea gone now. "I know, but, Greta, I've got to tell Peter about your charging the dress to his account."

"Are you going to tell him about my dinner with Bryan too?" Greta's face fell.

"I will because the Cristinis are his friends and you shouldn't have done that when you were entrusted to them overnight. And this is his home. You need to abide by our rules while you live here."

Greta sat next to her sister on the bed, looking regretful. "I'm sorry."

Catharine knew that Greta was determined to live her life by her own set of rules. What could she do or say? She still remembered her first love and how she'd felt. "Greta, as long as you live under this roof, you will have to tell Bryan that he must court you properly. If not, you're surely asking for trouble. Hiding the truth will only bring you heartache and pain. I don't want that for you. If he cares for you, then tell him to come to our home. Unless you have something to hide. He may be honorable, but passion can interfere with good intentions. I'll not have it any other way. Can you understand?"

Greta was crying softly now. "Yes." She hiccuped.

"Trust me, Greta. I haven't been totally honest with Peter about things, and it's caused unnecessary heartache."

Greta's eyes flew open. "You haven't told him, Catharine?"

Catharine swallowed hard. "No. I know I should have . . . but I've been worried about what he'd think of me." Now she sounded like the one needing guidance.

"My sweet, sweet Catharine. Peter will understand and love you just the same. You should tell him."

Catharine bent to give her sister a peck on the cheek. "Don't look so glum. I'm just protecting you from yourself. But you're right, once you're eighteen, you're really an adult. So make adult decisions, please."

Greta walked her to the door. "I understand, Cath. I'll send a letter to Bryan at Fort Russell. I don't know when he's off duty again." She paused at the doorway. "But, Cath, you should know . . . I think I love him." Her eyes sparkled, and the way her tear-stained face softened when she said his name, Catharine knew she did.

20

Clara stared at her reflection in the mirror, smiling. There was more color in her face now, and she noticed her eyes appeared brighter, reflecting her renewed interest in living for the first time in years. She felt excited about what each day would bring since getting to know Mac. He'd taken her to dinner, for long walks in the park, and for drives in the country, and he'd promised to accompany her to church soon. *I wonder what he's doing at this moment. Is he thinking of me too?* Her heart fluttered. She hoped so. She'd almost forgotten the original purpose that had brought them together. They always had something to talk or laugh about, and she hung on to every word he said. The way he told a story or described a situation made her laugh.

On their drive in the country, he'd parked the buggy under a huge cottonwood tree, then pressed warm kisses to her waiting mouth and along her neck until she drew up short and cautioned herself. He was romantic, yes. But there had been no declarations of love. Yet. Surely it was just a matter of time before he declared his intentions. He'd brought her flowers and taken her to afternoon tea last week. All promising . . . very promising.

Tomorrow Mac was taking her to see Sarah Bernhardt perform at the Cheyenne Opera House. She wanted to look her very best as he paraded her amid the other "important" socialites of Cheyenne. He must do very well as an investigator. Several times he'd traveled out of town, saying how much he'd missed her when he'd returned. He'd only asked her once for an advance to continue the investigation, and when before she was reluctant, now she was eager to give him what he needed in order to speed up the process.

Clara had seen Peter and Catharine at church and was cordial to both of them, preferring to be civil until she had proof of a prior marriage. Peter seemed even more distant, and though he continued to respect her as his mother, he spent very little time talking to her. It had been a long time since he'd come to visit her. It pained her deeply to think she had such little place in his life now.

She turned her attention to the chifforobe, where she'd hung a royal blue dress of satin with black jets adorning the bodice and the back bustle. It was one of the finest gowns she'd bought in a long time. She fished around in her jewelry box for the jet earrings that were a present from her deceased husband. She sighed as she remembered the Christmas he'd given them to her. It was one of the few things he'd bought her in all the years they were married.

Clara wiped away an unbidden tear and shook her head. Well, that was in the past, and when she'd least expected it, Mac had become a part of her life. While she'd loved her husband and respected him, she'd never felt for him the way she did for Mac. Besides Peter, she now had a purpose for living.

Later that afternoon, Peter stepped from the barn and watched as Catharine lugged a pail of water to her ever-drooping flowers. A sorrier site he'd never seen, but she was determined to keep them watered. He glanced up at the sky for any sign of a cloud, but it was as vast and empty as the desert. Looking back at his wife, he saw the heat was getting the best of her as she stood and fanned herself with her apron, gazing at her sad little flower patch. Her calico work dress was stained with perspiration, and dirt clung to the hemline. Now was the time to ease her burden, just as she'd tried to ease his concerns about the crop. Peter had seen more than a few grasshoppers about, which was normal . . . but he felt a strange foreboding.

He lumbered over and slipped his arms about her waist, then picked her up and spun her around until her hair fell from its pins and they were both dizzy with delight.

"Peter," she exclaimed, "what's gotten into you? Put me down." But her eyes told him a different story.

"Baby," he whispered in her ear, then leveled a gaze deep into her sparkling green eyes. "You need to rest. You look plumb tuckered out." He still held her against him, and as usual he felt an intense rush of emotions. A slow smile crossed her face, and she kissed the tip of his nose.

"I'm nearly finished here and feel like resting in the shade of the porch with something cool to drink. What do you say . . . interested?" She flashed him a coy look and ran a finger along his brow.

Peter gave her a lingering kiss and then released her. He loved her lips and their softness as they yielded to his kiss. "We've been working too hard around here without a break, and I think we could use a trip to town to see that play at the opera house featuring Sarah Bernhardt."

"Oh, Peter!" She clapped her hands. "When?" She had the enthusiasm of a young girl, and it did his heart good to see her smile light up her tired face.

"How about tomorrow night? I spoke to Dorothy after church, and she'll meet us there with the tickets." He saw her smile fade. Was she jealous of Dorothy? He couldn't believe it but felt a twinge of flattery that she would be. "I thought it'd be nice to take Greta and Anna too. It can be a birthday celebration for Greta."

"What a wonderful idea, Peter. You're so thoughtful. You spoil them, you know." She took his hand, and he picked up the water bucket as they walked back to the house.

"I hope so, because I'm rather fond of them." They stepped up to the porch and plopped onto the porch swing. "Ahh, it's cooler here."

"Let me get us something to drink." Catharine started to get up, but he pressed her back into the swing.

"No. You sit, I'll go. You've worked hard enough for one day." Peter rose and disappeared inside the house.

Catharine refastened her hairpins again, creating a neat bun at the nape, and closed her eyes.

That evening Peter slipped out of the house once Catharine was fast asleep, which lately seemed to be almost as soon as her head hit the pillow. Concerns over his wheat crop were nagging him. The last couple of years, the locusts had been a huge problem, and he was seeing evidence of the insects again. He learned from the Department of Agriculture how to plow a strip between his wheat field and the sod land when there was evidence the grasshoppers were hatching. Then

187

he would fill the strips with bait to kill the grasshoppers, thereby saving the crop . . . at least he hoped. He'd already inquired around town to hire some laborers to help him. Come Monday morning, that's just what he'd be doing. But tomorrow he intended to show Catharine a good time away from the farm.

If the crop was good, he'd hire someone to help in the house. Greta and Anna were not cut out for housekeeping. He gave a little chuckle. Bless their hearts. They tried, but mostly they gave just halfhearted attempts in order to help their sister.

With the weather so dry, Catharine's little flower patch was a pitiful sight to behold—he could see it clearly with the light from the full moon. Even after they fertilized, the ground needed moisture. And they sure weren't getting any rain.

Besides the crop, he was worried about the chasm between him and his mother. He'd seen his mother only a handful of times at church and was cordial to her, but he wasted no time getting out of the building, afraid she may have more accusations about his wife. He couldn't be happier with Catharine than if he'd known her for years, and that was good enough for him.

Before returning to the house, Peter leaned against the fence post, admiring how the silvery moonlight illuminated the prairie. The wind whispered through the trees, and he felt a peculiar need to offer up a prayer from his heart.

Lord, I stand amazed in Your presence that You love me and care about my every need. I thank You for this land, for I know it belongs to You. I'm happy living here doing what I'm doing. But most of all I want to thank You for my sweet wife. I consider her a gift, because I asked You to send me someone special and You did. She's worked hard learning to pitch in around the farm just for me. I'm asking You to remove this nagging doubt I have about her. I want to give my entire heart to her. I don't know how to handle this. If what my mother says turns out to be true, then I need direction. I want to turn it all over to You. Amen.

Feeling a weight lifted, Peter made his way back to the house, eager to snuggle against his sweet woman.

Excitement filled the farmhouse while everyone hurried around with last-minute touches to their toilette before leaving for the opera. Catharine was filled with love for Peter that he would do this for Greta's birthday. He looked so handsome, stirring her heart in his pinstriped trousers with leather braces. She'd ironed the white shirt he'd paired with a brocade burgundy vest, then helped him tie his black string tie and tuck it into his vest. Finishing off his look, Peter sported a wool felt-top hat with grosgrain ribbon around the band and a black frock coat.

"You look dashing, my love." Catharine watched him as he admired his reflection in the hallway mirror.

"Thank you, but I'm already feeling quite warm." Peter removed his coat. "I'll just wait until we get there, then put the coat on." He turned around to get a better look at her, and his jaw dropped. "Catharine, my dear, you are simply stunning! I'll be proud to have you on my arm, and I'm sure the envy of my friends." He held her hands at arm's length to admire her outfit, then leaned in to kiss her brow.

"I'm glad you like my gown. It's not new, but I hoped I'd get the chance to wear it again," Catharine said, then walked over to the mirror. The off-shoulder, jewel-green taffeta with its daring décolletage complemented her auburn hair. She had dusted her face to tone down the freckles and smiled at her reflection. "Do you think my hair is all right?" It was pulled up into a pompadour with a few curls tickling the nape of her neck and the sides of her face.

Peter reached for her and pulled her against him with a mischievous twinkle in his eyes. "Maybe we should just let the girls go and we can stay here."

Catharine stepped away from his grasp and whacked him playfully on the arm with her fan. "I think not. Nothing you could say could keep me from the play tonight."

"I bet I can change your mind . . ."

A rustle of silk and the flurry of footsteps descending the staircase thwarted Peter's teasing. Greta and Anna stepped into view, and Peter said, "My, my, but don't we all look so elegant and grown-up. Quite a switch from the calicos and brogans. Guess I'll have to play the knight in shining armor to keep the men away."

The sisters giggled and Catharine remarked with a smile, "You're already my knight, Peter."

"Let's cut the sweet talk, you two, or we'll be late," Greta teased.

Anna gave a quick curtsy. "Do you think I look older now?"

Catharine laughed and winked at Greta over Anna's head. "Indeed you do. Why, I hardly recognized you with your hair curled!"

Greta was wearing the pretty blue gown that she'd charged to Peter's account, and Anna wore a mint-green gown with velvet bows on the skirt that lifted the frothy material in peaks all around the hemline.

"You two are beautiful!" Tears sprang to Catharine's eyes. "I have the loveliest of sisters, don't you think, Peter?"

"Absolutely!" Peter laughed. "But I think we've stood here admiring one another long enough." He opened the front door, offered his elbow to Catharine, and escorted her to the waiting surrey. Peter had spent the afternoon polishing the surrey used for special occasions, cleaning it until it shone like a new penny. Catharine was impressed at the great lengths he'd gone to in order to make the evening perfect for all of them.

Moments later they were all settled and off on an adventure to Cheyenne, their laughter and chatter spilling out across the yard. Catharine couldn't remember the last time she'd seen this much excitement on her sisters' faces. *They've needed this outing.* She felt a twinge of regret that they had had to leave the city life of Amsterdam behind. Not so much for her but for her sisters.

Cheyenne, or Magic City, aptly nicknamed by a newspaper journalist because of its rapid growth, boasted the finest opera house in the West, Peter told her, and Catharine was in total agreement. An air of excitement filled the streets as carriages and people on foot lined up in front of the impressive building. Peter lined his carriage up with the rest of those arriving, then assisted the ladies down, being careful not to catch their gowns in the carriage door or wheels.

Catharine and Peter headed toward the huge double doors with Greta and Anna following. Dorothy was waiting inside, dressed in a deep ruby gown of silk and lace, and looked lovelier than ever.

"So wonderful to see you all again." Dorothy hurried over, passing a handful of tickets to Peter. "Our seats are up in the

balcony. I think we're going to really enjoy this performance."
Then before Catharine or Peter could answer, she turned to
Greta. "I hear birthday greetings are in order for you."

"*Dank U wel*. My birthday is next week, but this is a gift
from Peter."

"I appreciate you getting the tickets for us, Dorothy. Look
there, I see Francis and Helen Warren." Peter waved to them
from across the room and they smiled back, then continued
into the theater to locate their seats.

"Goodness! This place is spectacular!" Anna looked around
the hall in amazement.

"Yes, it is. I'm on the Cheyenne Opera Committee," Dorothy said. "The opera house holds 860 people."

"That's a lot of folks," Greta acknowledged.

Peter took Catharine's arm with one of his and Dorothy's
with the other. "Follow me, ladies," he said to Greta and
Anna.

Catharine took in the gas lighting throughout the vast
foyer, where a fifty-two-light chandelier hung from the ceil-
ing. A gas reflector above illuminated every corner of the
auditorium. "So beautiful, isn't it?"

"Indeed it is," Greta said. "Even the railings have upholstery. I'm impressed."

"There's a large banquet hall for refreshments on the second floor too," Dorothy added.

Catharine was in awe of the rich, carved woodwork that
gleamed from the soft glow of gaslights and the three large
cathedral windows at the back of the balcony. The hundreds
of colored glass panes were impressive. Her gaze traveled up
the grand stairway to the balcony. "Is that where our seats
are?" she asked Peter.

"Yes, my sweet. We'll have a grand view from there. Shall we go find our seats?"

"I think we should," Dorothy said with a nod. "Later, at intermission, we can have refreshments."

That sounded good to Catharine since she was already hungry. She'd been a little too excited to spend much time in the kitchen for supper, and now she regretted not eating more.

Once they were seated, Greta remarked at the perfect view of the stage. "I like it up here. I can watch everyone below before the shows starts."

"There are many truly magnificent gowns being worn tonight," Dorothy whispered. She sat on the other side of Peter and Greta, with Anna occupying the seat on Catharine's left.

Catharine wasn't sure how to respond to Dorothy, and she'd felt miffed that Peter would extend his arm to her as well. Maybe he was just being a gentleman. But my, he looked so handsome, and she'd seen the way Dorothy glanced at him from time to time. Was she thinking it could have been her who had wed him?

Catharine felt foolish with this kind of thinking. Dorothy had been nothing but friendly to her. Perhaps all the unkind thoughts had been placed there by Clara's mother at their wedding. *Well, I'm going to sit back and enjoy my evening, because I know tomorrow I'll be the one by Peter's side. I'll choose to remember this special outing with my husband.*

Peter held her hand and pointed out the arched stage supported by Corinthian-Doric columns, and an elaborate curtain covered with a portrayal of Roman chariot races. She knew he was proud to have brought them to the opera.

Soon the curtains were drawn, and for the next hour or so, Catharine settled back with nothing but rapt attention at Sarah Bernhardt's acting.

193

21

Intermission came quickly, Peter thought. The play was a good distraction from his earlier worries, and from the looks on the ladies' faces, they felt much the same way. He rose from his seat to suggest refreshments when suddenly he spotted his mother in the crowd below, being assisted down the aisle by an attentive gentleman. His mother had a big smile on her face and was dressed to the nines, and he had to admit she looked wonderful. *Could this be . . . please, don't let it be . . . the private investigator she hired?* Hopefully he could avoid a confrontation tonight.

"Shall we go have a glass of lemonade in the banquet hall?" Peter asked, turning back to his party.

"Wonderful suggestion, Peter. I'll lead the way," Dorothy said, getting up from her seat.

"I don't know when I've enjoyed myself more. This is such a treat for us, Peter." Catharine smiled at him.

Peter thought she'd never looked more beautiful than she did right at this moment. Well . . . maybe that wonderful night they'd spent in the city. His heart rate increased when he thought about it. He swallowed hard, feeling the heat rise up his neck. "I'm so glad you're having a good time. That's why we're here. Everyone needs some fun to look forward to."

Anna stood on tiptoe to reach Peter and gave him a peck on the cheek. "Thank you so much!"

Peter was flustered. "Well . . . goodness, you're welcome."

"We'd better hurry," Dorothy urged. "Intermission is not long and I'm sure there'll be a line."

They joined the throng of people and headed for the banquet hall, where refreshments were being served. No sooner had they walked in than Peter saw his mother with a glass of lemonade in her hand. When she spotted him, she waved.

Peter groaned. He couldn't avoid speaking to them. "Catharine, I see Mother with a friend. We should go over and say hello."

"Of course, Peter." She dipped her head in agreement.

"You all go ahead and I'll be back in a few minutes. I see someone I want to talk to." Dorothy slipped away from their group.

"Peter, what a nice surprise to see you," Clara gushed as they walked closer. She greeted Catharine and her sisters. "Greta, I see we meet again. How's that nice soldier boy you were with?"

Greta's eyes shifted to Peter, then met Clara's gaze. "I believe he's just fine."

"Pity he couldn't escort you tonight." Clara turned to her escort. "This is Mac Foster, a very dear friend," she said, her face coloring. "Mac, this is my son Peter and his wife Catharine, and her sister Anna. You met Greta at the Tivoli."

Mac bowed slightly and squeezed Catharine's hand. "You never told me how beautiful Dutch women were." He winked at Catharine, then shook hands with Peter. "I'm glad to have finally met you. Your mother is extremely fond of you, but I'm sure you know that."

Peter responded with a hello but couldn't help thinking what a smooth talker Mac was. He appeared to be around his mother's age, with a dusting of gray at his temples and intense eyes. He could tell by his mother's expression that she really fancied Mac. Did she imagine herself in love with him? Peter was shocked at the thought, but the look on his mother's face said a lot. Why shouldn't she seek male companionship? She'd been a widow for years, but somehow Peter had never given it much thought. Of course she was lonely. And with Mac's arm encircling Clara's waist, it looked like they'd built a close friendship.

"You must come back and have dinner with us again sometime, Mrs. Andersen," Catharine said.

"We'll see," was all she said, then engaged Anna in conversation about her plans for high school.

"Mac, why don't you and I get these ladies some refreshments? I see you've already had yours." Peter indicated the empty glass in Mac's hand. "There's only ten minutes before curtain." Mac acquiesced and Peter steered him toward the huge counter for their drinks.

"Mac," Peter said as soon as they were out of earshot, "I know all about my mother hiring you to get my wife's past history. I want to know if there's any proof to what she told me." Peter pressed his lips into a thin line, and his jaw twitched.

"You like to get right to the point, don't you?" Mac chuckled. "Since you're Clara's son, I don't want to start off on the wrong foot."

"I prefer not to waste my time. I don't want you to take advantage of my mother."

Mac drew his shoulders back and frowned. "Now what's that supposed to mean? I was hired to investigate your wife, like any other client."

"I'm well aware of that. And that's just my point. Have you uncovered anything about Catharine?"

Mac leveled a gaze at him. "First of all, your mother can take care of herself. Second, I don't discuss my business with anyone but the person who hired me, and that's your mother. It's her business to discuss it with you if she so chooses." He lifted two glasses from the counter. "You have a very beautiful wife, Peter. I'd be more concerned with keeping her if I were you. Someone could snatch her up. Now, if you don't mind, this conversation is over."

Peter touched Mac's sleeve. Without batting an eye, he said, "If that's a threat, that will never happen with Catharine. We're very happy. And just so you know, I don't really trust you or your methods with my mother." Peter lifted two glasses and spun around to rejoin the waiting ladies. He tried to quell the anger boiling inside. Mac was trouble—Peter smelled it.

The Cristinis had joined the small group, and Angelina walked toward Peter and gave him a kiss on the cheek in greeting. "I know that look, Peter. Is everything okay?" she whispered.

"Nothing that I can't handle. I didn't know you and Mario would be here tonight."

"We wouldn't miss it! Who is that man standing over there with your mother?"

Peter watched as Mac handed drinks to Greta and Anna and suddenly remembered that he held Catharine's drink. He strolled toward her with Angelina following. "That's Mac, Mother's . . . er . . . friend." He said hello to Mario, ignoring Angelina's look of surprise.

Grateful for the bell signaling that intermission was over, Peter gulped down his lemonade and they all hurried back to their seats.

For the rest of the play, a young understudy by the name of Maggie O'Neal delighted the audience with her perfectly delivered lines and performance, but Peter had a hard time concentrating, thanks to his exchange with Mac. It was a hard fact to swallow that his mother, Clara Andersen, was seemingly taken by Mac.

Catharine leaned over and whispered, "Anything the matter, Peter?"

He patted her hand and said, "Everything's fine, dear." He could tell that somehow she knew he wasn't being truthful.

On the ride home, the chatting from the females was a delightful sound to Peter's ear and a great change from his former life. He shoved his negative thoughts about Mac to the recesses of his mind. He had a hard time seeing Mac and his mother together, but there was nothing he could do about it now. He listened to the conversation flowing around him.

"I declare, Maggie O'Neal is going to be quite a performer," Greta said.

"Maybe so, but she's no Sarah Bernhardt. She's the ultimate actress," Catharine said, snuggling close to Peter's side.

Anna chimed in, "But you have to admit she has a way about her, and such striking features. I liked her even in a minor role." She yawned. "I'm so sleepy."

Greta patted her legs. "Come, put your head on my lap, my little peep." That's all it took for Anna, who settled in for the rest of the way home.

With Catharine's body tucked close to his side, a warm sensation flooded Peter's chest. But he was still alarmed by the comment Mac had made about Catharine being a beautiful woman who could be taken from him. He wasn't sure what Mac had meant by that. *He's just all talk. I wonder what Mother sees in him. Other than a means to an end.*

An end that might harm his relationship with Catharine.

Clara invited Mac in for coffee after the play, and they were hardly in the door before he grabbed her and planted a kiss on her lips. "You look good enough to eat. I've thought about your kisses all through the play tonight, Clara." His breathing was ragged, and he pulled her tight against him. "Mmm, you smell good too. Do you know what you do to me?"

Clara tried to calm her heart pinging rapidly against her corset, which was already cinched so tight she could hardly breathe. All in the name of vanity. She'd wanted her waist to look small, and the corset flattered her bosom. Truth was she loved his kisses too. They were like an elixir for her thirsty soul, and while she wanted more, she placed her hands on his chest and pushed back slightly. "No, but maybe you should tell me while I make the coffee."

Mac clasped her hands and kissed them. "It's not coffee I need. It's you, my sweet Clara. Beautiful you. You make my senses reel. I long to make love to you." His eyes were dark and smoldering as they searched hers.

Clara drew back, alarmed, and licked her lips to steady

her voice. "Well . . . I . . . I'm very flattered, Mac, and while I want that too, I've not heard you say one thing about love or marriage after spending all this time together."

Though she said one thing, her heart said another and tried to rule her head. She wanted nothing more than for him to sweep her into his arms, vow his love, and declare he didn't want to live without her, then carry her up the sweeping staircase.

"Marriage!" He chuckled and kissed her on the tip of the nose while stroking her back. "We're older adults, and since we both know what we want and need, how can it hurt?"

This time Clara moved out of his embrace. "Because it's the right thing to do, Mac. Let me ask you, have you ever been married?"

"What has that got to do with us?" He frowned.

"It has everything to do with us. I do feel a lot for you . . . I may be in love with you." She made no move to leave the foyer but stood waiting for his response.

Mac sighed. "Clara, I was married years ago, but it didn't work out. I do care for you, maybe more than I've ever cared for any woman." His eyes softened and he took her hand. "I care for you a lot . . . a whole lot."

Tears threatened when she didn't hear what she longed for him to say. She chewed her bottom lip to keep from saying something that might push him away, and she didn't want that. "But you don't *love* me?" Her voice sounded flat and seemed to come from far away.

"I didn't say that. What is love? I'm not sure if I know. I know that I love spending time with you even when we are at odds. You're pretty and smart, and I enjoy your quick sense of humor." He gave her his most endearing smile and tucked a loose curl behind her ear, then stroked her cheek with his thumb. "I think you're special . . . very special. But I need time to figure this all out."

She swallowed hard. Perhaps he was right. She wouldn't want him to say he loved her just to make her happy, but oh, how she longed to hear it. "Meaning what, Mac?" Her voice trembled.

"I'm not really sure if I can be tied to one place. Many times I'm on the road and you would be left alone."

Ah, so he *had* thought about marriage, if he was worried about her. She felt somewhat relieved. She would give him the freedom to choose.

Clara searched his handsome face. It would be easy for her to let him stay the night. No one would know, and she wanted to feel his arms wrapped around her. She mentally shook her head.

"Mac, I'm going to have to ask you to leave now." She moved to open the door, but he brushed against her and she was filled with desire—something she'd felt only in the early days of her marriage. Right now she didn't trust herself at all. This had gone too far.

"Please, Clara." He stroked her arm. "Let me show you how you make me feel . . ."

She faced him and felt a poignant sadness. "Mac, there's nothing more I'd like than to have you do that, but I just can't."

His face grew solemn. "All right. I'll leave. Does this have something to do with my not going with you to church? If so, I promise to go with you. But I personally don't need church."

Clara blinked at him. She knew he had no clue. "That's only part of it, Mac, and if I have to tell you the other part,

well . . . I pity any man who thinks he doesn't need God."
She felt tears threatening, but she fought them back.

Mac's face looked like a thundercloud. "I'll be back tomorrow to take you for a drive, and we'll talk then." He squeezed her hand, then slipped out the door, closing it behind him.

Clara leaned against the door, her hand against her mouth to try to hold back the sobs, but it was no use. How she wanted him. She loved just being in his presence. He was charming and delightful and made her feel so womanly and desirable. Hot tears flowed down her cheeks. *Oh, God, help me be strong.* She slid to the floor, her dress ballooning up around her in a heap and the corset cutting into her stomach, then yanked the jet earrings off and threw them across the hall.

22

First thing Monday morning, before Catharine finished washing the breakfast dishes, two hired men arrived with their plows to help Peter make a trench around the wheat field. Earlier, when she'd dug into the flour barrel, she squealed when she found grasshoppers, and everyone had come running. This was not a good sign, and she prayed the bait Peter was putting out today would be enough to kill the locust eggs in the fields. Today she would make certain the men had plenty of water to drink and a hearty lunch.

Anna bounced into the kitchen just as Catharine was finishing up. "I've been wondering, Cath. Could I help you make a cake for Greta's birthday on Friday?"

"Of course you can. Maybe between the two of us it won't be half bad." Catharine smiled at her baby sister.

Anna giggled. "I think your cooking has improved. Since I don't know the first thing about baking a cake, I figured I might as well learn, and now is as good a time as any to start."

Catharine gave her a funny look. "Did I say anything about knowing *how* to make one? I'll have to resort to a cookbook again." She snapped her fingers. "I just had an idea! What about getting something from the bakery in town or getting Mario to make something special? His desserts are delicious."

"Whatever you decide is fine with me, but if you do bake something, I want to help. I can't think of a single thing for her present except . . . one of the puppies." Anna picked up the dried glasses and carried them to the cupboard.

Catharine shook her head. "I don't think that's such a good idea. Peter's already told you that you can only have one. Remember?"

Anna's face fell. "I know, but I'm hoping he'll change his mind. I think he really likes them, don't you?"

"I really haven't noticed, Anna. I've been too busy. In fact, I could use your help with making lunch for the men when they finish plowing." She finished drying the last dish and laid the cloth aside.

"Where's Greta? I thought she was helping. After all, I fed the livestock so Peter could get on with the plowing."

"She's doing some mending. It won't take us long to make sandwiches for the men."

"Do you mean right now?" Anna whined.

"*Nee*. I have to bake the bread first and I'm just about to shape the loaves now. The dough has been rising since dawn." Catharine sighed.

"Cath, you look tired. Maybe I'll stay and help with the bread."

Catharine glanced over at her sister with fondness. "I'm fine. You're free for a couple hours, but come back and we'll make lunch. Was there something you wanted to do this morning?"

Anna shrugged. "I'm going to give the pups a good brushing. The little darlings' fur mats easily, especially with this heat. If you're sure . . ."

Catharine propped her hands on her hips, cocking her head to the side. "Would I lie to you?"

"I guess not." She gave Catharine a quick squeeze. "I'll be back soon to help." In a flash she was out the door.

Catharine watched through the window as Anna hurried outside to the small pen that Peter had constructed for the pups after the last incident in the kitchen. How she envied that Anna hadn't a care in the world. Part adolescent, part woman, she thought affectionately. It wouldn't be long before she'd start noticing the opposite sex like Greta. *Heaven help me!* She guessed that was part of the reason Anna wanted to be certain the chores were divided equally. Just like a schoolgirl would think. Tit for tat.

She moved to the counter, quickly shaped the dough into four loaves, and slid them in the oven. She wiped her brow with the back of her hand and decided to work a little on the chair for Anna. It was too hot to stay inside, so she dragged the chair to the front porch, where the cottonwood tree shaded one end. While the bread baked, she went to work on the chair, removing the old fabric with an upholstery tool, humming cheerfully.

When the men returned from the field, Peter suggested they eat outside under the trees since they all were dirty. "We don't want to track dirt in the house, and we won't change clothes until we put the bait out."

"*Goed*," Catharine said. "I'm not interested in washing the floors today, and for certain it's a bath you'll be needing." She held her nose between two fingers, then swatted him with her dish towel. Peter skipped sideways, pretending fear, and the other men laughed good-naturedly.

"You men wash up at the well. I left bars of soap and fresh towels there for each of you. We'll bring your lunches out momentarily." Catharine hurried back inside where Greta and Anna were slicing the bread and meat.

After everyone had their fill and heartily thanked Catharine and her sisters, they used rope to fasten their coveralls to the tops of their boots. "This will keep the poison from touching our skin," Peter explained to the women. "The mix could easily burn us. That's why I had you sew my pockets closed last night."

"Yours is definitely not a job I want," Greta said to Peter.

Catharine handed Peter a pair of soft cotton gloves, and after he'd put them on, he pulled on another pair, a leather gauntlet type. The other men followed suit.

"Catharine, we'll mix the bait near the fields, then fill the plowed furrows with the bait to kill the hoppers. I suggest you ladies stay indoors for the next couple of hours. If the wind decides to kick up, I don't want you ladies to breathe this stuff. Promise?" His unshaven face held concern.

"We promise, Peter." Catharine bit her lip.

"My clothes will have to be washed, but I'll do that myself." He leaned over and kissed her head. "Don't start fretting. We'll be through before suppertime." He turned to the others. "Ready?" They nodded and he said, "Then what are we waiting for? We'll cover our faces right before we mix the bait." The men climbed in the wagon and rumbled out of the yard.

Catharine stood watching until they were just a mere speck on the edge of the wheat fields. She silently prayed for Peter's safety and for the wheat crop.

"Come on, Cath." Greta took her hand. "Let's go inside and take a break."

"I know," Anna said. "Why don't we plan your birthday dinner?"

A big smile crossed Greta's face. "I'm all for that. I'll make us some tea."

They crossed the yard to go inside the house. Catharine, for one, wanted to be out of the heat. She paused as they passed the yapping puppies and said, "You know, maybe we should bring them in. The cow and horses are protected in the barn in case the poison gets carried on the wind. It won't hurt this one time for the puppies to come inside."

That's all it took for Anna's face to light up. "Cath, you and I can carry them in while Greta makes the tea."

"At least they can entertain us while we stay indoors. I'm glad Peter told me not to wash clothes today." Catharine was glad to go sit in the living room and prop her feet up on the footstool. She'd been up before dawn and suddenly realized how tired she was. One of the puppies curled up in her lap, and she and Anna dozed until Greta returned with the tea. She poured the fresh brew into Catharine's favorite Blue Willow teacups.

"Anna, you need to give these puppies proper names so they can get used to coming when they're called." Catharine picked the puppy up from her lap and kissed its little head, then put him on the floor. "They are so adorable and soft."

"Do you think that's a good idea, since I won't be able to keep them?" Anna asked.

"Mmm . . . I don't think it would hurt."

Greta sat next to Anna. "I like the name Sugar for this one. She's my favorite." She bent down to pat the puppy on the head, and the pup settled down next to her feet.

"This one is the cutest and the smallest, so I'll call her

Baby," Anna said, holding the pup in her arm. "And this one"—she pointed to the fireplace where another puppy had plopped down—"I'll call Prince." Anna looked over at her sister. "So . . . Catharine, what will you name your favorite?"

"Let's see . . . how about Ginger because of her mixed coloring? What do you think?"

"It's perfect, but you better not get too attached, Sis." Greta took a sip of her tea. "You know how strict Peter can be sometimes."

Catharine laughed. "But I know his soft spots."

Greta raised an eyebrow. "I'll bet you do," she said with a knowing look.

A loud knocking at the door interrupted their dog-naming session. Catharine jerked up, hoping there wasn't a problem in the wheat field. She moved to rise from her chair, but Anna was quicker.

"I'll get it!" Anna hurried to the door as Catharine watched. "Bryan. Was Greta expecting you?"

The handsome soldier took his hat off and stood waiting at the door. "No, but I was out on patrol and my shift just ended, so I thought I'd drop by for a few minutes, if that's all right."

"I—" Anna stammered.

"Bryan! What a nice surprise," Greta exclaimed. "For heaven's sake, Anna, let the man come in."

Anna threw the door wide open, and he nodded a thank you to her. "I hope I'm not interrupting or keeping you from anything."

"No, we're all in the living room having tea. It's been a busy day around here. I'll have to fill you in." Greta handed his hat to Anna to hang up, then hooked her arm through his. "Come and join us." She led him to the living room with Anna close behind, and the puppies came racing toward him. "What have we here? Not one but four puppies." He smiled down at them.

"Look who's here, Catharine." Greta propelled Bryan directly in front of her, and Catharine couldn't help but notice a tinge of flush that crept down Bryan's face to where the top of his double-breasted uniform met his neck.

"Hello, Bryan. So nice of you to stop by. Will you have some tea with us?"

"Don't mind if I do. I can't stay long," he said, turning to Greta.

"Anna, we need another cup, if you wouldn't mind fetching one." Catharine looked at Bryan and felt she had to explain. "I'm sorry. I don't own the full set but still enjoy using it."

"Oh, a mug will work just fine. I'm not particular." He bent down and inspected the tea set. "Very pretty. I can see why you're fond of it."

"It's the last of our mother's china, and Catharine always fancied the Blue Willow. An unfortunate storm at sea broke all but these pieces," Greta said.

"Have a seat, Bryan, and make yourself comfortable." Catharine was glad that he'd finally come to call on Greta in the proper way. She could tell that her sister was in love with Bryan by the way she gazed dreamily at him and by the blush on her cheeks. He seemed to be smitten by her as well. *Maybe this will all work out. I'm glad I had that talk with her.*

The puppies gathered at Bryan's feet and yanked on his pant leg. When he shook his leg to shoo them away, they seemed even more determined. He laughed at their antics until Greta took control and made them settle down.

Anna returned with a mug and Greta filled it with tea. Bryan took a sip, gazing at Greta over the mug's rim. "I'm more of a coffee drinker, but I think I like your tea."

"Thank you." Catharine set her cup down. "We were about to plan Greta's eighteenth birthday party for this Friday. Perhaps you'd like to come too."

"That all depends on the army, I'm afraid, but I'd like to." When he smiled, his teeth shone white.

"Maybe we can make sure it's when you're free then," Greta piped up, glancing over at Catharine for approval.

"We can do that." Catharine watched as a smile crept across his handsome face.

"I have army duty this Saturday, but I'm free Friday evening. I'm so pleased that you've asked me." He set his mug down.

"Then it's settled. We'll have a small party Friday night," Catharine said.

"Could we invite the Cristinis?" Anna asked. "I enjoy being with them."

"If Greta wants to. It's her party."

Greta refilled Bryan's mug. "Certainly. I like them too. But I don't know of anyone else to ask who knows me, other than Clara and Dorothy. Shouldn't we ask them too?"

Catharine was thoughtful for a moment as she carefully set her teacup down. "If they don't have other plans, sure. This is sort of late notice, you know."

Bryan stood. "I need to get on back now." He turned to Greta. "I look forward to Friday."

"I'll walk you to the door, Bryan." Greta quickly rose.

"Don't dawdle outside, Greta. Remember what Peter said about the bait," Catharine reminded her.

Bryan's forehead wrinkled in question. "I'll explain," Greta said as they left the room.

"Guess we'd better make a list, Anna," Catharine said, walking over to her desk. "This party is getting larger by the minute."

Anna clapped her hands with excitement.

Living in the country had been such a shift for all of them, Catharine thought. Just one visit to town for a play was hardly enough excitement for two young women. She'd try hard to keep that precious smile on Anna's face for as long as she could. But right now, she needed a snack before supper.

23

Peter removed his overalls after the others had left, then rinsed them in a washtub of water. He wrung them out as best he could, then refilled the tub with soap, pushing the overalls under the soapy water for a good soak. That should do it.

He was mighty tired. It'd been a long day and he wanted to have supper, but first he'd bathe. He removed the gloves, then threw them into a sack and headed for the creek. The smell of fried chicken and gravy wafted on the breeze. He hoped Catharine had made whipped potatoes too. His stomach growled and his mouth watered.

He had to chuckle. Sweet Catharine was trying so hard to become a better cook. It was hit or miss at best, but he always ate whatever she put in front of him. He'd seen the concern on her face this morning and he didn't want to worry her, but the spreading of the bait was little more than a trial effort. Without rain, the crop was suffering, as were her flowers, and the dryness and heat only made a better breeding ground for locusts. *It's out of my hands now, Lord.* He'd done all he could to protect the wheat.

As he slid into the cool creek water, he wondered about

Catharine's past. He noticed that Catharine was always anxious to go pick up the mail in town. What was she expecting? Her parents were dead and she said she had no surviving relatives. Who would be writing her? Another man? Anger flashed through him. That would be impossible . . . unless that was what Mac had implied.

Sometimes he worried about Catharine. Many nights she tossed in her sleep, although she hadn't had any more nightmares to his knowledge. He got the distinct feeling that she was hiding something.

He finished washing, slipped on his pants and shirt, and hurried back up the trail to the supper awaiting him. He didn't want to keep his family waiting.

Now that's a thought! It was the first time he'd ever considered them his family, but that's just what they were. He smiled when he saw his wife standing on the front porch waiting for him.

"The girls and I are going into town to pick up a few things for the birthday party, so I'll put a handwritten invitation to Dorothy and your mother in their mailboxes," Catharine said to Peter the next morning. "Do you want to come along, or is there anything you need?"

Peter finished tucking in his shirttails. "I don't believe so." He stepped over to where Catharine was making the bed. He leaned down and planted a kiss on the nape of her neck, and she whirled around and slid her arms around his waist. "Catharine, I'm sorry about last night. I was just plumb wore out." Her eyes latched onto his. Peter loved how her irises were rimmed in a deeper color of green.

213

"I know you were, Peter. Sometimes it's nice just to be near you." She laid her head on his chest and listened to the beat of his heart beneath his chambray shirt.

"Then our winters should be most interesting." Peter kissed the top of her head, then moved away. "I'd better get out of here now or we'll both be in trouble and you won't get your shopping done."

"You're right, my handsome husband. I'll let you go as long as you promise to give my flowers a drink of water before I return."

"You drive a hard bargain, ma'am! But I'll see what I can do." He scratched his chin. "With taking care of the farm and those little critters of Anna's, I'm not sure I'll have time," he teased.

"Speaking of which, would you consider keeping more than one of the puppies?"

Peter raised an eyebrow. "What? Are you all trying to wear me down?"

Catharine gave him a sheepish look. "Well . . . would you just give it some thought, Peter? There's been very little that I've seen Anna excited about. Greta has a beau to entertain her, but Anna . . . well, she hasn't met any friends her age yet."

"And what about you, my sweet? I've seen how you've taken to Ginger, and she follows you around when you're outdoors."

Catharine grinned. "I have to admit, I do like the puppies. But if you *really* want us to have only one, then we'd best be considering which one to keep. It won't be easy."

"Tell you what—I'll give it some thought. You and the girls have a fun excursion, and I might even have supper waiting for you if you're out very long."

"Then I'll be sure to hang around town long enough for

that to happen!" She giggled and tweaked his nose. "I must hurry. I have a lot of shopping to do."

Peter shook his head. "Women. I'll never understand 'em. I'll go hitch up the team for you while you finish getting ready."

"Thank you, my dear. Now I need to get my hair pinned up. Are you sure there's nothing you need from town?"

"Not a thing . . . only for you to hurry back." He touched her cheek, reveling in its softness.

Catharine left Greta and Anna talking with Angelina about the cake she would bake for Greta's birthday, promising to return shortly so they could all go to the mercantile store. She hurried on down the sidewalk, reaching the post office in a matter of minutes, but when the clerk checked her mailbox, it was empty. She thanked him and sighed. Her father's solicitor had promised the proper documentation would be arriving soon. *Apparently he doesn't mean this century!* But there was no use fretting about it.

She walked over to the postmaster. "Excuse me."

The portly man behind the counter smiled. "Yes, ma'am. What can I do for you?"

She handed him the handwritten invitations for Dorothy and Clara. "I'd like to mail these, please. I'll pay for the postage." She handed him the correct change.

"No problem. Will that be all?" He stamped the invitations and put them aside.

"Um . . . I'm expecting a very important letter from a solicitor from Holland. I was wondering, rather than drive all the way into town several times a week, is there a way to know when it arrives so I can retrieve it?"

The postmaster chuckled. "Not really, but if you'd like someone to deliver it to you, that'll be an extra charge."

Catharine nodded. "That would work perfectly. Thank you so much."

She walked back to Mario's Ristorante and found everyone just as she'd left them—laughing and discussing the menu.

Angelina looked up as Catharine walked over. "I have the perfect plan, if you'll go along with it." Her dark eyes danced.

"What have you all cooked up? I was gone only a few minutes."

"Here, take a seat and we'll tell you," Angelina said, indicating an empty chair at the table. "I have customers to wait on, so let me tell you quickly."

"We don't want to keep you from your work," Catharine said, hesitating to sit. "We should leave."

Angelina threw up her hands. "What? And keep me from my friends? Not a chance. Anyway, what would you think if Mario and I cater Greta's birthday party?"

"But how? Your restaurant is open on Friday nights." Catharine secretly loved the idea but didn't want to put her friends out.

"We are, but I've asked Mario if we can let our staff handle it for just the night. We could certainly use the break. What do you say?"

"Please! It would be wonderful to have some Italian cooking again," Anna pleaded.

"Not that yours isn't good, Cath," Greta quickly added.

Catharine chuckled. "We all know that my cooking leaves a lot to be desired, so you don't have to tread lightly on that score."

"So it's yes?" Greta's eyes were wide with hope.

Catharine looked around, pretending to look stern and unmoving. Her sisters' faces dropped, then she exclaimed, "Yes! Let's do it! I believe Peter will be relieved that he doesn't have to help me."

Greta grabbed her hand. "*Dank U wel*. This will be a wonderful birthday."

"Well, it is your eighteenth, so it should be special, like you." Catharine squeezed her hand. She knew she wouldn't always have Greta around, but she wouldn't think about that now.

"Then it's settled." Angelina stood. "I'll be back in a few minutes and I'll bring you some coffee, Catharine."

Greta turned to Anna. "Why don't you and I go on ahead to the mercantile and let these two plan everything?"

"Good idea. Is that okay, Cath?" Anna hopped up.

"Yes, and I'll walk over as soon as Angelina and I plan the menu. I won't be long."

Not long after they left, Angelina poured a cup of coffee for both of them and sat across from her. "Mario will take care of the customers for a few minutes. Angelo and Alfredo cleared the tables for me." She cocked her head. "Now tell me, how've you been?"

"A little more tired than usual, and Peter is working hard to save the wheat crop from locusts. He told me they were a problem last year too." Catharine told her about how he'd dug trenches and filled them with bait.

"They were a big problem, but maybe this new idea will work this year," Angelina said. "Let's hope so. I'd hate for you to have to borrow money from Clara. She's a little tight-fisted, I hear."

Catharine raised her eyebrows. "I had no idea. I've not

217

been around her a lot. I have a feeling she doesn't care for the Dutch."

"Then she's the one with the problem. Don't worry, she'll come around. She's just miffed that Peter didn't marry her proper Dorothy Miller. She had it all planned out for him."

"I know, but I wish she'd give me a chance. She seems to like Anna for some reason."

"Maybe because she never had a little girl of her own. I know I'd like to have one myself." Angelina paused and set down her cup. "Catharine, what is wrong? You look so sad."

Catharine's shoulders slumped, and she stared down at her coffee cup. "To tell you the truth, I haven't been feeling well. At first I thought it was the heat, but I think I might be pregnant."

Angelina's face burst into a broad smile. "But that is wonderful news, is it not? You don't seem very happy about it."

"I am, Angelina. I guess I just wasn't ready for it so soon." She faced her friend. "I'm not ready to announce it because I'm not positive. So please don't say anything, all right?"

"Not even to your husband or sisters?" Angelina gave her a quizzical look.

"No. I'll tell them when the time is right. I just can't yet."

"If you are pregnant, you won't be able to hide it for long." Angelina patted her hand. "You have my word, my friend, that I won't say anything."

Catharine knew that Angelina had more questions, but she was grateful that she didn't ask anything further.

"I will pray for your health and the baby's as well," Angelina said.

Catharine was comforted by her friend's concern. She took the last swallow of her coffee. "Thank you. But I should let you get back to your customers soon. I've kept you long enough."

It wasn't long before Angelina and Catharine decided what they could have for a light supper, and Mario would make his special tiramisu rather than cake. Angelina promised that Greta would love it, and Catharine heartily agreed.

Looking quite pleased, Angelina said, "I'll see you all Friday about six and bring the food. It'll be fun. It's been a long time since we've had a party around here."

"I'd better get on over to the mercantile. Who knows what those sisters of mine can get into." Catharine hoped her voice sounded more cheerful than she felt right now.

Friday came quickly, and with it, Catharine's nausea. Thankfully, Peter had risen before her and didn't see her make a mad dash for the chamber pot. Then she trudged back to bed and lay down until her stomach settled. A fresh realization hit her that she was indeed going to have a child. She closed her eyes and thanked the Lord for the fruit of her womb, praying that no harm would come to this little one and it would arrive healthy.

Would Peter be happy about the baby? She hoped so, but for now she hugged the secret to herself. Besides, Peter was worried enough about the crop, and she wanted Greta's birthday to be centered on her. The news would keep for now.

Feeling better now, Catharine pulled on her robe, patted her braid smooth, and went to the kitchen to start breakfast. From the smell of it, Peter was already frying bacon. She fought the rising nausea again and paused in the hallway until it passed.

He looked up from the stove where he was turning strips of bacon and smiled at her. "Good morning. I didn't want to wake you since we have Greta's party tonight. What can I do to help?"

Catharine loved the blue-gray flecks in Peter's irises and the way his eyes crinkled at the edges when he smiled. His face and arms were deeply tanned and muscular. In her mind he was a beautiful specimen of a man, but she knew better than to call a man beautiful.

Instead she kissed him and said, "Really, Mario and Angelina are doing most of the work. Anna and I will set the dining room table and wrap our presents. That about does it."

"Would you like me to scramble you an egg?" He stood holding the spatula in one hand, his other hand on his hip.

The thought of an egg didn't sound appealing at all. "I think I'd just like some toast this morning."

Anna bounded into the kitchen with her usual sunny disposition. "How is everyone?" She reached over and took a slice of bacon off the plate next to the stove and devoured it.

"Just fine. Where's Greta?" Catharine asked, pouring herself a cup of coffee. Peter layered sliced bread on a pan and shoved it into the oven.

"I tiptoed around this morning getting dressed so she could sleep in on her birthday. After all, it only comes around once a year."

Peter handed her a plate with eggs. "That's very thoughtful of you."

"Well, she *is* eighteen today. She's a grown-up now." Anna sighed. "Ah, if only I were eighteen . . ."

Catharine laughed softly. "You would . . . ?"

"Oh, I don't know. Travel to New York and go to art school or maybe medical school or something equally important."

Catharine shot Peter a look and glanced back at her sister. "Really? Why don't you try finishing high school first and we'll see what comes next? You may change your mind by then."

Anna shrugged. "Perhaps, but I've been thinking about my future. I can't live with you and Peter forever."

Catharine walked over and gave her a hug. "Who said? We're not complaining." She was amazed. Anna was starting to act as though she'd aged one year overnight. "You won't turn sixteen for six months."

Peter lifted the pan out of the oven and put some toast on a plate for Catharine as she sat down next to Anna. "Peter, aren't you eating?"

"I've already had breakfast. I've got lots to do before our guests arrive. I want to clean up around the porch and outside."

"I can help with that," Anna said as jam slipped off her toast onto her fingers.

"No, you have enough to do helping Catharine out. But thanks for the offer." He walked over to the back door and fetched his hat. "I'll see you ladies a little later. If you need me, just holler. I won't be too far away."

24

Promptly at five thirty, Mario, Angelina, and the boys arrived, carting all the goodies in the back of their buckboard. Catharine finished ironing the linen napkins while Anna set the table. Greta was going from the dining room to the front door with such frequency that Catharine told her she would wear out the hardwood floor.

"I'm just watching for when Bryan arrives," Greta said.

"He didn't even get off until five. Why don't you just relax?" Anna was carefully setting the good dishes at each place setting, next to the silverware. "We could use your help bringing the glasses in."

Greta poked her tongue out playfully. "I'm the birthday girl, and I love watching you work."

"Maybe so, but our work would go quicker if you'd assist us," Catharine admonished.

The front door opened, and Peter entered with the Cristinis, carrying a large pot, its delectable smells permeating the house.

"Greetings, everyone!" Mario boomed. "Where's the birthday girl—or should I say young lady?"

222

"I'm here, Mr. Cristini," Greta said, rushing to help. "I'll take that pot for you."

"I can handle it. It's pretty heavy." Mario stopped to lean over the pot and give Greta a peck on the cheek. "Happy birthday! I have the best pasta fagioli for our supper, and Angelina is carrying my delicious tiramisu for dessert."

"What is pasta fagioli, Mario? It smells wonderful!" Greta said, lifting the lid to peer inside.

"It is!" Angelina said. "Mario makes the best soup this side of Italy. Just wait until you taste it. *Bellissimo!*"

"I can hardly wait." Peter led the way to the kitchen. "Just put the big pot on the stove."

Catharine looked up from the napkins she was folding. "It's so good to have you all in our home," she said warmly.

Angelina gave her a quick hug. "We wouldn't miss the opportunity, my friend." Her eyes were bright with enthusiasm.

Alfredo and Angelo carried loaves of bread wrapped in muslin cloths. "Mama baked the bread and wrapped the loaves right before we left." Alfredo smiled broadly. "It was all I could do not to tear off a hunk on the way over."

Anna took the bread from them. "I'll set them inside the oven until we're ready to eat. Everything smells wonderful!"

Catharine's stomach rumbled. Maybe she'd be able to eat a little tonight. She loved Mario's cooking and couldn't wait to try the soup. She watched from the kitchen window as a carriage driven by Peter's mother pulled up. Catharine's heart sank. She prayed this visit would be entirely different from her first one. *Will she notice the gloss on the woodwork and furniture? I hope everything is to her liking today . . . after all, she is going to be the grandmother of this child. Will she be happy about it when we tell her?*

"Your mother's arrived, Peter," she said quietly. Peter nodded and excused himself to greet his mother. Catharine shooed everyone out of the kitchen and back to the living room.

"Miss Catharine, where should we put Greta's gift?" Angelo asked, pushing a package at her.

"I'll take it. We can put it on the sideboard for her to open later. Don't you think that's a good place to put the gifts?"

Angelo nodded shyly, then followed the group back to the living room. Catharine placed the gift next to Anna's and the one from Peter and herself. She took a deep breath to calm her jitters, then pushed open the door from the kitchen to greet her mother-in-law.

Angelina caught her by the sleeve and pulled her aside before she had taken two steps. "How are you feeling? You look a little pale."

Angelina's dark eyes mirrored concern. It warmed Catharine's heart that she had a friend like Angelina to confide in. "Good right now. I was sick this morning, so there's no doubt about it, I'm pregnant."

Angelina beamed, a smile widening her face. "I'm happy for you! We need a wee one in our circle of friends."

"Are you coming, Catharine?" Peter called out.

They both moved through the door to the living room. "I'm here," she answered. Dorothy had arrived and was seated next to Clara on the couch. "Dorothy. Hello. I wasn't aware that you'd arrived." Turning to Clara, she said, "Hello, Mrs. Andersen."

Clara murmured a hello, but Catharine couldn't read what she was thinking behind her unsmiling face.

"Thank you for inviting me." Dorothy smiled up at her.

Catharine smiled back. "We're glad you could come." She was unsure of whether to take a chair or just stand waiting. She wondered what Clara would do. Suddenly she felt at a loss for words.

"I think the only one we're waiting for is Bryan before we have supper." Peter sat in his high-back chair with Angelo hanging off the arm.

Seeing Angelo sitting with him got rid of any doubts Catharine had about Peter wanting to be a father. The boys seemed to care for him like an uncle. *He'll make a wonderful father.*

Almost on cue, boot heels sounded against the porch steps, and Greta hopped up from her chair. "That must be Bryan."

"Right on time. Angelina, let's go heat up my soup so that it'll be piping hot," Mario said.

Clara's head shot up. "You mean you didn't prepare the meal, Catharine?" She directed her gaze to Catharine. Peter shot his mother a disapproving look as he and Mario left, but she continued on. "I must say I'm not at all surprised."

Catharine felt her face flame hot, and tears began to rise while she searched her mind for a reply.

Angelina regarded Clara coolly and responded, "Matter of fact, it was my idea. They enjoyed our spaghetti dinner once, and Mario and I wanted to make something special for Greta's birthday."

"Yes, that was very sweet of them, and I know Cath appreciates not having to spend another night in the kitchen after helping Peter in the fields, caring for the animals and the house, and weeding the garden," Greta said. "I don't know how she does it without servants. It was very thoughtful of them to offer."

Catharine knew the smile on her sister's face was forced,

but she wanted to hug both Angelina and Greta for coming to her rescue. "Mrs. Andersen, Dorothy, would either of you care for something to drink while we wait for the soup to heat?" she asked.

"I'm perfectly fine, thank you. I can wait." Clara sniffed into her lace hanky.

"No, I'll wait for dinner, but thank you," Dorothy said, giving Catharine a sympathetic look. Did she have an ally in Dorothy? What a surprise. Maybe she'd misjudged the facts. Maybe the entire idea of Dorothy and Peter being a couple was purely Clara's own idea.

"Well then—"

"Can we go see Anna's puppies before we have supper, Mama?" Alfredo begged.

Anna turned and asked Catharine, "Would that be all right?"

"It won't be long before supper, but there may be time for just a quick look, boys," Catharine said.

"And don't come back in here dirty. You can go see them, but then come right back." Angelina cocked her head, narrowing her eyes at the twins.

They scrambled up to follow Anna outside. "I'll go too if you don't mind," Dorothy said, getting up. "I love dogs."

Anna looked surprised. "No, of course not. Come along." Anna chatted about the naming of the puppies as they left the living room.

"Next thing they'll be wanting one of those pups," Bryan said. "And I couldn't blame them. If I was in one place for more than a few months, I'd have a dog too."

"But I thought your orders were to be stationed here awhile." Greta flashed him a worried look. She sat as close to him as humanly possible, Catharine noted.

Bryan put his arm around her. "The army is the one in control and can move you to where they decide you're needed the most."

Catharine watched the couple interact. Bryan was too handsome for words, and she thought they made a nice-looking couple. She wondered if they would eventually get married. She knew young love all too well and how easy it was to lose one's heart.

Greta pouted. "Well, you're here now and that's what counts, and I don't want to think about anything else."

Bryan gave her a hug. "Me too. Tonight is for celebrating."

Catharine wanted everything to be perfect. Thankfully, by the time the pasta fagioli was dipped into Clara's old rose china bowls and the thick, crusty, buttered bread was on the table, her nerves had calmed down a little. She asked everyone to come to the dining room and have a seat.

Mario strolled to the front door. "I'll call Anna and the boys and tell them everything is ready."

A loud crash sounded in the hallway, and the children ran into the dining room, Angelo hot on the heels of one of the pups. "Prince! Come back," he shouted, but the puppy seemed frightened and ran all the more, looking for a place to hide. "I'm sorry," Angelo called over his shoulder, breathing hard while he chased after the feisty puppy. "When Anna opened the front door, Prince slipped through."

Clara screamed as the puppy ran between her legs, and she lost her balance, careening right into the beautifully set table and jarring the large soup tureen. Soup splashed out of the bowls and onto the linen tablecloth Catharine had spent all morning ironing, staining it as well as Clara's pretty moiré gown.

"Oh! Oh! My goodness! Catch that confounded dog!" she shrieked, jumping out of the way. Peter reached out to steady her, his face furrowing into a scowl.

"For heaven's sake! Somebody grab Prince before he destroys my birthday dinner!" Greta bawled.

Bryan went one direction and Mario another, but Prince eluded them while the others moved chairs aside, yelling and trying their best to grab the puppy.

Alfredo quickly scooted underneath the tablecloth and found the trembling puppy while the adults looked on, horrified. Peter's jaw twitched furiously as he muttered something under his breath. Mario grabbed Angelo by the ear and pulled him toward the hallway as Anna took the pup. She kept her head down and avoided looking at Peter, hurrying out to put Prince in his cage.

Angelina scooted to the kitchen and returned in a flash with a dish towel, trying to soak up the mess created in the center of the table, a frown across her face. Catharine stood rooted to the spot, not daring to even look Peter's way. She felt embarrassed for Clara as Dorothy took a napkin from the table to blot the front of Clara's dress. Couldn't they just have one decent meal with Peter's mother?

"Boys, go to the kitchen and wash your hands, then come back and apologize," Mario said sharply. The twins scurried off to do his bidding, heads hanging in remorse. "I'm so sorry, Mrs. Andersen. I'm sure they meant no harm."

"I've told Anna that those dogs have to be watched closely," Peter said in a clipped tone, the muscle in his jaw twitching. "I thought she knew to put them in the pen when we have company. This has to stop."

Catharine met his level gaze with a pleading look. Didn't

he know she was uncomfortable enough without him getting upset too? His expression made her feel as though she couldn't control her household.

Dorothy said sympathetically, "I'm sorry. Since I was with the children, I should have made sure the door was closed."

"I'll talk to Anna about it, Peter. But please, let's all sit down before the soup gets cold." Catharine huffed in exasperation just as Anna and the twins returned and sat down.

"Mrs. Andersen, I'm very sorry if that upset you," Alfredo said.

"Me too," Angelo muttered.

"Apology accepted." Clara gave the twins a hard look.

Mario grunted. "Good! Now let's try what's left of the pasta fagioli."

Everyone took their seat, and after Peter prayed a special birthday blessing for Greta and blessed the food, Catharine passed the bread around. She'd forgotten to light the candles, but it was a good thing she hadn't or it could've been disastrous. And that definitely would have sent Clara into a tizzy! Catharine nearly giggled out loud at the thought.

Clara leaned into Peter's side, talking too low for Catharine to hear what was said. *How can I make her like me?* she wondered.

When the last bite was gone from the soup tureen, with compliments to Mario that it was the best soup they'd ever had, everyone sang "Happy Birthday" to Greta and settled back with coffee and dessert. Even Clara seemed to be enjoying herself.

Catharine pushed her chair back and reached over to the sideboard for the gifts to hand them to Greta.

"Open mine first," Anna urged.

"Nice wrapping. I'm surprised." Greta gently unwrapped her sister's gift. "Oh, Anna. This is wonderful!" She held the gift up for everyone to see the watercolor of Crow Creek, with the filtered sunlight kissing its bank and overhanging trees.

"I know how you like to stroll down there to think or meet Bryan," Anna declared.

"Anna!" Greta rolled her eyes.

Bryan laughed and said, "Very observant, Anna. Nicely done."

The Cristinis gave Greta a stylish hat, which Greta immediately donned, preening this way and that. "For your next trip to the Cheyenne Opera, Greta," Angelina said.

"I may have to borrow it myself." Catharine admired the hat with a grin.

"I hardly think you'd catch me without this hat on the next time I go to town." Greta gave a soft giggle.

"You have excellent taste, Angelina," Clara commented.

"How do you know I didn't pick it out?" Mario laughed.

Clara shot him a glance. "Really?"

"He's only teasing, Clara. You can't get him to shop for anything unless it's food." Angelina poked her husband and everyone laughed.

Dorothy smiled as Greta opened her gift. Nestled inside was a delicate lady's writing pen and embossed stationery. "Dorothy, thank you for your thoughtfulness." Greta looked pleased as she set the box aside, then picked up Catharine and Peter's gift. She tore off the wrappings and exclaimed, "A leather Bible! Oh, Catharine and Peter . . . it's so wonderful," she said, almost reverently running her hand across the smooth leather. "Thank you both so much," she whispered, her eyes glistening.

"You're so welcome," Catharine said. "Let God be your guide for the future."

Catharine's heart felt full. Here was her sister, a woman, now ready to be launched into whatever life brought her way. She prayed life would be full of wonder and happiness for Greta.

Catharine felt Peter's eyes on her, and her gaze swerved toward him. His eyes held hers for a long moment, and she felt flushed.

Bryan stood up and fished in his pocket for his present. "I have something for you too, Greta." He handed her a small box, then sat down.

Greta looked at him in surprise. "I wasn't expecting anything, really." She flipped open the box and pulled out a small locket in the shape of a heart. "Oh, goodness . . . Bryan, it's perfect. Will you put it on me?"

Bryan placed the gold chain around her neck. It twinkled in the light against her pink gown. Greta reached down, touching it. "It's simply beautiful. Thank you so much, Bryan."

Bryan turned a light shade of pink. "You're welcome. Now, how about that walk you promised me?" He winked.

Everyone was quiet, watching young love unfold right before their eyes. Even the twins seemed to sense something special happening.

Greta shoved back her chair and looked at the group around the table. "If you all will excuse me, I have an appointment to keep."

25

A strange, distant buzzing penetrated Catharine's sleep, and with a drowsy gaze she glanced around the bedroom, looking for its source. It had been a fitful night filled with a haunting dream.

She saw nothing, but the sound was real. She lifted Peter's arm off her hip, quietly slipped out of bed, and made her way downstairs to the porch. It was a warm night again, and her nightgown was sticking to her. Leaning against the post by the porch railing, she looked out across the yard and beyond the grassy fields of wheat illuminated by the moon. All was still, and with the breeze absent she could hear the locusts.

The party had been a great success, despite Prince's frolic and Clara's disapproval on so many levels. But on Catharine's mind now was the dream she'd just had. It was exactly as she remembered it when the events happened.

The gavel of the judge had rapped hard on his massive desk, executing his verdict. Accidental death. She'd been glad that her parents hadn't had to witness this. Catharine stole a glance at Karl, fighting the huge lump in her throat. In slow motion she moved through the filmy haze to do what she must now, her heart broken. When she walked past him, his eyes pleaded, but she was devoid of any feeling of love she'd had for him before. Eerily, she continued out of the courthouse, remembering . . .

Catharine shuddered from a sudden chill. Would she ever forget? She patted her abdomen to reassure herself of the life within her. Karl Johnsen had been a smooth talker, handsome, and oh so incredibly charming. It had been a whirlwind romance, and her parents had warned her, just as she'd tried to warn Greta. But at least Bryan had come courting in the proper manner now, and he did seem to really adore Greta.

Catharine's heart was full as she prayed. *Lord, watch over the unborn baby You've entrusted me with. Thank You for my sweet Greta, a young lady now. Give her a good future with whomever You have planned for her. Watch over my little Anna with her tender heart. And, Lord, I know Peter is worried about the wheat crop, but I know You will provide if we trust You. Thank You for loving me. Amen.*

A sudden wind blew, and she heard an owl hoot from its roost in a nearby tree. It was a lonely sound, but she wasn't feeling as sad now. She heard the door open and Peter stepped behind her, encircling her with his arms and pulling her back against him so they both faced the field.

"Couldn't sleep?" he asked.

She could feel his warm breath against her ear, and she snuggled back further. "The sound of the locusts interrupted my dreams. Can't you hear them?"

Peter sucked in a deep breath. "Yes, and that's what concerns me now. Last summer was so hot and winter was the coldest one on record, which resulted in the grasshoppers. I feel a repeat coming."

She lifted one of his calloused hands from her waist, brushing it lightly with a kiss. "I pray not, Peter. Maybe it won't be as bad as last year."

"In a couple of days I'll be able to know if the bait we put out is working. Anything is better than nothing at all, considering last year's swarm."

"Tell me, how did you know to do all that?" Catharine listened to the hum of the locusts and shivered.

"Congress created a commission to respond to the grasshopper plague and how best to stop it. The bait is part arsenic and part sawdust. So we'll just wait and see."

She turned around to face him, gazing into the kind blue eyes she'd come to love. "It was a nice party today and the food was so delicious. What a relief for me not to have to make it."

He cupped her chin. "Don't worry about what my mother said. I swear she's just jealous that she never thought to do that. However, we will have to do something about all those puppies." His mouth twisted sideways. "Agree?"

"It was almost comical seeing your mother so undone. Anna told me later that she forgot to put the puppies in the pen. She felt badly about it."

"I should hope so. I know she's only fifteen, but don't you think it's time she started to be a little more responsible?"

Catharine splayed her hands against his chest and felt his heartbeat underneath her palms. "I'm trying, truly I am. Anna is different somehow. She's more of a free spirit than Greta or I."

"I'll give you that. But you still have to talk to her." Peter's face was serious.

She cocked an eyebrow. "Does that mean you might let us—I mean her—keep all four puppies?"

Peter laughed softly. "You little minx." He kissed the tip of her nose. "What I was thinking was maybe she could part with two of them for Angelo and Alfredo. That's if Mario will let them. He may refuse outright."

"Good idea. I knew you were a smart man," she said, playfully running a finger along his mouth. "Anna will feel better knowing they have the puppies." She yawned, trying to cover her mouth. "I'm getting sleepy. Let's go back to bed." She felt the pressure of his hand massaging her lower back, and her pulse quickened.

"Only if you let me hold you close."

"I think that can be arranged."

The owl hooted in agreement from his perch high atop the elm tree.

The day after the play, Mac didn't return to Clara's as promised. She'd wanted to bring him along to Greta's party, but apparently he'd gone out of town once again. She wished he'd at least told her. Every time he returned to Cheyenne from his trips, he was so charming that he won her over with his attention, so she was never miffed at him for very long. She was finding it hard to concentrate on much of anything without his face swimming before her. She felt like a silly schoolgirl.

She took great care picking her dress today, wanting to look her best. She intended on walking to Mac's office on the chance that he might be there. She couldn't wait any longer. She selected a day dress the color of bisque, which was cooler for summer wear with its lightweight fabric. Staring at her image in her mirror, she felt satisfied with her look and glad that she'd maintained her slender figure as she'd aged. The conservative dress held an open neckline and a lightweight chemisette that ended in a small V. Coral piping continued down the length of the bodice to meet her waist, making it appear even more slender. The sleeves were full at the shoulders, but the skirt remained narrow with a soft bustle at the back. Perfect, she thought.

She gave her cheeks a slight pinch for a hint of color, then picked up her reticule, praying that Mac would be in his office. Not wanting to appear in a hurry, she strolled down the sidewalk to the center of town, nodding to passersby here and there, then waved to Angelina, who was sweeping off the sidewalk in front of their restaurant across the street. It surprised her that she really liked Angelina and Mario. It was obvious they were becoming fast friends with Catharine and her sisters.

You could too, if you tried.

Clara gave a soft grunt. *I'm trying, Lord. But how can I trust someone who hasn't told Peter the truth? Maybe if I hadn't started prying in the first place, I would be none the wiser. But then I wouldn't have met Mac, would I?*

At her destination, she slowed her steps and reached for the door handle when suddenly an arm reached around from behind her, unlocking the door. Turning, she looked into the smiling face of Mac.

"Good morning, beautiful! You look wonderful. Perfect timing, I was just arriving."

Clara had to still her heart. Was she old enough to have a heart attack like her husband did? She sucked in air then smiled back. "Mac, I'm so glad you're back. Where on earth have you been?"

His eyes swept over her in admiration. "What kind of greeting is that? Have you missed me?" He took her hand and pulled her inside, shutting the door behind them. He pulled her to him, giving her a long, deep kiss until she thought her lungs would burst from lack of air. "Ahh, your lips are so sweet, Clara."

"Mac." She moaned, then staggered back, her heart hammering. "Yes, I've missed you." Had he said he missed her too? She couldn't remember exactly what he'd just told her.

"That's more like it." Mac's dark eyes penetrated her. "I had to make a short trip to Denver. Come on in. What have you been up to?"

Clara swallowed hard. "Is that all you can say? You couldn't drop by and let me know you were leaving? You promised the night of the opera that you'd come back the very next day so we could talk." She would not let him skirt the issue this time.

"Clara, I meant to. Really, I did. I just got busy and forgot."

"At the very least, you could have sent me a message." She stiffened as he reached for her again. She could smell his aftershave, and she loved how the dark hair at the edge of his neck curled into his collar. "I went to Greta's birthday party without you." She pouted, folding her arms across her.

He stepped closer. "I know, my sweet. I'm sorry. That was just an oversight. How about I make it up to you and take you to lunch?" His lips descended on hers again, and she let them linger there, allowing the pleasure that shot through her.

She'd longed for his touch when he was away. Clara struggled to keep her head this time—business first. "I'm really not that hungry. Have you found out any more about Catharine yet?"

He eyed her. "Come sit down and we'll talk." He patted

the leather chair next to his desk, which Clara noticed was devoid of his usual clutter. He pulled out a folded piece of paper that appeared to be a wire and pushed it across his desk toward her. "This is proof that she was married to a Karl Johnsen. What I don't have is proof that she was ever divorced from him."

Clara stared at the wire confirming from a solicitor in Amsterdam that Catharine Olsen indeed was married. She moistened her dry lips. "Was she divorced or not? This could totally ruin my son and my reputation! I must have proof, Mac!"

He turned in his chair and looked briefly out the window, his fingers tapping together while he pondered her demand. "And you'll get the proof you need. I promise. I have my contact working on it, and he believes she was never divorced before leaving the country. Unfortunately, I've run short of cash with my last trip, and my contact in Amsterdam won't send any more documents until I wire him more money." He swiveled in his chair again to face her, imploring her with his eyes. "You can understand that, can't you? The solicitor there has done quite a lot of research for me, and he's not cheap."

Clara's heart fell. More money? "How much?" she asked, compressing her lips into a thin line.

"About a thousand dollars should take care of it." He leaned over and lifted her hand. "All in all, that's not a lot of money to get to the truth, is it?" He turned her hand over and kissed her palm tenderly, gazing at her with half-lidded eyes.

She found his endearing smile irresistible and sweetly romantic. "All right. I'll go over to the bank and have a draft written for you today, and I expect to get some answers right away. But I'm afraid this is all I can spend on this investigation, Mac."

"Perfect!" He pushed back his chair and rose. "Now let's go have lunch and forget our troubles. Does that sound good to you?" he said, slipping his arm about her waist as she stood. "My, but you smell divine."

Clara felt a surge of love so strong that it dazed her. She wanted nothing more than the pleasure of his company.

26

Morning light cast streaks of red across the horizon. Peter stalked toward the fields, his legs feeling heavy, to survey what was left of his wheat. Normally this was his favorite time of day, with the quiet likened to the hush of a lover's sigh. But not today. He knew the wheat, which had grown nearly two feet high, was now reduced to about a fourth of its size from the Rocky Mountain grasshoppers. In the last few days the humming had gotten louder in warning, and though the bait had killed many of the eggs buried during the winter, yesterday afternoon he'd witnessed a swarm of grasshoppers a half mile wide. He'd told everyone to hurry inside and stay indoors, and to close the windows to seal off the house. Frantically, Catharine and her sisters hurried to do his bidding, with Anna snatching up the puppies to carry them to safety.

Peter stood surveying the ravaged field with despair. Now where would the money come from to run his farm? Not only that, but he had three more mouths to feed. He stuffed his disappointment deep inside. He mustn't let Catharine know how really bad this could be for the farm. He wasn't about to ask his mother for an advance, at least not until the next crop yielded. He'd had to do that last year, but not now with their strained relationship.

At least he hadn't lost the entire crop this time, but he blamed himself. Could be he hadn't gotten the bait down in time, or for whatever reason perhaps not all of them took the bait. *Maybe I'll just become a rancher.*

Catharine's flower bed was destroyed, as well as the vegetable garden—after all her backbreaking work. The grasshoppers had gnawed nearly every plant in sight.

Shoulders slumped and head down, Peter turned to go back to the house. He'd figure something out. The Lord hadn't ever let him go begging. When he finally looked up again, Catharine was walking toward him, a sad look on her weary face. Somehow he would find a way to make it all work.

"I'm sorry about your flower bed." His voice was barely above a whisper as she took his hand in hers.

"That's the least of your worries, Peter. Don't even give it a thought. I can plant another one." She rubbed her hand across his shoulder, and he felt comforted as they walked in companionable silence.

What had he expected? That she wouldn't support him? He needn't have worried. Catharine had come to accept her role as a farmer's wife with enthusiasm, despite her background, and he was proud to call her his wife. He stopped and turned her to face him. He could get lost in those sparkling eyes so full of life, and he felt an instant tingle of desire. That's what she did to him every time she looked at him. He stared into her lovely face as she stroked his jaw. No words were needed when she slipped her arms about his waist and held him tight against her.

Later that morning, Catharine watched as Peter started plowing under the field. Other farmers had been hit just as hard, so there was no use whining. They'd all help each other out. That's what neighbors did around here, she was learning.

She hummed a tune, trying to stay cheerful as she raked away the ravages of her flowers, then went on to what was left of the vegetable garden. She'd go to town again to look for some vegetable seedlings to plant. If they were to be found at all. Thankfully, Peter had canned tomatoes and beans with the help of his mother last summer, and there was still a good supply handy. So they wouldn't starve.

"I'm finished cleaning the porch," Anna called from the steps. "Is there anything else you want me to do?"

Catharine tilted her head back in order to see from underneath the brim of her bonnet. "Why don't you see if Greta needs help getting supper started? I'm nearly through here."

Anna flung the broom aside and hurried back inside. Catharine smiled to herself. Her sisters were becoming indispensible to her. They would be a great help when the baby arrived.

She wanted to tell Peter about the baby, but now was not a good time with the failure of the crop on his heart and mind. But soon she would. Perhaps in a week he'd have a better grip on things and she could tell him. *I want a little boy that looks just like him.* Catharine hugged her arms across her chest, daydreaming. Soon she'd have Peter bring his childhood cradle down from the attic.

Supper was a somber affair without the jovial talking and discussions normally heard around the dinner table. Everyone sensed Peter's mood, and they were also tired from the long day of cleanup.

"Peter, thank you for letting the puppies come inside during the grasshopper swarm." Anna spoke softly as everyone concentrated on their simple dinner. "I'm sure they would've been so scared. I know I still have to give three of them away."

"You're welcome," he said with a grunt, setting his fork down. Catharine knew Anna was expecting him to agree that she'd have to part with the puppies, but he seemed too dejected to even care. "I'm going to Cheyenne in the morning. I'll pick up some more flower and vegetable seeds. The UP railroad will deliver fresh vegetables to the market up from Colorado, so I'll buy some. Need some fertilizers too . . ." His voice trailed off. He seemed to be going over his mental list out loud.

"I could go with you," Catharine said.

He gave her a steady look. "Not this time. It's going to be a fast trip . . . unless you just want to go for the ride."

"Not really. I have plenty to do. Tomorrow is laundry day."

"Ugh." A groan escaped from Greta. "We just did laundry."

"It just seems that way," Anna piped up. "It always does when it's the least favorite chore."

"But we can get the task accomplished pretty quickly," Catharine said while she began to clear the dishes. "Whose turn is it tonight for cleanup? Yours, Anna?"

Anna rolled her eyes. "I guess."

Peter rose from the table, thanked Greta for supper, and strolled quietly from the kitchen. Catharine started to go after him, but Greta stopped her. "Give him time, Cath. He just needs to be alone for now."

Maybe she was right, but Catharine's heart ached to soothe him. "You're probably right."

From the kitchen window they watched him wander off toward the barn. He waved to Bryan, who rode past him and stopped in front of the house.

"Oh, what a nice surprise. I didn't know he was coming over tonight." Greta never waited for a response but threw her dish towel to Anna. She patted her hair and smoothed her dress, then hurried to the front door to meet him.

"In that case, I guess I'll stick around and help you, Anna. You wash, I'll dry," Catharine said, stacking the dishes in the sink.

"That's sweet, but you don't have to." Anna put water in the kettle to heat for washing the dishes.

"You know, Anna, I'm really proud of how you and Greta have pitched in with all the chores. There seems to be an endless supply of them." Catharine gave her sister a hug.

"What will you do if I live in town this fall to finish high school?" Anna asked.

Catharine shrugged. "That hasn't been decided yet, but I'm sure we'll manage—"

Greta poked her head back into the kitchen. "It is all right if I go for a walk along the creek with Bryan?" Her cheeks held a bright flush that made her even prettier.

"Yes. You really didn't have to ask—you're eighteen now. But I'm glad you told me just the same."

Greta flashed Catharine a broad smile. "Thanks!" She whirled around and hurried out of the house on Bryan's arm.

The tack room was always Peter's favorite place to piddle around when he had something heavy on his mind. He liked the smell of leather and metal permeating the small cubicle in the barn. As he reached for a frayed rope that he wanted to mend, his eye caught a small note leaning against an oilcan. He grinned as he opened it.

> Peter,
>
> I've watched you agonize over losing most of the crop. I'm so sorry, but together we can survive this. As you said, it wasn't the first time. If you really are serious about giving cattle raising a try, I will stand behind you. I wish I could make everything better, but the Lord says He will restore the years the locusts have eaten. We must rely on that promise. I think it also means the lonely years you and I have had will be in the past. I just wanted to remind you to be strong in the Lord. We're in His hands.
>
> With deep devotion, Catharine

Tears filled Peter's eyes. He was supposed to be a man of faith, but instead he'd been whining. Maybe not verbally but by his attitude. Catharine's gentle note reminded him to cast his burdens on the One who cared most about him. His Creator. He felt guilty now even doubting his wife's past and believing his mother's accusation.

His heart was torn about Catharine. He knew she had much faith, but was his mother right? He couldn't bring himself to ask Catharine . . . not yet.

❧

When Peter returned, he seemed tired but in a better mood, and he squeezed Catharine's shoulder affectionately. Maybe he'd seen her note. She and Anna had long since finished in the kitchen and were sitting on the front porch, relaxing. Anna was at the other end of the porch, sketching with her colored pencils. Peter plopped down in a rocker, stretching his long legs out, and leaned his head back against the chair. "Did Greta leave with Bryan?"

The weariness in his face and voice troubled her, but Catharine was helpless to make it all better. How she wished she could. "They went for a walk along the creek. It's a nice night for a walk. Seems to have cooled down, which is fine by me." She hesitated and murmured under her breath, "Is there anything I can do to help?"

Peter lifted his head and studied her. "No. I just have to think this through. Don't you go worrying, you hear? I figure I can plant winter wheat again in September, if I don't decide to raise cattle instead," he said with humor in his voice.

Catharine wasn't sure if he was serious or not.

"It's a possibility worth considering."

"But I thought you told me last year that a lot of cattlemen gave up after that terrible blizzard and left the territory."

"They did, but the ones who stayed behind are starting to get their herds back in operation now." He paused, running his hand through his thick hair. "I'm about ready to drop. Think I'll go to bed."

Anna got up from the swing, shoving her art supplies aside. "Wait, Peter. I have something for you." She held out a heavy piece of paper.

The look of surprise on his face turned into a smile. "Anna, when did you do this? It's wonderful." He stood, holding the paper at arm's length to study it better.

"I did it right after I sat down tonight. I didn't get to take my time before you got back, but I thought it might cheer you up."

Peter showed the drawing to Catharine. It was a beautiful field with golden wheat stalks, their ripe seed heads nodding in the prairie breeze against a bright, cloudless sky. At the bottom was written, "There's always hope," followed by a Scripture: *"Let both grow together until the harvest: and in the time of harvest I will say to the reapers, Gather ye together first the tares, and bind them in bundles to burn them: but gather the wheat into my barn." Matthew 13:30.*

The drawing took Catharine's breath away and brought tears to her eyes. "My goodness! This is beautiful, Anna!"

Peter wrapped his arms around Anna's slender shoulders. "Thank you. What a precious reminder that God will provide. I'll treasure this, Anna." His eyes filled with tears and he coughed. He took the drawing from Catharine. "I'm off to bed now," he said, shuffling toward the screen door. "Are you coming?"

"I'll be in directly. I want to enjoy the cooler night air we've been blessed with," Catharine answered.

No sooner had the door closed behind Peter than they saw Greta and Bryan walking back up the drive as they held hands, but Greta's eyes were red-rimmed. What now? She had been all smiles when they left.

Catharine watched as Greta stood by Bryan and he gave her a long kiss, then mounted his horse. He gave her one last look, tipped his hat, and then was gone, cantering away without looking back.

"What's wrong? You've been crying." Anna approached Greta on the steps. Greta opened her mouth to speak but burst into uncontrollable sobs.

Catharine turned to Anna. "Gather your things and go on in and get ready for bed."

"But—" Anna started to protest, but Catharine gave her a gentle push, indicating she needed to be alone with Greta. Anna reluctantly plodded back to the other end of the porch to gather her art supplies, glancing one last time at them.

Catharine laid an arm across Greta's shoulder and pulled her to a chair next to hers. "Greta. Whatever is wrong?" It hurt Catharine to see her sister this way.

Greta hiccuped, and Catharine reached inside her pocket for a handkerchief. Greta blew her nose but continued to cry softly, not meeting Catharine's eyes.

"Whatever it is, do you want to talk about it?" Catharine asked.

Greta finally faced her sister. "Bryan has been reassigned from Fort Russell to Fort Bridger. He came to tell me good-bye." More tears fell as Greta fingered the locket around her neck. "We love each other, but what can we do? He leaves in the morning at dawn." Greta's eyes searched Catharine's for answers.

Would it never end? Just when she thought things were going to get better, now she had a brokenhearted Greta on her hands. "For how long? Did he say he'd come back for you?"

"At this point it's permanent. No, he didn't say he was coming back for me, just that we could write to each other, and that if he got leave, he may be able to come see me." Greta's face crumpled again, and Catharine held her hand and let her cry it out.

"I'm so sorry, Greta. But if it's meant to be and he loves you as much as you say he does, then he'll be back or send for you."

Greta's eyes glistened through swollen eyelids. "You really think so?"

"Yes, I do. And you can write him every day." Catharine hoped she was right. She knew Greta's heart was shattered, but Bryan had never said he wanted to marry her—at least, she wasn't aware of it.

Anna tiptoed over, her art box stuck under one arm, and reached over to pat Greta on the shoulder. "I'm sorry," she whispered. "It's his loss, you know."

Greta turned in her chair, her face twisted in a frown. "He didn't *want* to leave me, Anna. The army is making him!"

Anna clamped her mouth shut and backed away, then reached for the screen door. "Sorry. Good night."

Anna never ceased to amaze Catharine with her keen sense of intuition. She hoped she and Anna were wrong in this instance. Time would tell. She reached down and pulled Greta up by the hand. "Let's go inside now. Go get your nightgown on and hop into bed, and I'll fix you a nice cup of chamomile tea. Tomorrow you'll feel better, after a good night's sleep. Things won't always look so bad."

Catharine led Greta to her room, then returned moments later to find her in her gown sitting on the bed. She was thankful that Anna was still downstairs cleaning her paintbrushes so she could speak with Greta alone. Greta's eyes were swollen and her face blotchy from crying as she idly braided her hair.

"I've brought you a good cup of tea. The chamomile should help you sleep." Catharine handed her the Blue Willow cup and saucer.

Greta murmured her thanks and took a few sips. "Thank you, Cath. I'm acting like such a baby, aren't I? It's not anything like your own trials. It's hard to imagine how you must have felt about Karl after what you went through."

"Each person's problems are not insignificant. Even though someone else might have had a worse situation, yours is still real and important to you . . . and to me." She took a seat on the edge of the bed, not wanting to think about the past.

"You are the most understanding person. I think that must be your gift." Greta sniffed into her hanky, then gazed at her sister. "You know, Cath, I feel terrible thinking only of myself. You've been more distracted and tired lately—and I don't mean since the grasshoppers descended on us. Are you feeling well?"

Catharine sucked in a deep breath. *Might as well tell her, I've already told Angelina.* "I'm going to have a baby."

"*What?*" Greta squealed. "And you haven't told me or Anna? Does Peter know?" Greta jolted up from where she leaned against the headboard, nearly spilling her tea. "That explains why you've looked a little peaked lately."

"There was just so much going on. I wasn't certain until your birthday and didn't want to take away from your day. Then the grasshoppers came, and Peter's been so down . . ." She stared down at her hands and rubbed them together.

"This is wonderful news, especially for you. I can hardly wait!" She leaned forward and hugged Catharine. "But you must tell Peter."

"I intend to. I just wanted to give him a little time to absorb what's happened to the crop. The grasshoppers didn't leave much that was green around here."

"But this will make him so happy." Greta swallowed the last sip of tea and set the empty cup on the nightstand. "God has blessed you again, and that's a precious thing."

"I'm not sure if Peter will be happy. He has more of us to take care of. Last year he had only himself to be concerned about."

"Will you tell Anna?" Greta asked, scooting back down against her pillow.

Catharine got up to leave, giving a low chuckle. "I will now. Angelina knows too. I hadn't intended to tell her—I just blurted it out when we were planning your birthday." She leaned down and smoothed the hair on Greta's brow. "Try and get some sleep."

Greta grabbed her hand. "None of us deserves your devotion, but I'm so glad that we have it."

"I'll always watch out for you and Anna. Don't ever forget that."

Greta smiled and closed her eyes, and Catharine quietly slipped out.

27

Peter was loading the fifty-pound bags of fertilizer he'd bought at the general store when he heard someone call his name. Turning around, he spied Thomas Sturgis—Tom to his peers—walking toward him.

Tom extended his hand in greeting. "How are you, Peter? Were you hit hard by the grasshoppers?"

Peter gave his hand a hearty shake. Tom's warm, friendly nature made him a favorite of the community and of the Wyoming Stock Growers Association, where he'd held the office of secretary for many years. He was struggling to maintain his own ranch after the winter blizzard.

"Unfortunately, yes. I didn't lose my entire crop, but most of it. I won't make much money this year, that's for sure, but last year it was far worse. It really gets a man down, you know?"

"I'm really sorry about that. You can always consider ranching, but I have to tell you, I can't promise cattle ranching will ever be the same again. Many of the ranchers have already left to head back East or look for more lucrative work."

Peter chuckled. "I've given it some thought before, but not seriously."

"Tell you what." Tom rubbed his jaw. "Why don't you come to our annual reception at the end of the month at the Cheyenne Social Club? You can be my guest and rub shoulders with the ranchers and get their take firsthand."

Peter propped his foot on the back of the wagon and crossed his arms over his leg. "I'll give it some thought and ask Catharine. I've heard it's quite the event. Would that mean she'd need a new dress?"

Tom leaned his head back and laughed heartily. "You know women—any excuse to buy something new. But yes, it's definitely dress-up time. You'd have to wear black and one of those stiff white shirt fronts."

"You mean those fancy things I heard call *Herefords*?"

"Yep! That'd be it." Tom tipped his hat. "I gotta run. I have an appointment to keep. I hope to see you there."

"You just might," Peter called out, watching Tom walk away. Well . . . it could be an alternative, and something he'd have to learn along the way, since he knew nothing about cattle. Who was to say another blizzard might not hit next year?

Leaving the wagon, he hurried over to the post office, but there was no mail, and as he was leaving, he ran smack-dab into his mother on the sidewalk.

"Son, you nearly toppled me over," Clara said as he steadied her by the arm.

"Mother, I'm sorry. I wasn't paying attention to where I was going. I had other things on my mind."

"I can see that, but I'm glad that we ran into each other. It's all over town that east of the city, grasshoppers descended on some of the farmers again. How did the crop fare?"

He heaved a sigh. "Not good, but not a total loss. I dug

trenches and set out bait, but I don't think I did it soon enough. I wasn't expecting it." They started walking down the sidewalk in no particular direction.

"I'm very sorry." She laid a hand on his forearm. "You know, I have a little money set aside if you have need of it."

Peter had no doubt that she would loan him the money, but he didn't want to be beholden to her. "I'll be all right."

"But, Peter, what will you do? It takes money to run a farm. Why not take the money from me?"

She gave him a look as though he was two sandwiches short of a picnic. He almost laughed out loud but stifled it, not wanting to rile her.

"Care to have a cup of coffee at Mario's place? I'd like to talk to you, but not out here on the sidewalk." Clara paused, looking up at him.

"Mother . . ." Peter put a hand on his hip.

Clara held up a hand in protest. "This is important or I wouldn't ask you." Her eyes were pleading. When had he ever been able to stop her?

"Okay, but I've got a lot to do back at the farm, and I told Catharine that I'd pick up some fresh vegetables since our garden was mowed down." They turned around and headed toward Mario's Ristorante.

Mario smiled as soon as he saw Peter, but his smile faded when he saw Clara. "Hello, my friends. You're too late for breakfast and too early for lunch. My guess is that you're here for coffee, no?" He indicated the first table they came to.

"Hello, Mario. You're exactly right. Could you seat us somewhere more private?" Clara asked.

Mario cocked an eyebrow at Peter, who only lifted his shoulders in resignation. "But of course . . . as you wish.

Follow me." He guided them halfway back where it was empty. "How's this?" He bowed slightly, draping a crisp linen napkin across his arm.

"Perfect!" Clara said. "Say hello to Angelina for me."

"She's gone shopping for britches with the twins. They're growing faster than we can keep them in clothes." Mario chuckled. "I'll return with your coffee in just a moment or two." He hurried off to the kitchen and soon returned with their drinks.

Clara waited until Peter had taken a drink of Mario's strong brew before saying a word. Peter felt uneasy. He thought this must have something to do with Catharine again, and he readied himself.

"Peter, Mac gave me more information about Catharine—"

"Why are you still digging into Catharine's past?" he said, his jaw clenching. "I'm married to her now, so what difference will it make?"

Clara blinked. "I'm afraid that you acted in haste where she's concerned. Mac has found proof from his solicitor in Amsterdam that she was married before." Her face was dead serious.

"I don't believe Mac," he said.

Clara reached inside her reticule and pulled out a piece of paper, opening it flat on the table between them. "This document is proof enough. It's a signed copy by Catharine's own clergy in Amsterdam."

Peter's blood turned to ice as he read the document. So it was true! And her husband's name was Karl. He swallowed the lump in his throat. Why hadn't she told him? She'd had three months to do so.

"Just because she was married before doesn't make her

unworthy of marriage to me." Peter tried to sound convincing, but his brain was scattered. He didn't know what to think.

"Peter, it gets worse. They can find no proof that she was ever divorced." Clara leaned over to bridge the space between them. "I'm sorry, but I felt you had to know. I wanted to make sure she wasn't just a gold digger and a ticket to America at your expense. She was probably flat broke, you know." Clara chewed her bottom lip.

Hot anger flashed through him. He was mad at his mother for investigating his wife, but most of all he was angry that Catharine had never told him. He tried to collect his thoughts as he thumped his thumb against the document, staring at the name of her husband. Karl Johnsen. He had a name. She was his first love, not him. Why would she hurt him like this? There was no way he could begin to understand her deceit.

"Peter . . . are you all right?"

His heart had all but stopped and he felt numb. Lifting his head, he studied his mother for a long moment. No doubt she cared for him and wanted to make sure no one took advantage of him, but now she'd just destroyed the one sweet thing he thought he had in his life.

"Of course there has to be a divorce decree, or she wouldn't have married me. Catharine is not like that." Peter could feel the thudding of his pulse in his neck. *Am I sure she wouldn't do that to me?* He didn't feel sure about anything right now.

"I'm telling you what Mac uncovered, and so far no record of divorce was found on file at the courthouse."

"Now, let me tell *you* something about Catharine, because you've never even asked me about her. She was from a very wealthy and prominent family, and her father was a shipping magnate. Her parents were on a buying venture to France when they encountered a terrible storm at sea. The boat sank, and with it, the entire inventory he was bringing back to Amsterdam. Catharine is well bred and well educated, yet she decided to become a wheat farmer's wife. We began to care for each other through our correspondence, no matter if she was married before!"

"That's all very well and good, and I'm sorry she lost her parents, but, Peter, don't you see? Even if she was divorced, where was she to go without a dowry or any visible means of support?"

"Did it ever occur to you, Mother, that she might have wanted a new life after her parents died, leaving her as guardian of her two younger sisters?" Peter expelled air from his lungs.

"I suppose you could be right. But why wouldn't she tell you about her first marriage? Perhaps she thought you wouldn't want to marry her then, and you could have married Dorothy." Clara drained her coffee and set the cup down.

Mario scurried over and they both became quiet. "Can I get you anything else? A refill perhaps?"

"No thank you, Mario. We're just leaving." Peter fished in his pocket for money and laid it on the table.

"Oh, so soon? But you've just arrived." He poured more coffee anyway. That was Mario's way. If you said you weren't hungry, he placed food in front of you, convincing you that you were. "I'll leave you two and go get ready for my lunch crowd." He backed away. Peter could tell that Mario knew something was up but had the good grace not to ask. "Ciao!"

"Goodbye," Clara mumbled.

When Mario was out of earshot, Peter answered his mother. "I don't know why she didn't tell me, but it's really none of your business now. It's time you accept the fact that Dorothy and I were just friends. Nothing more. Why don't you go see your dear friend Mac? He seems to have all the answers you could possibly ever want!" Peter rose and Clara did too.

"I'm really sorry, Peter. I truly was beginning to catch a glimpse of what it is you like about Catharine at the birthday party the other night. And as for Mac, he's become very dear to me."

"I'm not surprised, with all the money you paid him to do this."

"I'll have you know that he loves me and we've been spending a lot of time together, so you may as well get used to seeing a lot more of him around here," Clara said.

"You want me to accept Mac, Mother, but it's too bad you didn't do your part to get to know Catharine the way I do. When he gets the divorce decree, let me know. Notice I said *when*, not *if*. I've got to go." Peter stalked out of the restaurant without looking back. He passed Angelina returning from shopping with the twins, and though he normally would've stopped to tussle with the boys, today he only muttered hello and kept going.

"Clara, whatever is wrong with Peter?" Angelina asked as Clara was leaving. "Is he so upset about the crop that he can't talk to an old friend?"

"You'd be better off asking him. It seems Catharine is not at all what he thought." Clara huffed and continued on out of the restaurant without another word.

28

Never had Peter felt as alone as he did after the conversation with his mother. *Why, Lord? Why would Catharine withhold this from me? It makes no sense. Maybe she was afraid that I wouldn't send for her and marry her if she told me the truth. Would I?* Peter sighed and was overcome with weariness. It was hard enough just trying to hold the farm together, much less this.

An idea suddenly occurred to him. He'd overheard Joe Hankins in the general store saying the widow Lucy Hayes needed a handyman for repairs around her homestead before she left for England. He could stop at her place on his way back home. He considered himself a good carpenter, and it might be able to help him break even. That is, if she hadn't hired anyone yet.

Peter had met Lucy when she married and joined the church. Some people looked down their noses at her because of her reputation with the men at the local saloon. But that was in her past, before she'd given her heart to the Lord. Peter gave her the benefit of the doubt. After all, who was he to decide the condition of her soul?

With that in mind, he'd drop by her place before he went home. He needed the time to mull over what his mother had told him. He wanted to wait and find out if Mac got word of an official divorce before he confronted Catharine. But how was he supposed to act normal? She'd see right through him. *I'll just have to work longer hours. Lord, help me,* he pleaded. He clicked the reins, urging Star to pick up his pace.

It wasn't long before Lucy's homestead came into view, and he guided his wagon to a standstill just outside her picket fence. She must have heard him because the front door swung open. She smiled and walked outside.

"Well, land of Goshen! What brings you to see this ol' lady?" Lucy wiped her hands on her apron. Silver threads now dusted the hairline at her temples, and there were wrinkles around her eyes when she smiled. She was still a good-looking woman but was older than he remembered, and there was more meat on her bones than the last time he'd seen her. She'd taken her husband Lefty's death hard.

"Howdy, Mrs. Hayes." Peter climbed down from the wagon and walked to the porch steps.

"Oh, gracious, please call me Lucy. I'm not *that* much older than you," she said with a giggle. "Come on in and sit a spell. I'll get us something cool to drink."

"Thanks, but I'm on my way back home. I've spent the last several days trying to clean up the debris left behind from the locusts." Peter propped his foot up on the steps, removed his hat, and ran his hand through his hair. "I bet you're glad you're not farming now."

"I certainly am." Her face softened. "I heard about the grasshoppers. "I'm sorry. Were you hit hard?"

"Not as bad as last year but bad enough, which is the reason

I stopped by. I overheard in town that you needed a handyman before you take a trip. Have you hired someone yet?"

Peter couldn't believe he was asking for a job. All he really had to do was borrow from his mother. On an ordinary day he would have, but not after today. He was too angry with her.

"I haven't. No one has even asked me about the job. But you're a true answer to prayer. I've heard nothing but good things about you. I want to leave soon for England for the winter, but before I close up the house, there are a few things that need fixing around here. Mostly outside repairs, but a few inside too."

Peter swallowed his pride. "Then I'd be mighty obliged for the work."

"Sure thing. That would benefit both of us then. When can you start?"

"Day after tomorrow. There are a few loose ends at my place to take care of first. Will that work?"

"It will indeed. Why don't you come inside and I'll show you the leak I have around the dining room window. Lucky for me, we haven't had any rain lately, but I know it's only a matter of time. I don't want my hardwood floors to be ruined."

He followed her inside and inspected the window, quickly locating a gap in the window seal around the frame. "I'll need to bring a few things to fix the seal. I can tackle that first thing for you."

She clasped her hands in front of her. "That'd take a great load off my mind. Sure you don't want anything to drink?"

"On second thought, I could use a glass of water if it's no trouble. My throat is parched from the dust."

"It's no trouble at all. Have a seat and take a load off your feet. I'll be back in just a moment."

She left him standing in the dining room. It was the first

time he'd ever been inside her home, and he was mildly surprised at how tidy and homey it was. She had the normal whatnots and doilies, but what caught his eye was the beautiful cherry hutch filled with Blue Willow dishes. Now wouldn't Catharine just have a conniption if she saw this? He walked closer for a better look. *Wait, I'm supposed to be mad at her. Why do I care if she'd like this display at all?*

Lucy returned and handed him a tall glass of water. "I see you're admiring my Blue Willow. Have you ever seen it before?"

"My wife Catharine brought a couple of pieces with her from Holland. She had a set of her mother's, but most of it was broken during a storm at sea, though she salvaged a few pieces. It's right pretty, ma'am."

"Yes, it is. Lefty insisted that I have it, though I rarely entertain. Most people around Cheyenne don't want to associate with me." Lucy's bottom lip quivered and Peter was afraid she was going to cry.

"I'm sorry about that. Sometimes people have a hard time accepting a big change in a person's character." He gulped the water.

Lucy's face turned pink. "I've tried so hard, but I can't do enough to prove to them that I've changed, can I?"

Peter searched for the right words to say. "Probably not for some, but you need to remember the ones who *do* accept you . . . kinda like the way the Lord sees us."

"You're right, and I'm very grateful for those few friends." She motioned with her hand. "Let's step outside and I'll show you where some shingles are missing."

He was glad she'd changed the subject.

Before he left, he asked her to make a list of everything

she needed him to repair, promising to return after breakfast in a day or so.

Peter was taking a longer time in town than Catharine thought he'd planned to today. He was in a mood she couldn't seem to penetrate. No matter, she had plenty to keep her busy. Tonight she'd boil chicken for the dumplings that Peter loved. She'd finally learned from watching him and was able to roll out the dough to make them light and fluffy. But she wanted to squeeze in a little nap before starting supper if she could. She was having trouble keeping her eyes open lately and knew it was from the pregnancy.

Catharine slipped off her dress before lying down. The sheets felt cool against her cheek, and the smoothness of the pillowcase was somehow comforting. After a few moments daydreaming of Peter's warm kisses and sweet embraces, she fell asleep. She dreamed of a gentle prairie breeze skimming the plentiful wheat fields, undulating like waves over the beautiful golden grains, their heads seeming to bow to their maker. Peter moved toward her slowly, holding out his hands to the child in Catharine's arms. Lifting the little girl above his head, he swung her around while sunlight played on their shoulders. Catharine breathed a deep sigh of contentment and love for the blessing of her new family . . .

Someone tapped on the bedroom door, pulling Catharine away from the tranquility of her dream. "Come in. I'm awake." Catharine looked at the clock and then at Anna. "Sorry, I should have been up by now. Is Peter home?"

"Hello, sleepyhead. I think Peter is in the barn, though he hasn't been back for long. Greta and I started supper."

Catharine got up and shimmied back into her housedress. "Oh my! He'll think I'm a lazy wife."

Anna giggled as she buttoned the back of Catharine's dress. "He'll think no such thing. Now that you're going to have a baby . . ."

"Shh. I haven't told him yet. He has too much on his mind at the moment. But I'm glad I told you and Greta. It was hard to keep the news to myself."

"I can hardly wait. It's so dull around here. But you know I'll be in school most of the time. I can't imagine how much fun it will be." Her face shone with excitement. "There, you're all buttoned now."

"I had the most incredible dream," Catharine said. "I had a little girl, and Peter and I were in a wheat field that was ripe for harvest, with the sun shining down on us."

"Mother always said that God speaks to some through dreams." Anna's face was serious. "Maybe that means the wheat will grow in abundance and your baby will be healthy."

Catharine pondered her words. "I think I'd like to believe it was a sign from God that everything is going to be all right this time." She grabbed her apron. "Let's go, I have dumplings to roll out."

Peter barely made it home in time for supper, and as soon as he'd eaten he made a hasty exit, mumbling something about working some more on clearing the field while the sun was still up. By the time he came in and washed up, Catharine was in bed, sleepy but waiting for him. He climbed in bed, and she marveled at the well-defined muscles in his biceps and across his chest and stomach.

She reached out to stroke his chest lightly and remarked, "You have a farmer's tan on your neck, hands, and forearms." She laughed softly. Peter flinched and didn't pull her to him the way he normally did. "Are you tired?"

"I guess I am. I want to finish clearing the field tomorrow." He folded his arms to his chest, then turned away from her.

"You know, I'll be glad to help you," she said, continuing to touch him, delighting in the feel of his skin. She scooted closer. She wanted him to hold her and kiss her and was surprised when he didn't.

"No, you have plenty to do with the garden and the cooking," he mumbled.

He must be really tired, she thought. She lay against him and listened to his breathing, wanting him as she finally drifted off to sleep.

Peter listened to the even breathing of his wife, steeling himself not to touch her in spite of the stroking of her fingers. He feigned sleep, but the image of her full breasts and shapely form that he'd glimpsed through her nightgown was embedded on his brain. She was beautiful, but he was hoarding anger and was torn in two—the desire was strong to make love to her and hold her all through the night, but at the same time he wanted to demand the truth.

He stifled the words. He'd know soon enough. Rest assured his mother wouldn't relax until she had all the facts.

29

Catharine lifted the willow basket with the sheets she'd laundered, and as she lifted her broad-brimmed straw hat from its peg, a folded note fell out. Her heart skipped a beat. Peter must have stuck it in there before he left. She hurried outside and sat down on the back steps, not far from the clothesline, before opening the note.

Catharine,

I know I've been a little short with you lately, and I apologize. I guess I've had a lot on my mind after losing the wheat crop. I'm still adjusting to having a wife and her sisters as part of my life now. Three totally different personalities can confuse a man just a bit. I pray that you won't have any more bad dreams since they seem to affect your normally cheerful spirit. Thanks for your sweet note to me. I know that I'm not without my faults, but I believe we can grow closer as we learn more about one another. Everything will work out if we give each other time.

Warmly, Peter

Catharine blinked back tears. She admonished herself for not being sensitive about his adjustment to all of them living in his house. Losing the crop income had been a big blow too.

A smile crossed her face at the mention of her note to him. Sooner or later they would have to be more comfortable to talk openly, and she would tell him about her past.

Catharine tucked the note in her apron pocket and hung the sheets in the bright sun. She loved the way the outdoor smell kissed the laundry with a fresh fragrance all its own. If she could only bottle the smell, she could easily supplement their income. She smiled at the thought. But it was one of those tiny gifts from God that most people never took the time to notice.

A bead of perspiration formed on her upper lip from the heat, so she finished hanging the last pillowcase, then picked up her basket and went back inside.

Greta was working the iron back and forth on a dress, her face serious. "You know, Cath, soon you won't be lifting a heavy laundry basket."

Catharine smiled at her sister. "Guess that means you'll be taking this chore over for me, then?" she teased, trying to get a smile out of Greta. But her sister's facial expression didn't change.

Catharine sucked in a deep breath, a pang in her heart for her sister's hurt. Bryan's leaving had been hard on Greta, and Catharine felt helpless. Only time would heal a broken heart—she knew that firsthand. But hearts did heal.

"You know I will," Greta said. "I'm almost through ironing, and if you don't need anything else from me, I'm going to go write Bryan a letter."

"You go ahead and do that. I think I'm going to lie down

before starting supper. Between the heat and this sleepiness, my energy starts waning about this time of day. What's Anna up to?"

Greta hung the freshly ironed frock on a hanger and put away the ironing board. "She mentioned something about going to the creek to paint, but what she *really* means is she's going to go cool off in the water to get out of doing chores."

"I can't fault her there. I hope this dry spell breaks soon. I'm tempted to join her, but I'm too sleepy to walk anywhere at the moment."

"Go on and rest. There's plenty of time before we start supper."

Catharine rubbed the small of her back. "I won't argue with that."

Later in the week a sudden rain hit without warning, drenching Catharine before she could reach the front porch of the house. Greta and Anna were right behind her, laughing with joy and thoroughly enjoying the pelting rain.

"Ahh . . . it smells so fresh and invigorating," Catharine said, hugging her arms across her chest. She looked out at the rain, wondering of Peter's whereabouts. Lately he'd been leaving right after breakfast and returning just in time for supper. She knew there was always plenty to do around the farm, so she didn't question that he rarely came in for lunch.

She stared hard as if he might appear through the pouring rain. *How foolish! He could be holed up in a line shack or under the protection of a stand of trees instead of fighting the rain just to come inside.* A large clap of thunder made her jump.

Greta shrieked and ran straight for the door. "We need

to get inside," she urged, just as lightning lit up the sky and the barren field.

"I agree. Come on, Anna. Let's go in and get out of these wet clothes. We'll have to plant the rest of the vegetables tomorrow." All three of them left their muddy brogans on the porch and padded inside in their socks.

"At least the rain will be good for the plants that Angelina brought," Anna said. "I love tomatoes and those other funny plants—what did she call them?"

"Summer squash and eggplant. They're supposed to be quite tasty, according to Angelina. She cooks them in place of meat sometimes in her dishes."

"Humph! I can't imagine," Greta said as they climbed the stairs to change clothes. "I wonder if Bryan has ever eaten that."

"You'll have to ask him in your next letter," Catharine said. "Why don't we meet back downstairs and have some hot tea and cookies while we wait for the rain to stop."

"Sure thing," Anna agreed, moving past Greta through their bedroom door.

Catharine hurriedly slipped off her work dress, draped it across the back of a chair, and toweled herself dry. She rubbed her hair with a towel while gazing out the window. The rain was coming down in torrents. Where was Peter? Was he safe? She prayed he was, then plucked another work dress off the hanger and quickly donned it. With a swift stab of a couple of pins, she knotted her long hair into a chignon, picked up her Bible, and headed back downstairs.

Just as Peter was packing up his tools outside the dining room window, he heard the rumble of thunder. He had just enough time to store them in his canvas bag before the rain fell in sheets. *Lucky I got that window sealed properly in the nick of time.* The wind blew hard, and he held his hat down on his head to keep from losing it.

Lucy opened the front door, motioning with her arm for him to hurry inside. As he hesitated, she waved harder, so he went up the steps and placed his bag next to the door.

"You can't be out in this weather, Peter. Time you took a break," she said once he was inside. "Come on into the kitchen. I just took out apple cake. I'll pour us some coffee."

Peter knew it was no use protesting. Once the lightning stopped and the rain slacked, he'd be on his way home. These storms never lasted long. "The apple cake smells wonderful," he said as he pulled out a kitchen chair.

"It was Lefty's favorite. Not too sweet, but sweet enough." Lucy busied herself slicing them both a huge chunk of cake, then poured two steaming cups of coffee.

"These apples from your orchard?" Peter asked, lifting a forkful of cake.

"Gracious, no. I couldn't grow an apple tree if I tried. They're canned by Dorothy Miller. You know her, don't you?" Lucy took a chair across from him.

This close to her, Peter could see how much she'd aged, but she had a spark in her eyes and a lot of energy in her step. A fully alive attitude. That must be what had kept her going since her husband died. "Yes, I know her. Nice lady." He savored the taste of the warm cake in his mouth and chased it down with the coffee.

Lucy eyed him. "That's right . . . weren't you two court-ing at one time? Seems I remember seeing you together at church." She lifted her cup and looked at him over its brim.

Peter shifted in his chair. "We were together a lot . . . and still are friends, but no, we were never serious, much to my mother's disappointment. But I did care for Dorothy."

"I see. Tell me, Peter, are you happy with your bride?" Her eyes penetrated his but softened with sincerity. "What is her name again?"

"Her name is Catharine, and of course I'm happy. Why do you ask?"

Lucy lifted the coffeepot from the stove and poured them each another cup. "I'm not rightly sure, but I sense something amiss when a man married only a few months doesn't rush home as soon as his work is done. And you don't smile much for someone who says he's happy. Of course, you can tell me to shut my mouth and I'll just mind my own business. I reckon I always speak my mind." She laughed. "Lefty always said I had the eyes of a hawk when it comes to seeing right through people."

Peter wasn't used to someone talking so bluntly and realized how intuitive Lucy was. He glanced up from his dessert and swallowed hard, then expelled a deep sigh. "There's a problem with my mother . . ."

"Well, that's not so unusual. Mothers feel like they've lost their sons when they get married. But I know your mother. She'll get used to the idea, as long as you include her in your life—"

"I'm afraid it's not that simple, Lucy. I didn't tell her I was getting married or, for that matter, corresponding with a mail-order bride. She handpicked Dorothy for me, but she just wouldn't listen. So I never told her about Catharine. When she found out, she was certain that Catharine was after my money, my land, and a chance to go to America."

"Well, let her think what she wants. The truth will bear out." Lucy wiped the crumbs from her mouth with a napkin.

"If only it were that simple. Mother hired an investigator and told me that Catharine has been married before." Peter's heart squeezed as he said the words out loud.

"It doesn't make Catharine any less your wife and someone you love." Lucy's forehead wrinkled as she regarded him with concern.

"That's not all the story. The investigator believes she was never divorced." Peter spoke the word *divorced* so quietly that he wasn't sure Lucy had heard him, because she didn't react immediately.

"Oh . . . I'm so sorry. Catharine never told you any of this?" The surprise was evident in Lucy's face.

"No, never. It's bad enough that she kept it a secret from me, but worse if she never got a divorce in the first place." Peter clenched his fist on the table. "Then there is no real marriage." It was embarrassing to admit this, and now he'd be the laughingstock of Cheyenne, not to mention a lawbreaker.

Lucy reached over, taking Peter's clenched fist in her own until his fingers relaxed. "Peter, try to remember things are not always what they seem. If there's one thing I've learned from my past mistakes, it's not to take everything at face value. I trusted no one until the good Lord came into my heart. Now I listen to His direction. Maybe Catharine is having a hard time trusting anyone completely and there's a reason for it." She patted his hand and leaned back in her chair. "What do you really believe? Didn't you trust her before all this?"

Peter lifted his head to look her in the eye. "I did. I cared deeply for her and thought there were no secrets between us. We knew everything there was to know about each other."

"Mmm . . . so you'd told her about your relationship with Dorothy then? Seems as though I remember watching Catharine from across the room at church that day when you introduced them. She seemed very surprised, almost hurt, and I could tell she thought Dorothy was competition."

Peter jerked up in his chair. "You could tell that from a few short moments? It never entered my mind." He was quiet for a moment. "You know, I didn't tell her about Dorothy in our correspondence. Maybe I should have, but I never intended on marrying Dorothy."

"But don't you see, you held back a part of yourself—"

"That's not a fair comparison. Catharine already being married is something altogether different!" Peter felt the heat rising up his neck in his defense.

Lucy sat quietly as he contemplated the truth. He guessed she was right. He hadn't told Catharine about Dorothy. He had no real motive not to—he'd conveniently just omitted it.

The rain had stopped and it was time to leave. Peter reached for his hat on the chair next to him.

"I think you should go home and have a talk with your wife," Lucy said, stacking their dishes. "Ask her about her past and tell her how you knew. Give her a chance to defend herself, and you'll find out the truth."

Peter stood, holding his hat in his hands. "Thanks for the cake and for your advice, even though it stings. I'll try talking to Catharine, but it won't be easy."

"Swallow your pride and don't let it come between you two. It won't be easy, but you can't go on this way either. You've already lost most of the wheat crop. Admit it, you don't want to lose Catharine too."

He clapped his hat on his head a little harder than he'd

intended. "I reckon not, but she's gonna have a lot of explaining to do."

Lucy followed him to the door. "I'll be praying."

Peter's shoulders drooped as he sighed. "I appreciate it, and I'm going to need it. Thanks again, Lucy. You're a wise friend."

Lucy smiled and waved goodbye while he strapped his canvas tool bag to the back of his horse, then headed home to Catharine.

30

The rain fell in steady sheets, and the wind howled about the farmhouse, but Catharine and her sisters were safely ensconced in the cozy living room with hot tea and ginger cookies. The ginger kept her queasiness under control. *Please protect this child growing inside me, Lord.* Catharine patted her abdomen.

Greta was working a cross-stitch sampler, and Anna was reading Mark Twain's *Huckleberry Finn*.

Catharine set her cup down and picked up her Bible. "I'm glad we're getting rain finally. Perhaps now it'll cool down a little. But the rain makes me think of home."

"Me too. Amsterdam had cool springtimes and summer showers." Greta paused in her needlework. "Cooler temperatures would be nice too. I wonder if Peter is holed up somewhere in this downpour."

"Mmm, I don't know, but surely he would seek protection. I think the worst of it has passed now. I haven't heard any more thunder." Catharine smiled at her sister. "I'm glad you received a letter from Bryan. I believe that's the reason for the perpetual smile on your face?"

Greta giggled. "It's obvious, huh? Yes, he says he misses me. He'll come to see me the first weekend he has free."

"He's more than welcome to stay with us."

"I'm glad he's coming. I like Bryan. I think he'll make you a good husband," Anna said, peering over her book.

Greta shot her a look. "He hasn't spoken of marriage yet." Her face colored.

"Just a matter of time, dear sis." Anna went back to her book.

Greta turned back to her sewing and Catharine opened her Bible, but her mind wandered back to yesterday when she and Anna had driven to town to check the mail. On the way back home, she passed Lucy Hayes's farmhouse. She spotted the attractive widow standing outside talking to Peter. Had he just stopped in to say hello?

Something was dreadfully wrong. Peter hadn't touched Catharine since the day after the locusts came, other than a perfunctory kiss when he left after breakfast. She sighed and started reading in Matthew where she'd left off yesterday. She wanted to finish chapter ten. The first part of verse twenty-seven pricked her conscience: "What I tell you in darkness, that speak ye in light."

You should tell Peter the truth about your past. The voice in her head was almost audible.

I know, Lord. He deserves the truth. Catharine decided to tell him tonight when they retired to their room, away from her sisters. *Lord, give me the right words to say . . .*

Peter braced himself for what he knew would be a difficult evening. On the way home, he decided there was no use putting off the inevitable. He would talk to Catharine right after supper. Clear the air and get it all out in the open, letting the chips fall where they may. That's what his father always told him when he had something unpleasant to deal with. Which was most of what Lucy had said to him this afternoon.

He led Star to his stall and, after a quick rubdown, gave him some oats and fresh water. He wiped his carpentry tools and put them away. "Time I faced the problem, Star, and quit stalling for time," he said, stopping to pat his neck affectionately before leaving. Star snorted as if in total agreement, and Peter laughed softly.

When Catharine saw him come into the kitchen, she laid the ladle down and walked up to him, giving him a kiss. Her cheeks were flushed from the heat of the stove, and as usual she wore whatever she was trying to cook on her apron. It almost made him chuckle looking at her, but he gathered his wits about him and merely squeezed her hand.

"Go wash up. Supper will be ready in about ten minutes." She stepped back to the stove, opened the oven, and placed the rolls inside, then busied herself setting the table. "That was some kind of rain, wasn't it?"

Was she acting different somehow, or was it because his mind was in turmoil and he was imagining it? "It wasn't so bad. I've been in worse."

She started making gravy and stirred the bubbling grease until it browned, then added the flour. She poked out her bottom lip to blow away a length of hair that fell across her eyes. She'd never looked more adorable to him than when she was attempting to whip up an entire meal by herself. Her cooking had improved with the aid of a cookbook and occasional help from him.

He wished she knew how much he loved her, but his heart wrenched in pain with the knowledge that she once loved someone enough to marry him. He wished he wasn't jealous and confused. He wished none of this was true. He wished he could sweep her into his arms and take her to bed and cover her with his love. But he wasn't sure of the truth now, so that wouldn't happen. Not now. He gulped. He hoped his uncertainties wouldn't last forever.

She turned to see him still standing there looking at her, and she gave him a lopsided smile. "You're still here? Could you call the girls when you go wash up?"

"Sure thing." Peter knew his voice sounded flat. She smiled, and he twirled on his boot heel, hurrying from the kitchen.

When Greta and Anna went up to their room early, Catharine knew she would have to make a move to open the conversation with Peter, who sat in his favorite overstuffed chair, flipping through the Montgomery Ward catalog. It was as though her sisters sensed she needed to be alone with him. He'd been quiet throughout supper. She couldn't put her finger on it, but something wasn't right. Did he already know?

Catharine took the seat closest to him and leaned over the catalog. "What are you studying so intently in the catalog?" She was close enough to smell the scent of fresh soap from his quick wash before their meal. Her hands felt clammy and she licked her lips, trying to get the nerve to broach the real subject on her heart.

"I was looking at all the latest farming implements. I wonder if I shouldn't take a harder look at raising cattle after the last couple of years of locust problems." His eyes locked onto hers.

"Next year will be better."

"How can you possibly know?"

She smiled. "I dreamed of a beautiful field full of ripe grain ready to be harvested."

Peter raised an eyebrow. "Is that so? I'm not sure I believe in dreams."

"Well, it was a most pleasant dream, and I believe God speaks to us sometimes through dreams." Catharine fingered the ring on her left hand. She wanted to tell him the rest of her dream, but her tongue felt thick.

"I'm not sure about that either. But we were invited to the Cheyenne Social Club's annual reception."

"I thought that was only for cattlemen."

He continued flipping the pages of the catalog. She loved his hands and long fingers, wishing she could feel them gripping hers in love.

"I reckon they can invite anyone they want to as their guests."

"Peter . . ." She didn't know where to start.

"Hmm?" he said without lifting his head.

"Could you please look at me?"

"What, Catharine?" He glanced at her, then studied the images of new plows.

Catharine wanted to snatch the catalog from his hands. She moved closer, and Peter looked up with surprise. "I need you to look at me, please."

"I'm looking. What do you wish to talk about?"

Her shoulders lifted, then sagged. "For starters, where have you been going every day after breakfast?" Catharine's heart was in her throat as she waited for his answer. All she could think about was the lovely widow Lucy.

Peter turned in his seat to face her squarely, his eyes not revealing anything. "I guess I should have told you . . . I've been doing carpentry work for Lucy Hayes."

"You have?" Catharine felt a moment of relief. "But why?"

"Because the crop failed, I now have four mouths to feed and bills to pay, and I refuse to borrow from my mother!" he spat out.

His reaction alarmed her, and she wasn't sure how to proceed. He didn't know that he'd soon have five mouths to feed.

"I'm sorry. I didn't mean to raise my voice. There's a lot on my mind."

"Yes, I've noticed. We don't talk anymore, and you kept your working for Lucy a secret. I'm your wife—you could've confided in me."

Peter stood up, raked his hand through his hair, and paced the floor before speaking. "Confided in you? You mean have confidence in you?"

She looked at him in surprise. "Of course."

He shook his head. "Of course . . . just like that . . . just like you keep confidence in me?"

"Certainly I do."

He bent over and stared into her eyes until she felt pinned in the chair. "No, you don't," he whispered. "You keep secrets, Catharine."

She felt her heart plummet. *He knows* . . . This was not going the way she'd planned at all. "What secrets?" she asked under her breath.

"Your first marriage—or have you totally forgotten about it?" Peter's face was dark with fury.

Catharine froze, feeling all the blood drain from her face, feeling light-headed. She'd wanted to be the one to tell him. So much for her best-laid plans to be honest about everything. Slowly she rose from her chair on wooden legs. "How . . . did you find out? That's what I was going to talk to you about tonight . . ."

Peter flinched. "Is that so? Then why, pray tell, did you keep something like this from me?" he said through clenched teeth. She reached to touch his sleeve, but he pulled his arm away, and as he did his hand knocked over her Blue Willow teacup and saucer, sending them crashing to the floor and breaking into a thousand pieces. "I can't believe you would do that. You held my heart in your hands." He clenched his fists.

If he was angry enough, would he strike her? She shrank back. Catharine didn't think he would, but one never knew another totally, completely.

"I . . . didn't want to tell you . . . because . . . you may not have wanted me then. I know that was wrong to do, and I'm sorry."

"You're right! I wouldn't want to be married to someone who is still married to someone else. Now what do we do, Catharine? *Tell me that!*" he yelled. Drawing closer, he pointed his finger at her. "So it is true! I knew I should've believed the facts my mother discovered."

He said it with such anger that she recoiled. The blood rushed to her stomach, causing instant nausea, and she swayed on her feet, but Peter seemed unaware or didn't care one way or the other.

"Like the way she believed Dorothy was better for you than me?" Her voice wavered and her mouth was as dry as flour. She held her hand across her stomach to keep from heaving.

Please, Lord . . . help me. Keep me from being sick. "Peter, I can explain. It's not at all like you think!"

He spread his legs apart and crossed his arms across his chest. "I'm waiting."

Catharine gulped in air, then expelled it. She couldn't bear to look Peter in the face but stared past him, gazing out the window at the prairie beyond. "I fell in love with a man named Karl Johnsen. My parents disapproved, but I was in love and wouldn't listen to their warnings. Later he started drinking, and I found out there was another woman . . . and then another . . . but by then we had a baby girl named Lina." Catharine choked on the words and paused to calm her racing heart. She blinked back the tears flooding her eyes and tried to stay in control enough to finish her story.

"Lina was a colicky baby and cried a lot, which was something Karl could not tolerate. One evening when Karl was out drinking with his friends, Lina was particularly fussy. I got her calm, so I stepped out into our garden, just to hear the silence. It wasn't long before I heard her crying again, so I went back inside to soothe her." Her chin started to tremble and her breathing became shallow. "As I reached the nursery door . . . Karl was holding Lina, shaking her hard." Catharine squeezed her eyes shut. "Before I could get to her . . . the crying suddenly stopped."

Tears slid down Catharine's face, and she felt numb at the retelling of the worst moment of her life. "Lina's face was blue . . . and she . . . ." Catharine put her fist to her mouth and opened her eyes. "Lina wasn't breathing . . . We both stood there. Then Karl suddenly ran from the house. Even today, I can still smell the alcohol on his breath."

Shifting her gaze from the window to Peter, still rooted to

the same spot, she saw the look of shock in his eyes. Catharine felt nothing in her heart but pain—and a sharp pang of love for the babe she was carrying. But now Peter would never know that because she had seen the disgust on his face.

She knew that her reaction was in part displaced anger from all the past hurt in her first marriage and from losing Lina. At the same time, she felt justified withholding the truth because Peter had distanced himself from her in more ways than one. First with believing his mother, and then with his working secretly for Lucy Hayes. Catharine admonished herself for thinking it had been more than that with Lucy. Her heart knew better, but he should have talked to her about it.

With a flat voice, she said, "I realize now that you *never* really trusted me but trusted your mother."

Why wouldn't he say something? Anything? She'd hoped in the last few months that Peter had grown to love her. She stared down at her prized Blue Willow, representing the pieces of her heart that had just shattered.

"Would you like to see the divorce paper or the death certificate of my baby before you'll believe me instead of your mother?"

He opened his mouth to speak, but when not a word came out, Catharine felt she had no choice. She whirled on her heel and fled up the stairs. By not answering her, he gave a clear indication that he didn't want her as his wife anymore. When she reached the landing she called out to Greta and Anna. Looking surprised, they rushed into the hallway.

"Whatever is wrong, Cath?" Greta asked. Anna's blue eyes were wide with unease.

She turned them by the shoulders and pushed them through the doorway of the bedroom. "Hurry, pack a small bag and meet me downstairs in ten minutes. I'll explain when we're on the road to Cheyenne!" When they hesitated in disbelief, their mouths open, she snapped, "There's no time to quibble. *Schiet op*. Hurry up. *Now!*"

Catharine was sure they thought she'd lost her mind, but in fact, she believed she'd just found it.

31

It was several seconds before Peter moved in the direction of the stairs. He had to go to her. He'd never imagined she'd hidden behind a mask of pain so terrible. It was even harder to believe that a man would shake his baby hard enough to cause her death. Bile rose up in his throat when he tried to imagine the scene and suffering Catharine had endured. He couldn't begin to imagine. Somehow it didn't matter that she had kept it from him now. He'd misjudged her.

He took the stairs two at a time and was breathing hard when he reached their bedroom. The door was standing wide open. "What are you doing?" He watched her as she slammed her satchel on the bed and hurriedly started filling it with her clothes and sundry items.

"I'm leaving, and my sisters will come with me. Our marriage is not based on mutual trust, and not love either, I guess."

He slumped, his hands on his hips, not daring to touch her when she was so furious. "Catharine, I'm so sorry. I should've been more forthcoming."

"Sorry?" She harrumphed, then walked over to the dressing table to pick up her brush and comb. He thought she might

285

throw them at him and was ready to duck, but instead she crossed the distance to their bed, her heels striking sharply against the hardwood floor. She tossed the dresser set into the bag with fury. Peter had never seen her this angry before.

"I want to take a horse and wagon, and I'll have them returned to you as soon as I can." Her movements were so jerky that her hair came unpinned and tumbled down about her shoulders.

"Where are you going? Stop this nonsense!" Peter knew his attempts to stop her sounded lame.

"No, *you* stop it, Peter! You never trusted me, and I suppose your mother gave you reason enough not to. I'm sorry I kept it from you, but I trusted *you*. When I met you, I had no idea that you'd had a relationship with Dorothy just short of marriage, so I wasn't sure how to act when I was around her. I figured she was in love with you, and that hurt. And now you tell me you've been at the widow Hayes's, and you talk about trust to me? I knew when I finally got the courage to tell you about my past, you'd be angry." She hung her head, then snapped the bag closed. "Please step aside."

"Catharine . . ."

Peter felt helpless and emotionally drained. There was nothing he could do but let her go. Maybe she was right . . . they shouldn't be married. He was confused but at the same time felt pity for her sad past. He moved just as Greta and Anna arrived at the doorway with questioning faces.

"Peter . . . what's going on?" Greta asked.

He looked from Greta to Catharine. "Ask your sister."

"Catharine, can I please take the pups?" Anna pleaded.

"*Nee*. I'm sorry. Peter will have to find homes for them. Let's go hitch the wagon, Greta."

Anna started to sniffle, apparently thoroughly confused at the situation that had developed, and stared at Peter. He couldn't bear to meet Anna's or Greta's eyes, but stood help- lessly by with his hands at his sides while all three raced down the stairs. He heard the slam of the front door, and their chatter followed them out to the barn.

His eyes took in the rumpled bed where he and Catharine had become man and wife a few short months ago. In the beginning he'd felt a strange distance between them. Then later total abandonment as she came to trust him. Now he understood why, and his heart squeezed in his chest. It was like Lucy said—Catharine had terrible pain in her past but was willing to leave her homeland to try and start over again.

His head ached. He walked over to the dressing table, picked up her lilac toilette water, and sniffed it. A tear slid out of the corner of his eye as he remembered her soft scent and the feel of her against him. God help him. He knew that he loved her despite her hiding the past, but how could they make this all work? He believed the tragic tale of the baby and didn't need to see a death certificate, but what about the divorce from Karl Johnsen?

Suddenly he realized that it didn't matter anymore—the man was out of her life now. Peter loved her and knew deep in his heart that Catharine was worthy of his love.

He was thoroughly bewildered about what to do now and felt deep compassion for her loss. He could understand why she would divorce a man who had killed her child, and one who wasn't faithful as well. In part, he could understand her reasoning for *not* telling him for fear of rejection and humili- ation. She had no parents and had to care for two sisters she was deeply devoted to.

What had been her motive for wanting to marry him? He wasn't sure, but he intended to find out.

Clara smiled when she read the note a messenger had delivered to her earlier in the morning. Mac wanted to take her on a trip with him to Boston and asked her to meet him at the Rollins Hotel to discuss the details. Excitement filled her. Was Boston where his family lived? It seemed he had mentioned that once before. Surely he wanted to introduce her to them. Clara was breathless at the very thought, not to mention being with Mac. Maybe then she would get his undivided attention for once. *Oh, goodness, what should I pack for a weekend? I want to look my best. Perhaps a new hat?*

The sun felt good on her back as she strolled to his hotel, and her spirits were high. Never in a million years would she have guessed she could feel like this about someone again. It was hard to hide her smile as she entered the hotel lobby.

"I'm here to see Mac Foster," she said to the manager. "Please let him know Clara Andersen is here for our appointment." Clara squared her shoulders.

The manager gazed at her. "He said he was expecting you but had to run out for a few minutes. He asked that I give you a key to his room and said to tell you he'll be back shortly and to make yourself at home."

Clara was mildly surprised but tried not to show it. It was just like Mac to think of a last-minute errand that he'd forgotten. "Of course, thank you," she said, taking the key in her hand.

"It's the second floor, fifth room on your right." The manager smiled. She walked up the stairs, pretending not to be aware of his eyes on her.

She felt a little uncomfortable meeting in Mac's room, but she knew it was just until he arrived and they went to have lunch or whatever he had planned. The thudding of her heart kept time to the sound of her heels against the carpeted hall runner.

She could hardly wait to see him again. He exuded energy and excitement, even if he was forgetful. She'd have to learn to overlook that bad habit of his. She loved his contagious smile. Even when they didn't agree about a particular subject, their disagreement always ended amicably. After all, she was sure that at her age, there were probably one or two things he didn't like about her either.

She slipped the key in the lock, turned the knob, and stepped into the living quarters that Mac called home for the most part. It smelled of stale air and cigars. Funny, he'd never smoked around her. She went over to the window and shoved it open to get some fresh air inside. Turning around, she saw a pair of pants slung over a chair, a shirt hanging haphazardly from the knob on a chest of drawers, and a pile of papers strewn about the small desktop next to the bed. An ironing board and iron stood in the corner with a suit coat that had been freshly pressed laying on it.

She began to tidy up to waste time more than anything. Besides, she didn't mind doing this for the man she loved and took her breath away. She hung the pants and shirt on hangers, then walked over to the desk. She thought to merely shove the stacks of paper together to form one tidy stack, but they were in such disarray that she had to divide the mess to make any headway toward creating a neater stack. Just as she was about finished, one document in particular caught her attention. It was dated April 20 and had the crest of a solicitor in Holland. She squinted to read the details, then carried it over to the window for better light. She skimmed the paper and her hand began to shake. It was Catharine Andersen's divorce decree, dated nearly six months ago!

Clara's wobbly legs carried her to the side of the bed, where she sank down onto the lumpy mattress. A sick feeling clenched her heart. Mac had known all along that Catharine was indeed divorced. Why hadn't he told her?

Reality hit her hard in the chest. *Because he simply didn't want to!* Her mind reeled and tears burned her eyes. Peter would never forgive her even when she told him the truth. Regrettably, she wished she'd never felt compelled to delve into Catharine's background. She knew it was, in part, because she'd felt slighted when he hadn't told her he'd been corresponding with a mail-order bride all those months.

Clara stood and squared her shoulders. Mac better have a good reason for not telling her. But no answer would be good enough, she reasoned with herself. Had she gotten mixed signals from him? He'd told her more than once how much he cared for her and missed her when he was on an investigation trip. But did she mean as much to him as he did to her? A pounding headache was beginning to build behind her eyes.

The sound of a key in the lock snapped Clara upright as she held the paper in her hands.

Mac hurried in and flashed her one of his endearing smiles. "My sweet, I'm glad to see your pretty face this morning!" He kissed her soundly on the mouth, then pulled her close to nuzzle her ear. His lips tasted of mint mouthwash, and their delicious softness gave her pause, but she stiffened, determined not to respond to his touch. He released her and stepped back. "What's that look on your face for?" His eyes studied hers intently.

"This!" Clara waved the document in front of his face. "What is the meaning of this, Mac?"

"Calm down and take a deep breath, then tell me what you're talking about."

"You know very well what I'm referring to, so please don't pretend you don't!"

Mac looked at the paper she held in her hands. "Oh, that," he said quietly. "I planned to tell you this weekend."

"Why? How long have you known?" Her heart sank when he didn't say there had been some mistake. She stuffed the document into her reticule.

Mac stroked her arms. "I didn't want to lose you, so I waited, wanting to get to know you better. I've been so happy since I met you. Haven't you felt the same way?"

She pulled away from his embrace. "Yes, I have . . . but you've withheld the truth, Mac, and let me accuse Catharine of something far worse than was fair. And I've created a big rift in my relationship with my son. How could you do that to me?" Clara's voice trembled.

Mac's face became sober. "I told you. I thought if you knew that I'd already uncovered the divorce decree, you wouldn't have anything to do with me. I don't have a big home to take you to or money to support you in the style you're ac-customed to here in Cheyenne. I thought you knew that." His eyes softened as he gazed longingly at her. He'd never looked more serious than he did at this moment. "I'm always on the road traveling to wherever my next investigation takes me. But this time I want to take you with me."

He reached in his coat pocket and pulled out two train tickets, holding them up in front of her to see. "I've bought us tickets to Boston for a week. Say you'll go with me and we'll have a grand time, just you and me, Clara. I don't want to go alone this time."

"Is that where your family lives? Are you taking me to meet them?" she asked, trying to sort everything out.

"No. I just wanted you to go with me on this trip. My family is scattered around—it's just the way I live. Please say you will forgive me, Clara. You can tell Peter that Catharine was divorced properly and we can be on our way. No harm done."

He put the tickets back in his pocket, then pulled her into his arms. Cupping her neck in his hand, he tenderly pulled her to him, gently kissed her brow and cheek, then tasted her mouth again with deep longing. She slid her arms around his waist, feeling his strong back muscles.

Clara longed to stay in the tenderness of his embrace. It would be so easy to give in and travel with him, enjoying the fun his energy caused. Life would not be dull with Mac. But would she ever be able to trust him? He'd broken his word to her more than once, but this was the worst.

Slowly she removed herself from his grip and stared into the face of the man she loved so much yet knew so little about. "I'm sorry, I can't do this, Mac . . . it wouldn't be right. Unless . . . you're proposing marriage?"

Mac looked befuddled. "Well . . . I . . ." He shoved his hands in his pockets and didn't meet her eyes.

"Exactly. Just what I thought." Clara backed away toward the door, tears streaming down her face. Her heart turned to stone.

"Clara, wait!" Mac rushed to the door, trying to block her.

"I can't, Mac. I wish I didn't love you . . ." Blinded by tears, Clara turned and ran down the stairs, shutting out the future she'd thought she could have with Mac.

32

Catharine saw Clara trip at the bottom of the hotel stairs, and she ran smack into Catharine, who reached out to break her fall.

"Mrs. Andersen! Are you all right?" Catharine was surprised to run into Clara at the hotel, and she looked like she'd been crying.

"Excuse me . . . I'm sorry," the older lady gasped, holding her handkerchief to her mouth. She hurried on.

"What in heaven's name is wrong with Mrs. Andersen?" Anna asked.

Greta and Catharine started up the stairs to the room they'd all share. "I wish I knew," Catharine said.

They didn't have long to find out. Clara stopped at the hotel's front door and whirled around. "Catharine! Wait!" she called out, stepping toward them.

Catharine and her sisters stopped dead in their tracks and turned. Clara, her face crumpled in sadness, sniffed into her handkerchief. "I . . . need to tell you something. I'm sorry . . . so very sorry." She hiccuped, then wiped her eyes.

Catharine stood rooted to the spot. Greta and Anna stood on the stairs, peering from behind her shoulder.

"Peter's probably told you that I . . . I hired an investigator to look into your background. It was a stupid thing to do."

"Yes, he did, Mrs. Andersen . . . but please continue."

Clara met Catharine's eyes, pursing her lips tightly, then continued. "I was duped by Mac in more ways than one. I'm sorry for that. I never should've considered it in the first place. He first told me you weren't divorced, but he knew almost from the beginning that you were."

People in the lobby slowed as they passed, curious at the crying woman's apology, but Clara didn't seem to care that they were staring. "Please accept my sincerest apology. I can see now it was a thoughtless thing to do, and I know that I've caused you and Peter grief by my actions."

Catharine was more than surprised at this quick change of heart in Peter's mother, but her apology did seem sincere. She knew what she must do. With all the effort she could muster, she said, "Apology accepted, Mrs. Andersen. I should have told Peter the whole truth a long time ago."

Clara sniffed again, her lips trembling, as she fished in her reticule and handed a paper to Catharine. "Here's the proof of your divorce, in case you didn't have a copy."

Catharine took the document without even looking at it. "Thank you, Mrs. Andersen. I've been waiting for my copy to be mailed."

"Well then . . . I must go."

Anna slipped past Catharine and put her arms around Clara. "It will be all right, Mrs. Andersen. If Catharine says she forgives you, then you can believe she truly means it."

Clara nodded. "Thank you, Anna." She scurried out, leaving the three sisters stunned by the turn of events.

"Whew! This has been some kind of day, Cath," Greta said.

Catharine sighed. "Yes, it has. I don't know about you and Anna, but I'm really tired."

The accommodations at the Rollins Hotel were simple to nearly bare but clean. Very different from the Inter Ocean where they'd stayed when they'd first arrived in Cheyenne. Catharine couldn't afford the luxury of the Inter Ocean anyway while they decided where they would go. She wanted to catch the first train away from here, but to where?

There were two regular beds in the sparse room, two sitting chairs, and a small necessary room. Anna and Greta would share one bed and Catharine would take the other.

Anna looked around, setting her bag on the floor. "Mmm . . . I'd make us some hot tea, but we'd have to call room service," she said. "And you left your Blue Willow tea set behind."

"Ha! I don't believe this hotel has such a thing as room service, Anna!" Greta laughed. "You are just too spoiled, my little sister."

"I am not!" Anna protested with a pout, then smiled over at Catharine.

Catharine lay back on the bed pillows, closed her eyes, and covered them with her arm. "She's only teasing you, Anna. I don't plan to stay here any longer than we have to," she declared.

"We could go back now, Cath. Mrs. Andersen apologized, and she has the proof you need to show to Peter. The proof you've been waiting so long for." Greta took a seat next to her on the bed. "What do you think?"

"I think not! Why would I want to go back? He doesn't want me! Not after I kept the truth from him. When we're settled, I'll send Peter money to ship my tea set along with the rest of our belongings. "

Despite trying to stay in control for her sisters, Catharine started weeping and turned on her side, facing away from their pitying eyes. The pain in her heart was too much to bear. Even if she had proof of her divorce, she'd kept it from him, along with the truth of her baby. That was wrong.

Lord, please forgive me. I didn't mean to cause Peter any pain. But he wouldn't want me now. I just didn't know what to do, and now I've made a mess of things. She wondered if he would miss her, and her mind began reeling. *I'll soon be divorced again, with no home and a baby on the way and two sisters to provide for.* She groaned. Even with her sisters, she felt alone.

I'll never leave you or forsake you . . . you're not alone.

Catharine knew that in her head, but she couldn't make her heart understand.

Greta and Anna said nothing. Greta got up and pulled the side of the bedspread over Catharine to let her cry it out. "Anna, let's decide what we can do for supper," she whispered. Anna agreed and they moved to the other side of the room, talking softly.

The house was too quiet and the bed empty without Catharine, and since Peter couldn't sleep anyway, he went to sit on the porch to think. The evening prairie wind was peaceful, but it couldn't settle the restlessness he felt in his soul. Catharine was the best thing that had ever happened to him, but he'd have to face it—he may have lost her forever. He wished he could take back some of his words that he knew had hurt her, but he hurt too. His heart had ached when she'd said she'd been in love with Karl. Was she still? What happened to him after that night? Peter might not ever know and didn't really care as long as Catharine was free of Karl.

Peter had completed his work for Lucy, and she'd be leaving any day for England. Tomorrow he'd go over to pick up the pay she promised him and perhaps get her advice on what to do.

Prince and Baby bounded up the porch steps, begging for attention. He scooped them up and they licked his face, yapping. It wasn't long before their barking woke the other two puppies. Ginger and Sugar decided it must be playtime, and they came out from under the porch where they usually slept. Peter enjoyed the pups, but they only made him think of Anna and then Catharine. *Guess I'll just keep the little fellers.* He couldn't help smiling as they fought for a spot in his lap. But he dragged his feet when he went back inside to a silent house.

Fitful sleep and bad dreams left Peter feeling wiped out when the sun streaked through the sheers that draped the bedroom window. He grumbled about having overslept to the sleepy-eyed puppies, which were curled up at the foot of the bed. *Wouldn't Catharine be shocked if she knew?* He hurriedly dressed, gulped down his steaming coffee as soon as it was made, and munched on a day-old biscuit. After picking up his pay from Lucy, he'd consider whether to drive into Cheyenne to see if he could find Catharine. Would she give him an audience? He didn't know, and he surely didn't know what he would say, but he'd think on it.

He fed the farm animals, turned the cow out to pasture, and took the puppies outside to fill their dishes and water bowls. When he was in the barn to saddle his horse, he heard a horse and buggy drive up, and the puppies started yapping. *Catharine! She decided to come back!* He dropped the harness and raced out of the barn to the front yard. Disappointment filled him as she saw his mother pull up.

"Peter, Peter! I have to talk to you immediately."

He certainly didn't wish to chat with her. But for her to drive out to his farm at midmorning meant something was up.

Clara scrambled down from the wagon, laying her buggy whip aside. From the looks of the horse's heaving sides, she was in a rush. What was it this time? Confirmation from Mac that Catharine was divorced? *God, help me* . . . How had things gone from happy to dismal so quickly?

Standing inches from her, Peter could see her eyes were swollen. Apparently she'd been crying and hadn't slept much, from the look of the dark circles beneath her eyes. She was clearly upset. "Mother, what is wrong this time? More news from your hero, Mac?" he asked sarcastically.

Clara's face caved, and tears splashed down her cheeks. Peter hadn't seen his mother cry like this in years. He wasn't sure what to do, so he waited until she blew her nose and exhaled.

"Mac is not my . . . not my anything. It's terrible!"

If he wasn't sure before, Peter was certain now, from the sorrow on her face, that his mother was in love with Mac. It pained him to see her this way. "Mother, I'm so sorry—"

"Just listen to me, Peter. What I did was a terrible injustice to Catharine. Mac knew almost from the beginning that Catharine was divorced. He continued to lead me on."

Peter was confused. "He *knew*?"

Clara twisted her handkerchief in her hands. "Yes. He

298

received the paperwork proving it. Peter, can you ever forgive me?" Her bottom lip quivered. "I've driven a wedge between you and your wife, and I'm deeply sorry. I'm just a foolish old woman. I let my heart control my head." Her admission brought more tears.

He sucked in air and released it. "You're not a foolish old woman, and you know it. But because of all this, Catharine left."

Clara lifted her head and stared at her son. "Oh no . . . now I know why she was at the hotel when I left. I never thought to ask why she was there."

"You saw her?"

"Yes, and I apologized to her for my part in this. Peter, you must go to her."

"I'm the last person she wants to see. Come sit down and tell me everything." His anger mixed with pity as he guided her to the porch steps. The puppies followed, but Clara paid no mind. His once vital mother now looked small and frail somehow, and his heart squeezed tight. Lately that had been happening a lot.

"You said Mac had the document? Where is it now?" he asked once they were seated.

"Catharine has it now. I gave it to her. After all, I did pay for it. Peter, I'm so truly sorry to have caused her all this trouble. What a fool I've been. I wonder why she didn't tell you from the beginning."

Peter propped his elbows on his knees and clasped his hands together, closing his eyes briefly. "Because of the suffering she endured with her first husband, that's why." He related the story of Catharine's husband Karl and the death of their child. When he'd finished, Clara was weeping again. Peter reached over to take his mother's hand. "We'll get through this . . . but I don't know if Catharine can get past it. I'm so glad you apologized. That's a good start."

Clara wiped her tears. "That has to be the worst story I've ever heard."

"Can you imagine how Catharine felt as a mother?"

She shook her head. "No, I honestly can't." Clara shuddered. "Do you think we can start over, Peter?" She compressed her lips.

Their eyes met. "Only if Catharine wants a new beginning, but I wouldn't count on it. Right now I'm not high on her list of favorite people, and she was really angry when she left. I said things I shouldn't have, and regrettably, I didn't speak when I should have."

Clara rose. "I'm going home now, Peter. I'll take my cue from you, so let me know where I stand. But go find her. She's staying at the Rollins Hotel on Sixteenth Street. Maybe she hasn't left yet."

He stood too. "I will, but I have something that I need to take care of first." Peter walked his mother to the carriage. When she started to climb up, he stopped her long enough to give her a brief hug. "Mother, I'm sorry if Mac has hurt you, truly I am, and I want you to know . . . I forgive you. Sometime soon you can tell me all about Mac, if you want to."

Clara flung her arms around him, hugging hard, then pulled back and kissed his unshaven face. "Thank you. I love you, Son, and I do want to make it up to Catharine, if she'll let me."

After he assisted her up to the carriage seat, Peter said, "I'm not sure she'll come back. She was very upset."

"Nevertheless, you must try." Clara clicked the reins against the horse's rump and trotted out of the yard.

33

Catharine tied her bonnet tightly under her chin to ward off the brisk wind before leaving the hotel's lobby. During breakfast in the hotel's restaurant, she kept one eye on the door, hopeful that Peter would come charging in to declare his undying love for her, but there was no sign of him. No knight in shining armor.

Catharine's stomach had settled down by breakfast, allowing her to eat a few bites of toast and sip a cup of hot tea. She missed her coffee with Peter and realized she liked it almost as much as her tea. Almost, but not quite.

Greta was worried that she'd lose contact with Bryan, but Anna concerned herself only with the fate of the four puppies and Clara. She'd taken a liking to Clara for some reason that Catharine couldn't understand.

Catharine had suggested that they go as far as Fort Collins and then maybe on to Denver. She wanted to say goodbye to Angelina, then check on the price of tickets, so she left her sisters quibbling about their destination while they finished breakfast.

Hastening down the busy streets of Cheyenne, Catharine

was struck at how much she'd enjoyed living in Wyoming in her short time and had thoroughly embraced the West. She'd just have to get used to the idea of living in another city, another place, and another lifestyle. What kind of life, she had no idea. She certainly wouldn't be a mail-order bride again! Besides, who would take in a woman with her two sisters and a baby on the way?

Her heart felt like it might burst, and her shoulders sagged in despair. Perhaps Angelina could give her some advice. Catharine's money wouldn't last very long, and she hoped that wherever she was, she'd be settled long before the baby arrived and winter set in.

Stepping through the doorway of Mario's Ristorante, she saw Angelina in the back of the restaurant behind the big glass-encased counter, where delectable pastries were lined up to entice patrons. She was slicing cheese and looked up as Catharine approached.

"Hello, my friend." She laid the knife down and walked around the counter. "You're in town early. Are you here to shop?" She drew back when she caught the look on Catharine's face. "Is something wrong? You look terrible. Is it morning sickness? Is one of your sisters ill?" Angelina shot out her questions like a cannon.

"Oh, Angelina. I need some good advice, because I surely can't think straight." Catharine removed her bonnet as Angelina led her to a small table off to the side.

"Whatever is wrong, my dear?" She wiped her hands on her apron and sat across from Catharine.

Catharine took a deep breath. "Peter and I had a fight. I never got a chance to tell you that Clara was having me investigated by Mac Foster. She believed I was a homeless waif looking for a way to come to America and only after Peter's land and money!"

Angelina stared with obvious surprise. "Oh dear."

"I haven't told you the entire story—it gets worse. I . . ." She looked down at her lap. "I . . . was married before." It was hard to say the words out loud. *What must she think of me?*

"I see . . . So Clara told Peter, and—let me guess—you hadn't told him?"

"Right. I'm ashamed that I didn't, but I thought he wouldn't want to marry me if he knew my past."

"That's not so terrible, and I'm sure he would understand if you talked to him about it."

"I tried, but all we did was wind up arguing with each other, and then Peter yelled at me. Angelina, I left my husband because he . . . accidentally shook our baby until she stopped breathing . . . but that's not the only reason." Her voice trailed off, and she waited for her friend to say something.

Angelina's olive complexion drained of color. "Lord have mercy. How terrible, just terrible. Whatever did you do?"

"We divorced later because I could no longer live with him and look into his eyes every day, but my loathing for him started long before that." Catharine spoke in a monotone voice, devoid of emotion now.

Angelina reached over and laid her hand on top of Catharine's. "This must have been a nightmare for you." Compassion was evident in her face and voice.

"It was the worst day of my life. My husband started drinking right after our marriage, and there were . . . other women . . . but I forgave him. But after this, I couldn't stay married to him, even though I know he hadn't meant for our baby to die."

Angelina leaned back in her chair. "Peter didn't understand that?"

"No, because I kept it from him, and now he doesn't trust
me. Why would he?" Catharine dabbed her eyes with the
handkerchief Angelina offered. "I was afraid he still had feelings for Dorothy, and lately he'd been leaving every day and
not returning until supper, so I imagined all sorts of things."

"So it was an issue of trust for both of you." Angelina
shook her head. "This is a difficult thing you did—not telling Peter."

Catharine knew it wasn't a statement of condemnation
but of compassion. She looked Angelina squarely in the eye.
"I know that now, but I was so afraid. I didn't know what to
do. Can you understand?"

"Of course I can, but since you were divorced, I guess I
don't understand what the problem is." Angelina frowned.

Catharine chewed her bottom lip. "I was divorced for a year,
but my father's solicitor never sent me the sealed document as
proof, and for months I waited. During that period of time, I
started corresponding with Peter and never received my copy
before I left Amsterdam. I wrote my solicitor and gave him
my new address, and I've been looking for the document to
arrive in the mail any day now. The solicitor said the paperwork got lost or something and wasn't forwarded to me."

"Did Peter need actual proof over your word?" Angelina
pursed her lips and her brows shot up.

"Mac told Clara that they weren't able to find any proof
of a divorce, and that's all it took for her to turn against me.
I believe she thought she was protecting Peter." Catharine
rubbed her brow in frustration. "But she somehow found the
document and gave it to me last night. She also apologized."

Angelina tilted her head in surprise. "Clara apologized last night? Incredible!"

"I left Peter last night, Angelina. I figured he really didn't trust me. I haven't told him about this baby either, and I won't!"

"Tsk, tsk," Angelina said. "You're in troubled waters, my friend."

Catharine fell silent. Angelina was right.

"But that doesn't mean it's not fixable. With God all things are possible, especially when they look grim."

"My sisters and I are going to Fort Collins, then on to Denver. We can find jobs or something. I couldn't bear to live here and see Peter all the time."

"Don't do anything hasty. Peter deserves to be told about his baby, don't you think?"

The bell over the restaurant door jangled, and Angelina excused herself to go wait on a customer, leaving Catharine with her head in her hands. When she shut her eyes, all she could see was Peter.

Balmy skies and wind made for pleasant weather, the temperatures not as hot as the week before. But all that was lost on Peter. He had one thought, one focus in mind. He'd say goodbye to Lucy, wish her a pleasant trip to England, and thank her for the work she'd found for him to do. After he picked up his pay, he'd go straight to Cheyenne and find Catharine. There was already a hole in his heart from her absence, and the funny thing was he actually missed her sisters too. He prayed that God would put the right words in his mouth when he talked to Catharine. If he found her.

As Lucy's house came into view, he slowed the wagon and saw a large box on the front porch. She must've found something more for him to work on. Well, it would just have to wait.

Peter halted Star, then hopped down and strode up to the porch, glancing at the box as he passed it. He rang the doorbell, waited for a few minutes, then knocked. Where was Lucy? Hands on his hips, he turned around, considering what to do, when he spied a white envelope taped to the box. He pushed his hat back, squatted down, and lifted the envelope addressed to him, using his thumb to slide under the flap to open it.

Dear Peter,

I'm in Cheyenne to catch the train for my trip to England. I've written you a check for all the work you did for me on the house and barn, and I'm leaving a little bonus for you and Catharine in this box. It's my wedding gift to you, and I pray you'll have many happy days of using it. All I ask is a favor that you will watch over my place for me while I'm gone. I'll return in the spring, thus avoiding the harsh Wyoming winter.

I've been praying for you and Catharine, and I hope that everything will work out.

All my best,
Lucy Hayes

Peter whistled when he saw the check and put it and the letter in his shirt pocket.

Taking his pocketknife out, he popped the nails holding the top edge of the crate and loosened the lid. Pushing aside a mound of tissue paper, he was shocked to find the set of Blue Willow dishes nestled in the box. *Mercy me! Lucy, you shouldn't have done this.* What a wonderful thing for her to do.

He recalled their conversation the first day he'd been in her house. She'd remembered what he told her about Catharine liking Blue Willow but losing most of it. He thought of yesterday when he'd accidentally broken one of Catharine's Blue Willow teacups. He knew how much it meant to her and felt terrible, but it had been an accident. Peter struggled with the weight of the crate but managed to slide it into the back of the wagon. He was touched that Lucy would do something like this. If he could make amends with Catharine, she would love Lucy's gift, no doubt about that.

He flicked the reins and shouted "giddyap" to Star, and the wagon lumbered toward home. After a few minutes on the bumpy road, he pressured Star faster. Instead of going home first with the china, he'd go straight to Cheyenne. He had an idea . . .

Clara awoke sprawled facedown in her bed, one arm dangling off the bed where she'd dropped from exhaustion. Through the bleary, swollen slits of her eyes, she blinked, looked across the room, and moaned. For heaven's sake, her day dress was crumpled! Her nose was stuffy from crying and she was finding it hard to breathe with her face against the bed. She struggled to sit up, and the weight of all the recent events hit her like a hot prairie wind, burning her face with humiliation and hurt. She'd cried herself to sleep with thoughts of Catharine's shocked face, Peter's anguish, and Mac's admission. It was bad enough that she'd caused trouble for her son and his wife, but saying goodbye to Mac had torn her heart out.

How could she have been so blind? She had been certain he loved her. She shook her head and walked to the sink. After pouring water from the pitcher into the bowl, she splashed her face. She'd thought about it most of the day and hadn't wanted to believe the quiet voice in her head implying that there were differences in their beliefs. Mac had said as much before, and he said he didn't need to attend church and didn't need God. That's why he would promise to go but never showed up.

Had she let the desires of her heart overrule her head? A thought popped into her head and she tried to think it through. *"Don't cast your pearls before swine,"* or something *like that?* Now where had she read that? Somewhere in Matthew? She'd look it up later. But there was significant meaning in that verse for her, regarding Mac. There was much she had to make amends for. But first she'd have to find a way to get over her heartache.

She dressed and made herself some strong coffee, but she couldn't bear the thought of eating. Her stomach was in an uproar. She put her dishes in the sink and stood wondering what she should do as the long day stretched out before her.

The doorbell rang. She hurried to the front door and saw a messenger through the window. "Yes?" she asked when she swung open the door.

The adolescent delivery boy jumped back a step with her questioning frown. "Ma'am, I was to deliver this to you this morning."

"I'm sorry, I wasn't expecting anything this morning. I didn't mean to shout at you," Clara said, taking the small wrapped package from him.

"Aw, it's okay, I don't mind. But could you sign here for me?" The boy held out a tablet, and she scrawled her name on the printed space and dated it.

She reached inside her dress pocket and handed him a few coins. "Thanks, son."

He bobbed his thanks and traipsed back down the stone steps.

Clara went to the living room and sat by the window overlooking the street. She untied the string around the box and peeled off the paper wrapping. A letter and a set of beautiful tortoise-shell hair combs took her breath away. *Who in the world . . . ?* Opening the folded paper, she started to read the note.

My sweet . . . can I call you that? I think I always will. I'm sorry if I've hurt you, but I just couldn't see this working out with us. With me on the road all of the time, I couldn't expect you to give up your home in Cheyenne, or your church, or your son and, perhaps soon, grandchildren. I won't let you. And I do not want to be someone who wrecks lives or homes. Please understand it's not about love but practicality. And truth be told, I don't think I have your kind of strength, your accountability to life and love.

I'm enclosing a check for that last advance you gave me on the investigation. I never used it—it was just a way for you to think I needed further work on the case and to prolong our time together. We have had good memories together with lots of laughter.

*I care for you deeply, but I think this is best, so this is
goodbye. I hope you'll wear the combs in your beautiful
hair and think of me.*

Always,
Mac

Pain tore straight down the center of Clara's heart, ripping
it in two until it felt like stone. She stared at the letter, unable
to cry anymore. It was apparent that Mac had no concept
that God couldn't be confined to a building. God dwelled in
her heart. There were many churches where she could've felt
at home, as long as the truth was preached. Clara knew that
she'd made some mistakes and wasn't perfect, but God's love
for her and His forgiveness would see her through.

Mac spoke out of both sides of his mouth. It finally hit her
how selfish he was. Yes, he'd told her once that he *may* have
been in love with her, and he said all the right things when
it was good for him to do so. He was handsome, intelligent,
and full of energy, and she was going to miss that. He had
his faults, but she overlooked them, and her love for him had
been unconditional. That was the problem. Love sliced both
ways, but he took the choicest portion for himself—and gave
very little in return.

Clara leaned her head back in her chair, dropped the letter
to the floor, and closed her eyes. She prayed . . . prayed like
she never had before.

34

"Are you sure you want to do this?" Angelina crooked her arm around Catharine's and tilted her head to the side, giving Catharine a penetrating look. "I wish you'd at least think on it another few days."

Mario stood by with a sad look on his face, whether for Peter or for her, Catharine couldn't tell. "You all can stay with us instead of running away. We'd be a little crowded, but just until you made other arrangements." He scratched his head, thinking aloud. "I could use the extra help in the evenings. We're very busy at the restaurant, you know."

Catharine wiped a tear from the corner of her eye and sniffed into her handkerchief. She knew that Mario was just offering to hire them out of his desire to help, not because he really needed help. "I truly appreciate your thoughtful consideration to hire us, but I have no other choices. Staying here and running into Peter would make our lives too hard. I should have been honest with him from the beginning. He's never going to forgive me now." She crossed her arms and glanced over at Greta and Anna, who were sitting on a nearby bench surrounded by their bags.

The Union Pacific depot was bustling as usual with the arrival and departures of passengers, and any other time Catharine would be energized by all the activity. But now the beautiful depot only served as a reminder that she'd once been excited to meet her future husband.

"I can't thank you both enough for what your friendship has meant to me and my sisters. How can I ever repay you for your kindness?" Catharine sniffed again. "Where are the twins this afternoon? I wanted to say goodbye."

Mario twisted the ends of his mustache and looked around nervously, as though he expected them to come screaming through the depot. "You know how fickle kids at their age can be. Plus they don't like goodbyes and prefer playing in the park when they aren't helping out at the restaurant."

Anna left the bench and sidled up to Angelina. "You will check on the puppies or maybe help Peter find them good homes, won't you?"

Angelina hugged the girl. "I'll see what I can do . . . maybe we'll take one of them, right, Mario?" she asked.

Mario's eyes grew large. "Well . . . I can't say for sure . . . but yes, we'll give it some thought and I'll ask Angelo and Alfredo if they'd like one."

Anna seemed satisfied with Mario's answer, but Catharine was sad that they couldn't take them along.

Greta walked over to the group, saying, "Our train will be here in a few moments, Cath. We should say our goodbyes now."

"Yes, you're right," Angelina said. "We don't want you to miss your train. Once you're settled in Denver, please write us." Her eyes expressed warmth but threatened tears.

Catharine couldn't help but notice that Mario glanced

around in agitation, then pulled out his pocket watch to check the time. *He's probably not good with saying goodbye either.* Catharine knew it was hardly likely their paths would cross again, which made their goodbyes all the more poignant.

The UP personnel shouted the announcement that the train for Denver would be boarding in the next fifteen minutes.

Catharine twisted the wedding band on her finger. "Oh dear . . . I guess we must go now."

Mario smiled, looking past her shoulder, then leaned over to give her shoulder a squeeze. Angelina's sad face lit up and her mouth dropped open. Catharine turned to see what she was so shocked about, and her heart skipped a beat.

Peter's hands were shaking so hard that he thought he might drop his end of the box. Thankfully the twins carried the other side.

Before going to the hotel, Peter had dropped by and spoken briefly with Mario about his plan.

"Excellent idea! I'm glad you are going to go talk to Catharine." Mario shook his head. "Angelina and I were so saddened about all of this. You are doing what's right, Peter." Mario popped him on the back.

"I sure hope so, Mario. I don't want to live without her."

"Then go tell her. She's still at the Rollins Hotel for now, but Angelina said she didn't expect her to stay."

"I'm heading that way just as soon as I run by the bank with a deposit."

"Ciao!" Mario waved, watching Peter hurry off.

When he arrived at the hotel fifteen minutes later, the clerk told him that Catharine and her sisters had checked out moments before. He muttered under his breath in frustration. "Do you know where they might be headed? Another hotel?" he asked the doorman.

The doorman shrugged. "Mister, I don't have a clue where they were going, but they mentioned the UP depot. It's really none of my business, sir."

Peter took a silver dollar out of his pocket and slapped it in the doorman's hand. "Thanks!"

The doorman smiled broadly and yelled after him, "Thank *you*!"

Peter flew down the stairs to his wagon. Maybe he'd get there before the train left—it was just down the street. In moments he was zipping past carriages and buggies and flying past the park in front of the train depot. He spied Alfredo and Angelo playing catch with their baseball and mitts, right where Mario had said they'd be.

Peter stopped the buggy and hopped down. He called out to them and they ran up, hugging him. "I'm so glad you're here! Would you like to make some change helping me with a surprise?"

"Sure!" Alfredo said.

Angelo nodded eagerly. "Whaddya need?"

Peter leaned down to the twins and told them his plans. The boys were only too happy to help him out and scampered behind Peter to his wagon.

Now, as they entered the huge atrium of the Union Pacific depot, several curious passengers stopped to watch as Peter paused to look for Catharine. He spotted Mario smiling as he was giving Catharine a hug, and he winked conspiratorially at Peter over her shoulder. She was dressed in a green traveling dress with a crisp white blouse beneath her matching jacket.

Peter watched as Catharine slowly turned and saw him. Her drawn and pinched face shocked him. He froze. A sadder face he couldn't ever recall seeing. Not even his mother's crying had moved him the way the look in Catharine's eyes did. *A look of a crushed spirit or of resignation?* Peter swallowed, and his tongue stuck to the roof of his mouth, denying him the eloquent speech of forgiveness he'd planned. In that long moment they exchanged looks of hurt and raw feelings, and it was as if the two of them were all alone in the noisy, bustling train depot. Neither moved—each full of selfish pride.

Catharine didn't say a word but turned back around to continue with her goodbyes, then picked up her carpetbag.

"This crate's getting heavy. Can we please set it down now, Peter?" Alfredo begged, jarring Peter back to his senses.

"I'm sorry, boys. Yes, let's set it down right here." They set the crate on the floor.

Mario shot Peter a look of impatience, then motioned for him to go ahead and make his move. Peter was determined in his purpose.

"Catharine," he yelled across the wide atrium. His heart pounded as Catharine slowly turned back around and mouthed, "Peter . . ." She moved closer to him.

"Catharine, I'm sorry. I . . . never meant to say all the things I said. I don't care who or what has happened before. I only know I don't want to spend my life without you. If you'll forgive me, we could give this another try based on trust and love." Before she opened her mouth, Peter turned to the twins to whisper, "Okay, now, boys."

Alfredo lifted out a Blue Willow platter and handed it to Peter while Angelo was bent on one knee digging into the crate. Peter crossed the few feet to Catharine, holding the large platter at waist level as if serving her a meal. "If you will let it, this Blue Willow platter can represent my promise to fill your life with my trust and love and a houseful of children." He thrust the platter into her hands as Mario reached over and took the carpetbag from her. Surprise filled Catharine's face as she held the platter, looking unsure of what to do with Peter's apology and admission of love.

Peter turned, and Angelo handed him a teacup and saucer. "This is to replace the one that I accidentally broke. May your cup run over with goodness, mercy, and the plans we'll make together."

Peter enjoyed watching Catharine's reaction, which looked to be something between disbelief and pleasure. Greta was speechless for once. Angelina held her hands together in rapt attention, while Anna watched the scene unfold with her wide, innocent eyes.

Catharine clutched the dishes to herself. No doubt she was wondering where he'd gotten them. Hopefully there would be plenty of time to tell her later.

"I . . . I . . ." she stuttered.

Peter noticed the softening of her face. He was making headway and was encouraged by the look in her beautiful eyes. He continued on, aware that some people had stopped to watch. Alfredo stepped up and handed Peter a beautiful soup tureen.

"This, my dearest Catharine, can represent all the family and friends that gather around our table to celebrate holidays and good times."

She balanced the dishes stacked in her arms, but not a soul moved to assist. He saw the edge of her mouth quiver. Was she trying not to smile?

He wasn't through yet. Angelo handed him the salt and pepper shakers. "This is the spice you have added to my life so far, and without it I don't think I can exist." Catharine blinked at his admission. She stared agape at his unconventional method of apology.

Peter wondered if he looked like a fool, but he pressed on. He stepped over to Greta, and Alfredo handed him something. "Greta, I know you've had a rough time since Bryan left, and I don't know what the future holds for you, but I want you to take this Blue Willow cake server and slice your wedding cake with the groom God has for you."

Greta looked completely caught off guard. "Peter, it's beautiful. I promise you that I will use it for my own wedding." She stared down at the knife in her hand, turning it over to admire the delicate blue pattern on the china handle.

Peter turned to Anna. "Anna, I want you to take this cup and saucer to build your own Blue Willow set, but I don't want to see those puppies drinking out of the saucer." He chuckled, and he heard Angelina, Mario, and Greta laugh.

"But . . ." Anna looked at him curiously.

Peter snapped his fingers, and the twins lifted the puppies' box out of the crate, where he'd placed them before leaving for town. The boys placed the box of wiggling puppies at Anna's feet. "Now don't let the puppies out of the box here, but if each of you will come back home with me, you can keep all four puppies. I promise." Peter looked at Anna and felt fatherly tenderness toward her. "The house is lonely and quiet without all of you."

Anna's tears of joy spilled down her cheeks, and she was in Peter's arms instantly.

"Oh, Peter . . . I do hope we will," she said. She turned

to Catharine, who stood motionless, the Blue Willow dishes heaped high in her arms. Everyone held their breath, but Mario cleared his throat loudly, then nodded his head at Peter while the twins moved away. The train whistle blew, announcing its departure, and Catharine started.

"What's it going to be?" Peter strolled closer to Catharine. "Are those getting heavy? You don't have the bear the burden alone, Catharine. I'm sorry for all you've been through. Say you'll come back home where you belong."

"Oh, Peter," Catharine murmured, and Peter saw her eyes fill with tears. "I'm sorry for not telling you everything. Can we learn to trust again?" Catharine looked up at him, openness and honesty reflected in her eyes. "Are you sure you still want me—and my sisters—in your life?"

Peter could hear the twittering between the other three women. He reached out to take the dishes and handed them to Angelina and Mario. "We *are* family, aren't we?"

Catharine gave a slight nod and sniffed into her hanky.

"In that case, we can work through anything," he said, bracketing her face between his hands. He tenderly brushed a single tear from her cheek and felt love flow into his heart until every vein in his body tingled. "I love you, and I guess I did right from the start." She was his lovely, devoted Catharine, always concerned for others.

Catharine fell into his embrace, crying, and he showered her face and eyes with kisses. She whispered "I love you" in his ear.

The small group around them echoed their agreement with soft *ahh's* until finally Peter and Catharine pulled apart, but he didn't let go, and he promised himself that he never would. They stood leaning against each other, her head resting against his shoulder, overcome with emotion.

The twins expressed their feelings above the yapping of the puppies. "Yippee!" they yelled almost in unison. "Now can we go home?"

Everyone laughed, and Mario and Angelina carried the dishes back to the crate to pack them back up. Angelina wiped a tear or two from her eyes and sighed. "Ahh . . . so romantic, don't you think, Mario?" She gazed at Mario, who simply smiled at her and winked at Peter.

Anna knelt down to soothe the puppies clamoring to get out of the box. She lifted Prince and hugged him tightly to her chest while he nuzzled her with his nose. She stood and turned to them and said, "It's time to feed the puppies. Let's go home."

35

A happier group didn't exist, Catharine thought as the chatter and laughter spilled from the Andersens' wagons rumbling down the road. They had waved goodbye to the Cristinis with promises to have lunch after church on Sunday. Greta drove the wagon they'd taken to town, three of the puppies piled in the back and one in Anna's arms. Catharine pressed close to Peter's side on the wagon bench they shared, not wanting one inch to separate them. Her heart was full of gratitude and love that God had seen her through the defining exposure of her and Peter's wounded hearts. She remembered her mother saying once, "What man meant for evil, God meant for good." From now on, when she faced a difficult problem—and without a doubt there would be a few—she'd claim that promise.

She stole a glance at her husband's lean and handsome profile, letting her eyes slide down to his square, strong hands and nicely shaped nail beds. She remembered the way those hands had caressed her with tenderness and fervor. Catharine felt sudden desire surge through her, and her face grew warm at the thought. She would tell him about the baby when they got home, praying silently that he would be pleased about his new role as a father.

Peter took his eyes off the road a moment to smile back at her, a mischievous look in his eye. Blushing, she looked out across the field to enjoy the common yellow dandelions dotting the landscape. Purple pasture thistles nodded their heads at the tall yucca plants loaded with white blooms. The gentle motion of the wagon after a while made her eyes droop, and she struggled to keep them open. Besides the pregnancy making her tired, she was behind in the sleep department. Catharine felt like she could sleep an entire week.

"What are you thinking? Are you happy?" Peter broke her reverie.

She laid her hand on his knee. "Yes, Peter. I'm very happy and can hardly wait to get home. I've so much to do."

"Mmm . . ." He gave her a sly gaze. "Most of it can wait. It'll all be there tomorrow. If you're like me, you didn't get much sleep, so we can make up for that."

Catharine got his meaning and smiled shyly, patting his knee. "Yes, we can."

In a short while they were driving down the lane lined with maple and ash trees. "Those trees will be a scarlet red in the fall," he told Catharine.

"I'm really beginning to appreciate the unique beauty of Wyoming. It would have been hard to leave it."

He reached down and squeezed her hand. "I'm so glad you didn't."

"Peter, I should tell you more about my first marriage," Catharine said softly.

"There will be plenty of time to talk later on. I should

explain a few things myself." He patted her knee. "But let's just celebrate our love for now."

Catharine lifted her eyes to meet his. "That, Mr. Andersen, will be fine with me."

When they arrived, Peter set the brake on the wagon, then assisted Catharine down, holding her in his arms to give a welcome-home kiss, which lasted a little longer than was proper in the yard. They unloaded the dishes with Greta's help, and Anna let the puppies loose. They bounded from the wagon and ran around the yard chasing each other, happy not to be confined. Anna's laughter was music to Catharine's ears.

Like family once again, they shared their evening meal together, enjoying thick slices of roast beef piled high on creamy whipped potatoes and smothered in onions as Peter liked it. "I do believe you are fast becoming a good cook, my dear wife!"

"I agree," Greta said, wiping the last crumb from her mouth. "Either that or we're starving. I don't recall having lunch before we went to the railroad depot."

"We didn't," Anna said. "Catharine was afraid that we'd miss the last train. I'm so glad you got there before we boarded, Peter."

"And so am I, Anna," Peter said, giving her a wink.

Catharine rose, taking her plate to the sink. "I'm thinking you had a little advice and help from Mario," she teased.

"I'll never tell." Peter picked up his dish and walked over to caress Catharine on the nape of her neck, just below where her hair was pulled up into a chignon. "Why don't we put the

Blue Willow in the hutch while the girls clean up the kitchen? What do you say?"

"Okay . . . but what about your mother's rose china?" Catharine wiped her hands on the dish towel, anxious to be alone with Peter to tell him about the baby.

"I'll put it in the crate and she can have it back."

"Then let's get started. Greta, you and Anna don't mind, do you?"

"'Course not. It won't take long to clean up. Then I, for one, am headed to bed early." Greta gave Anna a quick look and a nod.

Anna frowned, then, seeming to suddenly understand, replied, "Oh . . . yes . . . so am I."

Catharine giggled and followed Peter to the dining room. She knew exactly how Greta's mind worked and was grateful.

With the rose dishes packed into the crate and the Blue Willow gracing the dining room hutch, Peter and Catharine stood back to admire their work. "It's so beautiful, isn't it? I don't think I told you thank you." Catharine scooted up to him and threw her arms around his neck. She touched her lips to his, lingering against his mouth until he pulled her tightly against him, kissing her with all the passion he'd been holding back the last few weeks.

She pulled away, teasing him with a soft laugh. "My goodness, Mr. Andersen . . . I can barely breathe."

"You can't stop love, and I love you, Mrs. Andersen." His eyes traveled to her throat, where her pulse beat rapidly. He stroked her arms, then pulled her against him again.

"Ahh . . . I love you too!" She led him toward the stairs,

untying her apron and letting the ties trail behind her pro-
vocatively. She paused on the first step to remove the apron
and laid it across the handrail, then grabbed his hand.

Peter looked thrilled at her open playfulness and followed
her up the staircase. Halfway to the top, they paused to embrace again, and she laid her head on his shoulder as they
continued up to the landing. Right before reaching their bedroom, Catharine paused in front of the attic door.

"Come with me," she said, turning the knob.

"What?" He regarded her with a confused look.

Catharine crooked a finger, motioning for him to follow her
up the dusty steps. Once in the attic, Catharine stopped and
knelt down to remove the heavy cloth covering Peter's baby
cradle. "Would you carry this down to our room, please?"

"Well . . . er . . . sure. Are you planning on decorating our
room with it? It's really dirty and old." Peter scratched his
chin.

Catharine knew he didn't have a clue. She stepped around
the cradle and lifted his hand to her lips and kissed it. "Peter,
how does the name Willow sound if we have a little girl?"
Her heart pounded in her chest as she waited for his answer.

"Willow . . . a little girl?" A look of incredible delight lit
up Peter's face, which then softened with tenderness. "Do
you mean that you—?"

Catharine nodded, barely able to breathe, tears welling up
in her eyes. Peter lifted her, swinging her around wildly until
they were breathless in the narrow space of the attic. Their
eyes locked and held with their own special caress.

"Willow, huh? I like it. I like it a whole lot, my love."

Epilogue

A few days later, Clara heard someone run up her porch steps and ring the doorbell. She peeked through the sheers, not sure she wanted company today, but was pleasantly surprised to see Anna. Swinging open the door, she immediately waved for Anna to come in before she noticed a puppy tucked under her arm. "Oh dear. You can't bring that thing in here, Anna!" Clara quickly moved aside, but Anna thrust the puppy into her arms, and it started licking her hands and squirming.

"Her name is Baby and she's already housebroken," Anna said, setting down the luggage she held in her other hand. "I thought since Mac left, she'd be a great companion for you . . . you know, to take your mind off of him."

Clara continued to hold the ball of fluff while Baby nipped at the pearls dangling from her neck. "Well . . . I've never had a dog of my own." In spite of herself, Clara stroked the puppy's back. It was so soft.

"She won't hurt you. See there? She likes you." Anna patted the puppy on the head. "She's one of my favorites of the

325

litter and she minds well, which I suppose you'd like. And we can fix her up a bed next to yours."

Clara watched in total surprise as the young slip of a girl picked up her suitcase and started up the stairs, her luggage banging against her leg with each step. "Where are you going, Anna?"

"You *did* ask me to live with you when school started, right? Well, I thought we'd better get more acquainted the week before. Which room would you like me to use during the week?"

Clara stood holding the puppy and looked up at Anna's bright blue eyes. "I . . . I guess you're correct . . . I did. Use the second room on the left."

"Well then, I guess it's settled."

"Will everyone else be coming over today, Anna?"

Anna turned at the top of the stairs and answered, "Oh, yes, ma'am. They're outside right now. I ran on ahead of them." She moved to the landing but paused to say, "Oh, and you'd better make room for grandkids, because one is already on the way."

Clara snapped her head around with an audible gasp, but Anna had disappeared. In just a matter of the ringing of a doorbell, her life had suddenly, drastically, and wonderfully changed . . . for the better.

Author's Note

Cheyenne, Wyoming, was aptly nicknamed the Magic City of the Plains and frequently referred to by its nickname in the local newspaper, the *Cheyenne Daily Leader*, as early as 1867. I was fascinated to learn that it was dubbed the Magic City because of its boom and rapid growth, after starting from a ramshackle city on the empty plains. Early on, bullwhackers, thousands of men, and a few hundred lewd women drank and gambled in the raw railroad town, bringing debauchery and violence, which left a stain on Cheyenne's reputation. Thankfully, Rev. Joseph W. Cook, an Episcopalian, set about to institute order in the community with the aid of other urban pioneers, starting churches and schools and civilizing its inhabitants.

I was simply in heaven on this trip of research, because this was, after all, cowboy country. When I visited, the first thing that struck me about Wyoming was the windswept prairie and wildlife. Walking the historic district of Cheyenne ignited my desire to photograph and read about the old buildings and homes that are still intact today. With such rich history, I tried to give a glimpse of its details in my story, but there is so much more that could be told.

Mail-order brides were a huge part of settling the West. My heroine was from Holland and many Dutch brides settled in Minnesota, but I took the liberty of having her travel to Wyoming to marry a wheat farmer.

Grasshoppers, or locusts, were a severe problem, not only in Wyoming but in many parts of the West. For reasons unknown, the Rocky Mountain grasshopper or locust is extinct now, as a result not of pesticides but of habitat loss. They destroyed entire crops very quickly. In 1877, Congress created the United States Entomological Commission to deal with the plight of the farmers caused by major locust crises.

My first glimpse at the Union Pacific depot as I entered the city of Cheyenne left a lasting impression on me. With its multicolored sandstone and pitched roof resembling a castle, I decided it would be the starting point in my novel. I marveled at the details of the building and enjoyed the museum there. By the time my heroine arrives, the clock tower has not yet been erected and wouldn't be until 1890. There was a beautiful park in front of the depot with trees, a bronze cannon, and a fountain, all of which is still there today.

Most of the government, commercial, and residential buildings owe their significant design to William Dubois, a prominent architect of Cheyenne. The Inter Ocean Hotel on Sixteenth and Capitol Street is the hotel where Peter arranged for Catharine to stay when she arrived. It was built by Barney Ford, a former slave, and was considered one of the finest in Cheyenne.

Laramie County courthouse on Eighteenth Street was built in 1872, with an adjoining structure in the rear that was the jail and sheriff's residence. In 1903, Tom Horn, a notorious hired assassin, was hanged in the jail's yard.

Bryan takes Greta to a classy speakeasy, the Tivoli. The three-story Victorian brick building is still standing today and is being restored. It was rumored that the upstairs was a brothel and had hidden passages.

The Rollins Hotel where Catharine takes her sisters was one of the first hotels constructed in 1867. It boasted a bath house, a bar and billiard room, and a barbershop and could accommodate two hundred guests. The Depot Exchange Café was a popular café owned by Leopold Kabis, a restaurateur and caterer.

The stylish brick Terrace Row where Clara lived was built in 1883 on Eighteenth Street and was nestled between Capitol and Carey Street.

Warren's Emporium, where Peter takes Catharine when she arrives in Cheyenne, opened in 1884 to provide women with an extraordinary shopping experience. It was built by Francis Emroy Warren, an ambitious and successful mayor who became governor of Wyoming territory from 1885–86, and again later in 1889–90. The building is no longer there.

Helen Warren, the first lady of Wyoming, was a sweet and gracious woman. She was a prominent member of Cheyenne's society and was responsible for helping establish the First Baptist Church, of which she was a stalwart member. The original church building became unsafe, and a new church was constructed in 1894. I took the liberty of making Helen a friend to Clara.

Ester Hobart Morris was the first woman appointed as a justice of the peace. Wyoming was the first state to allow women the right to vote and hold public office. Ester's marrying Peter and Catharine is purely a work of fiction for my story.

Sarah Bernhardt performed *Fedora* with her company at

the Cheyenne Opera House. Her understudy, Maggie O'Neal, was created from my imagination and was named after my oldest granddaughter, who loves acting and singing. Maggie O'Neal was also my mother's name.

The hero in the book was named after my dear grandson Peter.

Angelina Cristini was named after my sweet granddaughter Angelina.

Thomas Sturgis, briefly mentioned, was the secretary of the Wyoming Stock Growers Association (WSGA).

Crow Creek, which runs north along Cheyenne, is where I placed Peter Andersen's farm. It once caused incredible flooding of the town.

Since I mention it in my story, I should point out that Fort Russell established its military headquarters three miles northwest of Cheyenne in 1867. After Francis Warren's death in 1929, it was renamed Fort Francis E. Warren Air Force Base.

There are differing opinions as to when tiramisu, meaning "pick me up" in Italian, was first invented. Some say it was a "Tuscan trifle" created in Siena, Italy, for the visit by Grand Duke Cosimo de'Medici III in the seventeenth century. He brought the dessert, called *zuppa del duca*, home with him to Florence in the nineteenth century. Later, it was taken to England and grew popular, making its way to Venice.

Others say that tiramisu was a favorite of Venice courtesans who needed a "pick me up" between their encounters above the Le Beccherie restaurant, where it was created. Still others say it was invented by a chef at Trevso near Venice in 1969. Whatever the case, it makes for a lively story. For my purposes in the story, I decided to go with the earlier proposed date.

Acknowledgments

I'd like to acknowledge my son-in-law Bobby Christine's father, Alexander Christine, who died when I was near the end of writing *Deeply Devoted*. It was from the Christine family that I portrayed the Cristinis in this book. When Al's family came to this country from Italy, they changed the spelling of their name from Cristini to Christine. Many Italian immigrants brought art, culture, and much more to America to make it what it is today.

Al was deeply devoted to his family and country, and it seemed appropriate for me to dedicate my book to him since he touched our family's lives, including my grandchildren. He served three tours of duty in Vietnam and was honored with three Purple Hearts. Bobby is walking boldly in the shadow of his dad's footsteps—he is a lieutenant colonel in the Army Guard and served time in Iraq.

Thanks to all the folks at The Bookmark at JFBC who are big supporters of my books.

I especially want to thank my personal prayer team, Mag's

Peeps, who prayed for me every day as my deadline loomed, after my brother died, and with my own personal issues. Many thanks to Sheri Christine, Kelly Long, Karen Casey, Gaye Orsini, Connie Crawford, Linda Underwood, and Linda Hoffner. May God bless you richly!

Thanks to my readers for their continued support and interest in my books.

Maggie Brendan is a bestselling author. She is a member of the American Christian Writers (ACW), the American Christian Fiction Writers (ACFW), the Romance Writers of America (RWA), and the Georgia Romance Writers (GRW). She was also a recipient of the 2004 ACW Persistence Award. Maggie led a writers' critique group in her home for six years and was quoted in *Word Weavers: The Story of a Successful Writers' Critique Group*. She was a guest speaker at a recent Regional Church Bookstores and Libraries conference in Marietta, Georgia, on the value of Christian fiction.

A TV film version is currently in development for her first novel, *No Place for a Lady*, book 1 of the Heart of the West series. *Romantic Times* awarded *No Place for a Lady* a 4.5-star review and also gave *The Jewel of His Heart* a 4-star review.

Maggie is married and lives in Georgia. She has two grown children and four grandchildren. When she's not writing, she enjoys reading, singing, painting, scrapbooking, and being with her family. You can find Maggie on her website, www.MaggieBrendan.com, and on her blog, http://southernbelle writer.blogspot.com. She is also a resident blogger on www.bustlesandspurs.com.

Journey into the
Heart of the West

Can a Southern belle tame the heart of
a rugged cowboy?

Sweet Romances
That Capture the Heart

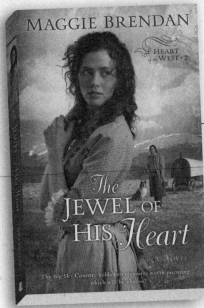

The Big Sky Country holds two treasures worth pursuing . . . which will he choose?

Her father's money could buy her anything except true love.

Be the First to Hear about Other New Books from Revell!

Sign up for announcements about new and upcoming titles at

www.revellbooks.com/signup

Follow us on twitter
RevellBooks

Join us on facebook
Revell

Don't miss out on our great reads!

Revell
a division of Baker Publishing Group
www.RevellBooks.com